Kiss Them Goodbye

A Novel

JOSEPH EASTBURN

WILLIAM MORROW
An Imprint of HarperCollins*Publishers*

KISS THEM GOODBYE. Copyright © 1993 by Joseph Eastburn. All rights reserved. Printed in the United States of America. No part of this book may be used or reproduced in any manner whatsoever without written permission except in the case of brief quotations embodied in critical articles and reviews. For information address HarperCollins Publishers, 195 Broadway, New York, NY 10007. HarperCollins books may be purchased for educational, business, or sales promotional use. For information please e-mail the Special Markets Department at Spsales@harpercollins.com.

FIRST WILLIAM MORROW PAPERBACK EDITION

The Library of Congress has cataloged the hardcover edition as follows:

Library of Congress Cataloging-in-Publication Data
Eastburn, Joseph.
Kiss them goodbye : a novel / by Joseph Eastburn.
p. cm.
ISBN 978-0-688-04598-2 (Hardcover)
ISBN 978-0-06-244402-8 (Paperback)
1. Police—New York (State)—Fiction. 1. Title.
PS3555.A6958K57 1993
813'.54—dc20   93-10405
----

16 17 18 19 20   OV/RRD   10 9 8 7 6 5 4 3 2 1

For my father, Joe

Kiss Them Goodbye

1

NIGHT AIR EXPLODES past me. I hit the roof and roll, moving, brain thundering at shock pulse.

At the roof door, I brush tar from my soles. The door opens so quietly. Inside, the heavy smell of trapped air in the stairwell. Filling the lungs like fuel. Head swimming now. Racing down flights, the old frenzy filling me. Feel the banister. Spindles blur past my shoes, faster, faster, feet almost on fire. Thoughts burning up into my skull. Have waited so long for this . . . I want to scream—but clamp glove on my face.

On the floor now. Here I am. Fourth floor—smells like ammonia. Wombats have been here. Can hardly keep to the wall. Legs tingling as I run. Fingers grip the molding. Eyes glued to the plaster. Now STOP. A rush of air from my mouth. Am I here? The door. The pounding in my head rising on chords of sound, howling. A storm raging inside. Have to stop it . . . but no time. Now the sound is coming closer. Louder. Closer. In a fury now, white-hot, seething.

Turn the knob. See it turn. A flash of brilliant light. Enveloping me. But it can't be, not here. A Day-Glo playroom. A child's mad colors. Bright oranges, reds roaring, blues that cut. Colors that erupt, burst across walls, great swaths of color, splattered upward at sharp angles.

Try to focus . . . see the room as it really is. A great silence inhabits me. I see it now. No color. Drab. Dark wooden desk. Closet door ajar. Dust on the floor. Close my eyes . . . the playroom again— flashing back—cutting in, burning through my eyes.

Open the door wider.

A blade of light falls across a sleeping face.

Crawl to the edge of my bed. There I am, sleeping. Skin so white. Jet-black hair. Someone creeps into my room, brushes my hair. Hands so soft. So nice.

This won't hurt.

2

WHEN THEY FOUND fifteen-year-old Eddie Crawford, he was tucked upside down in one of the garbage cans under the massive windows on the fourth floor of Ardsley Hall. Another freshman, Brad Schwerin, always the first in line at breakfast, was emptying his garbage on the way out when he discovered the body. He could only see the scuffed heels of Crawford's shoes when he lifted the lid. Even before enduring his slimy oatmeal and powdered eggs, the boy thought he was seeing things and walked calmly back down the squeaky hallway with his garbage, only to stop in his tracks and start screaming.

Mr. Toby, one of the masters, looked out of his door and ran to where the boy's pink, trembling hand pointed down at the shoes; he then called to one of the other masters, the German teacher, Mr. Carlson, to help him hoist the body.

By the time Crawford was lifted out of the can, the hall was full of boys milling around. They moved in closer, their eyes widening in disbelief. Crawford's face was indigo. His neck was wrapped in the school tie with gold crests that all the new boys had to wear. When the body was turned upright, the thin piece of silk suddenly peeled away. Shrieks of fright echoed through the hallway. Crawford's throat had been cut, and the blood that had poured over his features into the garbage can had left tracks racing up his face. On top of his head was a frozen clump of brown hair that had been swimming in a pool of his own blood.

Cary Ballard was there that morning, but stood away from the others as the screams went up into the rafters of Ardsley's hallway. He remembered reaching suddenly for his own throat, as if someone were about to grasp it from behind. He wheeled around, but there was no one there. All he could say was that a fear gripped him. He turned toward the back stairs.

He was a large boy, already over six feet with broad shoulders and strong arms, yet something about him was frail, even delicate. He was also painfully shy and he hunched in a conscious way as if to apologize for his stature. At times, despite this, he rebelled against his own dispirited nature by losing his temper or talking back—bold actions for which he was usually reprimanded. He was fourteen, handsome in a boyish way, had clear skin and some freckles across the bridge of his nose. His eyes were green.

Cary slouched down the back stairway. The sight of the dead boy's body had terrified him. He ran down the stairs until the dank smell of the hallway faded. On the steps between the second and third floors, his palm skimming the banister, he stopped suddenly on the stairs. Out of the corner of his eye, he saw the familiar shadow, the tall, slightly pitched parody of that figure, that presence he remembered so well. It was coming up the stairs. He was sure his own footsteps had already been heard. All he could manage was to pin the back of his head against the wall, waiting, hoping the shadow would stop, retrace its steps and go down. It didn't. He tried to contain his breathing, which came in short spurts that stalled in the back of his throat. He knew who it was. There was no question. Whatever fight he had left seemed to turn inward. As he watched the shadow on the landing below make the final turn to the third floor, he listened to the steps and for the first time was unsure. Now the shape of the image racing up the wall took flight in his mind. The shadow whipped across the surface of the cement. He saw a hand. He panicked, plunging down the stairwell. He ran right into Mr. Allington, a tall master who dropped down a step as the boy bumped into him.

"Whoa, young man!" he said. "What's the hurry?"

"Oh, sir, sorry—I thought it was someone else—I'm not feeling well, I—I—"

"What is it?" A warm hand fell on his shoulder.

"Nothing, sir—it was just the smell up there—I couldn't . . ."

As assistant headmaster, Elliot Allington had been present in Ballard's initial interview. The boy always remembered him as the only person behind that long reef of a table in the Admissions Office who had smiled.

Allington looked down at Cary, concerned. The boy sensed the master staring at his shirt.

"What were the screams on the fourth about?"

The boy could not respond at first, but looked right through the man toward the end of his fear. "I . . . don't know what . . . happened, sir. There was no air. I couldn't breathe—had to go."

The master's eyes began to tighten. "Cary, just sit down and relax, all right?" Climbing the stairs two at a time, he disappeared.

The boy felt as though he was in shock and didn't remember how he got to the hill overlooking the town, but felt he could not get his breath until he was away from the muffled gloom that floated through that stairwell. He was numb. He looked down at himself just to make sure his body was still there. His tie was gone. That's what the master had been looking at. He had lost it, no doubt, between the fourth floor and the hill outside. Then he began to question whether he had ever put it on.

As the wind began to whip yellow leaves around him, his mind tried to retrace the steps he had taken. It was all a blur. He would have to go back upstairs to get another tie before class.

As he stared down at the front lawn of the school, the way it rumbled into town, something occurred to him. He turned back to look at the stone arch that joined Ardsley and Booth halls. For an instant he imagined he saw the murdered boy, Ed Crawford. There under the vaulting gray stones, he remembered, was the last time he had seen Crawford alive. It was the day he had first thought of leaving Ravenhill School. Recalling the incident kept the fear at bay. He thought back, devouring the memory.

At lunch that day, Crawford had attacked him in front of the others at the dining table. He told Cary that he was worthless for having declined to fight him after history class. The class had met in the dank basement of Booth Hall, near the labs.

Crawford, a light-skinned boy whose fiery pupils seemed to glow in the dark, and another boy, Gluckner, a big football player, had been sitting sullenly on either side of the locked door to the history classroom like Japanese guard dogs.

When Ballard walked down the basement stairs, he spoke to them but they didn't answer. They just looked at each other during a kind of tense silence. Ballard set his books down on the floor. Suddenly Crawford spit on Ballard's books, then stood up, smiling. When Ballard pushed Crawford against the windowpane in the oak door, the old glass echoed down the hallway. Crawford's eyes became oddly distended as if filling with chaos. He slapped Ballard hard in the face and told him he'd better show up after class to fight. Ballard said yes but he didn't show.

Instead he slipped into the dining room for lunch. Then he realized Crawford was nudging him from behind, kicking his heels to unnerve him. Crawford didn't have to say much. He just sat at the same table, right across from Ballard, and stared at him. He leaned the patched elbows of his sports jacket on the white tablecloth and hissed across at him. "You're a wimp." He rolled the word around in his mouth and spit it out, much the way he had spit on Cary's books in the first place. "You know what you are, don't you, *wimp*?"

Cary looked down at Crawford's elbow patches and got the idea that the sports jacket must have belonged to someone's father. His own father had died so long ago he couldn't remember what he looked like. Cary heard the other students snickering. When the main course came, they refused to pass him any food and he sat, unable to look at any of them, staring out the window.

Then he saw it. The same hand he had seen so many times. It reached slowly out of the same black cuff and moved across the outside of the window. The hand rested against the window glass, as if waiting. No one else saw it. The boys were lulled by the din of voices, of forks scraping plates, the crisp rubbing of linen jackets as the scholarship students pitched stainless steel bins of food onto the table. No one seemed to care that someone's arm, draped in black, was poised in the window near their table. Ballard knew whose hand it was. He wondered why so many years had passed since he'd seen the stranger—and why now?

He thought back to the first times he had ever noticed it. The figure would appear at a distance, just standing there in a black cloak and hat, staring. Ballard often thought it must be hot in those clothes. A black scarf was always wrapped across the bottom of the face.

When he was a child he remembered seeing the figure one time standing on the grass outside his bedroom window. It was a bright summer day. The hill sloped down to a cement wall where his father was busy tending a thin bed of petunias. Ballard had opened his window, noticed his father squatting over the flowers and, on the hill above, seen the stranger standing there, staring. The way the eyes above the scarf burned, the boy imagined it was smiling. This sent shivers up his spine, but he kept looking at the stranger until it went away.

At the table Ballard's eyes followed the black sleeve as it moved slowly across the pane, bringing with it a shoulder, and finally, the wrapped face. The same smiling eyes. The figure was wearing the dark hat and filled the entire window, looking down at Crawford in a very careful, attentive way. Again, Ballard stared up at the stranger until it went away.

As Cary stood now in front of the school, lost in these images, he understood why Crawford had died in such a grisly way. A police siren could be heard whining in the distance; it turned the corner at the light in town, followed by an ambulance, and complained as it climbed the hill to the school.

Ballard turned now and saw a horde of students and faculty members spilling out from under the arch as the vehicles came to a halt. In the crowd, he picked out the red face and blond hair of Mr. Carlson. He saw Mr. Toby talking excitedly to one of the officers and he saw Schwerin standing in the doorway crying.

The ambulance team walked into Ardsley. Ballard saw the edges of their white jackets as they climbed past the windows in the stairwell. Soon they would reach the fourth floor, he thought. They would bring Crawford's covered body down on a stretcher, slide him in the ambulance, and drive back down the hill. People would wonder for years who could have done such a thing. As he took a deep breath, Ballard didn't need to wonder. He thought he knew.

3

NICK FOWLER HAD been a cop in Buffalo for ten years, a sergeant for the last four, and had just made lieutenant. He had been trying to get a transfer to Ravenstown for years because the fishing was great and he was tired of the city. With the breakup of his marriage, he was spending more and more time out of town. When the call came that same morning, he was on vacation, eating breakfast at an angler's lodge twenty miles upriver from Ravenhill School.

A half hour later he was in a squad car, still wearing his waders, speeding along the blacktop. His old precinct approved his transfer by policefax, and the local force hired him on his way to the scene. He guessed it was his strong background in assaults, evidence gathering, and maybe a little luck. Besides, he was in the neighborhood. His first case as a lieutenant too.

He pulled off his waders in the backseat of the car. The driver, a sergeant, said he would stash them for him in a locker down at the station house, handed him his gun and temporary badge, then peeled away leaving him standing under a stone arch. It was only then that he realized he was wearing a plaid shirt, frayed jeans, and a pair of hightops.

When Nick Fowler ambled onto the scene, an hour and a half after the body was taken downtown, he met Sergeant Robby Cole. Cole had gotten the call initially and was now coordinating technical services. Nick nodded to the sergeant. He skimmed Cole's typed report and looked around the hallway, trying to yank himself out of a vague feeling that he was out of place. He was still surprised at how fast all this had happened; he was even a little sleepy. He couldn't seem to focus.

Then he saw the blood.

It was on the floor, on the walls, everywhere. Something took a hold of Fowler inside. He looked down at the victim's name and address on the report, his chest knocking, his own blood beginning to throb. He felt a little dizzy. He steadied himself, closed his eyes and stood quite still for a moment, as if his thoughts were suspended. He had seen bodies before. He had read the names of murder victims before on plain white pieces of paper, the forms recopied so many times they had to be committed to memory. He saw the face of a man appear in the back of his mind. It floated there like an apparition, then faded.

Fowler opened his eyes. He scanned the hallway and couldn't help but notice that nearly all the cops were looking at him.

He started to move anxiously around the room. By that time, more and more policemen were arriving to take a look—most were standing around drinking coffee from Styrofoam cups. The first thing Fowler did was raise his voice. The cops turned around with blank stares to hear this new guy, however politely, ask every man not involved in the investigation—including a lieutenant from the county—to leave. That didn't win him any friends. He even walked up to his new boss, Captain Allen Weathers.

"I'd like to ask you to leave too, Captain. No offense," he explained with a reluctant smile, "I need to seal the scene. Make sure no evidence is destroyed."

"Who's stopping you?" Weathers shot back, bristling as he stared up at the tall blond man, eyeing the prominent cleft nose, the wide jaw, the blue eyes. He had gone out on a limb to bring this guy in.

"Sorry, sir," he said, unable to contain a frown, "if you'll just step over here, the bloodstains under your feet might get to the lab." The captain suddenly rose up on tiptoes and hotfooted it toward the wall. Fowler kept a straight face.

He set up a temporary office in an empty room on the floor, ordered his team to block off the corridor, asking the prefects to require their students to use the back stairwell. He then installed a police line of yellow tape bordering the scene. He also requested a barricade downstairs on the third floor, which blocked off the old wooden staircase.

He asked to be briefed on exactly what trace evidence had been found. He requested the immediate presence of the master who had found the body. When he was told that Mr. Toby was teaching, Fowler had him called out of his class.

Only one gloved technician had arrived. Nick fidgeted and watched as the man worked carefully around the place where the body had been found. Having read the initial report, Fowler knew the throat wound had been inflicted with a sharp, thin blade, possibly a fillet knife. Before he supervised a second thorough search of the scene, Fowler set up a schedule of interviews with faculty.

He then walked up to Robby Cole, who stood pushing a hand through his dark hair. Nick asked if he had gotten any leads on the victim.

"What?" Cole said distractedly, staring down at his report.

"Ed Crawford. Would you please find out what he's been doing? If he had any enemies? Were there any witnesses? Like that."

" . . . Oh sure."

Fowler looked at Cole. "Are you with us today, Sergeant?"

"I'm here," he said curtly.

"You're handling the prints?"

"Sir?"

"Elimination prints of all the boys, prefects, and masters on the hall. Should have those by now."

Cole glanced again at the report he had written two hours ago and shook his head. "No prints yet."

"Well, get some techs up here," Fowler said. "Standard samples are only now being taken. We waiting for Christmas or what?"

Cole's gaze hardened. "I put in the call, whaddaya want me to do?"

"Call them again."

Now Cole had his back up. Nick Fowler didn't pay attention as the sergeant stalked away. He got on another phone himself to connect his forensics team with the county coroner. He wanted an acid phosphatase test to discover if there were traces of semen on the dead boy.

He was starting to unwind.

A photographer finally arrived. Fowler watched him take endless shots of the bloodstains above the wainscoting. He made sure the photographer took enough pictures for a full sketch of the scene and pointed out more bloodstains under the window behind the garbage can.

Fowler was studying the shape and position of the stains when the rest of the team arrived. He put one technician on prints and pointed the second tech across the hallway, where at eye level there were more blots and smudges of blood along the white walls. He watched as the man carefully scraped a crusted sample loose with a razor blade. This would go for a serology test as to blood type; it could also provide genetic markers for a whole DNA workup of the victim or assailant.

Fowler wanted a lot of blood samples, hoping the killer had shed some in the process. He paced, wondered to himself how many hours the stains had been there. The photographer finally stood up.

"I want ultraviolet too," Nick said to the man before he could speak. The photographer shrugged, reached into his kit, and reloaded his camera. Fowler felt sweat building up around the holster of the police-issue .38 under his arm. He fanned himself and turned around to see a technician dusting the window ledge. His eyes were drawn to the soft brush in the man's hand as it kept going over the same spot in the corner. "Got something?"

"Yeah," said the print man. "He must have taken off his gloves for a minute. Three or four points here, a loop, an arch. When I lift it, I might have something—but without a whorl, Lieutenant, forget it."

Nick Fowler knew he was right. The signature of a print was the whorl at the top center of each finger. He sighed and looked out the windows. The field van that the state police had sent over was now parked down near the stone arch. He knew they could process some of the evidence here, but most would have to be taken back to the lab. As he stood gazing through the glass at the manicured lawns of the back campus, he wondered if the autopsy had begun.

He was trying to reconstruct the crime in his head. He couldn't imagine the boy being murdered in front of these large windows. He called over one of the men assigned to him, a young cop nervously tapping his foot by the banister.

"I'm sorry, what's your name?"

"Marty Orloff."

"Marty, see if you can find out who last emptied the garbage cans up here, and if there's a regular schedule of collection."

"Okay," the young cop said, a small smile appearing on his face.

"These men are going to comb this whole area for fibers, hair, soils, fluids, the usual. There's something strange about these bloodstains."

Marty grinned as he rocked on the balls of his feet. "Covering all your bases, huh?"

Nick raised an eyebrow. "Why not?"

"You don't have to go so hard, Mr. Fowler—we know you're a lieutenant."

"Thanks for reminding me," he said. "Just do it."

4

RAVENHILL WAS ONE of the finest boarding schools in New York. It sat on a hill that sloped down past a lake toward a small town that jealously guarded its eighteenth-century buildings against the march of time. All along the main street, the old structures were dilapidated, in need of paint, and many of the residents left their houses in their original condition, holding up the layers of grime as an emblem of pride to the passing years.

Dr. Brandon Hickey was sitting alone in his office overlooking the town. His phone was ringing. He insisted on an old rotary phone in an antique black case. The tapered handle vibrated slightly in its cradle as the phone continued to peal. Fourth ring. Dr. Hickey leaned forward at his desk, staring at the noise. He didn't move but the gray hairs in his mustache worked all around the tense circle of his mouth. Sixth ring now. He finally reached over and yanked up the receiver.

"Yes? . . . Who is this?" One hand flapped impatiently across his desk. "Yes, Lieutenant, what can I do for you? . . . What? . . . I would be of no use to you. I was asleep when this tragic incident occurred . . . I'm sorry, Lieutenant, my plate is very full, as I'm sure you can imagine, and I—no, I'm explaining to you, I am unable to be interrogated . . . Why? . . . Because I'm in a board meeting . . . All day . . . Yes . . . Not tomorrow either . . . I'd be glad to tell you right now where I was last night—no, you listen, sir, I am the headmaster of this institution; I do not go around slaughtering students in the middle of the night. I need students. Ergo, I encourage our boys. I even chastise them at times, but I most certainly do not—you're wasting your time . . . Fine, well you do that . . . Another day, yes . . ."

He slammed down the phone. It was immediately ringing again. He picked it up, pressed down the receiver button, and left it off the hook. He stood up, his bony shoulder blades rotating as he pulled his sports jacket down repeatedly, straightening his tie. He was trying to ground himself and looked astonished when his oak door swung open and Elliot Allington stepped quietly in, gesturing toward Earl Hungerford, a stout, red-faced businessman wearing an open collar and polyester grays. The folds in Earl's neck extruded like the bellows of an accordion. He was wheezing as he entered.

"Brandon, I just wanted to say how sorry I am."

Dr. Hickey's face was twitching, his mustache turned up at the ends. "Sure do appreciate you stopping by." A glare at Allington. "Normally we make appointments in the office."

"As your chairman—with half the board on vacation, Brandon, I felt we *had* to talk."

"Won't you sit down, Mr. Hungerford?"

The man frowned, glanced back at Allington. "Elliot, get the door, will you? Hungerford's wheeze segued to a drumroll of throat clearing, Dr. Hickey blinking to punctuate the interval. The door closed.

"Brandon, I don't think we need a board meeting to know that the school should be closed for a week, until things cool off, am I right?"

"I'm sorry, that is out of the question."

Hungerford, owner of a chain of odd-lot stores, was not used to being refuted. He rattled his jowls as if he hadn't heard correctly. "What?"

"Send them home now and half of them won't return. The answer is no."

"You're not going to be pigheaded about this, are you?"

"Rational is the word. A kind of thinking that is beyond certain people around here."

Hungerford thrust his neck forward. "Do you realize what the papers are going to say about this?"

"We're having a memorial service. We'll invite them." Mr. Allington nodded in agreement.

"What the hell good is that? The gossip, Brandon, is already spreading out of control down the aisles of my stores, if you want to know."

"The aisles of your stores do not part the Red Sea, Mr. Hungerford, but the tuition invoices *do*. They are owed on the fifteenth. I have no intention of letting any of our parents fall behind on their payments."

Hungerford looked at Allington in disbelief. "I'm talking about damage control here. Close the school for two days, then . . . dedicate the time to young Crawford. Let us release a statement about increased security for the boys."

"I'll take care of all that."

Hungerford stared at him. "Why, you stubborn old goat."

"Call the board members."

"By that time it will be All Hallows' Eve, you nutcase."

"I'm sorry, Earl."

"Oh, it's 'Earl' now?" His lungs gave a wheeze as he careened toward the door. "That tie is cutting off the circulation to your brain—if you have one." He jerked the oak handle and disappeared.

Dr. Hickey turned his stare on his assistant. "Why didn't you tell me he was out there?"

Allington blanched. "He just barged past me. I was on my way in to tell you there are some parents here to see you."

"Nothing but parents all day, Elliot. You'll have to tell them I'm busy."

"Dr. Hickey . . ." He paused. "It's Mr. and Mrs. Crawford."

The headmaster stiffened. The burnished wainscoting around his office reflected back a series of nervous movements—fingers pushed along the side of his hair, mustache thumbed; a deep breath was heard. The man seemed to shiver. Allington opened the door.

Dr. Hickey stepped into his outer office. His secretary was arranging stacks of paper with jittery fingers. Her strained eyes signaled him toward a small couch where a middle-aged couple, looking frail and small, were sitting, leaning against each other for ballast, their faces drawn, their eyes resting on the carpet. Mr. Crawford looked smaller than his wife; he seemed to collapse into his suit jacket, his face pale gray. Mrs. Crawford had put on weight, her blouse tight around her shoulders; a brown perm held wisps of white hair. She didn't seem to be breathing.

Dr. Hickey approached them. They saw him coming and both stood up, looking hopefully at the headmaster as if his face would hold an answer. When they saw his hollow cheeks, they knew there wasn't, and would never be, as long as they lived, an answer.

"Mr. and Mrs. Crawford . . . I'm terribly sorry."

Mr. Crawford just shook his head, lost deep inside himself. Mrs. Crawford lifted her face up, her eyes, imploring at first, then turning as hard as obsidian. "How could this happen?"

"Not in the history of the academy has a boy been . . ."

"You said his life would begin here. You said that the day of his interview."

"We're doing everything we can."

"There's *nothing* you can do *now*." Her voice was hoarse from crying. "What can anyone do *now*?" Mr. Crawford took a hold of his wife's shoulders.

"Nothing," said Dr. Hickey.

"That's right, nothing."

"I'm sorry."

"You let him be murdered in his sleep. *You* might as well have killed him yourself. His neck was . . ." Her composure vanished as her shoulders began to shudder in silent heaves, deep rolling waves, until the tears just came out. She started to wail.

Dr. Hickey was no longer shaking. Whatever movement his body was making had disappeared inside.

5

FOWLER HAD SITUATED himself at a boy's desk in an empty room on the fourth floor of Ardsley. He had been interviewing for several hours now. Ms. Coates walked in and sat down across from him on the edge of one of the twin beds.

She was in her mid-thirties and was the only woman master in the school. She wore her brown hair in a pageboy cut, her face almost pixieish. She had a diminutive nose, dappled with light freckles, and a flawless mouth—"toy lips" Nick had heard one of the students say under his breath—now he understood. She kept her lips slightly puckered as she stared at him, suggesting an inviolate sensuality. Her ample bosom seemed to back up the stare. Her voice was surprisingly deep, though, and for all her femininity, Ms. Coates was practically a baritone.

She was also very tall. Over six feet in heels, Nick decided, when she strode in. She seemed to wear the heels with a vengeance. She walked like a bodybuilder in stockings.

Fowler noticed her face was tight when she sat down. Her calf muscles rippled as she pressed her knees together.

"Ed Crawford was one of your students?"

"I teach algebra one. All the freshman get me." Another ripple in her face now, as if a muscle was out of control.

"What kind of student was he?"

"Average."

"Do you have any thoughts or impressions about him?"

"He was a difficult boy . . . strongheaded . . . unruly . . . not a great student . . . but he made up for it in other ways."

"What ways?"

"Oh . . . he was courteous. Turned in his assignments on time . . . he just couldn't get it."

"Get what?"

"Logarithms, mainly. And coefficients. Sine and cosine. They all just flew right out of his head."

"Was he distracted, worried about something?"

Ms. Coates adjusted her posture, a slight arching of the back. "Not that I know of."

"Did he ever look frightened, pensive—anything like that?"

"Not with me."

"I'm sorry?"

"He was not frightened with me."

"You brought him out?"

"Well, yes, I got along with him. I wasn't privy to his innermost thoughts, mind you, but . . ."

"Was anyone?"

"I doubt it."

"Why?"

"He was solitary. I recognize that in people because I am myself."

"He was a kindred spirit then?"

"You're a loner, too, aren't you, Lieutenant?" She was smiling at him now.

He looked at her. "Why the smile?"

"You seem different from the other policeman."

"How?"

"Oh, gentler, a little more refined." She was inching forward on the sagging single mattress, her dress riding up slightly.

His nostrils flared slightly. "That's a nice perfume you're wearing."

Her eyebrows went up in surprise. "Oh, I never wear perfume. That's just me." Another smile.

A tight smile back. "If you say so." Fowler cleared his throat. "Ms. Coates, where were you last night between two and four A.M.?"

"In my bed at South End."

"Anyone who can confirm that?"

"I was alone."

"The students at South End—might any of them have seen you retire?"

"Look, Lieutenant." The hips swiveled around so her knees were aimed at him. She tugged her skirt down, then smoothed her leg very slowly. "I don't check in with the dorm before I put on my nightie. Those boys are very impressionable."

Fowler was staring at her now, not saying anything. He noticed her return the stare, getting self-conscious, her allure suddenly tempered by an icy change of posture, her shoulders back, her face drawn.

"Something wrong?"

"Do *you* think there's something wrong, Lieutenant?"

"Well, you seem insulted, Ms. Coates."

"Do I?"

"When was the last time you saw Crawford alive?"

"In class yesterday, of course."

"Why, 'of course?'"

"Well, these questions are getting exasperating."

"Are they?"

"Yes! Can we please finish up? I have tests to correct." She was adjusting her skirt down now.

"What was he wearing the last time you saw him?"

"How should I know? I have a class full of boys."

"Where did he sit in your class?"

Again the hips swiveling like a turret, knees apart. "Look, in the front row, for God's sake . . . he probably had on a pair of slacks and a sports jacket like all the boys."

"White shirt?"

An impatient glare. "They're required. What does this have to do with anything?"

Fowler watched the anger flow into her features. "Ms. Coates, the deceased's parents identified certain things as missing: pictures of the boy, a letter jacket everyone saw him wear. Name tags were ripped out of his underclothes."

Ms. Coates suddenly looked very saddened.

He watched her. "Who would do that, Ms. Coates?"

"How should I know?"

"Did he have any enemies?"

"Crawford was a good kid," she said wistfully. "I'm sorry this happened to him."

"Why did you get upset just now?"

"Well, I don't care for your tone."

"What is my tone?"

"I take back what I said before—you are like the other men." She was shaking her head. "Typical, emotionless male."

"My *job* is to be emotionless."

"It's more than that, Lieutenant. There's something— disconnected about you."

Fowler felt the sting of that. He worried for an instant that she might be right. "In case you've forgotten, Ms. Coates, we had a gruesome murder here last night. A boy was very likely tortured."

"Oh, please don't."

He was staring at her, more curious, watching her squirm as if her clothes were too tight. "All right."

"Can I go?"

"Ms. Coates, who do you think killed Ed Crawford?"

"Look, I don't know. One of the janitors, maybe. They give me the creeps."

"Why not a faculty member?"

Overly casual. "Why not?"

"I may need to speak to you again."

She looked him in the eye. "My pleasure."

She sprang off the mattress and stood in front of him. She shook her hair out and did a runway turn.

BALLARD AWOKE BEHIND the oak tree on the edge of the hill. He rubbed his eyes. The town looked like a burning postcard.

He wondered how long he had been sleeping, then noticed the sun was high now. He was afraid to go upstairs, afraid to go to class. He turned around and caught a glimpse of Mabel shaking a dust mop into the air outside the basement door of Madison Hall. Mabel was the old, gray-haired matriarch of the wombats.

The wombats were the school janitors and cleaning ladies, usually old arthritic men and bearded women, some nearly illiterate, most were—at least according to the students—feebleminded.

They were not, but their labors could not remove the stain of ridicule, as the boys laughed at their humped and withered bodies, their sweaty armpits, their wild, haggard, frightened faces. They had small, dingy closets in each building, where—as they wrung out washrags and dumped water into cast-iron sinks—their gray backs protruded into the hallways.

As Ballard stood up, trying to get his bearings, Mabel looked over at him; for an instant he imagined she was a savage. As if by some unwritten law, both he and the woman turned away from each other.

Ballard walked toward Ardsley and saw another wombat, Stanley, meander under the stone arch, swaying side to side, bowlegged as a cowboy. The lines in his old face traveled from his forehead down his cheek, around his chin and up the other side. His skin was a pale yellow. Stanley spent most of his time in the power plant, where he tended the boilers. He watched the oil heaters and made sure the temperature gauges held true. He usually had a grimy cloth dangling from the back pocket of his khaki trousers. He was known to show up during morning break under Madison Hall, where the cleaning ladies drank coffee. That's probably where he had just been.

Ballard's stomach began to churn as he entered Ardsley Hall. He turned abruptly on the stairs once and jumped. There it was again, that dread, that fear.

STANLEY WAS CLEANING gauges when the little cop, Marty, came shuffling down the long hallway into the boiler room. Marty took off his hat and had to duck his kinky hair underneath the pipes that were wrapped with insulation.

"You Stanley?"

Stanley was startled, but smiled immediately, sending a stream of spit through the gap in his front teeth as he talked. "Yes, I am. I'm Stanley, keeper of the keys, lord of the manor."

"That so."

"What can I do you for?"

"Well," said Marty, "all I want to know is who emptied the garbage on fourth floor of Ardsley Hall last night. Somebody said you would know."

"I know all."

"Okay, who?"

"Lydia. Lively Lydia, lithe Lydia, Lydia of Ravenstown, that old, once divine, dark-haired beauty of Greek parentage, who is now my girl."

"What time does Lydia do her thing?"

"Four-thirty."

"P.M.?"

"Of course, otherwise how could she get her beauty sleep?"

"Look—could you tell me where this goddess is right now?"

"In the basement," Stanley said.

6

IN THE CANTEEN, Mr. Toby was still shaking from his interview with Lieutenant Fowler. He sprinkled salt and pepper on an egg sandwich at the counter, squeezed some catsup on the paper plate, and turned around to look for a chair. There was a hushed buzzing in the room. Most of the faculty members who were not teaching during third period were there, sitting in small groups, shaking their heads and talking about the murder.

Toby saw Mr. Allington sitting at a table with Dr. Nathan Clarence, the school psychologist. They were both sitting in silence staring out the windows. Toby pulled a chair out at their table.

"Hello Elliot . . . Nathan."

Allington looked up. "Hi, Bill . . . aren't you the one who found the body?"

"Schwerin did actually," Toby said, sitting down. "He came and got me. Poor kid was in a state." He took a wary bite out of his sandwich. "That lieutenant certainly is thorough."

"Thank God for that," Allington said.

"What did the headmaster say?"

Allington ran a palm over his gray wiry hair. "He went calm almost immediately, like the eye of a hurricane." Dr. Clarence snickered, uncrossing his legs, gazing at Toby.

"What's he going to do anyway?"

"Well, his decision not to close the school for a few days has infuriated almost everyone."

Mr. Toby was chewing ravenously. "Of course, he should have. The man is . . ." He waved his hand absently.

"Out of touch," Dr. Clarence offered.

Allington nodded. "Well, he thought if the routine were broken, students might drop out, but actually it's money—every headmaster's undoing."

The three men fell into a silence as Toby gulped his sandwich, staring straight ahead. Dr. Clarence lit a cigarette and glanced around the room.

"Well, what do you think?" Mr. Toby had wiped his mouth with a napkin and was looking at Allington.

"About what?"

"Who do you think . . . I mean . . . who could have done it?"

Allington sipped his coffee thoughtfully. "I'd hate to think it was one of the students." He stood up. "Sorry, I have to get back."

Dr. Clarence sat up and stretched. "Why do you say a student?"

Allington reached down for his cup and drained his coffee. A worried expression crossed his features. "Because . . . think how awful it would be if it were a teacher."

The two men at the table seemed to pall. They stood up so they were at eye level with the assistant headmaster, traded meaningful looks, and stared around the room at the other faculty members.

Mr. Toby rubbed his neck. "We're all shuffling around, on edge, looking over our shoulders. It's . . . crazy."

"It is," said Clarence.

Allington sighed, patted Toby on the shoulder, and walked out of the canteen. Toby and Clarence blinked at each other, turned away, and looked out the window.

ON THE BACK stairs, Ballard sat down between the second and third floors where he thought he had seen that shadow. Now the place felt empty. Two prefects, the upperclassmen who monitor each floor, had to step over him; they shot him nasty looks. He overheard one say that the police technicians were still studying the scene of the crime. Cary finally started up the stairs. As he neared the fourth-floor landing, he prayed the fear would go away.

He remembered he was supposed to look for his tie on the stairs. He hadn't seen it.

When he reached his floor, he saw the yellow police line bordering the area where the body had been discovered. The light from the windows revealed a lot of men, but Ballard noticed the figure of one man on his hands and knees; he seemed to be crawling up one of the walls. Ballard approached the yellow tape out of curiosity. He looked at the man, who now was beginning to stand, inspecting the wall.

Nick Fowler heard the old floorboards creak in the hallway. It made him think of something. He turned and saw the boy staring at him.

"You live on this hall?" he said.

"Yes."

"Did you hear anything last night, any struggle—sounds of any kind?"

The boy raised his shoulders silently, opened his palms, and shook his head. The shake seemed to vibrate down the boy's legs. "No," he said almost inaudibly.

A technician turned his head, then went back to work.

Fowler lifted the tape and ducked under it. He looked down at Ballard as the scuff of his own shoes echoed in the cavernous hallway. The boy was shivering.

"Don't be afraid. This happens sometimes."

Ballard blinked. "Does it?"

"What's your name?"

"Cary Ballard . . . in four-oh-one, right here." He pointed at his door.

"Did young Crawford have any enemies among the boys that you know of? Anybody threatening him?"

Cary started to shiver again. " . . . No."

"Was *he* out to get anybody who might have wanted to get him back?"

"I don't think so." Ballard realized his palms were lined with sweat.

"What's the matter? You seem . . . upset."

Ballard put his hands in his pockets. " . . . Do you know who did it yet?" he said.

Fowler itched his nose. "Would I be standing here with this serious look on my face if I did?" He smiled, then looking down at the boy's white shirt, his expression changed. "Did you forget your tie?"

"I lost it."

"Where?"

"I don't know. On the stairs, I thought, but . . ."

"What color was it?"

"Blue with gold crests . . . the school tie . . . we all get them."

Nick Fowler studied the boy's face. "Cary, I'm going to need to take a statement from you. Don't worry, it's just routine. Do you have any time this afternoon?"

"Uh—"

"Two?"

"No, I've—"

"Got a class?"

"An appointment."

Nick smiled in spite of himself. "I hope you can fit me in—what kind of appointment?"

"Therapy."

"Oh," he said. "What about after that? Say, three?"

"Okay."

Fowler patted him on the shoulder. "Just come back up. I'll be taking statements from everyone on the floor. Don't sweat it."

"See you then," Ballard said quietly. He slumped only a few feet to his door, the same planks squeaking under his shoes.

Fowler watched him intently. Ballard unlocked his door and disappeared.

Fowler stood for a moment, collecting his thoughts. He walked back to the bloodstains.

IN HIS ROOM, Cary stared down at the green blotter on his desk. The color relaxed him. He could collect himself, even try to figure out what was happening to him. He thought back to when the head-master, Dr. Hickey, had approached him the second day of school.

It was a month earlier, as he was changing classes. Ballard heard someone call his name as he was walking under the stone arch. Dr. Brandon Hickey had come walking briskly up to him. He always wore a tweed check blazer, and the thin strands of hair pulled across his bare sunburned head made him seem like a specimen from a museum, with a mustache.

"Could I speak to you for a moment?" he intoned.

Ballard looked up at him. Dr. Hickey smiled down at him as if looking into a microscope.

"What is it, sir?" Ballard said.

Dr. Hickey lifted his flat nose in the air. "Let's take a walk." He put his hands in his blazer pockets, starting out from under the shadow of the arch toward the athletic fields.

"I have Latin out at language arts, sir."

"Mr. Curamus?"

"Yes."

"I'll write you an excuse. This is important."

As they strode in silence past the boiler plant and the infir-mary, past the chapel, the gymnasium, toward the football field,

Ballard watched the headmaster's profile. He was unusually serious today. The boy studied the way the man's blunt nose seemed imbedded in his brow, how the corners of his eyes wrinkled when he was about to speak.

"How are you ... feeling?" he began. "I mean, are you all right?"

"Yes."

As they crossed the cinder track, the white uprights on the football field seemed to sprout out of the grass. Dr. Hickey stopped. "Tell me, how did you feel when you were accepted here at Ravenhill?"

Ballard seemed confused standing there in the morning light, trying to remember. "I—I was very excited, sir."

"Did you know that my assistant, Mr. Allington, insisted that you should be accepted here as an experiment?"

"An experiment, sir?"

"Well, given your recent suspension from Fieldcrest Academy, your problematic history, Elliot felt we should reach out and give students like yourself a second chance. It was entirely his decision. What bothered me was the scholarship ... but that's another matter."

"I don't understand."

"You see, the school psychologist, Dr. Clarence, felt very strongly from your tests that—due to your somewhat difficult childhood, your history of classroom outbursts—you might, well, the doctor felt you might not respond well to this environment."

"Respond?"

"Don't take this too hard," Dr. Hickey said. "It's part of what happens with evaluations. Dr. Clarence can tell you more about the tests. The point is, a number of people on the admissions committee also registered some doubt that Ravenhill was the right place for you. You were, after all, dismissed from your last school for fighting, wasn't it?"

Ballard felt a sinking sensation in the pit of his stomach. "Why are you telling me this now, sir?"

"We've all been troubled, Ballard. Given the early loss of your father, and your mother's situation, we felt you needed a chance. So, we twisted a few arms."

"I don't like feeling beholden to—"

"Don't be silly, you're not."

Dr. Hickey looked out across the end zone to the trees in the distance. They formed a tight border along the edge of the practice field; they seemed to contain his racing thoughts. "I'd like you to see Dr. Clarence, Ballard. I'm sure you wouldn't hurt anyone. In fact, I know you wouldn't, but I—"

"You think I'm crazy?"

"I didn't say that. I want to make sure you're all right. Seeing the doctor is only a precaution. None of the students have to know."

"Yes, sir."

Dr. Hickey reached his bony hand down, as if asking to be forgiven. Ballard shook it without looking at him.

On the green blotter the whole scene flared up before him. There in his room, Cary saw the seeds of fear. He saw them all trying to tear something out of him—some knowledge—now a small hell inside his head.

7

At 1:15, INSTEAD of a lunch break, Nick Fowler drove down the hill into town to the Edwin R. Koenig Funeral Home. The elderly woman at the front desk said the autopsy was in progress and went back to her magazine. *Vogue.* Fowler cleared his throat.

"Studying for the bar exam?"

The woman looked up, squinting at him. "Just what can I do for you, sir?" she said coldly.

"I'd like to speak to the medical examiner for just a moment."

The woman leaned forward, leveling her jaw at him. "As I just said, sir—"

Fowler flashed his identification.

She paused, stood up quite imperiously, marked her place, and marched down the hall. Fowler noticed the all too familiar smells even out in the lobby. A moment later he heard the woman's high heels clicking along the linoleum tiles. It was his turn to look up.

"The medical examiner will see you," she said, "but only for a few minutes."

"That's all I need."

Inside the room, Dr. Koenig turned around from the white Formica counter where his instruments lay. As he washed his hands in a small basin in the counter, he nodded at Fowler. He was a tall man, with a gray receded hairline, a reddish complexion. His body was festooned in a long white coat. Dr. Koenig was not only the county coroner, he owned the largest funeral home in Ravenstown.

On a long table, a sheet covered the body. In the corner, one of the detectives from the police team, Bill Rodney, looked apprehensive. Fowler could see he was filling out a report.

Koenig reached his hand out.

"Lieutenant Fowler. I understand you're in charge of the investigation."

"That's correct." They shook hands.

"You want a report?"

"As much as you've got so far."

Pulling on a fresh pair of elastic gloves, Koenig turned toward the body. "Normally the neck is the no-man's-land of the autopsy." He pulled the sheet back. The first thing Fowler noticed were the boy's eyelashes, he didn't know why. Koenig's white hands hovered above Crawford's blue neck. "Well, here is a large incised wound, which severed the larynx. This was done with a sharp instrument, perhaps a stiletto or a simple deboning knife, or a fillet knife found in most kitchens."

"Right."

"There were some defensive wounds, scrapes along the posterior aspect of the left forearm, and on the palmar surfaces of the fingers of the right hand."

"He put up a fight."

"Yes. But there is where we leave solid ground, Lieutenant."

"What do you mean?"

"Well, if you look closely, there are visible cutaneous injuries to the area, underneath the knife wound. Notice the inclined furrow along the sides of the neck, which duplicate the pattern of either a small rope or a cord of some kind."

"He was hanged?"

"Further testing will be needed to verify this, but . . . cause of death, as far as I can see, was cerebral ischemia, brought on by compression of the vasculature here"—he pointed to the furrow—"thus halting the venous return from the head—here you can see engorgement above the level of where the ligature was tied." He lifted Crawford's eyelids. "And here, you see the bulging of the conjunctivae. He was hanged."

"Then had his throat cut?"

"Yes, killed twice, it seems."

Fowler absorbed this. "Okay."

"Toxicology may reveal any number of causes. The deep cut could have the effect of hiding the real cause of death. For instance"—he pointed above and below the large incised wound—"notice the smaller cuts."

"Made when he was still alive?"

Koenig paused. "Perhaps." He lifted an arm up and, straining a little against the rigor mortis that had set in, traced red blotches around each wrist. "These abrasions almost certainly point to the victim being bound."

"Rope burns?"

"More likely, a thin gauge of cord."

"Any semen, Dr. Koenig?"

"No. Acid phosphatase reveals no semen at this point, but on the genitalia we found traces of cervical secretions."

Fowler looked up at him. "A woman?"

"That's correct."

"Anything else?"

"A rectal swab did not reveal penetration . . ." Koenig's thin white fingers suddenly probed Crawford's mouth. Fowler thought the boy's lips would break like the petals of a pressed rose. His mind began to drift, but Koenig's voice made an incision in his thoughts. "A hint of lipstick left in the corner of the mouth, the rest removed presumably by alcohol—evaporated by now; we're checking for color and composition of the lipstick. Swabs of the face and neck exhibited an alkaline pH; traces of mucus and the enzyme amylase point to intense salivary activity."

"Suggesting what?"

"The victim was kissed, certainly licked. A lot."

Nick absorbed this. "Can you get a DNA workup from saliva?"

"I wish we could."

Nick Fowler stared down at the body. "The wounds suggest a strong person, don't you think?"

"I can't be sure." Koenig said, peering up. "But that's your department, Lieutenant."

Fowler felt the bite of Koenig's remark because he knew it was true. "Thank you, Doctor. I have one question."

The doctor looked up, startled.

"There were bloodstains in the hallway . . . lots of bloodstains. Would the victim have bled profusely *after* being hanged?"

"Not as much as while he was alive, naturally."

Nick Fowler was thinking. "Let me know as soon as you have anything else."

Edwin R. Koenig smiled slightly, nodding his head. "I will." The circles under his eyes became the shadows of a half moon when he ducked his head.

When Nick Fowler returned with Bill Rodney in tow, the afternoon light on the fourth floor of Ardsley was streaming through the windows. The phone rang in the office. It was Marty saying that the garbage cans had been emptied the afternoon prior to the crime, about 5:00 P.M. Fowler covered the mouthpiece while he thought for a moment; he knew most of the boys on the hall had been interviewed and printed. He wanted to review the statements. He put the phone back to his ear.

"Marty, I want you to roam around and talk to students the rest of the day."

The voice crackled through the receiver. "About what?"

"Anything. What do they think? What do they care about?"

"I found out where the kids smoke—that interest you?"

"Yeah, where?"

"In the tunnels."

"Tunnels?"

"That's right, Lieutenant. Some kids from Ardsley Hall told me about it. They were built during the war when the school was used as a military base for two years."

Fowler listened intently. "What did they say was down there?"

"Cigarettes and rats—but I think the kids do things and talk about stuff down there that they can't talk about up on campus."

"Great. Put that in your report, and try to find anything you can about Crawford—what he was doing yesterday, who was the last person to see him alive. Like that."

"Whatever you want . . . sir." There was a slight insinuation in the tone, then a click on the other end.

Fowler frowned, asked Bill Rodney to take a scheduled 2:00 interview with a student.

He needed quiet.

He ambled up two flights and, finding a metal door unlatched, stepped out onto the roof to get some air. He took deep breaths, leaned against the south wall, looking out across the immense green lawns, all edged with Belgian block. When he felt a tacky sensation underfoot, he lifted up the soles of his shoes, touched tar, cursed, and scraped his shoe on a clean shingle.

He got a weird feeling then, a vibe that was unmistakable. He turned around, his eyes panning the roof, the walls, cornices, chimneys, the false pediment on the west wall—a nineteenth-century homage to Greek architecture facing the stone arch that stretched across to Booth Hall. He looked the other way, more chimneys, the old water tower, more cornices and rooftops stretching into the distance.

He walked around the water tower and looked over the hill that slanted down into town. Suddenly he felt a cold wave, a heavy dark feeling, a shudder up and down his spine. There it was again, a cold wash, a hollowness, an empty chill. He leaned against the tower. The feeling left him.

The door to the roof whined as he latched it. When he walked down the stairs, another eerie sensation overtook him. The wheels in Fowler's head were spinning. He stood up on the railing, looking under the stairway for places where a loss of paint or rubbed wood might indicate a rope had supported the weight of a body.

Nothing.

He doubted that Crawford had been hanged on the stairs—possibly on the floor itself. He came down another flight of stairs to the fourth floor. Looking at the bloodstains along the wall unsettled him. He wondered if the patterns on the wall had a ritualistic significance. But why? And why all the blood?

He studied the ceiling fans, glanced at the light fixtures above the old blades twisting in the half-light. His eyes dropped. High up on the walls, above a strip of molding, there were water sprinklers. Fowler pulled a chair out of room 401, the nearest to the blood-stained wall. He stood up on it and examined a sprinkler head jutting out above the door. The fixture was bent down slightly as if pressure had been exerted on it. He stood down on the floor, his eyes still on the sprinkler valve.

His gaze moved slowly down the wall. He studied a series of bloody handprints on the plaster: blots instead of palm prints that looked—from the snakelike imprint of veins—like the top of a hand. A boy's hand. These were enclosed by smudges that looked like gloved fingers. All along this area, the white wall above the wainscoting carried the same odd imprint.

Drops of dried blood trailed away in spirals across the floor. Fowler now climbed the stairs to see if the swirls spelled out something. All he could determine was that the trails of blood drops seemed to travel in oblong shapes, distorted figure eights, moving away from the wall toward the garbage can.

He walked back up to the wall, his mind a blank. He sat down in the middle of the swarms of dried red blots and—gazing down at the dirty floor—saw a fresh indentation in one of the floorboards.

On his hands and knees now, he decided the notch in the wood might be from the end of a knife. Inside the impression, some unvarnished wood peeked above a small cavity of dried red blood. His mind kept thudding up against the same dull question: Why the overkill? He was still kneeling down, staring at what looked like a place of sacrifice.

It was then he realized the killer had brought the boy to this spot during the night, strung him up to the sprinkler while he was still alive, partially slit his throat, and flung the knife so it stuck in the floor, while he—this was where it all collapsed—walked the body around? The body was not dragged. There were no smears, except for the occasional skid of a heel mark.

Suddenly Fowler got an eerie sensation. Goose bumps rose up on his forearms as he reread the report, documenting the position of the stains on the victim's clothing. The blood had poured down the front of the boy's shirt, and carried impressions of another garment, the killer's, forced against it. From these marks, he had decided the killer was wearing a dress shirt or blouse with buttons down the front. *Then he saw it.*

On the shoulder of the boy's shirt were gloved palm prints from a left hand with long thin fingers. Fowler stood up, rested his own left hand, as if he were the killer, on some air the size of a boy's shoulder, this leaving his right hand free. Sure enough, the fingers of his right hand copied the odd imprints above the wainscoting. There was no palm print between the finger smudges because that was where the top of the boy's hand was pressed against the wall.

He held the imaginary boy in his arms and moved out across the floor following the trail of drops, and back. That was when he realized he was dancing. YOU SLIT HIS THROAT, AND WHILE THE BLOOD POURED DOWN BETWEEN YOU, YOU DANCED HIM AROUND THE FLOOR, YOU SON OF A BITCH.

Nick Fowler knew in his bones that's what had happened. The rickety ceiling fans must have muffled the steps. Something bothered him, though, as he moved above the constellations of blood on the floor. The hands were reversed. It appeared as though the victim had been leading.

8

BALLARD WALKED UP the limestone steps to Dr. Clarence's office on High Street. His legs wanted to give way as he thought about discussing the personality tests. Dr. Clarence had said they would get to that.

Nathan Clarence answered the door the same way he had each Tuesday. He pulled opened the door, smiled slightly, dropping his eyes beneath the clear pink frames of his glasses, then—as he pressed the screen door open—Ballard would slip in.

Ballard always sat in the corner of the office on a stuffed sofa, while Dr. Clarence sat at his long mahogany desk where he could peer through the venetian blinds down at the quiet street. Ballard had often looked at the side of the doctor's head, studying the hair that was cut so close it seemed nearly shaved. The doctor had, on many occasions, offered Ballard the choice of lying down if he so desired, but the boy hadn't done that yet.

As always, there was a long silence, but today Ballard really didn't feel like talking. His head felt as though it were full of explosives.

"What are all those thoughts?" the doctor said finally. The words seemed to drop out of the sky like napalm.

"Nothing," Ballard said.

"Seem to be doing a lot of thinking over nothing."

"Yeah."

"Want to talk about it?"

"No."

Another silence. Ballard realized he was angry as he recalled what the headmaster had said to him a month before, but *he* wasn't going to be the one to bring up the tests. Then he thought about the fear.

"Want me to ask what's bothering you?"

"No."

"Well," Dr. Clarence said quietly, "let me try." Ballard was silent. "You're upset about what happened last night."

Ballard wondered what Dr. Clarence was referring to. "What?" he managed to murmur.

"The murder."

"I wasn't thinking about that."

"Well, what is bothering you?" Dr. Clarence said.

"Whatever you want to know about me, you end up finding out."

The doctor leaned forward. "Did that ever happen to you before—with your parents?"

"Never mind," Ballard said, the desultory whine in his voice turning harsh suddenly.

The doctor's tone changed. He said sharply, "Why are you afraid to tell me about this?"

"Because I don't want to!" His voice rising.

"Why not? Which parent did that to you?"

Something detonated inside. Ballard leapt off the couch, stalked to the venetian blinds, and turned so he was facing the doctor. "My father, okay!" His face was red, his hands shaking. "Are you satisfied?"

Dr. Clarence blinked, but looked evenly at him. "How did he do it?"

"Different from you!"

The doctor put down his pencil. "Why are you so angry?"

"You thought I shouldn't be admitted to the school—because of some tests!"

"Who told you that?"

"The headmaster. Second day of school."

"How did that make you feel?"

"How do you think?"

"Why don't you tell me?"

Ballard clenched his fists. "I was angry!"

Dr. Clarence smiled slightly. "You may sit down now, Ballard. That was very good."

"Maybe I won't." He stared at the doctor defiantly, their eyes locked on each other. The doctor was the first to look away. Ballard abruptly slumped back to the couch, lay down, and fell silent.

Dr. Clarence wheeled around in his chair and was surprised that Ballard was lying down. It was the first time. He began again, his voice now low and soothing. "You were about to tell me how your father found out your secrets."

"What?" Ballard said impatiently.

"How did he do it?"

Cary Ballard saw his father standing in a sea of color. He started talking. "In the flower shop, he would dote on the tulips or the mums, the hydrangeas, the geraniums. He would—I don't know—just talk to them. Take care of them."

"Why?" said Dr. Clarence.

"Because they were good—they did what they were supposed to do."

"They—what?"

"Grew up, straight and tall, they bloomed. Had colors."

"And you didn't?"

" . . . I guess not."

"What did your father look like?"

Cary thought about that. "Hefty. Kind of bulky. Dressed like a typical florist—green slacks, a green jacket. He drove a green truck."

"I thought you were going to say he was dressed in black."

The room grew very quiet. "Why would I say that?"

"Before you mentioned seeing a large shape of some sort in black. I thought it was your father."

"I never said that." Ballard felt his voice rise.

"You identified some black shape—some figure—in unconscious ways. First in the tests."

"Here we go."

"Do you want to tell me about the figure?"

"It doesn't exist."

"It doesn't?"

"I have these thoughts, that's all. I see this figure, this thing. I hadn't seen it since I was a kid. Now it's back. Someday I'm going to be free of it."

"*It?* Isn't it you?"

Ballard was silent for a long time. "That figure is my future," the boy said finally, his voice far away, a plaintive whisper in the distance. "It won't let people hurt me."

"How?"

" . . . It stops them. I have to sleep now." Ballard's breathing worked now into a steady rhythm.

"How does it stop them?"

" . . . I don't know—I can't tell—I . . ."

As Dr. Clarence began asking Cary questions about his test responses, he noticed the boy's uncanny ability to fall in and out of a deep sleep. He decided the boy was dissociating.

They talked about pictures from the Thematic Apperception Test. At one point, the doctor thought he had identified some violent behavior. It occurred to him certain desensitization techniques might help.

Ballard felt better when the screen door closed behind him. Walking back down the limestone steps, he rubbed his eyes. All he knew was he felt lighter.

SCHWERIN PRESSED HIS glasses up nervously and squatted down near the fire. "Why did you bring me down here?" he asked. No one answered. The glow illumined the old railroad ties spanning the shaft. The ties that held up the tunnel flickered far into the distance.

Schwerin watched the boys' faces glow, their eyes strange, even translucent. They were sitting, in silence, gazing into the fire they had built out of wood shavings, branches gathered from the woods.

"Tell him about the ghost," muttered Finkelstein, a red-haired boy sitting cross-legged by the fire.

Schwerin looked up. "Ghost?"

"Tell him, Gluckner."

The big football player looked up, shrugged. "You tell him—you saw it." He was lighting a cigarette, staring down the tunnel. "Hey, Goodson, you saw it too, didn't you?"

Goodson leaned forward, as if on cue, rolls of fat creasing his shirt. "Yeah, but not until I got initiated."

They all smiled. Finkelstein poked the fire. "See, Schwerin, this ghost was a student we figure died when the other tunnels collapsed."

The pupils of Schwerin's eyes were expanding. "What does the ghost look like?"

Chung leaned forward and laughed silently, sucking air. "Uh-uh, not yet. First you've got to do something."

Gluckner snorted in the boy's direction. "Schwerin found fucking Crawford's body. He's not scared . . . are you, Schwerin?"

Schwerin pushed up his glasses. "NO."

"What a dick." Gluckner was disgusted. He looked the other way.

Walsh, a skinny kid from Philly who still wore a Chicago duck's ass, pulled out his comb. "Shut up, Gluckner." He combed his greased hair back, was up on his knees. "Look, Schwerin, the ghost is still dressed like a student, right, Fink?"

"He's older," Finkelstein nodded. "But still dressed the way students dressed a long time ago. But his face is white."

Schwerin was squirming. "What do I have to do to see him?"

Gluckner threw a wood shaving at him. "You gotta write something on a bathroom wall, okay, douche bag?"

Schwerin looked confused. "What?"

Finkelstein smiled at Gluckner, whose eyes were gleaming back at him. "Think he could do it?" They traded meaningful stares.

Schwerin was looking around, calculating his exit. Gluckner stretched over, seized Schwerin by the collar, whispered in his ear.

"It's real simple: you write something about Ms. Coates on the wall in any bathroom, okay? We check it out—then we show you the fucking ghoul."

Schwerin was panicking. "Wh—what do I write?"

"Whatever moves you," said Finkelstein, laughing.

The grip around his neck made Schwerin's teeth lock. "You mean, about her body?"

"Do we have to spell it out, stupid?" Gluckner was twisting the collar, beginning to cut off Schwerin's air.

Finkelstein leaned over. " 'The words of the prophets are written on subway walls . . .' "

"And bathroom stalls," Gluckner said. "Remember that."

"Oh?" said Schwerin. He looked around at the boys. They were grinning. "You want a poem about . . . the last time Coates and I did it?" He rolled his eyes. Laughs echoed through the shaft. Slaps on the back, his hair jostled, noogies from Walsh, tits pinched.

Schwerin had arrived.

Finkelstein and Gluckner clapped hands in the air.

9

THERE WAS A pause on the other end of the phone line. Nick Fowler had just called down to the state police station, asking them to run a check on dancing schools in the Hudson Valley area.

Judy Bayard, the dispatcher, had taken the call. She had just spent the day listening to certain comments, mostly out of jealousy, by some officers working out of the station to cover Reliance County. She knew these cops and understood their gripe. The first really unusual killing in years and it got farmed out to a rookie lieutenant from upstate.

She had drunk coffee with these policemen, had sucked down beer chasers with them down at the Thirsty Moose. She had dated two of them. One cop she had even slept with until she found out the fussy roommate he complained about all the time was really his wife. Still, they were all pretty decent guys and she was a loyal person.

When Fowler specified ballroom dancing as the focus of the search, she laughed in his face. Until that moment she hadn't realized how much she had soaked in the opinions of the other cops. She checked herself, apologized, and said she would get right on it.

Fowler slammed down the receiver. He was getting ready to write up his report. He decided to fingerprint and interview Schwerin, the boy who had discovered the body. He didn't find out anything new. When he asked the boy which direction the shoes in the garbage can were pointing, Schwerin contradicted himself, reversing the position of the shoes at least five times. Fowler noticed there was some nervous exhaustion in the boy. He called the infirmary and suggested to one of the nurses on duty that the boy be given some time off, maybe a free weekend.

Ballard walked up the stairs around 3:15. Fowler liked to interview the boys in their own rooms to get a sense of who they were. He wanted to take this one's statement himself.

In room 401, Nick Fowler asked Cary to sit at the desk, where he placed the black print pad on the green blotter.

"Don't worry." He smiled.

He pulled the ends of the boy's fingers, and after he had rolled each finger on the ink pad and pressed it into the squares on a large white card, he handed him an alcohol wipe.

Bill Rodney rapped on the door, asking to speak to the lieutenant. They stepped out into the hall, where Rodney signaled him into the empty room that had become their temporary office. Fowler looked down at the receiver lying on its side on the table. He thought it might be Judy Bayard, the girl he had just spoken to.

Fowler picked up the phone. "Hello?"

On the other end he heard the precise, formal voice of Edwin R. Koenig through a thread of static. "Lieutenant Fowler?"

"Yes."

"We just got the toxicology report. It identified a large dose of tranquilizers taken approximately an hour before death."

"Anything else?"

"Very severe bruises on the heels."

"Interesting."

"Yes."

"I appreciate your work, Doctor."

"Not at all."

Fowler hung up. Bill Rodney closed the door; his tired face looked like it was hanging from a clothesline. The old detective lit up a nonfiltered cigarette.

"Uh, Nick," the tired voice said, "this just in: Latent fingerprints were lifted from the tie found wrapped around the victim's neck. It looks like the print of an adolescent."

Fowler watched Rodney's face fade into a cloud of cigarette smoke. It gave him an instant to think. As the crusty face reappeared, he placed the prints he had just taken from Cary in the gnarled hands.

"Push a check through on these, just in case—they're the Ballard kid's prints. He was the one missing his tie."

Back at the boy's room, Fowler knocked. Waiting for Cary's reply, he glanced up at the sprinkler above the door. He looked down again, turning the knob, and something caught his eye. Peeking out from under the lip of the old painted doorknob, he could see something sticking out. Then he noticed marks that had worn the paint off the bottom of the door. He pushed the door open. Inside the boy was waiting, sitting on the side of the single bed, looking at the floor.

"Just a minute," he said to Ballard. He fished out his pocket-knife. He was able to slip the blade of the knife under the metal knob, working something out through the crack. It was a tiny piece of brown rubber, used in extension cords. He couldn't help but notice that the old white paint was rubbed brown along the neck of the doorknob.

"What do you remember from last night?" he said. "Exactly."

"Nothing," said Ballard.

"Do you know what this is?" He held out the fragment of the electrical cord under the boy's face.

"No."

"It's a torn piece of an extension cord." Ballard shrugged. "Do you mind if I have a quick look around your room?"

"No."

Fowler opened the closet door, searched under the shoes on the floor. A pair of Cary's bedroom slippers had tar on the soles; Fowler touched them—still tacky. He put them aside. He then scoured the top of the shelf above the rack of hanging clothes—there was an old tennis racquet, scrapbooks, old sweats, a jockstrap, and knee pads. He ran through the pockets in Ballard's coats. He found some laundry tickets, some notes from a classmate in study hall.

Finally in Ballard's winter coat, forced against the wall of the closet, he saw something bulging out of a pocket. Using his handkerchief, he pulled out two pieces of extension cord, one long, one short.

"What's that?" Ballard said.

Fowler didn't hear him. He combed the surface of both pieces to find a mar in the sheath. He sat down at the desk, turned on the light, and worked the long electrical snake through the cloth, staring particularly at the edges. Toward the middle of the small cord, he found it. A piece of the rubber had been shorn off, possibly by the lip of the door knob. When he placed the small piece near the tear in the cord, it fell into place.

Fowler quietly placed the cord on the desk, dropped the piece in the handkerchief, and looked up at Ballard. "Did you leave your room at any time last night?"

"No."

"Did you go to the bathroom for a long time? Did you take a walk?"

"No."

"Were you out of your room at any time during the night?"

" . . . Not that I remember."

"What does that mean?" Fowler remembered his interview training, not to push too early, but he felt impatient. "Are you in the habit of not remembering?"

"No, I just mean I don't remember going out."

For a long time Nick Fowler stared at the door, then back at the boy. He abruptly opened the door, pointed to a semicircle of scuffs in the old white paint on the outside of the lower end of the door.

"Know what these are?" he said, looking up at Ballard.

The boy looked at the marks, shrugged, and looked back at Fowler. "No. What are they?"

"Heel marks."

"So."

"We just found out the body of the deceased sustained severe bruises on the heels." Nick Fowler stood up. He looked down at the boy. "Ed Crawford was strung up out here in the hallway. After the killer had some fun . . . the boy's hands were bound and tied . . ." he said quietly. "To this doorknob, with this extension cord."

Ballard's eyes grew to twice their size. "That's impossible," he said.

"I hope, for your sake, it is."

Ballard was now gasping for breath as he took in the full weight of what the man was saying. "I didn't kill him," he blurted out, his voice up an octave.

Nick Fowler looked at the boy's eyes. "Suppose you tell me then how this could have happened if you were here sleeping."

Now Ballard was shivering. His eyes had welled up. His head kept drooping as he shook it, repeatedly, to clear his thoughts. "All right, I did slip out."

"How early?"

"Around two."

"Why is there tar on your bedroom slippers?"

"I—I had to go up on the roof, then down the fire escape. They have electric eyes on the administration floor."

Fowler felt heat hovering over the skin on his face. He knew he was reddening. "Where did you go?"

"I—I can't tell you."

"I'm going to ask you to make a statement, Cary, which you will have to sign, so I want you to listen to me very carefully. Whoever you're protecting, whatever reason you have for withholding evidence, stop. It's not worth it."

"I'm not protecting anyone."

"Then where did you go?"

"You won't tell anyone?"

"If it's not admissible, then—"

"What?"

"If it's not evidence that can be used in court, then it'll be . . . between you and me."

Ballard rubbed his thin palms together. "I went to the graveyard."

Fowler impatiently flipped out his pad and pencil. "What graveyard?"

"The old one above the lake—on the hill that looks over the school."

"Why?"

"There's a girl that . . ."

"I'm listening."

"They say she does things."

"You went to meet her?"

"No, she doesn't know me—she meets, I mean, they said she meets football players there and—you know. I wanted to see."

"Did you?"

"No," Ballard said, his voice getting quiet. "There was no one there."

"What time was this?"

"Three—three-thirty—I think."

Fowler studied the boy's pale face. "What's the girl's name?"

"I don't even know."

"How would you know who it was then?"

"I heard what she looked like."

Fowler adjusted his tensed shoulders. "All right, what does she look like?"

" . . . Blond hair, bleached. Pretty, but hard looks. Wears a lot of makeup. Tight black jeans—look, don't tell her I sent—"

"Who told you this?"

" . . . Gluckner. He's a football player."

"You're sure this was three-thirty?"

"Yes."

"Try to think," Fowler said quietly. "The crime was committed around that time. You were in the graveyard?"

"Yes."

"I'm going to have to seal this room. Don't touch anything. Just stand up. Walk with me."

Nick led Cary out of his room. He kept his eyes fixed on the boy as he stood in the hall, his face lit up as he stared toward the windows; he was crying.

Fowler got on the phone and ordered the print man back in. He dropped the cord and torn piece of rubber into a plastic bag, labeled it, and asked Bill Rodney to find out what student was living just under Ballard's room on the third floor. Rodney already had it charted out. He flipped through his clipboard—the room was empty.

Fowler decided to take Ballard to the infirmary. He could stay there the night while the team combed his room for evidence. As the bell for the memorial service rang, Cary thought the entire student body must have seen him walking next to the lieutenant on the sidewalk in front of the chapel.

IN THE WHITE-TILED admitting office of the infirmary, Ms. Ross, the school nurse, a woman with inclement gray eyes and a lined face, seemed confused at first by Fowler's request. She nervously adjusted the small white folded hat across the top of her silver hair as she watched both sets of eyes fixed on her. Ballard thought her hat looked like a large origami bird.

"You see, ma'am," Fowler explained, "the boy's room has been sealed pending the accumulation of data."

"What does that mean, Lieutenant?" she said.

"It means, until we can clear the room, we need Mr. Ballard to stay here, as if he's sick."

"Is he?" she said as her jaw began its ascent.

"If you have a toothbrush and a towel for him, I'd like him to be excused from classes."

"I can't do that, Lieutenant."

Fowler craned his neck as he sized the tall woman up. Her jaw was now firmly installed at an acute angle high above her small, quivering Adam's apple. "Let's put it this way, Ms. Ross, Mr. Ballard is a suspect—but I'd rather not let that get around."

The nurse's eyes immediately fastened on the boy with horror. "What did he do?"

"Nothing that we can prove yet, but I need some time. I also need your assurance that what I've said is confidential—that means no one—not even your husband."

"My husband wrapped a Ford around a tree last year, Lieutenant. It took them two days to cut him out. I doubt he's in the listening mood."

"I'm sorry," Fowler said, dropping his eyes for a moment. "I'd like one of my men to sit outside the boy's room while he's here."

"Why?"

Fowler planted his feet as he stepped closer to her. "You see, Ms. Ross, this boy may have to interviewed, even interrogated before we're through. He may also be in danger."

Ms. Ross led the boy and Fowler to a room on the second floor. Before he left him, Fowler asked Cary if he could bring any books or personal possessions back for him. The boy asked for his schoolbooks, his diary, his warm-up clothes, and the picture of his mother on top of his dresser. Fowler nodded and pushed the hair out of the boy's eyes.

When Ballard heard the door close, he felt the fear come back. He couldn't say what it was, but it slowly took hold. His heartbeat instantly began to pound as the lieutenant's footsteps retreated down the stairs.

On Fowler's way out, Ms. Ross stood up at her wide oak desk and walked out to the foyer, holding a manila folder.

"Lieutenant, I was looking at the boy's medical records. He is in the care of a doctor." She turned so he could peer over her shoulder.

"Who?"

Her finger ran down the page. "Dr. Clarence, who is also the school psychologist."

"Does it say why?"

"Some sort of disturbance. It says here . . ." For one moment they both silently read a paragraph from the boy's doctor. One recurring symptom made Fowler very curious. It said that Ballard would often "disconnect and slip in and out of reality."

He looked up, blinking into the woman's gray eyes. "Where can I find this Dr. Clarence?"

"Well, he's at the murdered boy's memorial service now. So is the whole school." She rubbed a bony finger over her bottom lip, then looked down at her wristwatch. "Here," she put down the file and picked up the school yearbook lying on a table by the entrance and began leafing through the pages. "Here he is. You can spot him coming out of chapel."

Fowler looked down at the clear pink glasses, the severely trimmed hair, the skull-like head, the perfect bow tie of Dr. Nathan Clarence. He thanked Ms. Ross and left.

10

Inside the chapel, the students shuffled in and took their assigned seats. A few boys flinched when the sacred music began to blare from the massive gold-leaf pipes of the organ behind them.

Usually the music lifted the boys' minds away from their studies into a strange, exalted world. Those who weren't believers could contemplate the supernatural aspects of blood turning into wine, of bodies rising high above the earth. Mostly it was a time for reflection. And sleep.

Today was different. There were no heads nodding. Agitation was everywhere. The boys seemed uneasy, sullen, quick to anger, their emotions threadbare after the day of tension. There was a rumor the school might be closed; on that they could only hope. They had all heard the gruesome descriptions of Crawford's death.

As the light outside the tall windows was fading, the assistant chaplain, with the aid of a grid on his lectern, subtly recorded attendance. Then a loud major chord announcing the opening anthem descended on the boys, and they fumbled for their hymnals.

After the anthem, there was a breathless silence in the room. Mr. Fitz, the chaplain, stood up, adjusted his wire-rimmed glasses and smoothed his vesper garments. "Faculty and students of Ravenhill School," he said. "Today the worst tragedy in the history of the academy has befallen us. A terribly inhumane crime has been committed—and one of our own has fallen."

He walked slowly to the podium. "I read to you now from the

Book of Job, chapter two, verse three." There was a pause as his fingers lifted a wilted page out of the book. His voice echoed off the back walls. " 'And the Lord said unto Satan, From whence cometh thou? And Satan answered the Lord, and said, From going to and fro in the earth, and walking up and down in it.' "

The chaplain cleared his throat.

He walked around the podium, leaned on the side of the lectern, and took off his glasses. "Now, boys, I didn't read this quote to suggest that Satan himself is walking up and down in our midst. Rather, consider for a moment what might happen if we ponder the lessons of Job, how we might steel our minds against the panic that is clearly sweeping our campus." The chaplain's fierce eyes panned the rows of rapt young faces. "Think for a moment how, even though it appears that a kind of Satan is going to and fro on our campus—although we may be forced to acknowledge that presence—we *must not* curse God for our misfortune. We must hold fast to our faith and recall how, even though Job was set upon a dung heap and covered with boils from head to toe, he never renounced his belief in God. And in the end, the Almighty returned to Job twice as much as he had before."

A strange pall fell over the room. For the next ten minutes, Mr. Fitz extolled Ed Crawford's virtues, his good study habits, his interest in extracurricular activities. Anecdotes were mentioned of the boy's kindness toward his fellow students. During this eulogy, a strange phenomenon was taking place. There were murmurs across the audience. Students all around the room were looking from side to side, staring behind themselves as if they might actually behold Satan in their midst, standing perhaps by the back wall, sitting calmly on the aisle.

When the chaplain turned the program over to Dr. Hickey, the

headmaster seemed flustered as he stood up at the podium, grop-
ing for his speech inside the incalculable expanse of his gown. He
too had been looking uneasily around the room.

This left him no choice but to make some impromptu remarks
on his pet peeve—chewing gum wrappers on the grass—as he
searched for his speech. When he found it, he gazed solemnly down
at the boys and began to talk about the ideals that Ravenhill ascribed
to. He became vehement when he began to express how nothing, no
tragedy, no act of violence could shift the firm bedrock upon which
the tenets of the school were founded back in 1852.

At that point, Dr. Hickey had actually redeemed the service.
However, he then chose to ask faculty members to stand and offer,
from their own experience, any words they could pass on to the
boys about death occurring close to them. To his surprise, something eerie had taken place. No one had the strength to stand up
and speak. It was as if the whole congregation was under a spell,
all thinking the same thought: Satan *was* in our midst. The faculty
members who were usually so vocal seemed mesmerized, unable
to get out of their seats.

After the recessional, a number of masters regretted how many
of the students left the service walking out, numbly, in shock.

FOWLER LEANED ON the wrought-iron railing of the stairs near
the entrance to the chapel. He could get a good look at the faculty
members coming through the tall wooden doors, between the
Doric columns, down the long set of steps.

Dr. Clarence was walking alone. Nick Fowler approached him.

"Dr. Clarence?"

Taken off guard, the doctor drew back, carefully looking the
tall blond man over. "Yes?"

"I'm Lieutenant Fowler," he said, flipping his ID open.

The man paused, still staring. "Let me see that," Dr. Clarence said, reaching for the leather folder. Fowler opened it again, without releasing it. "All right," Dr. Clarence said finally. "One can't be too careful these days."

"May I speak to you for a moment, Doctor?"

"I thought we were speaking," the doctor said with a trace of innuendo. Fowler frowned. The two men eyed one another, turning up the sidewalk.

"We're trying to learn as much as we can about the students living on the floor where the crime took place."

"I see."

"I understand you're seeing a student named Cary Ballard."

"That's correct. I saw him today."

"Does he have a particular problem?"

"I've only been seeing him for a month."

"Well, Doctor, what I'd like to know is—can you briefly state what you think may be bothering him?"

"Not briefly."

Fowler looked over at the thick pink frames. "Well," he said, "take as long as you like."

The doctor's neatly cropped head had not moved but was facing forward as if there were a wall between them. Another pause. "Have you ever been in therapy, Lieutenant?"

"Yes."

"How long?"

"Not briefly."

Fowler thought he actually saw a faint smile flicker across Dr. Clarence's features. The man just kept looking forward as he walked. He lit a cigarette with a gold monogrammed lighter;

Fowler noticed how the butane flame was adjusted to exactly the right height. "His sessions are confidential, you realize."

"Can you give me a general overview, then, Doctor?"

After a pause, Clarence said finally, "He doesn't seem to be suicidal. He is depressed, however. His tests reveal a high level of paranoia."

"How can you tell?"

"His Wechsler results, where he was hypervigilant in math, particularly the matching exercises, and the digit symbol sections—reflected part of his anxiety. His Rorschach tests also revealed an overattention to detail, an obsessive nature. I could go on and on about his TAT cards, but I will leave it at . . . a preoccupation with sex."

"Sounds like a normal fourteen-year-old."

Dr. Clarence stopped in his tracks. "Lieutenant, for your information, he also does something that healthy children never do. He hallucinates."

"Can you tell me what he sees?"

"As I told you, that's confidential."

"If what he might see, or not see, has any bearing on the case, I'll find out anyway when I have you subpoenaed, so why don't you—"

"I can wait."

"Is there anything else, anything unusual—anything I might—"

"That's enough, I should think."

Fowler stopped in the middle of the sidewalk under a giant maple. "Doctor, excuse me for pressing you, but we think the Crawford boy may have been killed right outside Cary Ballard's room. Is there any condition, any occurrence that he has told you about—when he might *not* remember things?"

"No."

"Then how do you explain your statement in Cary's file at the infirmary, which says—"

"If you don't mind." Dr. Clarence turned to face him, planting his feet. "I think I've answered enough questions."

Fowler was frustrated. "I'm afraid that's not good enough."

"I beg your pardon?"

"You're withholding information that is valuable to this case."

Dr. Clarence swallowed to contain his emotion. His eyes became impermeable. "Lieutenant, someone should teach you some manners." He pivoted on his heel and disappeared into the evening shadows.

From his window in the infirmary, Ballard had witnessed the conversation between the two men. They were out of earshot, strolling along the sidewalk by the chapel.

His mind worked feverishly. He imagined the leaves in the green maples above their heads, full of sensitive surveillance equipment, the stems carrying wires, the leaves installed with a unique fabric of microphones that turned with the wind to record any nuance in the human voice.

There were light sensors, he was sure, computer screens concealed beneath the bark that registered any change in blood pressure between the two men, any emotional change that might reveal to the boy from a distance what they were saying.

Ballard knew his imaginings were defensive. He knew the longer he kept fantasizing, the longer he could keep the fear out. Still a terror seemed to pry open his thoughts as he thought of heels striking the door enough times to wear off the paint. He tried to remember what he had been dreaming about last night at four A.M.

IN HIS OFFICE in Ardsley, Fowler was just finishing his preliminary report. The end of his first day, and all he had was a few leads. He was going blank. He threw down his pencil.

He closed his eyes.

His mind was already racing back, searching every memory like a computer, trying to find out what was stirring deep inside him. The last image in the back of his mind died on a blank screen. The face he had seen before reappeared—it was his father— surrounded by white; more police forms? No, white sheets. The face leaned forward . . . to say something, and . . .

Nick opened his eyes, shook his head. He sipped some cold coffee, started pacing. He had to concentrate now. He picked up the report to review outstanding questions, facts.

He called the coroner once more. A last-minute report from the lab yielded an interesting discovery: On Crawford's pajamas, the transfer of fibers, presumably from the killer's clothes, had the thickness, the type of weave, and the dye content to reveal that the killer was wearing the type of suede often used on the lapels of vintage gowns and tuxedos.

This gave credence to Fowler's theory. The shape of the bloodstains, splashes that had struck the floor from an elevation of fifty-three inches—the exact height of Crawford's neck—all were in the same oblique patterns that showed the victim had been moving continually.

Fowler sat writing his report between an open encyclopedia and a forensic text. He was surprised that the small library in town had so many reference books on ballroom dances. He determined from the oblong trail of stains and heel smears that the killer—though allowing the victim to appear to lead—was doing the American Waltz. In fact he or she was doing a basic box step, where the quarter turn on the accentuated beat—from music in the killer's head, no doubt—created the spirals of blood.

He wrote a personal note to Captain Weathers asking him to at least give this theory a try. He provided pictures of the stains from above, matched with foot positions of the waltz from *The Encyclopedia of Ballroom Dancing*.

He mentioned the discovery of the place of death, by hanging, out in the hallway, but left Cary Ballard's name out; he didn't know why yet—just a hunch. He checked and rechecked the report, then signed it.

There was a sudden scraping sound out on the fire escape. He glanced out the window, but didn't see anything. He was in a hurry, so didn't bother to open the window.

HE STEPPED OUT into the night air. As he turned the corner toward the squad car, he saw two boys kick gravel with their shoes, trying to get away from the car.

"Hey!" he yelled after them, but they bolted out of the light down into the trees by the power plant. Fowler looked down at the old brick smokestack in the darkness.

He noticed one of his tires was low. Kids had been letting the air out. He half smiled. He wondered how Dr. Clarence would classify these boys. Hardened criminals, no doubt.

He drove down the hill, across the highway, and into the parking lot of the station house. He waved the file at the booking sergeant, who nodded, and put the report on the captain's desk himself.

Then he decided to go out for a late dinner.

The dispatcher, Judy Bayard, was just coming out of the ladies' room when Fowler breezed out the front door. She saw the venetian blind on the door swinging back and forth as she peered through the slats. She turned to the booking sergeant.

"What'd he come in for, free coffee?"

The sergeant's feet were up on the counter. He peered around the side of his shoes, his attention on a television set in the background. "Naw, he brought somethin' in."

"What?"

"Somethin for the Cap. Put it on his desk."

Judy cocked her head. "Really?"

11

SILENT. EDGE OF *the roof. Crawl around a chimney . . . over the edge of the wall, cinders under gloves, shoes on metal stairs. Down. Kneel. See into the fourth-floor window. The blond hair slumped forward, writing something. There he is. Case work.*

Eyes and mind intent. Threw down your pen, why? Something keeps you away from the others. What is it?

Want to catch me, don't you? Before I kill you, I'll tell you who I am, with thoughts. Just read the mind. Ready? Now, concentrate.

Court took me away from my parents—beat me so much. See it in your mind, Lieutenant. My father tied me to trees, whipped me while my mother screamed and threw herself at his feet. But she didn't stop him, did she?

The drums inside again, beginning to pound in the distance. A vein throbbing, tapping—bumb—bumb. Touch it—oh, shoe off the step—losing my balance—a ringing sound, echo down the fire escape.

You move toward the window, stare through the glass, seeing nothing. I jump over the wall. Back on the roof, hyperventilating. Terrible cadences in my head. Can you hear? Can't stop them . . .

that's why I stayed in my room and painted with bright colors— streaks on the walls—craving my parents' blood.

Wait. Lights out. Your shadow in the stairwell. Down more flights. Listen. Neighbors reported the screams . . . Lieutenant, I'm following you . . . down the fire escape . . . thoughts searing me . . . years in an orphanage . . . feet on metal stairs, racing to keep up . . . they threatened me with knives. I'm catching you now. Down. Terra firma.

Into your car, start to drive under the arch. I'm right behind you. Now running . . . thirty feet behind the car . . . your brake lights . . . see my parents' fins, tiny taillights over a cliff—meteors exploding . . . bastards killed in a car crash . . . never a chance to say thank you, fuck you. Listening, Lieutenant? The meter inside me pulsing now, veins beating again . . . accentuated . . . coming closer, taking me. Grandparents took me out of there and gave me a home, a life, an education. End of story. The cadence inside screaming now. I seeeee yoooou.

My grandparents loved me. That's not why I killed them. I corrected them for giving birth to monsters.

12

IN THE DINER, two blocks down from the state police station, a woman was paying for her coffee and rice pudding at the register as Nick Fowler strode in, shimmied onto a seat at the counter, and ordered some food.

She asked the cashier who the man was and got a shrug. She brushed some change into her free hand and walked outside.

Through the glass she stared at the wide back of the man as he leaned against the counter. A strange sensation took hold of her inside. She liked the feeling, but it scared her.

She felt the hoods of several cars. When she found the warm one, she looked through the windshield at the small red flasher on the dash. On the front seat was a cap that said "Buffalo Bills." It didn't take long for her to figure out this guy was the rookie lieutenant from upstate everybody was heated up about.

In the reflection of the car window, she brushed out her long red hair. Glancing over, she applied a shade of dark pink in the side-view mirror, then pressed her lips over a tissue. She picked a cinder out of the corner of a blue eye with her fingernail, then standing up, pulled her gray-check suit down to her knee, only to fluff it back up again. She walked across the gravel and opened the door to the diner.

As she brushed past the register again, the cashier's eyebrows went up, but not very far—something about the mournful, imitation country and western Muzak coming from the speaker dulled her surprise at most things.

When the woman's heels clacked up behind Nick Fowler, he was just pushing his soup bowl away. She leaned over the red stool cushion beside him and placed her palm on the counter.

Fowler looked down at her hand. He could see her legs too. As his eyes climbed the gray business suit curving up to the white ruffle under the dark pink mouth, he blinked.

"Hey," he mumbled.

"Hello," she said quietly. "You aren't by any chance the cop from upstate everybody's talking about, are you?"

Fowler's eyes were glued to her face. She was a very beautiful woman. "Is everybody talking about it?"

"Like a public service announcement."

He smiled. "Have we met?"

"I think I would have remembered."

He smiled again, offering a hand. "Nick Fowler."

"Maureen McCauley," she said, shaking his hand.

Nick held on to her hand. "Would you join me?"

She released her hand awkwardly. "Sure, Lieutenant." She sat down on the stool.

"So, Maureen," he said, glancing over at her. "Who's telling you about me?"

"Ravenstown's finest."

The waitress dropped his platter with a steak on it down on the Formica. "Sour cream for the potato?" She flicked the pages of her order pad, found his check, tore it off, and slapped it on the counter.

Nick lifted the platter up and handed it back to the waitress. Her eyes looked down as if it was still alive.

"Could you keep this warm for me, please? I'd like to talk with this lady for just a minute."

"Allllriiight," the waitress said. Hoisting the platter. "Anything else for you, honey?"

"No thank you," Maureen said.

The waitress wheeled through the swinging doors.

Maureen swiveled on the stool. "That was nice of you. I'd like to talk to you too."

"Anything to please our women in the press."

She stared at him, slightly dumbfounded. "How did you know?"

Fowler shrugged. "You don't look like you work for the sheriff's department; too much quality for that. There isn't any industry around here. You could teach or work at a hotel or a travel agency, I suppose, except there's something vaguely literary about you, but you're too well dressed to be a struggling writer. Besides, who else would know about a flap at the department but a reporter?"

"You're good."

"You still haven't answered my question."

"Which one?"

"Who told you about me?"

Maureen unrolled her neck from her shoulders like a cat stretching. "I have my sources."

"I'm just doing my job, Maureen. I never meant to step on anybody's toes."

"You can't blame them. The only thing to happen around here, now and then, is when somebody gets run over. Suddenly there's a big murder case, and they turn their noses up at the local guys and call *you* in. Better watch your back."

"Thanks for the warning." He was staring. "So, who's upset?"

"Look around."

"You know, this is a very tricky case. Somebody should explain that to the men."

"Maybe I could do it."

"I meant the captain," he said. "I'm up against a frightening individual, after all."

Her eyes lit up. "Tell me."

Nick noted the eyes, admired the face. There was something yearning there, shining back at him with anticipation. "I wish I could," he mumbled.

"Come on." She leaned over playfully, nudging his shoulder. Nick caught a whiff of her hair. The smell was so sweet it actually startled him. He turned and looked at her again. He saw something in her expression that touched him, had a sudden presentiment that he had known her before. Couldn't help feeling, though, it was too close, too fast.

She realized he was studying her now, and smiled back. "Well?"

He was on the ropes. "Can't reveal my sources."

Maureen nodded slowly. "I don't blame you. My readers would sure like to know though."

"You with the *Tribune*?"

"Yeah, it's a rag, but when they made me feature editor, I knew my stay in this town would be longer than . . . well . . ." She adjusted herself on the stool. "Can I level with you?"

"Please."

"I'm stuck here . . . I mean, I need something to sink my teeth into. Let me help you with this case, Nick."

Fowler's brow was clouding over. "This isn't feature stuff. I'm getting inside the mind of a psychopath. It's dangerous, not to mention grim going; just legwork, details, layers of tests, evidence."

"I love details; in fact, I'm compulsive."

"You don't know what I mean." A little ruefully. "Look, just stick to . . . whatever it is you do."

Maureen's ruffle began to stand up. "Wait. You think all I do are garden parties?"

"No way, I just meant—"

A flash of anger across her brow. "I can't handle it—because I'm a *woman*?"

"Never said that either."

"Then why don't you give me a nibble?"

Nick tried grinning at her. "Where?"

"On the front page." Maureen didn't blush.

Nick laughed. "Look, I'd rather not tip my hand to the killer. Do you mind?"

"All right, then just let me dig things up, Lieutenant. I have a good background in forensics. I have strong research skills."

"I can't."

"You need a friend in court, don't you?"

"I've just always worked alone."

The wheels were turning behind her bright eyes. "You know, you could feed me false information—that might throw him off. He could make a mistake."

Nick looked at her seriously. "Who said it was a *he*?"

"Nobody."

Now they were both staring. Something about her was pulling him, beneath that wafer of ivory skin, something charged, utterly electric. He was attracted and threatened—all at the same time—what more could he want? He shook his head. "Better not."

"Rather play it by the book?"

"For now, yeah."

She swiveled, speaking toward the windows of the parking lot. "Well, some people say you don't know what you're doing, but—"

"Who?"

She looked back at him, her cheeks reddened slightly. "Look—forget it, I just—"

"Who?"

She could feel his blue eyes boring down on her. Maureen looked down at the stubble of facial hair along his chin. She saw the sensitive mouth closed insolently over his front teeth. She wanted to reach out and touch his face, but couldn't hide her disappointment. "I don't remember."

"Why are you doing this?" he said wearily.

She pulled her fingers through her red hair. "Why am I doing what?"

"Putting me on the spot like this?"

She stared at him. "I mean, you're saying some fairly irksome things to me—sure that's fine, isn't it?"

"What have I said?"

"You don't mind putting the moves on me—"

"Hey look, it was just a friendly—"

"But let me do something where I might have to use my head, well that's out of the question, right?"

Nick couldn't understand how he had gotten into an argument with this woman. He didn't even know her. Her bright eyes just kept staring at him. "Look," he said, "people's lives are at stake here. I can't play 'let's make a deal' with this case."

Nick stood up, grabbed the check, and reached for his wallet. The waitress looked over a Maureen, back at Nick. "It's six seventy-five," she said, pushing buttons on the register at the counter.

Nick gave her a ten, took back the change, put a dollar on the counter.

"Shall I wrap up the steak?"

"No, forget it."

Maureen was already standing with her back to him, silently looking out the window. He turned around and looked her over once more. The way her high heels were drawn together made him feel cold. He wondered if he would ever be able to get close to a woman.

She saw him give her the once-over in the reflection of the plateglass window. She smiled into the reflection. She was hoping he would take her shoulder, turn her around, and say he was sorry. At least, say goodbye. Anything.

He never did.

SHE STARED THROUGH the window as his car pulled out onto the highway and sent gravel against the metal foundation of the diner. She threw her purse over her shoulder, strutted out into the parking lot and over toward the Thirsty Moose.

She shook her red hair out as she put her heels down hard on the pavement. She passed by the neon beer sign in a porthole window and stopped, looking back across the highway toward the diner. She was half hoping he would still be there, his back blazing from the counter, looking like an advertisement for Soloflex.

She kicked the door open.

Inside the smoke rolled across the bar. The noise from the tables in the corner was deafening. The jukebox was blaring. She pulled up a stool, put her soft pink cigarette case down on the bar along with her keys, lit up, and when the bartender came over, she ordered a White Russian.

While she was sipping her drink, she noticed she had sighed again, almost not hearing the group at the far table yelling her name.

"Hey, Maureen!"

She was in a blue fog. The neon sign above the bar was a buoy on an endless sea of cigarette smoke; she had been on this ocean before, in countless bars, alone.

She wondered why she hadn't gone back to L.A. She could get a gig in San Bernardino easy; even her hometown, Bakersfield, which was the pits, had to be better than this.

Staring at the red neon tubes in the sign, she wondered if that was the size of the vessels carrying oxygenated blood to her brain. Her thoughts were racing. She thought—*no* newspaper job *in the world* is worth *this* humiliation.

Suddenly someone with nails was tugging at her blouse. "Yo, Maureen," a loud voice said. "Got cotton in your ears?"

She turned around and looked into Judy Bayard's oval face.

"Hi," Maureen said quietly. "Sorry, I guess I didn't hear—"

Judy's frosted hair flounced up and down. On her third vodka she talked as if everyone around her were deaf.

"What'ya sittin' up here for? We got a whole table of guys down there."

Maureen glanced through the smoke-filled room, toward the back of the bar. There, in the dull light next to the bowling machine, was a table of blue arms waving. A few whistles.

"No, Judy, really, I'm not up for—"

"*Come on,*" she said, practically lifting Maureen off the stool, "we're roasting Dudley Do-right."

Maureen's thoughts were switching gears, grinding. "Who?"

"That lieutenant I told you about—he's fucked. You wouldn't *believe what that fool* said in his report. The guy is *nuts!*"

Maureen put her cigarette down. "How did you find out what he put in—"

" 'Cause I *read it, honey.* Fuckin' guy brought it in tonight. Captain's gonna shit. You *can't believe.*"

Maureen tamped out her cigarette, grabbed her things off the bar, and jumped off the stool.

"I'd like to hear," she said as the girl led her to the back.

13

Nick was bare-chested, sitting on the edge of the bed in the motel room, his head hanging down. A white towel draped over his knees. He realized he had been staring at the white material for a long time. He was depressed. The fight with that intriguing redhead had left him alienated and edgy.

His thoughts found safe harbor with the killer. He wondered why a person would dance with someone as they were killing them. The killing must have come out of some kind of romantic alienation—much like what he was feeling now—only with a thousand times more rage behind it.

Nick thought about his ex-wife, Penny, the pert brunette social worker from the Buffalo suburbs. She had enough guilt to move to the inner city to work with minorities, and enough scotch to cope with it. He heard her voice now, which always struck him as condescending—as if she were sitting in the room—the way she had always accused him of closing her off, taking any excuse to be distant, to be away from her, whether it was the extra duty he took on for his career, drinks with the guys, or even a football game on TV. She always said he kept himself separate. Nick let himself feel his defenses rising. Just for an instant, while he visualized her, he let his mind wonder: What would it take to make a man actually kill? He couldn't think of anything . . . but betrayal felt close.

Had the killer been betrayed by the victim? Was the killer attracted to the young boy? Or did the boy represent someone else, someone from the killer's past?

Nick dropped his head down into the towel. He wanted to crawl into the killer's mind—but he had gone blank. While he stared at the items on the desk, feeling numb, empty, he got an idea. He dialed the phone, heard it ring on the other end.

An elderly woman's voice. "Hello?"

"Mom, it's Nick."

Warmer now. "Well, how's it going?"

"Not very good. Look, can I ask you something? I have this black hole in my memory about the night Dad was shot, would you—"

"For God's sake, Nick, I was having a nice evening."

"I just want to know what *I* did that night, that's all."

"Please don't make me go over it, dear."

"I have to know—it's important."

"See, there's a television program on I'm watching. I'm sorry, I can't."

"Why do you always do this?"

"I'm sorry, dear. It's just too painful. I have to hang up now."

Nick was aggravated. "Just tell me why I left that night—Mom?"

A pause on the other end, a sniffle. "Good night, dear." A dial tone.

He slammed down the phone, his head sinking down in the towel again. He forgot the shower had been running in the bathroom. Again his mind was leaping back. The images kept flying toward him; they went by so quickly he couldn't grasp them. Hospital beds. Pleated, white cotton screens. Empty gurneys rolling down hallways in slow motion. They seemed to float toward him. He was falling.

Then he was standing outside a hospital door. It opened as if a gust of wind had sucked it inward. Papers flew across a room, and out open windows where clouds hung in the distance. Dr. Koenig was standing in the room, over a covered body, pulling on his surgical gloves. He smiled, then ripped the white sheet down. An older man sat up, slowly, looked toward Nick and started to scream. The man was his father. His open mouth, coming closer, swallowed the room.

NICK SUDDENLY WOKE up. The steam from the shower was pouring out of the bathroom. He looked up just long enough to see a face in the mirror before it fogged over.

It was his father's face—then it became his own.

CARY WAS RIDING on a roller coaster. There was some man next to him he didn't know; he was laughing. As they came over the top of a hill, high in the mountains, the track seemed to veer around a dark rock formation. When they crested a steep hill, their car swerved at a sharp angle, the light changed, and they were thrown inside a cave heading toward a sheer drop into blackness.

The man got out and glanced down into the tunnel. Cary was trying to pull the car back up the steep tracks but kept slipping. The man was waving him forward when the boy lost his footing. The weight of the car suddenly dragged him over the edge. As the man waved, he plunged into darkness.

CARY OPENED HIS eyes. He could feel thousands of tiny stones under his back. Had he fallen through a cavity in the earth's crust? He lifted himself up and felt gravel under his elbows. He could see the smokestack of the power plant in the distance. He saw a few stars. The sky was wearing a fierce blue coat. In the distance he saw chimneys on buildings. One of them was Ardsley.

He looked down, noticing that he was still dressed. The four black chimneys on the infirmary gave the small building the look of a castle. He saw a poplar next to the building moving slightly, but there was no wind.

He heard a laugh coming from the dark lawn below.

The gravel crackled under the soles of his shoes as he crept toward the edge of the roof.

Across the lawn was a patch of undergrowth, some woods standing barren in a flat bottom of land where the power plant was almost hidden by vines. There was a bright white light on the top of the brick smokestack.

The light exaggerated the silhouettes of two figures running toward the woods. Their slanted shadows swept across the grass until they loomed, covering the lawn, then whipped back at an angle toward the plant.

Even from the roof, Ballard could see one of them was the kid named Finkelstein. He could tell from the gangly lurch the kid had used trying out for the track team. He seemed to be chasing someone.

Ballard leaned over the edge of a wall, focusing his eyes. The student *was* chasing a woman. He heard a giggle, then saw a flash of white material pass under the glow of the light. He thought for a moment it was Ms. Coates, his math teacher.

They disappeared between the boughs of the small trees that bordered the building. Then there were only footsteps, rustlings like the kind he remembered in the woods as a child. Animals. Creatures just beyond the naked eye. He stood at the edge of the roof blinking.

Cary thought he was still dreaming. His mind started to race. The old dread was coming toward him as from the horizon, huge, immense, relentless. Something kept him from seeing it, however, some sound, below.

Someone else was watching. He didn't know how he knew. He thought he had heard breathing underneath him on the ground, or was it the wind rustling leaves on the poplar at the edge of the building?

He found the stairs that led down from the roof. The hook that held the door closed was still unfastened. He stepped down into the dark stairwell, anchored the door, and half crawled down to the landing. There, across the dim hallway, was the policeman still asleep next to his door.

He watched the little man's nostrils flare as they sucked in the stale air of the corridor. Cary managed again to slither behind the chair that was tilted back against the doorjamb. When he was inside his black room, he eased the door closed.

He had gotten back in bed before he realized he still had his clothes on. He stood out on the floor, stripped off his jeans and, in his underwear, got back under the covers. He felt the stillness of the night come down on him. It landed like an extra quilt. The quiet became so heavy he actually thought that sound itself had disappeared from the earth.

That was when he heard the noise. He knew it was a tile. The eave that bordered the second floor, running all the way around the four sides of the infirmary, was lined with orange Spanish tile. Again, he heard it. The wind would have to be high to make the tiles shift. He sat up in bed and peered through the window that threw a pale cast across the sheets.

A face appeared in the window. Ballard lurched backward off the bed. He landed on his back on the floor. The face was still there, covered with the black scarf as always, the black hat, the eyes—even in the dark—carrying an inhuman, feverish glow.

Ballard's legs wouldn't move. He squirmed backward, something retching up from deep inside him, as he watched the eyes of the figure burn like torches. He flopped over, dragging his body across the floor with his elbows. His fingernails found an uneven slat of wood raised slightly off the floor, and he pulled himself toward the door, his mouth unable to make any sound, though he was trying to scream.

14

THE NEXT MORNING, in his motel room, Nick Fowler shaved, showered, and was dressed by nine. When he turned off the water and wiped his face, he heard a stream bubbling behind the flat pink building. He opened his bathroom window.

He put on a pair of slacks, a clean shirt, sports jacket. He straightened his tie and drove to the diner to get some coffee to go. He dropped a quarter in the slot of a newspaper machine in the vestibule, not really paying attention, and folded the paper under his arm as he paid for coffee and a roll, no butter.

When he was behind the wheel, he opened the container of coffee, took a sip, and casually flipped the paper open on the seat.

The headline hit him in the face. ROOKIE INVESTIGATOR THINKS KILLER IS ARTHUR MURRAY. Fowler swallowed hard, looked down at the byline, with his mouth open, his coffee hovering in the air. He was stunned. It said "Maureen McCauley."

First the feature article distorted his history with the police department, fudged the dates of his employment, making him sound inexperienced. Next, it hinted he had based his entire theory—that the killer was dancing with his victims—on his own deprived feelings of wanting to belong.

A few people working the night shift at the station house in Buffalo were carelessly quoted when asked—over the phone probably—if he could dance himself. They said, "No, he had two left feet."

The article called the investigation "misguided." It called for Fowler's removal from the case, "reflecting the outcry from local officials." As far as he knew, Fowler hadn't heard of any outcry— only some disgruntled cops who had missed their turn.

The final paragraph asked if the community was going to stand by while a "wallflower" danced (badly) around the real issues of what happened the night of the murder.

Fowler shoved the transmission in gear and gunned the car out of the diner. He made the engine bawl through the quiet streets. It roared up the hill. His face was a shade of vermilion, he was sweating through the back of his clean shirt, he had spilled his coffee already, and he was seething.

He stormed up to the fourth floor, burst into the temporary office, where Bill Rodney stood by the window with a silent look of anxiety on his face.

In the corner, sitting on a student's chair much too small for him, was the captain. Allen Weathers stood up as the door flew open.

His short gray crew cut, an homage to his days as a Marine, could not hide the red color that had risen up under his scalp. Some people felt he was too tough to be a country official, that he took his frustration out on the men.

Nick Fowler stopped in his tracks. "Captain," he said, giving him a short, grim nod.

"Sit down, Fowler," he said, and sat down himself.

He picked up a copy of the *Tribune*, glanced at it, then threw it against the wall. "What the fuck is this?"

Fowler opened his mouth. "Lies, Cap—"

"How the fuck did you manage to get—"

"*It's lies, Captain. That bitch* doesn't know her ass from—"

"I don't care if it's lies, I want to know *how in the name of Jesus*, she got—"

"I just talked to her for—"

The captain's voice was rising. "Don't you know who the fuck she is?"

"*No, I don't know who the fuck she—*"

Weathers stood up. "Don't raise your voice to me!"

Fowler was up on his feet too. "*Then don't play me for a fool. The whole story is a—*"

"*Shut the fuck up!*"

Nick Fowler shifted his weight. "Yes, sir," he mumbled, sitting down.

Weathers started pacing, his giant hands behind his back. "Look, Lieutenant, I went out on a limb to put you on this case."

"I know, sir. I appreciate that."

"You haven't shown it. You're supposed to work *with* my department, not against it."

Fowler swallowed. He was trying to get a hold of himself. "With all due respect, sir, I haven't been working against your—look, when I took control of the scene, I had to run some people off—yourself included. That pissed a lot of people off."

"Okay." Weathers's voice had dropped a few decibels.

"That's why they're out to get me."

"How about this girl?"

"I met her last night in the diner after I put the preliminary on your desk."

Weathers stopped pacing, staring right at Fowler.

"Didn't you know she was a reporter?"

"Within about a minute."

"So why the hell did you tell her anything about—"

"*I didn't.*"

"What?"

"I told her nothing."

"Then how the fuck did she—"

"It was *leaked*, Captain."

"You're shittin' me."

"Someone inside got to it. I didn't tell her a thing. Not a word."

Weathers turned toward the window. "Some heads are going to roll. I'll be *goddamned* if I'm going to let some half-ass newspaper girl run my life."

"I shouldn't have laid it on your desk."

"Next time, Lieutenant, lock it up."

"Yes, sir."

Weathers grabbed his coat off one of the single beds. He looked down at the floor, thinking. "I'd like to kick your ass all the way back to Lake Erie, but I have to stick by my decision, or we'll both look like shit."

Fowler stood up. His voice was quiet, but full of emotion. "Thank you, sir."

The gray crew cut got in close. "But don't fuck up." Weathers took a step toward the door. "As far as the dancing business goes, it was good police work—I commend you . . . but, I don't want to see another goddamned word about it in the paper, you understand? It makes us look like assholes." He paused and looked Fowler in the eye. "Unofficially—keep pursuing it."

"Okay."

"Now I want a full report on this kid. Keeping him under wraps is withholding evidence."

"There's a reason for it."

Weathers looked over at Bill Rodney who by now was beaming. "What are you smiling at, you old coot?" he demanded, his meaty red hand on the doorknob.

Bill Rodney lit a cigarette, turning to Fowler. "I got a couple new things on the kid, Nick. Cap'n, you might want to hear this."

Weathers looked impatiently over at him, waiting. "Well?" Fowler turned.

Rodney savored the moment and blew a smoke ring that sailed out into the middle of the room and hung there, slowly getting larger in the silence.

"Let's have it," Weathers said.

Rodney leaned against one of the desks. "Last night around four-thirty in the morning, Marty found the kid crawling all over him, in a sweat, screaming about some face in his window."

"Where's Marty now?"

" 'Cross the quad"—Rodney stood up, craning his neck—"You can see the infirmary from here."

"And?"

"The lab called this morning. Seems they put the prints from that tie around the deceased's neck next to those of the Ballard kid, and the band began to play."

"You're shittin' me."

Bill Rodney glanced uneasily at Fowler. "No, sir. I just got the call."

"Get that kid in here right now."

Nick Fowler turned, looking out the window.

"Okay," Rodney said, picking up the phone. He dialed an extension, waited an instant; there was a click followed by a voice on the other end. "Ms. Ross?" he said.

Her scratchy voice could be heard across the room. "Yes?"

"This is Detective Rodney over in Ardsley Hall. Could you have Sergeant Orloff bring the Ballard boy over now?"

"Now?"

"That's correct."

There was a long pause on the other end. "He wasn't sick when he came in here," she said, "but now he looks terrible and you want him running around in the cold—"

"Ms. Ross, it's important."

There was a pause on the other end. "You know that—what's his name—Lieutenant, uh . . ."

"Fowler?"

"Yeah, there's a letter for him here—looks like it was slid under the door this morning."

"Send that over with the sergeant too, if you will."

"It smells kind of funny."

15

CARY BALLARD WAS sitting on a straight-back chair in the middle of the room. He was facing the window, where he could see some trees twisting in the wind. He half expected to see the covered face again. He finished telling the men what he had seen the night before.

An old man with a battered face was blowing smoke out from underneath a hat.

The little cop was sitting on the bed staring at his feet.

A burly man with short gray hair was firing questions.

Interrupting occasionally was the lieutenant who, while taking notes, explained to the big man some detail that Cary couldn't understand, then the questions would start coming again.

Finally they asked Marty to take the boy outside. In the hall-way Cary was once again surrounded by a yellow police tape, facing the massive windows near where Crawford had been killed.

Inside the room, Weathers was pacing again.

The purple envelope was lying on one of the desks. No one had touched it, but it blazed with a smell of perfume. At the back of Fowler's mind—a thought kept tugging at him—he had smelled this perfume before. Bill Rodney's eyes kept falling on the letter, then darted glances at Fowler, who refused to openly acknowledge its existence. Never even looked at it.

The captain was staring at Fowler. "What do you think?"

"I have a theory."

"Let's have it."

"I think someone is trying to frame the kid."

Weathers frowned.

Rodney crushed out his cigarette. "What about Marty's report, Nick?"

"That's true," Fowler said, picking up a supplemental report from the desk. "It says here several kids knew that the Crawford boy and Cary Ballard had a fight the day before the murder—and that there was enmity between them."

Weathers's color was rising again like a thermometer. "I want a full, and I mean *full*, in-depth follow-up report, Lieutenant. This kid is a suspect. How much proof do you need? He might have been in the room near where Crawford was hanged."

"When I interrogated him, he said he went up on the roof and down the fire escape to the graveyard to see some girl. He also could have been out sleepwalking."

Weathers was shaking his head. "Fowler, don't start with me—"

"We found traces of tar on his bedroom slippers. It matched the tar on the roof of this building."

Rodney lit up again, listening intently. Weathers raised his eyebrows, then furrowed them. "Can you prove the kid sleepwalks?"

"A history of sleepwalking *and* dissociation was mentioned in his medical records. I'm sure this Dr. Clarence knows. We could put a wire on the kid, let him go into his session, and—"

"The kid's not ready for that, Fowler, come on. He was

shittin' in his socks just now." Weathers stood up, rubbing his brow. "When I spoke to the headmaster, he indicated the kid was half crazy. Says he sees things. Came from a troubled home."

"I'll run that down," Fowler said, thrusting his hands in his pockets. "But I know he's being set up."

"I hope, for your sake, you're not shielding him."

"Give me a little credit."

Weathers leaned in. "Right now he's nowhere in your report, Lieutenant, and we have at least five pieces of hard evidence against him." He took a step closer. "How the fuck can I justify his absence in the initial disposition when the data is already established?"

Nick Fowler looked hard at Allen Weathers. They seemed to be shadowing each other's thoughts in the silence. "Do you think he did it, Captain?"

"No, but . . ."

"Then I want to let him go, and put a twenty-four-hour tail on him."

Weathers looked over at Bill Rodney, rolled his eyes, and looked like a man being led to the gallows. "Jesus fucking *H. Christ.* They are going to kill me if you screw this up."

Fowler tapped his chest. "They'll kill me first."

Weathers's eyes instantly bounced off the purple envelope on the table. "I thought she already did."

Rodney was again smiling. His old, gnarled hand hovered over the envelope as he grinned at Fowler. He reached down and picked it up. "Why don't you read it to us, Nick?"

Fowler sniffed. "Sure." He walked over, ripped open the side of the letter, and unfolded a large piece of purple stationery. Then his face sunk.

The letter was written with a childlike scrawl in ink, then signed in lipstick. Fowler laid it on the desk, smelled quickly for lye or other poisons. He would fluoroscope it later. He decided to read the letter aloud. It said:

Dear Traveler,

How did you know I was dancing? At first, I thought you were inside my brain. I hope someday you will explain it to me in person.

When I kill you.

Unless there is something inside holding you back, some guiding principle that will keep you away from me.

Thinking of you,

Arthur Murray

P.S. Next: another enemy will prove Jesus could swing. You miss me by a hair.

There was a hollow silence in the room. Nick Fowler pointed a finger at the postscript. He turned to Weathers. "A clue to the next murder."

Weathers's stony expression did not change.

"This is a deadly game we've got here, Captain. That boy's the only card I can play. You going to let me follow him, or not?"

Weathers was staring down at the lipstick-scrawled signature on the paper. He swallowed hard.

"You got it."

16

THE NEXT DAY the Associated Press had picked up on the "Arthur Murray" story. Several national newspapers excerpted the entire article, and some, like the *New York Post*, splashed the story on the cover. One of the morning shows mentioned it in a news brief.

Now the killer had a name.

When Fowler read the morning papers, he got angry. He felt they had instantly made his job that much harder. He feared the attention would fuel the killer's ego, driving him to kill again.

What was he going to do with the baffling clues in the letter?—much less the strange intimacy he and the killer had established. He talked into the phone, glaring down at the *Post* headline on his desk.

"So what are you saying to me?" Fowler noticed the irritation in his voice. He was on the phone with a police handwriting examiner named Orin. The man reported that he had spent the better part of yesterday analyzing the purple stationery.

"I'm saying . . ." Orin's voice rose slightly. "Without known standards of comparison, I can't tell you nothin'."

"I haven't collected standards yet, Orin. Before I do, I want to get a sense of what you think. Come on, give me *some*thing."

"Look, Nick." Orin sounded edgy. "Every person's handwriting has a range of variations. It might depend upon the conditions under which the writing was executed, the type of writing instrument, the surface—"

Fowler cut him off. "For God's sake, just give me a qualified opinion, will you? I won't hold you to it. It'll be confidential."

There was another pause on the line during which Nick listened to the examiner's breathing through static.

Now he pleaded. "I need something, Orin, anything to hang on to here. Come on, do me a job."

More static, then the voice came through. "I can't prove it . . . but it's possible the letter was written with a nondominant hand."

Fowler's mind started racing. "That would account for the childlike scratch."

"Maybe."

"What else?"

"It might also be an intentional disguise."

"What do you mean?"

"If you collect standards, you might find—I mean, it's possible—the person who wrote this letter may have been trying to make it look like someone else."

"How do you know that?"

"Well, in tracing or copying another's signature, for instance, people tend to exclude their own writing habits and adopt those of the other person. So, in effect, they are drawing, not writing. This letter has trace—or at least draw—all over it."

"You're beautiful, Orin."

"This is just an inconclusive—"

"I'll call you back."

Nick hung up the phone and glanced out the window at the back lawns.

Bill Rodney clicked down the other phone. He had been on the line for several hours himself. He reached over, cracked another window an inch to let some air in, then lit a cigarette. He watched Fowler pacing.

"Of the three hundred and fifty-eight lipsticks available from fifteen different manufacturers that the beauty suppliers we checked carried . . . Nick?"

"Yeah, I'm listening."

"The lab determined it was a L'Oréal shade called *Sunset*, a dark pink."

Fowler stopped in the middle of the room, thinking. "That's why Crawford's lips had been wiped clean with alcohol—I'll bet you ten bucks."

Rodney inhaled. "The purple envelope had been doused in a perfume called Shalimar. I asked the druggist in town if he had sold the fragrance to anyone; he recalled a woman buying a bottle recently."

"Did you get a description?"

"I tried—nothing."

Nick was racking his brain. His interview with Ms. Coates suddenly came blazing back. "Bill, I just remembered where I smelled that perfume."

"Where?"

"Ms. Coates. During her interrogation."

"Mmm. I'd like to tail that one personally."

"You may have your chance."

"The lab called again, saying there were no latent fingerprints, no prints anywhere on the stationery—except of course, yours and Sergeant Orloff's. One breakthrough: The lipstick on the stationery is the same brand, same shade as that recovered from the victim's lips."

"Great." Fowler smiled. "Get Marty in here. Today he starts following the Ballard kid. And check on purchases at stationery and drugstores within a fifty-mile radius."

He grabbed his jacket and walked out into the hallway. He stood there, Ms. Coates's interview filtering through his thoughts.

How would he approach her? He wanted to slap her with a warrant right now.

The implication in Arthur Murray's letter that there was something "holding him back" was eating at him—he was getting psyched out—he knew it. He stood in the same hall where the bloodstains on the walls and floor seemed to bring screams of carnage, lust, and betrayal.

He listened now. He walked to the other side of the hall, knowing his own footsteps would bring him back to himself. He heard the screams again, but knew they were not the murdered boy's screams; the voice he heard was older, hoarse—from beyond the grave. A man, a father, a lost soul.

THE LITTLE MAN who showed up had a greasy complexion and wore thick black glasses. His body was so thin his dark suit looked like a sheath over exposed wires. The suitcase in his hand seemed too large for him.

Fowler had arranged to meet Ballard in his room with an operator from a private security firm to give the boy a lie detector test. Fowler had chosen not to use a police examiner, in case he didn't like the results. He was trying to free the boy from suspicion, but he wanted to control the information.

The little man stood in the small dormitory room, looking around as Fowler explained that the test was a way to clear Cary. By the time the man had opened his black suitcase, though, the boy was visibly nervous. Nick talked to Cary, calming him down. They waited a while, then decided to go ahead.

Cary was staring down at the four-channel polygraph machine as Nick walked over to the other side of the room. He stood by Cary's desk, staring at something as the little man unwrapped the wires. Skin-colored pads were placed on Cary's wrists. Nick stared at the boy's desk, wrapped with police tape marked "Ravenstown PD." He began reading the top page of a stack of papers the boy had turned in during his first month. He leafed through the stack. Everywhere was the soft scrawl of a boy's handwriting. He instantly grabbed the stack up in his hands.

"Cary, mind if I borrow these papers for a day or two?"

The boy looked up at him. "No."

Fowler stepped to the door and left. Outside the door, he heard the dark little man begin asking questions. He walked down the hall, put Cary's assignments in a glycine pouch, ziplocked it, and called Orin down at the station to tell him he was sending him "standards" to compare with the handwriting in the letter.

When he hung up the phone, Fowler thought back to the last time he himself had administered a polygraph test. He tried to concentrate; remembered that from simple questions designed to reveal patterns of truth and deception, the Psychological Stress Evaluator measures audible and inaudible voice modulations, and then displays them on a graph.

By the time the test was over, Marty was back in the office. Fowler stationed him outside Cary's door, told the boy to rest, and ushered the small man from the security company into his office. "How did it go?"

The man took off his glasses, cleaned them methodically, put them back on his face, and looked at Fowler. He reached in his black case and took out the graph from Ballard's test. His knobby finger pointed to the tracings. "Normally there's some kind of fluctuation, Lieutenant, but look at this . . . for long stretches . . . nothing."

Fowler looked at the relatively straight line on the graph. "How do you account for that?"

"It's hard to say. Tranquilizers can affect the GSR measurement of a lie detector test."

"Okay. What else could it be?"

"There isn't anything."

"So, what are you telling me?"

"The only other thing I can think of is—the polygraph has trouble with people that—I sometimes refer to them as 'psychologically dead.' "

"I see."

"It's difficult to get any kind of response from them. It just . . . doesn't register."

Fowler requested that the test not be reported and filed the results in a brown accordion file folder in his office he was keeping on all participants, suspects, even police personnel involved in the case. He stood up from the makeshift file, looked down, and realized that, without thinking, he had put the information under F—the first initial of his own surname.

MARTY WATCHED BALLARD shuffle down the back stairs of Ardsley. The boy walked over to the second floor of Madison Hall. Outside the faculty lounge he asked to see the assistant headmaster about a room change.

A prefect stepped inside to tell the master Cary Ballard wanted to speak with him. As the oak door opened and closed almost immediately, Ballard caught a glimpse of a tense scene around the table, where a room full of grim-faced teachers were sitting.

The door opened again and Mr. Allington stepped out. His somewhat imposing stature was leavened by an easy manner and a deep, calming voice. He smiled as he pushed the door closed. "Mr. Ballard," he said, "what can I do for you?"

Cary smiled. "Am I interrupting you, sir?"

"Not at all. Another faculty meeting. What's up?"

"Well, I can't really study in my room, after what happened, you know . . ."

"I can imagine."

"And I was wondering if you would recommend me for a room change."

"Sure . . . why not?"

"Thank you, sir."

"I don't know what openings there are. Any particular hall you have your heart set on?"

"No, but—as far away as possible."

Allington clamped his large warm hand down on Ballard's shoulder. "Call me tomorrow. I'll see what I can do."

Ballard's face lit up. "Thank you, sir."

Marty ducked into an empty classroom as the boy ran past him down the hall.

Inside the faculty lounge, Allington closed the door and resumed his seat at the large mahogany table.

Dr. Hickey had taken off his glasses and was rubbing his face feverishly. Dr. Clarence was there, Mr. Toby, Messrs. Curamus and Carlson. Ms. Coates. All of the faces at the table were grimly set, some staring bleary-eyed up at the fluorescent lights, others gazing down at the sheen on the wood table.

Toby leaned forward. "These columnists are breaking stories every five minutes. One story I read—"

"Please. I hear it from parents all day long," Dr. Hickey interrupted, "calling to withdraw their sons. I'm putting out fires from the minute I get up in the morning."

There was a pause in the room. No one wanted to say what they all feared.

Toby cleared his throat. "What I was going to say was, one of the columnists speculated that, with this kind of assault, it could happen again."

Dr. Hickey's head jerked up and down. "For God's sake, don't curse us with that."

Dr. Clarence lit his cigarette and placed the gold lighter neatly on the edge of the table. "It very well could. No one can foresee what may happen."

Dr. Hickey stood up, adjusted his shoulders stiffly, and glared out the window. After a silence, he turned around. "The trustees are up in arms. My board has become a lynch mob. The alumni association predicts fund-raising this spring will go dry. Enrollment is bound to plummet. I called you all here this afternoon—because we need answers. What are we going to do?"

"Meet them head-on," Mr. Allington said quietly. "Start fund-raising now. Let's strategize, Brandon. If we start a fund for the boy's family, even a scholarship in his name, we can contain the damage. Then elicit further support later."

The room fell silent. Dr. Hickey looked across the room with contempt at Allington. He knew it was a great idea. He shook his head stiffly. "It could backfire in our faces."

"We're going to have rebuild our integrity one way or another. Why should we wait?"

Several masters looked over at Allington, nodding in agreement.

Dr. Hickey's eyes ferreted the room. He could see the other masters saw some wisdom in this. He fixed his gaze on the tree outside the window and did not speak for the rest of the meeting.

At Fowler's motel, personal calls from old friends in Buffalo flooded the switchboard. At the state police station, where all communications were checked, there was a stack of messages. Several people had called in confessions, admitting to the crime. All these annoyances, as Fowler called them, had to be checked out.

Judy Bayard was not singled out as the person who had leaked the information to the *Tribune*. Captain Weathers warned her, along with the rest of the staff, he would not hesitate to fire anyone inflaming the situation further by talking to reporters, or anyone on the "outside."

That night Nick read Cary Ballard's academic file. It did not contain the in-depth psychological profile, which was in the possession of Dr. Clarence. It comprised only his transcripts, the results of intelligence tests, correspondence between Cary's mother and the school, as well as some typed observations by the admissions committee on the day of the boy's interview.

Several people on the committee used either the word "nervous" or "distracted." The headmaster was, in his own words, " . . . nonplussed as to whether the boy was right for Ravenhill."

Mr. Allington's notes, however, included the sentence "It's time we explore the underprivileged, the afflicted students who could not, without our help, create new lives for themselves. I wholeheartedly recommend acceptance *and* scholarship money."

An admissions assistant wrote that he was "appalled" that Ballard had been expelled for fistfighting from his last boarding school, Fieldcrest Academy.

There was, however, a notation in the margin in someone's harshly slanted script: "Find out the details of father's death." Why was that pertinent to his admission? Had the boy told them about his father?

He looked at the handwriting. It was nothing like the elongated scrawl from the purple letter, yet it occurred to him he should send it to the examiner anyway.

17

THERE WAS A wrenching account in the *Tribune* the next morning of Crawford's grief-stricken parents' journey from New York back to Evanston, Illinois, to bury their son. The article again was penned by Maureen McCauley.

By midday, Cary Ballard's request for a transfer from Ardsley Hall was granted and he moved his belongings to Brookside, a small house with eight boys on a country road just off campus, near a marsh.

He also walked over to the gym and requested a chance to try out for the cross-country team. He had placed well in several races at Fieldcrest before he was kicked out. The coach said it was too late, but suggested he spend the remainder of the fall training on his own; if he got in shape, he could try out for winter track.

Ballard jumped at the idea. As soon as he had thrown his suitcases on the bed in his new room, he put on his sneakers and sweats. He had to get out of his burning head. Away from the police.

Other times he had gone running, he had kept to the manicured fairways of the school golf course. Sometimes he took to the back roads that wore tiny threads through a fabric of cornfields. Today, however, he wanted to run around the lake.

He did some stretches and jogged out the back entrance to the school, set a brisk pace along the outside of the great fence as it snaked along the boundary of the school. He didn't see the unmarked car creeping along behind him.

The fence was ornate in the extreme: tall, wrought-iron shafts that rose out of the ground some eight feet into the air, girded at the bottom by two waists of scrollwork, encased at the top in horizontal steel struts.

As Ballard picked up the pace slightly, he counted the uprights as they whizzed by in the corners of his eyes. He shuddered when occasionally his eyes drifted up to the razor-sharp points that looked like medieval spears crowning each upright. From the apex of the point, the iron had been forged down on each of the four corners of the shaft, only to curl up again, causing each upright to look vaguely like a turret. A castle of knives, he thought. He tried not to imagine blood.

Cary brooded over whether the steel shafts that seemed to puncture the blue sky were designed to keep the students in or the real world out. He wondered why the same fence encircled the abandoned graveyard. He picked up his pace as he started down the last hill into town. He remembered some school facts as he felt the first beads of sweat run down his brow. Ardsley Hall and Booth Hall—joined by the stone arch—were the original academy and so were also surrounded by the same gigantic fence as a kind of memorial to the past.

He started down the main street, running at a good clip when he passed the barbershop. He noticed his reflection in the tall glass window. It didn't make him happy to see his thin legs and arms pumping furiously when he had imagined himself much bigger, much stronger.

He felt his calf muscles bulge, though, as he ran the metal stairway that led up to the bridge over the waterfall. Down on the street Marty got out of a car and watched him.

At the top of the stairs he turned out into the grass that ran up toward the graveyard. He felt the blood rush to his head as he sprinted up the hill, thinking he would work his way back down the other side of the lake.

When he ran by the graveyard's wrought-iron gate, he heard a voice. Behind a tombstone, he could see a blond girl bent over on her back, flailing her arms at a boy who seemed to be wrestling her down.

He stopped running.

Ballard caught his breath as he walked toward the wrought-iron door that was hanging by a single hinge. Through one of the iron scrolls, he saw the boy trying to get the girl's dress over her head.

Out of sheer wonder, Ballard opened the gate. The rusty hinge reported a low scraping sound that rose suddenly. The startled boy in the graveyard jumped up and ran backward, tucking in his shirt. The girl stood up, confused, her eyes staring at Ballard, committing his timid face to memory. The attacker, hiding his face, yanked her backward and Ballard noticed that she was still looking at him as she was pulled out of sight.

WHEN HE GOT back to the gym, Cary saw Harold Finkelstein coming out of the showers. He wondered what Harold had been doing the other night chasing Ms. Coates by the power plant. Finkelstein was a tall, muscular boy whose bright red hair was trimmed so close to his head that it made his ears look like they were sticking out. He was one of the eight students living in Brookside Cottage.

Ballard mentioned, offhandedly as they were both drying off, what he had just seen happen to the girl in the graveyard. Finkelstein sat listening on the rickety wooden bench between the lockers, rubbing the foreskin of his penis, inspecting it with great care.

"Watch out, she wants your dick," he said.

"What?"

"Yours and everybody else's."

Ballard felt his face flush and couldn't help himself saying, "I guess yours is already spoken for."

"What?"

Ballard threw his sweats in his locker. "Only you like them older."

Finkelstein looked up in shock, then laughed derisively. "Like your mother."

"Fuck off."

Finkelstein looked at Ballard. "That girl's the town whore, douche bag. Don't you know anything?"

"No, I don't know anything," Ballard said, still looking in his locker, his voice striking a note of sadness.

"Well, I've heard the upperclassmen talk about some townie girl with bleached hair named Janine that"—he noticed that Ballard was still looking away—"never mind," he said, "she probably doesn't mess around with virgins anyway."

Ballard felt an indignation rise inside him. "I guess that counts you out," he said resentfully. Finkelstein didn't argue. He just smiled, keeping his eyes trained on the dial of the combination lock as he slammed the gray door.

Ballard walked down the hall, weighed in, and took a whirl-pool before he left the gym. Marty was outside, grimly counting the leaves on a branch of ivy by the front stoop. When Ballard slammed out the door, he almost missed him.

THAT EVENING CARY had to walk out to the language arts build-ing on the outskirts of the campus to take special help in Latin 2. His teacher, Mr. Curamus, in addition to being the assistant foot-ball coach, was a man whom Ballard felt was solely responsible for the Latin language being dead.

Ballard would stare at the floor, his eyes occasionally darting to Mr. Curamus's pointed beak as it lunged up and down while he was attempting to read Caesar. No one could murder a line of Latin like Mr. Curamus. Ballard's eyes wandered from the gray floor tiles, trying to look outside at the trees—anything to assure himself that he was still alive.

Tonight it was nearly dusk and night was pressing in around the edges of the leaves, making them seem indistinct. Ballard's eyes fell back to the floor tiles, until something moved in the window that brought his head and shoulders up with a start.

Staring through the glass was the blond girl. When he looked up, she smiled, then pressed her lips down over what looked like braces. She kept smiling.

Cary's heart jumped. Out of embarrassment, he pretended he was writing something and glanced in earnest at Mr. Curamus as the man gunned down another line of innocent syllables.

Cary made a notation on the page in his text, then glanced back out the window. It was empty. The trees had almost disappeared into blackness and he felt his chest sink. He regretted he hadn't smiled back at the girl.

A half hour later, when he had finished the interminable review exercise, Cary Ballard thanked Mr. Curamus and backed out into the night, ready to make the trek back to Brookside.

A voice behind him called out.

"Hey."

He turned around. The blond girl was standing waist high in the reeds up a small embankment, on the other side of the gravel. "Who are you?" Ballard said.

"Janine."

"I'm Cary." He managed a belated smile.

"Thanks for distracting that guy in the graveyard," she said as she nervously pulled her hair out of her collar.

"What was he doing?"

Janine turned her head to one side, frowning at Ballard as if he ought to know better. "He was taking advantage." A kind of confusion darkened her features. "I don't know why it always . . ."

"Does that happen a lot?"

She nodded helplessly. "My mother says I was cursed with hard looks."

"I don't think you look hard. You're . . . beautiful."

Janine almost trembled, looking at him, then up at the sky for a full minute. Then she stared down at him a little baffled. "Would you like to be my friend?"

Ballard felt an emotion inside him that had no comparison to anything he'd ever experienced. "Yes."

She smiled. "If you hadn't come along today, I'd have had it."

He nodded, thinking that Finkelstein might be wrong. "I didn't do anything."

"Yes, you did. You think I do that kind of thing every day?"

Ballard stared off at the woods, then realized he might not be able to speak again if he didn't say what was on his mind. "Some people say you do."

Janine's upper body seemed to rise out of the reeds, revealing the tight creases in the thighs of her jeans. Through the small aperture between her legs, he caught a glimpse of the evening sky.

"Did somebody tell you about me?"

"Yes."

She stared down at him, and as her mouth dissolved before his eyes, she turned suddenly and disappeared.

Ballard ran up the bank, dropping his Latin book somewhere

in the reeds. When he got to the top of the rise, he could see a tousle of wheat-colored hair flying through the tall grass. He ran after her. What he couldn't hear were the footsteps of someone behind him, who stopped, reached down and picked up his book, and kept walking along the gravel.

Cary knew that to catch up with her, he'd have to run hard. He felt the blood pound up into his nostrils as his heels thudded down the hillside. Janine was running fast, her boots sending small stones back, one of which pelted him in the forehead. She ran with anger, he thought, so he let her wear down, keeping just about ten feet behind her, watching the steam in her legs start to give out.

Once she yelled over her shoulder, "Get away!" He didn't. Finally, when she had reached the soccer field on the other side of a pasture of tall grass, she collapsed and rolled in her jean jacket to a stop, her chest heaving in the darkness. Ballard stood over her, only slightly winded, but letting his breath sound more furious to match hers. They heaved together.

"I dropped my Latin book."

"You can eat your Latin book, for all I care."

"I'm sorry about what I said."

Janine forced her elbows under her. She was still breathing hard. "Who told you about me?"

"Finkelstein."

"Who's that?"

"Some kid who lives out in my new residence, Brookside; he's just a twerp."

"He's a liar."

"Well, who was that guy in the graveyard?"

"What difference does it make? I didn't ask him to maul me."

"Why do you hang around with him then?"

"I don't. He keeps following me. What else is there to do in this town, anyway, watch the trees grow?"

Ballard knelt down in the grass beside her. The grass was wet and he liked the feel of it. He leaned forward and put both hands in the grass beside her. He felt the soft flesh on her arm touching his knuckles as she breathed.

In the half-light, he could see her chest fill with air, pressing her firm breasts up into her yellow satin blouse. Her lips were parted and she stared up at him, her eyes quietly burning.

Ballard couldn't remember how much time passed as he looked down at Janine. He remembered her breath slowing down. Then time came unraveled. He seemed to drift into a fantasy that was played out on the soft landscape of her face.

Her mouth drew him down from a great height. He remembered his body arched forward. His lips landed on hers. They were so soft he seemed to go right through them until his mouth was almost underground. He sprang back up to the surface. With each kiss, he fell deeper into her mouth. It seemed there were undiscovered regions, vast precipices. He kept falling, his lips roaming a vast terrain, tasting a perfect land, but his hands, he made sure, never fell below her white neck. He just let them rest there as his mouth traveled back and forth.

An hour later Ballard walked Janine home. She lived on a dirt road that wound up the hill behind the town high school. They talked about their parents. Her mother worked part-time in town, she said. She didn't mention her father.

When he said goodbye to her, he kissed her sweetly and kept his hands on her neck. He didn't want to take advantage of her. Besides, he was afraid. She appreciated him for that. Her kisses told him that again and again.

18

LATER THAT NIGHT, Marty Orloff dozed off in the front seat of his Oldsmobile parked down the dirt road just below Brookside Cottage. He didn't see Ballard come in.

When Cary was climbing the steep stairs to the second floor, he saw Harold Finkelstein standing at the top of the stairs, leering down at him. On one side of him, smiling from ear to ear, was Bill Chung, a Chinese exchange student; on the other side, Jordon Goodson, a fat Jewish boy from Brooklyn.

The three of them stood at the top of the stairs in their underwear, swaying their torsos back and forth like hula girls, as they grasped their genitals and hoisted them up and down, rolling their eyes, and running their tongues around the edges of their mouths. The sound of their smacking lips stopped Ballard on the stairs. In one of Finkelstein's sweaty hands, his Latin 2 book danced above him like a ghost. His ears recoiled as the three of them warbled in high-pitched voices.

"*Janine!*" they crooned to the top of their registers. Ballard thought he was going to choke; the mere sight of them had killed all the available oxygen. "*Ohh, Janine? Is that you, honey?*"

Ballard decided to play it cool. He walked quietly up the stairs, grabbed his Latin book from Finkelstein's grimy hands, saying simply, "What are you guys, jealous?"

The three boys stared at him, then exploded into Goodson's room, landing in a heap on a single bed. As the springs squeaked furiously, Ballard walked into the bathroom and washed the front and back cover of his book. He pulled a paper towel and rubbed the stone visage of Caesar—camped in Gaul, no doubt—as he heard the boys howling.

"Yeah, we're real jealous," Finkelstein yelled toward the bathroom. "We want to get crabs too!"

Goodson burst out a laugh, his enormous stomach shifting up and down like the continents. Chung laughed silently, rolling over so that, with his back turned, his shoulders bounced to the four winds.

Ballard stepped back into the doorway. "You better watch your mouth, Finkelstein."

"Yeah?" he said, his face lifting up. "You better wash yours!"

"Shut up."

"How much does she charge?"

Ballard felt his chest tighten. "She doesn't do that. You have the wrong girl."

"That's not what Gluckner said." Finkelstein eased himself up to a sitting position. The other two boys went quiet.

Ballard felt as if his shoes were nailed to the floor. "What did Gluckner say?"

Finkelstein reached down and grabbed his crotch. "He said Janine fucked his brains out in the graveyard!" This set off another explosion. The three could hardly contain their laughter. They rolled against each other, kicking the air deliriously. They didn't notice that Ballard's face had gotten so red he almost passed out.

"Gluckner was never in the graveyard," he said. "It was somebody else."

Finkelstein sat up. "Yeah, somebody else letting her have it after he was finished!"

Ballard walked into Finkelstein's room, looking for something to break. He grabbed the plastic handles on the boy's stereo. He hoisted it up, completely beside himself, thinking he would throw it out the window. Then he saw something through the glass that stopped him. He sat the stereo down, his hands trembling.

Finkelstein walked in. "Hey, don't worry about it, Ballard," he said casually, leaning on the doorjamb. "Look at it this way, you got some ass, right?"

Ballard's attention seemed to be drifting. He turned listlessly. "No."

"What?"

"I didn't get any ass."

"You gotta be kidding."

"No . . ." he said, turning to Finkelstein with a shiver. "I only kissed her."

"You what?"

"I said I kissed her."

Finkelstein shook his head and yelled out into the hallway. "Hey, Goodson, he said he *only* kissed her."

Goodson's stomach preceded him into the hallway. "Wouldn't be surprised," he said. "He doesn't know what to do with it."

Finkelstein smiled at Goodson. "Yeah, but Ballard has principles, you know?" He turned back to Ballard. "Of course what Cary here doesn't realize, is that if he kissed Janine, he just kissed every cock in Ravenstown."

Goodson howled and disappeared back into his room. Ballard could hear him tell Chung what Finkelstein had just said. There was a pause after which Chung started to laugh and cough at the same time until he started to gag uncontrollably. Goodson could be heard slapping him on the back.

Finkelstein shut the door to his room, sat down again, his hairy leg up on the bookcase. He stared up at Ballard, who was looking out the window. "Just make sure you use Listerine, bro. Get rid of those nasty germs."

"Right . . . germs."

Finkelstein smiled. "You don't want to believe it, do you? I'm warning you, I know women. She's bad news." Finkelstein was admiring the red hairs on his calf.

"Yeah, you know women, all right—old ones."

Finkelstein now looked up at Ballard, again shocked, but not willing to betray that, his gaze resolved into a threat. "I don't know what you're talking about."

"How's Ms. Coates?"

Finkelstein eyes drifted to the side, then looked back at Ballard. "Least she doesn't train."

"What?"

"You know, Ballard—several guys at once."

For a moment Ballard couldn't get his breath. He thought he was going to faint. A hand appeared in the window. Ballard watched it through the glass as if from a great distance. A second hand joined the first, pulling the dark brim of a hat down onto a head. As the hat now tilted up, it revealed the face, partially draped in black.

It was the stranger.

Kneeling on the sill, dressed in the same dark cape, the same eyes shining. Ballard stared at it. The hands tried to lift the window, but it was locked. Ballard felt himself getting sleepy. He looked into Finkelstein's eyes. They were narrowed under his angled eyebrows, glowing with hostility. "Little boy," he said. "Ready for bed?"

The figure outside the window nodded at Ballard very slightly. Ballard felt sick to his stomach. He wanted to break Finkelstein's neck, but something was pulling him down. Some horror that drew all else in its wake was starting to engulf him. His fists began to unwind.

Shrouds seemed to float before his eyes. He looked down at Finkelstein's eyes; they burned far into the distance, like lamps across a river in some other world. A world where nothing was as it seemed.

Ballard didn't remember walking down the hall, closing his door, and falling asleep with all his clothes on.

19

THE URGE BURNING *in me again. Rhythms out of the night. Terrifying beats, drums. Air escaping—my head a sieve.*

Down the drainpipe, soles, knees at the siding, hands picking the ivy. The honeysuckle behind the hedge reminds me of a man I killed in the flowers. Around the back of Brookside, under the split rail. My breath like an engine, idling. Across the lawn, terrible thoughts like sores, lesions, sounds torturing me, poisons in my head, down behind the squad car parked up the road, crawling slow.

An open window. Rise up. Quick blow to the back of the head—stunned. Grab his baton. Hit him again. He slumps over, good. Need time. That cadence like a volcano inside me. Better put him out. Fumble inside the pockets, where is the fucking syringe? Okay, juice. Up with the jacket, honey, in the bicep. Sleep.

Now I can move. Feel the night bloom. The man in the flowers sending me strength—body long decomposed—so I can right so many wrongs. The night like petroleum, igniting me.

Screen door open, up the stairs. Down the hall by the bathroom. Inside, bare sink . . . see the mirror? Look at—eyes, oh no, lift the scarf. The mouth perfect, mother's mouth, full of longing, rage.

Out into a hallway cramped with snares and tambour—sounds

rising and falling. Never going away. So many hallways. The vein thumping in my arm. Sweat running. Open the door!

The Day-Glo playroom again. Paint thrown across the walls and windows. Colors crazed. Fury everywhere. Make it go away. Doesn't stop. Colors scream at me. Voices chanting, odes. Hymns. I'm home.

Open the door wider.

A blade of light across a sleeping face.

Close on knees. Up to the altar. Voices rising up, a crescendo. Look at your lips. Wipe her kisses off NOW.

White Jockey briefs glowing against dark skin. No moonlight. No sounds, but slow breathing. Eyes inside at rem speed. Final dreams. Just let me brush your hair. Your radiant black hair. A wisp behind the ear, off the forehead, like they did to me. Let me brush.

Your hair.

20

For the next several days, Finkelstein came up missing. First, the housemaster, Mr. Bendleby, noticed that he hadn't come down for breakfast.

Bendleby was the retired director of athletics for the school, an overweight man with white hair and an oval face that made him look oddly like an oversized cherub. He oversaw Brookside Cottage and coached winter track. The stories were legion about the day, a season before, he had spoken at the grandstand to all those who had come out for the sport. With an informal panel of judges, it was determined that he said "uh" four hundred and thirty-two times in his fifty-five-minute speech.

In one run-on sentence, or "collage" as Goodson liked to refer to them, Bendleby managed to squeeze in thirty-seven "uh"s and still hold the audience in the grip of his art. The fact that people were laughing didn't seem to penetrate his studied gaze. He just planted his cleats on the wooden track and kept on talking. It was later decided Bendleby secretly thought he was funny.

He wasn't laughing on the evening of Finkelstein's disappearance. The red-haired boy had not attended a single class, made an appearance in the dining hall, or even the gym. Bendleby reasoned that he had run away.

While his parents were informed, rumors spread throughout the student body that Finkelstein had eloped with Janine. It was said Finkelstein, who was a math whiz, easily first in Ms. Coates's class, had stolen away to Wall Street and become a runner on the floor of the Stock Exchange. It was said Finkelstein had disguised himself in woman's clothing with the intention of reapplying as the first female student at Ravenhill since 1903. Only Finkelstein could inspire this kind of gossip.

Ballard realized he couldn't remember very much about the last time he had seen Finkelstein. He remembered looking out the window. The rest of what he saw tore at the insides of his head, scratching to escape into words, but he never discussed it. He never discussed that he had woken up that night, sweating and covered with dirt on the roof of Brookside, or that his hands were smeared with mud. Or that the knees of his trousers were encrusted with dried dirt.

In fact, most of those next two days Ballard felt uneasy, disoriented. He noticed that Goodson and Chung kept away from him, sitting quietly in their rooms with their doors shut. This only fed the fire that already burned out of control in Ballard's brain. He could only sink beneath the covers, moving his body into a fetal position, moaning slightly, at times aware that people were climbing the stairs, but oblivious as to who.

At one point, he began to shiver so much he got out of bed. On his way to the closet to get his robe he noticed a police car parked down the road, its red floods revolving in the afternoon light.

In his closet, Ballard found his overcoat, which was warmer, and buried himself inside it. He was about to close the door when two white gloves fell down from the top shelf. He picked them up. They were damp. He couldn't figure out why.

Ballard stood quite motionless, trying to remember where he had gotten them. He knew that he had worn them the first day of school when he was selected at random to hold the chapel doors for the on-rushing students and faculty. He had been outfitted in a blue school blazer with a gold crest on the pocket, under which in Latin was displayed the words *Sine Macula* ("Without Stain"). He had also been given two pairs of white gloves, one for the morning, one for the afternoon. He looked for the other pair. They were missing.

There was a knock at the door of his room. Goodson cracked the door and pointed his stomach at Ballard, who quietly thrust the gloves into the coat pocket. Goodson's eyes dropped down to the pockets.

"What are you doing?"

"Nothing," Ballard said.

Goodson stood for a moment, puzzled, then slouched over to Ballard, pulling the gloves out of the coat pocket. He stared down at them.

"What the hell . . ."

"From opening day."

Goodson stared at Ballard, handling the gloves in silence. Then he noticed the slime on his hands.

"Ugh," he said, rubbing the film on Ballard's sleeve. "What's that?"

"I don't know. They need cleaning, I guess."

"You guess? Better come down. They found Finkelstein."

"Where?"

"In the marsh," Goodson said, touching his hands again as he looked at Ballard.

A FISHERMAN HAD discovered the body in the lower reaches of the marsh, a short walk below Brookside Cottage. He was an older man, the caretaker of several campus houses during the summer months, who had developed a taste for trout.

As it turned out, he had come down that particular morning with a jar full of fresh worms, only to become distracted by a piece of white material, cotton perhaps, billowing out of a natural pool that had been created during a recent storm when an oak had fallen across the stream.

The fisherman put on his waders and sloshed out toward the white thing. As he got closer, it looked to him like an undershirt. His old arthritic hands reached down, yanked the cloth, but found it wouldn't come. He cursed his father from whom he'd inherited his affliction and, this time grabbing hold of the cloth with both hands, heaved it straight up.

Something heavy emerged from the silt. It was Finkelstein's head. Rising up on either side of the head were the boy's hands—in white gloves—nailed to a two-by-four that stretched under the shoulder blades.

Around his neck his undershirt was knotted so tight that the boy's face had turned battleship gray; the tongue, covered with sand, protruding to the edge of the chin. His eyes had rolled back so far into his head that the blood vessels looked like they might have leapt down the paths that tears once had taken.

The old man took such a fright he started backward, falling into the stream, only to stand up again. With his eyes riveted on the gray face, he fell backward several times before he reached the bank, shivering, and as he later told the police, "plumb scared to death."

When Nick Fowler, Bill Rodney, Marty Orloff, and three policemen fished Finkelstein out, they saw he had been strangled by his own undershirt. Again, when the undershirt was peeled away, a knife wound gaped in the neck. The thing that shocked them, though, were the white gloves fastened down to the board with bolts. Once-red stains washed across the gloves. The men all stared at the Christ-like corpse. A chill passed through them. As the victim's lower body rose out of the water, the knee-high garters holding up a pair of black dress socks were dripping water over a pair of black patent leather shoes, recently shined.

Fowler was depressed. He knew that the body of this second boy was sure to have been washed clean of most prints or body fluids. He watched the body being covered, then loaded on a stretcher. He recalled Arthur Murray's letter and wondered "whose enemy"? He didn't have to wonder about the reference to Jesus dancing; Finkelstein had been crucified in evening clothes.

He turned around when he heard the siren and watched the ambulance roll along the county road that bordered the marsh, taking the body down to the coroner's office.

Fowler realized that, with one look, a part of his psyche had coalesced with this dead boy. A part of him was now lying in the back of the ambulance—rolling out of sight. He felt alone. When he looked up, his men were staring at him. He felt disconnected from them but struggled to look into their eyes. There he saw pain and shock. It brought him back.

He quickly gave assignments to his team. He wanted the foot size of the victim determined, and every store that sold dress clothes within a hundred miles checked to see if that size shoe had been recently purchased. He wanted tests run on the accessories themselves to see where they might have been purchased. He wanted the wood analyzed, and if possible where the bolts had been purchased. He wanted every student who was willing to talk interviewed. He wanted the entire faculty interviewed again if possible. He asked Bill Rodney to begin preparing the offense report. He told him he would prepare his own. The truth was, he couldn't deal with it. He had to think.

A police sketch artist snapped loose a tape measure from a tree on the far bank. He noted the distance to the body and, choosing a highway sign in the distance, directed Marty off toward a signpost by the road that he chose as his second coordinate.

Fowler pulled on a pair of police-issue waders and eddied out to a stake that marked the spot where the body had been found. He rolled up his sleeves, braced the camera and sample kit hanging from his neck behind each elbow, and dropped his hands through the clear water. He reached down to where Finkelstein's head had been partially buried in the silt at the bottom of the pool. He felt around for a few minutes and found nothing. The sketch artist was wading toward him with the tape drawn from the signpost.

Nick turned and made his way to the far side of the bank. He walked slowly around until he noticed a small opening in a curtain of shrubbery that lined the bank. He ducked under the limb of a white birch. When his foot caught on a vine, he looked down and saw freshly broken branches. Then he pushed aside a screen of small trees laced with spiderwebs. He stepped through. The trees and bushes whipped back into place, obscuring a new-mown field of rye behind the marsh.

On an elevated portion of ground he found the place of death. It was just a small, flat area by a fence where the grass was thick and soft. It reminded him of a primitive burial ground where people were sacrificed to uncertain gods.

The tiny blades of rye riffled in the wind as Fowler bent over, counting out the bloodstains that spread in patterns. Some of the grass had been pressed down.

He thought the patterns were different this time.

The edges of the grasses that carried the weight of the dried, reddish-brown substance were sometimes stuck together, fused by the blood that had been spilled, he guessed, two days before.

He looked up in the sky. He imagined the ceremony had occurred at night, when the sound of falling blood pelted the grass like a soft rain. As he shook his head to clear his racing thoughts, Nick Fowler worked his way around the extremity of the crude grasses bent under prints of shoes that must have determined this strange, primeval dance floor.

He knew, with all the nasty press he had gotten, he was bound to incur resistance from the department. Yet he also knew that one of the first rules of investigating was inclusiveness—it dictated that every piece of evidence be gathered and, when there was a question as to whether it actually constituted real evidence, to define it as such. He had to include a detailed report that he thought the killer was dancing with his victim, but he would confine the details to how the act functioned uniquely as associative evidence.

He couldn't minimize the details, but he could cling to a kind of police jargon that wouldn't threaten the brass. He also knew it was an important way he could prove the killer was a person strong enough to hold the weight of his victims as they were dying—but perhaps it wasn't the only way to prove that.

Then he saw a knee impression on the hallowed ground.

21

WHEN CAPTAIN WEATHERS'S car barreled to a stop on the country road beside the marsh, Sergeant Marty Orloff was standing sheepishly by the sign, holding the tape measure on the metal upright.

"Come over here," Weathers yelled to Marty. "I want to talk to you."

Marty pointed to the tape and shrugged. Weathers's face deepened its already burnished hue as he stomped determinedly over toward the policeman.

"You were on the kid?"

"Yes, sir."

"What the fuck were you doing—beatin' your meat?"

"No," Marty said under his breath. "I was knocked unconscious with a blunt object and drugged. Sir."

Weathers leaned over to look at the back of Marty's head. "What'd they hit you with?"

"A baton . . . sir," Marty said under his breath.

"Your own?"

Orloff nodded silently.

"The most basic fundamental, Orloff. Never leave your fucking window down."

"Yes, sir."

Weathers tramped his boots into the clumps of grass around the sign, shaking his head. "I oughta fire your ass. Parked in a vulnerable stakeout to begin with."

"Yes, sir."

"Stop saying that!"

"Yes. I'm sorry . . . Captain."

"I don't give a damn if you're sorry. You'll be really sorry if you pull any more shit with me. Now we have another dead kid on our hands. You think I don't have men who wouldn't love to be on this? *Huh*?"

"I promise I'll make this up to you. I'll question every student, every person who lives anywhere near here."

Weathers grunted and sunk his bull neck into the leather collar of his denim jacket. "You'll do what I tell you."

"Yes."

Weathers's sharp eyes lifted over the marsh to a clearing on the other side of the trees. He could see Fowler's blue windbreaker. He saw the flash of a camera aimed at the ground.

WEATHERS WORKED HIS way around the marsh on the far side of the curtain of trees. From a distance he could see Fowler's blond hair blowing around in the wind. He was meticulously taking photographs of the grass, then stopping to take field notes. The captain's boots were muddy and wet by the time he got within shouting distance of his lieutenant.

"Hey, Fowler, what have you got?"

Nick looked up and yelled into the wind. "Best thing I have is a knee impression in the ground here, ribbed cords, I'd say." He started in the captain's direction.

Weathers waved him back into place. "Stay put, I'll come to you."

Fowler continued talking into the gusty wind. "I've taken some macros of the impressions, several soil samples to compare with any trousers that might yield deposits. Plaster man's on the way to cast it."

By the time Weathers had made his way to the spot, his boots had sunk in over the lacing two times. He was puffing.

Fowler looked down, puzzled for a moment. Then he realized. "This little area must be the high ground—that's why it's not wet."

Weathers shook hands. "Look—I want Marty off this detail and on that Ballard boy's tail every minute of the day."

"Good idea."

Weathers looked down at his shoes. "Goddamnit."

Fowler pointed to the impression. "Over here it's dry. Place of death, Captain. See the blood?"

Weathers looked around. "Yeah."

"Severe wounds, again to the neck, probably the same weapon; again the wound wrapped, this time with an undershirt, and the body was propped into the silt thirty-five feet from here in the marsh. I located the path he took. The body was nailed, dragged, then lifted slightly through the curtain of undergrowth over there, then hauled into the water."

"What happened here?"

Fowler hesitated. "This time—go with me, Captain—this time, the stains are a little different. I think there's some kind of code here."

"In what?"

"The dance steps. Look."

Weathers bent down and stared at the bloodstains. He stood up. "I'm warning you, no newspapers—you got it?"

"I'm going to have this entire area studied for saline activity, fibers, cloth fragments."

"Look," Weathers said, "I don't need to know every time you go to the bathroom. I just want it taken care of."

"I think the killer, or someone, was on his knees for part of the time. It's hard to speculate why, but—"

"You gotta do better than that."

"What?"

"The governor called me today." He paused. "Do you have any idea what kind of pressure I'm under?"

"I know that you—"

"No, you don't—but just the same, I'll put it to you this way, Fowler. Maybe it isn't exactly your fault when your men get clubbed on assignment, but it does reflect, okay?"

"I know."

"It makes me wonder if I've got the right man on this case."

"You have the right man, Allen."

"The right man, Lieutenant, will give me a suspect in the next day or so, you understand? The right man will comb this county for the murderer instead of futzing around here in the make-believe ballroom."

Fowler's face turned crimson. "You're out of touch, Captain."

"What?"

"You want results, but you don't care if they're the right ones."

"Lieutenant, I suggest you—"

"You think this guy is killing young boys so his methods can fall out of a textbook into our laps?" Weathers was taken aback. Fowler had raised his voice and now was staring, his blue eyes bright with anger.

Weathers stared back. "These news stories make it look like we don't know what we're doing."

"We don't. We're stymied. This killer is smart and is going to be hard as hell to catch. He's just hitting his stride now—I can feel it. He wants to keep killing. And I certainly can't do my job with you breathing down my—"

"I'm going to pretend you didn't say that."

"If it makes you feel better, Captain."

"What would make me feel better, Lieutenant, is less time spent on theory and more time on law enforcement."

"Then why did you hire me? This is what I do. I get inside the killer's head. I try to understand who he is."

"I want a suspect. I'll give you forty-eight hours." Weathers glared at Fowler, turned, and padded back through the muck toward the other side of the marsh.

Fowler turned his attention back to the ground. He didn't see Weathers halt on the far side of the marsh and forge a path through the sludge over to Marty, who was now standing on the bank, still holding the tape measure. He couldn't have heard what the two men were saying, even if he had wanted to.

Maureen McCauley had just entered May Loon Kitchen, the Chinese restaurant out on the strip. Judy Bayard, the dispatcher, waved at her from a cloud of smoke at the end of the room. Judy had grown up with four brothers. With one leg thrust out into the aisle, she hunched over the table chewing gum like a truck driver in eye shadow.

"Haven't seen you in a while," she said, putting her gum in the ashtray. "How's it going?"

"Oh, I don't know," Maureen said, sitting down. "This story's so hot my editor thinks it has to go national. They're going to take it away from me, Judy."

"Have you heard the latest?"

"No," Maureen said, adjusting herself into the cane chair. "What's up?"

"Well, I usually work out Monday, Wednesday, and Friday at the club, you know." She smiled knowingly. "Got to keep this little body tight—all I own are tank tops, right? So . . ." She put out her cigarette, waved the smoke away. "It's hot in here, right?"

"Yes. So? What happened?"

"Well, I'm like stuffing my leotards into my gym bag when the captain storms in. I hear him yelling at somebody on the phone in his office. Somethin' 'bout this Fowler guy still using that dance crap on this murder too. Somethin' like he's fed up, he's going to personally send the guy back to the Thousand Islands. In a salad. You know—crazy stuff."

"Who was he talking to?"

"I don't know. His wife."

"He's going to fire him?"

"I wouldn't exactly shed a tear. Know what I'm saying?"

"Sure."

"Oh, he said something about the *Tribune*—I don't know what it was but he was pissed, so—"

A little Chinese man had shuffled up to the table, bowing slightly as he lifted his pad and pencil into the dim light. "Ready to order?"

Judy Bayard looked up. The hard lines of her eye makeup seemed to melt. Her eyes even crinkled. "Oh, we haven't even looked. Just give us a minute. Please."

Maureen nodded with approval, then smiling a little uneasily, she opened the menu.

HER CHICKEN WITH black bean sauce was still talking back to her as she drove up the winding country road toward Brookside Cottage. She stopped her blue Rambler a good two hundred yards up a hill, where the reflecting sun made the road look like the back of a snake. She stared down at the twisting cement sheath as it coiled around the marsh. She turned off the engine, put a mint in her mouth.

She could see several policemen combing the marsh area. From her crime reporting in California, she could tell the men were working the area in a grid search pattern. In a field beyond it, she could see a section cordoned off by the same boring yellow police line. There, by a long metal fence, she saw more men down on their knees, searching for an original thought.

She left her purse in the car but shoved her auto lens camera into her skirt pocket. As she approached the fence, she could see several technicians studying a section of grass with magnifying glasses. One man was placing something in a small test tube then into a black case; there were pillboxes clustered near his hands.

One man was surrounded by heavy manila envelopes, equipped with lock seals. He was writing furiously on a form that was glaring back at him in the afternoon light; Maureen knew this officer was launching a piece of evidence on the odyssey it makes toward the courtroom. She remembered the phrase "chain of custody" as she saw yet another man working with a mold of plaster of Paris.

One of the policemen looked up at her suspiciously when she leaned over the fence, looking over the yellow tape. His name was Robby Cole.

"Ow," she said, bumping her knee against a galvanized steel post.

"No one's allowed on the crime scene, ma'am. Sorry." The man had dark features, a widow's peak at his hairline.

"What crime?" she said.

"I'm sorry. We can't discuss that."

Maureen smiled. "I guess you can't stop me from standing on my cousin's own land, now can you?"

"Just stay on that side of the fence please," Sergeant Cole said wearily. "Collecting evidence here."

From where Maureen was standing, the sun was laid out at an angle across the grass; she could see small spots that shifted slightly when a breeze came up. She wondered what the spots were.

"You know, you look like my old boyfriend. What's your name?" Her dress rode up her thigh slightly as she leaned over the fence with her camera. Robby Cole looked at her now. She focused the lens on the spots in the light and pressed the shutter. "Mind if I take your picture?"

The policeman heard the click, sighed, and shook his head. Two other men were amused by this. They looked at Maureen. The dark tops of her panty hose were just beginning to peek from under her skirt as she leaned again, focusing on the grass just behind the policeman's hair. She clicked the shutter again. This time the policeman stood up. "Now listen, I told you—"

Another snap. Maureen was backing away, now snapping the angry policeman as he waved his arms moving toward the fence. She turned and walked down the path, smiling. That was one way to get a man's attention. Behind her, Sergeant Cole was staring at the way she walked. He watched her until she was out of sight.

"Nice," he said to himself. "Very nice."

An hour and a half later, in the darkroom at the newspaper, Maureen glanced down at the luminous dial of her watch, slipped the paper from under the enlarger, and plopped it in the solution.

She pulled on a pair of rubber gloves, lifting the paper gently from one pan to the next, as it finally curled in the setting solution. After she had checked her time again, she pulled the last print out. This time she had adjusted the brightness to compensate for the aperture setting on her camera. The spots on the grass were lit up in patterns that made her mind wander.

Something was going through her head as she hung the wet developing paper on a line with clothespins. It was a song. She couldn't remember the name of it, but it made her sad. She flicked on the light.

She started thinking about her senior prom from high school. The guys in Bakersfield all wore their hair greased up on the sides like the fenders of a Jaguar. They rolled their smokes up under the short sleeves of their white T-shirts—part of a uniform that included black chinos, white socks, those pointed black shoes with zippers or ties on the side—shined so you could see them in the dark.

She couldn't remember how long she had been staring at the L-shaped patterns of the spots before she heard the rhythm in her head. Her hands were drawn across her chest defensively as she hugged the outsides of her elbows.

Slow-slow-quick-quick-slow. She unclasped her hands when she realized her knuckles were white. She was one of those girls who could never follow. Her tragic flaw, she thought.

She had been stood up at her senior prom. It had a thirties theme, she recalled. She had spent most of the night with her hair pinned down like a flapper, wearing a pillowcase, trying to teach some greaser how to dance. Seeing a redneck attempt the Charleston is one of those sights that can stay with you for a lifetime. She remembered how, toward the end of the night, they played nothing but slow music.

Slow-slow-quick-quick.

The greaser never got it. He just wanted to hang on her and feel the flesh along the sides of her ribs, of which she felt there was a little too much. On the last dance, he had tried to reach up and feel her breast. She had grabbed his hand and tucked it behind her back.

Maureen McCauley shook her head, wishing, now standing there alone in the small room, that she had let him touch her. She wished a lot of things had gone differently. She looked at the spots again. Slow-slow-quick now.

She knew she had her story.

22

THE WHITE SHEET clapped like a sail. Fowler thought of the regattas he had seen as a boy. When he had taken sailing lessons with his dad those summers on Lake Erie, he remembered how, coming about in a stiff wind, the jib cracked like a rifle shot.

This sound was different. Edwin R. Koenig had whisked the sheet all the way to the ankles of Finkelstein's body. He brushed the boy's red hair back as if a gesture of deference would mute the grisly sight. He began to speak very softly.

"The cherry-pink discoloration of skin you see here is caused by the accumulation of reduced hemoglobin in the capillaries as it migrates under the effect of gravity. Normally it has a purplish cast, but here the body was cooled rapidly in the waters of the marsh."

"Cause of death?"

"This time we have a slightly different case, Lieutenant." His gloved fingers traced the edges of the gash in the neck.

Fowler's eyelids kept closing despite his efforts to keep them open. "First we have a laceration here. See how the wound has irregular, undermined margins that show bridging of the skin and subcutaneous tissues between the sides of the wound?"

"Yes."

"It also has a slightly different coloration."

"Two different wounds?"

"Exactly." Koenig picked up a magnifying glass. "But here, just below, you have an incised wound, much deeper with an absence of marginal abrasion."

Fowler looked in the magnifying glass. "What do you think?"

"The first wound was made earlier."

"How long?"

"It's hard to say, Lieutenant. Less than an hour."

"Was the victim alive for that time?"

"Here again, a gray area. But, calculating the development of rigor mortis, the amount of potassium in the ocular fluid, and what we've been able to discover about the state of the digestion, we place the time of death somewhere between midnight and five A.M. Tuesday morning."

"Can't narrow it down more than that?"

Dr. Koenig suddenly stiffened. "This isn't *Kojak*, Mr. Fowler. We're lucky to calculate to a twelve-hour period. Anything else is conjecture."

Fowler paused. "I'm just wondering if he was bleeding from his neck while still alive."

"It's possible."

"Was he alive when he was nailed to the board?"

"An analysis of the hands yielded sequestered blood clots in the area of trauma. I really can't be sure. He may have been alive, but I doubt he was conscious." The doctor raised his eyebrows. "What's intriguing is that this victim was dumped in running water which washed away a great deal of the actual evidence—if you recall, no traces of lipstick here, like on the first victim's mouth, or saliva on the face and neck, etc. However, in protected areas of this victim, the tip of the penis for instance, we still found traces of mucus."

"I don't understand."

"Vaginal activity."

"Again."

"When we combed the pubic area, we found any excess hair had washed away, but we found one plucked hair, a hair with roots, lodged in the elastic of a stretch sock. If the specimen belongs to the assailant, it will yield a genetic fingerprint."

"He's taking chances now."

Koenig paused and looked over the frames of his glasses at Fowler. "He?"

"Or she."

"Let's say, the more violent this killer becomes, the more an identity will be revealed to us."

"Is there anything else I should know, Doctor?"

"Only this." Koenig's delicate hands flew toward the furrows in Finkelstein's thighs. His elastic gloves fluttered down to a suck mark that appeared very faintly on the surface of the skin. "This obviously is the bite your print man tried to lift. If he can't get a dental imprint, I suggest we have a cast made."

Fowler stared down. "Right. I also have a forensic dentist I can call in. He's good."

"The lab, as you know, has given this its highest priority."

The formality between Fowler and Koenig had relaxed somewhat. Nick thought they had forged a strange bond, staring at dead boys under fluorescent lights. He simply nodded at the doctor, smiled sadly, and closed the door to the examining room.

Out in the night air, he took a breath. Fowler thought each of the dead boys held a mystery that the two men experienced as a part of themselves. He wondered if it was the part each felt they had lost.

23

Watching. Blond man out of the funeral home. Stops on the street corner, returns to a lit window—staring at the drawn shade.

Like the way I sculpt flesh? . . . give you a scenario out of limbs, a maze into which your mind collapses each time it enters.

You cross the street, climb the stairs into the campus. Veins jump in my arms. Impulses roaring. Cries have taken over my head. Each time I free one, a chorus of sounds, waves of voices, rising, timpani.

Do it NOW.

At the bridge over the spillway, your hands in pockets. My gloves on wet grass, soles jackknifing, silent. Slip under the bridge. Veins lunge to the skin. Quiet the blood. Just slip out the knife. Move behind you, one sweep, take off your head. NOW.

Your footsteps off the bridge. Climbing the hill.

I killed a man in the flowers. Came up behind him and just grabbed his neck. Rode him down into the petals, the pollen streaking his hair. Blossoms howling, stamens like tongues.

You're stopping at the graveyard. Perfect. Rasp of a hinge—the gate in the distance. Stepping inside, over several tombstones.

I move up on the bank. Up the hill to a tree. Just cut off his air. No marks on the neck. The police said it was a heart attack.

You're walking from stone to stone. Utterances. Voices coming from—? At the black fence now. I see graves looming. Through the broken place in the bars, I move quietly, behind the mausoleum— there you are. Closer now. Ever so silent. It's out now. Moonlight on the blade.

Three gravestones away. Rain and snow have worn the names from those stones. What is that?—moans on the air. Chorus of voices in my head, or—tears? That you, Fowler?

I hunch down—you're looking over here. Music now, voices clamoring, ringing my skull like a chime. Can't stand it. Need silence. One thrust, quiet the swarm. Along the hedge now, closer, my eyes on you. Veins in my forehead, going tap—tap—tap. You're not looking. Do it NOW. Knife to the gullet. But you're crying over an unmarked grave?

Kill you later. You're too surprising.

24

A PALL HAD fallen over the campus. Word had gotten around that locks of Finkelstein's hair had been pulled out. His collection of pennants from schools around the league had been taken, his yearbook missing, a picture of the boy on his grandfather's knee—stolen. Underwear, socks, assorted articles of clothing unaccountably missing.

The students walked around edgy, cranky, startled from several nights without sleep. Circles hung under everyone's eyes. There were reports of terrified boys huddled together through the night hours, telling ghost stories, tales of murder and horror. Often they were so giddy and scared they just fell asleep in their clothes wherever they were sitting.

The next evening, after another loathsome memorial service, the students filed anxiously out of the front of the chapel. Standing at a distance, Dr. Brandon Hickey watched the groups of boys meander under the arch, up onto the porch of Ardsley and through the door toward the dining room. He watched how some of the boys held the door for those following behind. He was touched by this display of civility. He felt the urge to hug certain students and wished he could comfort the boys more openly without people thinking it was unnatural. He realized his fists were clutched at his sides. His face was ashen, drawn tight around a distracted mouth. Which one of these young boys would be the next to fall? Which young body, full of the rush of life, would be cut down? The headmaster turned and looked toward town. He raised his clenched hands. They were shaking.

Five minutes later, he walked quietly into his assistant's office. Mr. Allington was working at his desk. "What do you think I have in my hand?" the headmaster said quietly as he leaned over one of the secretary's desks.

Allington looked up from the stacks of student progress reports. "Oh, Brandon, I'm sorry, I didn't even see you standing there."

Dr. Hickey dumped two handfuls of chewing gum wrappers, pine needles, dirt, tree leaves, and cobwebs, one with the spider still wriggling near a strip of tinfoil, right into the center of the secretary's blotter. He studied the spider trying to extricate itself from a crease in the tinfoil. His own predicament, he thought. Without looking up, he muttered "Go ahead, say it."

Allington was staring at him. "Say what?"

"You know."

"Look, Brandon, talk to Dr. Clarence, go fishing, do something to get yourself together. I can carry on—"

"You have such contempt for me."

"I don't have—"

"You think I'm incompetent, don't you?"

"No, I—"

"*You don't need to pretend.* I know. I can see it."

Allington paused. "All right, yes."

"Thank you." The headmaster's knobby finger was raised to his lip; his mustache was trembling. "You don't think I'm qualified to run this school, do you?"

Allington leaned back. "I never said that."

"It's written all over your face."

"Well, your priorities are skewed, Brandon. Parents are withdrawing their students every day, our funding is collapsing, we're all walking around terrified, and all you can think about is—"

"Don't you dare defile my efforts at keeping this school beautiful. If it wasn't for me, we would all be up to our ears in filth." He swept the gum wrappers and refuse into the wastebasket.

"Brandon, sit down, you're—"

"Beauty itself is at stake."

Allington stood up and reached out an arm to help the older man. "Just take it easy."

Hickey pulled away, staring at him coldly. "How dare you."

"What?"

Dr. Hickey's brown eyes filled. "You want my chair, and don't deny—"

"I most certainly—"

"Let's stop kidding each other, Elliot. I've known for a long time."

"What do you mean? I always support you. I—"

"You undermine me." Dr. Hickey raised his watery eyes to the ceiling. "You want it, all right." He finally turned, ambling toward the door, as the last students filed into the dining room. He turned back to look at Allington. "More than breath itself," he said almost to himself, then disappeared.

ALLINGTON WAS SHOWING the strain as he walked to the dining room a few minutes later. Table after table of students found themselves talking in hushed tones about the murders. Their voices seemed to reflect a pervading fear, a paranoia that no one was immune to.

The fact that Finkelstein had become idealized, however, brought ballast to the fears sweeping the school. He had arisen to the level of myth. When teachers spoke of him, he was extolled for his sense of humor, his direct, if candid personality, his participation in sports and school clubs. Finally Finkelstein was eulogized for his long-standing devotion to God. Now the customary sick jokes began to seep through the cracks.

When the students sat down at Mr. Allington's table, they were very quiet. After the pea soup, somewhere during a main course of thin scallops of beef floating in a watery au jus, Allington heard someone, he wasn't sure who, tell one of these jokes. Several boys had hunched over at the foot of the table, when one voice said, "Why didn't Finkelstein ask the Saint Ann's girl to the spring prom?" There was a pause. "He was already pinned."

Allington was incensed. He stood up at the table, threw his linen napkin down as if it were a gauntlet. "Any student caught telling another reprehensible joke will be expelled." He stood there daring them, his face flushed.

The boys at his table stopped chewing, went silent, and stared up at his immense frame towering above them. They noticed how the master's handsome face had changed; in outrage, it seemed to dissolve into weakness. His graying head of kinky hair combed flat across his head, his bushy black eyebrows, and his slightly hooked nose—made somewhat more severe by a pair of thin but sensual lips—all seemed to betray him. He sat down.

He took a more controlled tone of voice. "How would you like it if people made tasteless jokes about you before you were even in the ground?" He stared at no one in particular.

"Sir?" A fat but articulate finger wagged the air.

"Yes, Quigley," Allington said impatiently, as an overwrought, bespectacled boy stopped dumping pepper on his beef long enough to compose his hands devoutly in front of him.

"Sir, I truly believe we are celebrating Finkelstein's unique sardonic sense of self by telling these . . . these stories."

Allington stared down at Quigley's hands as if they were sausages. "I don't care what you're celebrating, I won't have it."

"But, sir"—Quigley's hands flew into the air—"if you think of it, we are marking his place in the universe. Engraving his memory on our minds so that we too may—"

"Be quiet, Quigley. I'm in no mood for your crackpot moralizing." The temperature at the table seemed to rise, but Quigley, editor in chief of the student newspaper, had already examined his lofty view of the situation.

"It's obviously a form of folk heroism, and I personally—"

"You personally may leave the table!" Allington's voice trumpeted across the room, enough to raise heads fifteen tables over. The dining room went silent for a moment, then slowly a ground swell of talk reignited the tables.

Quigley looked down at his uneaten strips of beef, shaking his head tragically. "Yes, sir," he whispered. He stood up, pushed his chair in without scraping it, and walked from the dining hall with his head lowered.

Allington never recovered. An unusually popular master, especially with the boys at his table, he became flustered now. The students were just sitting there, not looking at him, staring instead down at their thick, white plates in silence.

He picked up his napkin, dabbed his lips, and mumbled. "I apologize to the rest of you boys. I guess I've gone too far."

He left the dining room as well.

Dr. Hickey couldn't help but notice this display. A fragment of a smile flew across his features. He reached out and touched Allington's sleeve as the tall man brushed by the head table on his way out. Dr. Hickey then turned to someone at his table, mentioning how much pressure the assistant headmaster must be under.

He smiled when it occurred to him to apply some more pressure now. He would send a memo to Allington tomorrow, saying he should personally update the faculty on the status of the investigation. Then he would know what headmasters go through every day. Then he would know pressure.

One of the waiters brought Dr. Hickey his tapioca pudding and coffee. He felt more relaxed now.

25

THE NEXT MORNING Fowler overslept. He was awakened by the phone clanging next to his ear. His hand reached over, knocking the phone off the end table onto the green shag carpet.

He launched his body half out the bed and stretched his arm out toward the receiver.

"Hello?" he said, groggy with sleep.

On the other end he heard Bill Rodney's whiskey voice. "Well, must be nice. Wish I could sleep in."

Fowler was balanced on one arm, his other arm clamped with the phone to his ear. He groaned and stared at the clock. "Oh shit," he said.

"Stop and get the *Tribune* on your way over to the van, Lieutenant. It might interest you."

Fowler heard the insinuation in Bill Rodney's voice. It was without judgment; nevertheless, it was there.

"You're kidding."

"Wish I was."

Fowler hung up the phone, decided to forgo a shower, shaved too fast, cutting his chin, and found he was already cursing before he had even driven over to get the morning paper.

By the time he pulled the *Tribune* out of the machine in the vestibule of the diner, his nerves were frayed. He had been talking to himself on the way over in the car; he was expecting the worst. That way, if by chance he was treated more favorably, he would have already absorbed some of the shock.

But this was worse.

The headline read ARTHUR MURRAY FOX-TROTS AROUND INVESTIGATORS AS SECOND BOY IS CRUCIFIED. COUNTY IN TERROR OF SEX KILLER. There was a picture of the bloodstains on the grass. Next to it, was a diagram of the basic L-shaped Fox-trot step. The article again was by Maureen McCauley.

It contained a great deal of information from the autopsy report, which Fowler knew had to be from the locked report he had personally put in the captain's safe; it had lab evidence that only someone who had access to his reports could have gotten. There was a subtle implication, again, that he was not doing his job.

But what troubled him was the fact that the reporter had stolen his dance theory, turned it around, and used it against him. She implied that Captain Weathers might be stonewalling the "dance aspect" of the investigation, which was true, but it portrayed Fowler as a weak man who had thrown up his hands, in effect, giving up his own angle on the case. It openly chastised him for lacking the courage of his convictions.

How had she gotten that photograph? An analysis by a local dance instructor, a Mr. Pullen, was printed in the next column; it detailed the history of the Fox-trot, with its variations: the Park Avenue, the Conversation, the Arch Turn, the Forward Basic, etc. It even attempted a profile of a person who might have been deeply influenced by this dance—and at what ages the steps might have been learned.

Fowler's hand was shaking as he lifted the coffee to his lips. Here he was again, out in the diner parking lot, reading lies and distortions about himself, and again, there was nothing he could do about it. He had to take it. Nick Fowler hadn't had breakfast and was not really awake when he did something uncharacteristic. He decided he was *not* going to take it.

He drove over to the offices of the *Ravenstown Tribune*, got out of his car, and stalked into the building. The receptionist at the front desk tried not to look alarmed at the angry man who had pushed his badge into her face, demanding to see Ms. McCauley right away. She was new.

She rang back and found that the reporter was away from her desk. She was wondering how she could tell the man in such a way that it would not get him any more upset. When she looked up, though, he was gone.

Nick had marched past the front desk, down the hallway, and was directed to Maureen's area by two mailroom attendants, who stared at each other when they heard his tone of voice and saw the expression on his face. Finally Nick Fowler got to a small newsroom area, where feature reporters were scattered around, standing behind cluttered desks that hoisted up rows of computer screens.

In the center of the room, Maureen McCauley was seated at her desk, talking on the phone. She saw him coming, spoke a word into the receiver, and hung up. She wanted to smile but could see, as he approached her, the storm clouds racing across his brow. She wanted to glory in this moment. After all, this was what she wanted, wasn't it? Hadn't she written the article to get his attention?

He walked up and hovered over her. The nostrils of the cleft nose were flaring in and out as he breathed. His prominent brow bulged with color above two fiery blue eyes. She thought he was going to scream. He raised his fists over her. Then something helpless wrenched his gesture, in midair, as he dropped his hands, looking at her.

"What are you doing to me?" he said helplessly.

She was taken aback. She had expected him to hit her, to take out his gun and blast a hole in her computer screen, to kick her desk over. She melted.

"I'm not doing anything to you—I'm just doing my job, Nick."

His breath had evened out slightly. "Your job doesn't include humiliating me," he said. "It doesn't include calling attention to yourself by using my own investigative techniques against me."

"I'm sorry this upsets you," she said, standing up, "but people have to know." Hands on her hips now.

Fowler didn't even realize he was preoccupied by her strong, thin fingers, her red nails perfectly filed. "People don't need you in their faces telling them the police are incompetent. Don't you see how you're undermining what we're trying to do?"

"Trying to do, or doing?"

"You have no *idea* what we're doing, do you?"

"Neither does anyone in the country."

He looked away to control himself. "Whoever is giving you this half-ass information that allows you to distort what—"

"The public wants answers, Mr. Fowler."

Her flippant replies irritated him. "Cut the crap. I'm trying to talk to you. Don't give me stock, bullshit answers."

"I'm sorry if that's what you think I'm giving you."

He looked her in the eyes. "It's over—this little game—you understand me?"

"No, Lieutenant, it's just beginning." Maureen didn't realize her shoe was nervously working up and down, making the flesh on her thigh jump like an electrical current. She stilled her foot.

Nick Fowler had a dull feeling that he had already lost this round. He shook his head, staring at her. "What do you want from me?"

Maureen was again taken aback, touched by his sincerity. She tried to fight the impulse to touch his arm. She leaned forward. "Let me help you."

Nick looked at her. "I just need you to leave me alone."

"I don't want to leave you alone." Maureen was getting worked up again. Her eyes had welled up slightly. She was angry at herself for getting emotional.

Fowler leaned. "Just let me do my job. That's all I—"

"Use me. If the killer is reading the paper, then we could lure him into a trap."

"It's too dangerous for you."

Maureen smiled. "Why can't you share it?"

Nick shook his head slightly. "I don't trust you."

Maureen was thunderstruck. It had never occurred to her. She smiled ironically, turned, and sat down.

Nick saw that he had hit home. He said quietly, "If you were in my shoes, would you have any trust after what's happened? Seriously."

"No."

There was a static sound, a computer beep, and a voice-call from the girl at the switchboard. "Ms. McCauley, are you there?"

Maureen turned toward the phone. "Take a message, please."

"Someone left a letter for you."

"Just leave it out front. I'll get it later. Thank you."

There was a pause as Maureen looked back up at Nick. Another beep announced the switchboard operator again. "Sorry, Ms. Mc-Cauley, but the letter says 'urgent' on it."

Maureen sighed. "Look, I'll be out in a—"

"It smells kind of . . . weird."

Something shivered down Nick's spine. He reached over and grabbed Maureen's arm. "Ask her who it's from."

Maureen looked startled at Fowler's sudden intensity. She turned toward the phone. "Does it say who it's from?"

The girl's thin voice crackled again through the speaker. "Arthur Murray."

Nick Fowler was running down the hall with Maureen on his heels. When they got to the reception area, he already had his .38 out, had flung the door open in a crouch, both hands on his re-volver.

The lobby was empty.

Fowler rushed outside to see if a car might be pulling away. The parking lot was deserted. One car was parked along the road. There was a cloistered area in front of the building where trees had been cleared. The rest of the building was surrounded by woods. There was no one in sight.

He walked back inside. He asked the receptionist what the person looked like who had dropped off the letter. The girl seemed overwhelmed by the sight of the gun, the sudden barrage of questions. She was flustered, fanning her face. "I didn't notice anyone."

"You must have seen someone."

"There were several people waiting for appointments," she said, her voice getting more defensive. "And the phones were jumping—as always."

"When did you see the letter?" Fowler asked.

"I didn't see it," she said, remembering back. "I smelled it." She arranged the buttons on her blouse nervously. "That's when I called."

Fowler pulled on a pair of gloves and picked up the purple letter. It was the same stationery, and it was addressed, in ink, to Maureen McCauley, care of the Features Department, *Ravenstown Tribune*. Maureen motioned him into a conference room off the lobby.

Inside, Fowler set the letter gingerly on the table, sniffed it carefully for poison, again aware of the strong smell of perfume. He pulled out a pocketknife. When he slit open the envelope, another large piece of purple stationery unfolded on the conference table. Again, it was scrawled in the same infantile hand, again signed in dark pink lipstick.

Dear Ms. McCauley,

I have enjoyed your articles immensely. Perhaps you will take pity on Lieutenant Fowler. He is a man wounded by his affinity for the dead. Something beyond this life is drawing him relentlessly, like the tide.

I'm making a study of him. Saving him for last. I could kill you too, if you like. Forgive me for being so forward.

Shall we dance?

Arthur Murray

P.S. Next: another enemy kissed out in nature, where time no longer runs.

Fowler stood looking down at the letter. "How did he know that?"

Maureen's pretty round face was lowered, studying the scrawl on the letter. The face lifted up, it was blank. "Know what?"

"Is he reading my mind?"

"Maybe he's following you."

Fowler seemed to blanch. He reached down for the purple letter.

"That letter was addressed to me." There was a sharp tone in her voice. "Leave it there." Nervous now.

Fowler looked at how her jaw was set, the cheekbones flaring out, the skin flushed. How soft the nape of her neck was when she bent down.

"I'm sorry. This is police evidence now," he said. "After the investigation, it will be returned." He carefully picked the letter up, folded it into his pocket. "Of course, you could just get inside the station house safe and read it anyway, right?" She rocked back.

He walked out of the conference room.

In the hallway, he heard high heels behind him as he pulled the glass door open. He stepped outside. Maureen flung the door open behind him and stepped out as well. He turned to her. She was staring at him in defiance. He couldn't allow her to get involved. He was worried now for her life.

"No," he said quietly.

"You can't stop me."

"I have ways."

"What is it with you? You're like an automaton."

Fowler stared at her. "I'm asking you, for your own welfare, to back off."

"You know I can't."

"I'll speak to your superiors," he said strongly.

"You do, and I'll speak to yours."

"I hardly think after what you said about Captain Weathers that he would be likely—"

"Stop it!" she yelled. "Just—" She had raised her fists. "Look, it's too late to keep me out, I'm already in!"

"That's what I'm worried about. You could be the next one crucified. Wake up!"

A triumphant look spread across Maureen's face. "You're jealous."

Fowler frowned, looking away across the wooded area. He could still see a car parked out on the road. He then heard the faint echo of the engine turning over in the distance and noticed that the car now started up the hill and, backing out of sight, disappeared.

Fowler noted the make and model. He turned to Maureen. "You said it yourself: He may have followed me here."

"It doesn't worry me." Again her voice revealed a strange fragility coming through.

He realized what was in her eyes. It was fear. Nick watched her as he said, "He would just as soon kill you as look at you."

"Sounds more to me like he wants to kill you."

Fowler shook his head. "He wants to impress me—that could include killing people associated with me. Look, the answer is no. That's it." He started down the steps toward his car.

"Fowler," she said quietly, her tone uncertain, imploring, as she walked down the steps after him. When he opened his car door, she was next to him, in close. He smelled something aromatic. She grabbed his sleeve, twisting the material, her voice distressed. "This story is hot. It's going national. If I can get involved, as a liaison, I'm assured of keeping the story. I deserve it. I've worked hard for this."

"What perfume are you wearing?"

"I've—what?"

"What fragrance did you put on?"

She was flustered. "I don't know. It was a gift."

"From who?"

She stared at him, beginning to smile. "Wouldn't you like to know?"

"I would." Something bitter in his tone.

"Why?"

"Never mind." He got in the sedan, closed the door.

She yanked open the door. "Don't shut me out."

"Stick to reporting," he said coldly, and slammed the door.

Maureen's features seemed to thicken with sadness as she watched Nick Fowler pull out of the parking lot. Then she felt anger.

He was like all the rest of the men she had known in her life. They didn't want to yield one ounce of power to a woman. Nick Fowler would yield, she thought. He would succumb.

She would make sure of that.

26

MARTY ORLOFF HAD backed the car up so the line of trees in front of the newspaper building was drawn like a curtain in front of him. He then pulled the car around, drove the three short blocks through town, up the hill, crossed over High Street, then continued down the other side of the hill by the lake. He took the county road a few hundred yards more, turning into the back entrance of Ravenhill School.

He passed the crime van on the way, which was parked near the marsh, just below Brookside Cottage. He was afraid Fowler might have followed him, so he roared the vehicle across the macadam road that twisted through the campus. He passed the outbuildings, the language arts facilities, came around a small hill, slowed down, and pulled his car up behind Ardsley Hall, where the kitchen staff parked.

When he got out of his car, he glanced at his watch. He pulled the schedule of classes out of his pocket; he had gotten them from the assistant headmaster the day before. He had eight minutes before Ballard left his first-period English class with Mr. Toby on the fifth floor of Madison, then walked down four flights to his second-period math class with Ms. Coates.

He saw there was a pay phone behind Ardsley. He stepped up to it and put in a call down to the state police station house. When the switchboard picked up, he asked to speak to Captain Weathers. He waited, tapping his foot nervously on the gravel. Then he heard a click as the call was being transferred. He heard the gruff voice on the other end.

"Weathers."

"Captain, this is Marty Orloff."

There was a pause on the other end of the line. "Well, what is it?"

"Look, sir, you asked me to—"

"I know, I know. Go ahead."

Marty switched the receiver to his other hand. "Lieutenant Fowler did not come directly into work this morning, but drove to the diner, then the *Tribune*."

"You followed him?"

"Yeah."

"What the fuck was he doing?"

"I don't know, but he came outside talking to the reporter, what's her name."

"The one who wrote that goddamned article?"

"Yeah."

"You sure it was her?"

"A couple of guys pointed her out at the Thirsty Moose. It was her. Definitely."

"They were talking."

"Oh yeah."

Again there was a pause on the phone. "All right, Orloff, you've redeemed yourself. I'll take care of this. Just stick with that kid now, you got it?"

"You bet."

"Need some No Doz?"

Marty Orloff laughed. "No, sir. Uh, the lieutenant asked me to do some legwork on the victims. Want to hear this?"

"Of course."

"Turns out Crawford and this kid, Ballard, had a fistfight day or so before he was murdered. Now I hear from kids in Brookside Finkelstein and Ballard had an ugly argument about some girl the night he was killed."

"Think he's shielding the boy?"

"I'm not sure."

"You don't need to mention this to Fowler. Let me handle it."

"Right."

WHEN THE BELL rang, Cary Ballard slumped out of his English class. He was still shaking from being questioned before breakfast by the detective, Bill Rodney. On his way to math, he tried to keep his racing thoughts occupied.

Marty Orloff followed ten feet behind Cary. He was walking behind two other students and couldn't help but overhear them. The student doing most of the talking, Schwerin, was the same boy who had discovered Crawford's mutilated body the week before.

"I was down in the tunnels yesterday," he said.

"Was it gross or what?"

"Totally. They gave me an initiation to see the school ghost—that giant boy we always hear about."

"Yeah."

Marty walked a little faster.

"What did they make you do?"

Schwerin turned his head, pushed his tortoiseshell glasses up on his nose, and talked rapidly, his braces giving his words a slight sibilance. Like a steam radiator, Marty thought.

"They told me I had to write something on a bathroom wall about Ms. Coates."

The other student shook his head, smiling. "Did you?"

"Yeah," he whined. "But it wasn't dirty enough—I have to do it again."

Marty saw Cary turn off on the second floor. He leaned on a railing, knowing he had found a worthless lead to throw the lieutenant. He watched the boy enter his math class at the end of Madison Hall.

Inside the room, Cary felt nauseated as he took his seat in one of the wooden desks bolted to the floor. He didn't pay much attention to the other boys who were loitering around, waiting for class to begin. Three boys wrestled in the corner, giggling; they were trying to subdue one huge boy, a football player, who was wearing a black and yellow hat with the word "Cat" on the crown. He batted the other boys around like flies. His name was Ray Gluckner.

Ballard noticed there were two desks in the front row that were conspicuously empty. He stared out the window at the trees and seemed only mildly interested when Ms. Coates marched into the room, strutting toward the blackboard to signal that class had begun. The three boys in the corner blushed under her stern gaze, stopped horsing around immediately, and took their seats.

Ms. Coates's triceps began to ripple as she wrote the day's formulas on the blackboard. The boys watched her calf muscles bulging when she leaned over the desk to pass homework back. They also noticed how, like on so many other days, she had covered her large breasts with clingy material in a primary color. After writing the formulas on the board, she brushed the chalk dust from her sweater in a very suggestive way. This drove the boys to distraction.

Ballard was like all the rest of the boys. His collision with puberty had left him so vulnerable to the fabric of Ms. Coates's sweaters that her breasts became building blocks of pure science. Usually he would just gawk at her like the rest of the boys, his brain longing to calculate the area just beneath her rather prominent chin. Today he was distracted. He stared into space. He even gazed out the window.

Ms. Coates kept looking at his troubled face in between copying more algebraic formulas on the blackboard. She drifted to Ballard's side of the room, brushing the chalk dust from her sweater a little more emphatically. One student, leaning over to ogle her, knocked all his books into the aisle on the floor. She rewarded the boy with a smile, then glanced back at Ballard.

There was a knock at the door. A white piece of paper bearing the administrative letterhead was slipped into Ms. Coates's fingers by a messenger. Ballard didn't notice; he was adrift on the memory of his morning encounter with the police.

Ms. Coates read the note, smiled like an elf, and adjusted the hem of what had always been the equator of Ballard's attentiveness; her thigh muscles jumped as she turned and sashayed over to the front of his desk.

"In trouble, Ballard?"

"Excuse me?"

She held the piece of paper over his head, then watched it float down, missing his desk, to the floor. "Oh sorry," she said, with a smile, as Ballard reached down to the floor. "Got it?" she said, as the tip of her high heel came down on the message just as Ballard's fingers stretched out to get it.

Ballard had lurched his body out into the aisle to scrape up the piece of paper. He tugged on it, but Ms. Coates's foot had fastened it securely to the dust on the wooden floor. He was trying not to notice her stockinged ankle fixed like a colossus above the warped floorboards.

By now the other students were all bent into the aisles, trying to see what he was doing. Ballard slowly craned his neck and looked up as Ms. Coates's legs towered above him.

A voice came thundering down. "It seems the assistant head-master wants to see you."

Ballard's mouth went dry. As he attempted to pull on the piece of paper, he twisted his neck up farther to where he could see beyond her slightly protruding belly, past her breasts, to where her small petulant mouth was flattened across the horizon.

"You're standing on the message," he said finally.

She lifted her toe. "Oh, was I?"

Ballard pulled himself back to a sitting position. "Thank you, Ms. Coates."

"Get the assignment from one of your classmates," she said, her eyes adamant.

"Yes, ma'am," Ballard said as he stood up and backed into a desk next to his. "I will. I promise." The students laughed.

She smiled now as the boy moved sideways, awkwardly, out the door.

27

Nick Fowler was deep in thought as he pulled his car up to the crime van and turned off the engine. He had recognized Marty's squad car before parked outside the *Tribune* building, then had seen it pull away. He wondered why Marty was tailing him. This was a strange development, but he couldn't think about it.

He was more concerned about the killer. How had he or she known what Nick was feeling about his father? He knew he had to bear down. He was getting spooked. Was the killer observing him from a distance? If so, how could any person have known that right now he *was* feeling close to someone dead? Haunted was more like the word. A yearning. A cavity of pain he could never seem to fill.

Unless the killer felt the same way—unless Nick could use that as a scent to track this ungodly thing that fed on young boys. He thought back to his school days, his friends, the girls he had gone out with in college, before he entered the police academy. All of them, like his ex, like Maureen, had accused him of being "distant." He knew that was the way he had felt ever since he had arrived in Ravenstown. Even long before that, in fact. His whole life.

That's when he understood something that shocked him: He knew he felt more drawn now to the killer than to anyone living. As if he had entered an alien world inhabited by images of death, where his own intuition flooded down into an uncertain hell—his every waking moment touched by fear—preparing him for what would happen when he finally came face-to-face with the killer. That troubled him very deeply.

Nick got out of the car. He stood there, outside the van, thinking. He had another few days at the most before Arthur Murray would kill again.

If only he could find the key.

How did Murray choose his or her victims? Had he or she decided to dress them up in formal clothing because of all the press coverage? Almost certainly. Tuxedos, romance, ballroom dances. Was the killer from another generation? Had to be. Unless he or she was acting out some drama with phantoms from another time. Parents? Maybe.

He slammed the car door and walked toward the van.

Bill Rodney looked up at Fowler as he stepped up into the van. He saw that the lieutenant was preoccupied. He smiled slightly and handed the lieutenant his messages. "Rough start today?"

Fowler rolled his eyes. "Yeah. Anything going on?"

Rodney laughed. "You've got to be kidding."

Fowler realized it was a pretty dumb question. "I should say what isn't going on, right?"

"It hit the fan this morning."

"Weathers up here?"

Again Detective Rodney could not suppress a smile. He lit a cigarette, raising his eyebrows. "It's a good thing you overslept, Nick. He was here, chewing on everything but the trailer hitch."

"He must have an ulcer."

"After that article he does."

"Bill, were you able to run a background check on Dr. Clarence?"

"We're working on it." Rodney dug into his file. "Found some very interesting facts about the doctor. The administrator I spoke to claimed the hospital let him go because of 'staff friction.' That's the official word. We later talked to other staff members. A different story is taking shape. Have a feeling the incident was under-reported to save his reputation."

"When do I get to read the report?"

"Tonight."

"Good. Did you find out what kind of tranquilizers Marty was drugged with at the scene?"

"We're waiting on the lab."

"Anything on the spikes the victim was nailed with?"

Rodney wearily picked up his report. "Maintenance thinks they were taken from a group of rusted bolts in the power plant. We questioned the old janitor down there, Stanley." He handed him a sheet of paper. "Here's the transcript of the interrogation. My feeling is he's clean."

Fowler read the report. "How about the victim's clothes?"

Bill Rodney looked at Fowler like he was a child who had been misbehaving. "Shall I give you a dramatic reading from your messages, Nick?"

Now Fowler felt a connection with Rodney. A live person, too. He stretched the pile of yellow Post-Its in the old-timer's direction. "Why not?"

Rodney smiled. "I think I have them memorized." He took a drag on his cigarette. "One, the formal attire on the victim was used. We checked about fortysome thrift and antique clothing stores in three counties. The clothes traced out to a little place in Reliance, even the size eight and a half patent leather shoes."

Fowler seemed reflective. "Call them back. Find out if any other complete outfits have been purchased. Get the size."

"Okay."

"Were they able to reconstruct the knee impression?"

"Yeah, but here's the thing. It casts out as the knee of another adolescent boy."

"Not Finkelstein?"

Bill Rodney put out his cigarette. "Now you're going to love this, Nick. We questioned the Ballard kid this morning."

"Right."

Bill Rodney spoke slowly. "In his room we found corduroy pants with dirt encrusted on the knees."

Fowler was shaking his head as Rodney talked.

"Then I caught him in the bathroom trying to wash out the stains. Anyway, I sent him off to breakfast. They check out as the same type of corduroy in the cast of the knee impression. In the cuff was some dirt with a similar composition as the soil at the scene."

"Jesus."

"You'd better bring him in, Nick."

Fowler studied Rodney's old, lined face. "You think he did it, Bill?"

"Well, you can't rule him out—he's almost big enough."

Nick Fowler's eyes drifted out the small window of the van. His face went ash-gray. He stood up and put his hands in his pocket. "I want that in a separate report."

Rodney looked at him apprehensively. "You can't withhold that."

"It's just too pat, Bill. I have the feeling, the same feeling I've had all along: This kid is being set up. I know because *I'm* being set up. And the way our people are thinking about these crimes is so boneheaded they're likely to charge Ballard just to get themselves off the hook. I don't know how or why—I just have to find out more about this kid."

"Why are you risking your own neck for some kid you don't even know?"

Fowler looked at his associate. "I better get to know him, hadn't I?"

"They're going to nail you."

"I'll put it in a supplemental report. Call the school for me and find out the boy's home address. I want to talk to his mother."

Bill Rodney was staring at him. "Whatever you say."

Fowler nodded. "You have a schedule of Ballard's classes?"

"Yeah, Marty is on him now."

Fowler looked down at his messages. On top was one from the coroner. Fowler thought for a moment, then dialed the funeral home. When he got the receptionist, he asked to speak to Dr. Koenig; he was put on hold. Fowler sighed, looked over at Bill Rodney.

"Do you know why Marty was tailing me today?"

"What?"

"He was watching me when I came out of the newspaper building. Then he drove away."

Rodney smiled. "Weathers must be losing it."

"That's what I thought." Fowler heard a receiver pick up on the other end of the line. He then heard Dr. Koenig's precise voice.

"Lieutenant?"

"Yes," Fowler said.

"Some developments. Just a minute." Fowler could hear him shuffle papers on the other end of the line. "Okay," he said. "The plucked hair we found on the victim revealed a blood group: type A. It was a pubic hair. I can't establish this conclusively, but I believe it came from a woman."

"How did you determine that?"

"The fineness of the hair, and the root contained traces of progesterone, a hormone found in birth control pills."

"Wait a minute . . ."

There was a pause on the other end. Koenig spoke again. "Lieutenant?"

It was as if a light had switched on in Fowler's brain. "Of course, 'You miss me by a hair,' that's what he said in the postscript of his first letter."

"I beg your pardon?"

Fowler waved his hand. "I just realized something. Go ahead, Doctor."

"Now, the bite mark. The cast was to be made by the forensic dentist you recommended from Albany; he drove down yesterday. But when he started to make the dental imprint, he discovered it was not a bite mark at all."

"No?"

"The marks were caused by the impression of a necklace, perhaps a string of pearls, he thought. They may have been pressed against the victim's body in a struggle."

"Thank you, Doctor. That helps a lot."

"Not at all."

Fowler hung up the phone. He looked over at Bill Rodney.

"What is it?" Rodney said.

Fowler's wheels were turning. "Now it's a woman's hair, and the bite mark was a actually a necklace."

Rodney crushed another cigarette. "Change partners," he said.

"Yeah."

28

MARTY ORLOFF LIT his cigarette by the cement wall just outside the first-floor window of the math classroom. He took a few drags. He leaned his head back.

He wanted to quit smoking. He stared down at the three butts on the concrete near his battered shoes. He frowned. He knew he had just been sitting out there about twenty minutes. Had to cut down. When he leaned his head back again, this time he saw Nick Fowler's face upside down staring at him. He jumped up.

Fowler was standing above him on top of the concrete wall.

Marty sputtered. "Uh—Lieutenant—hey . . . what's up?"

"Thought I'd follow *you*."

Marty was off-balance. "I didn't hear a sound. You a second-story man in Buffalo, sir, or what?"

"Why are you following me, Orloff?"

Marty looked down at his shoes. "You know, Lieutenant, remember I told you about the tunnels?"

"Yeah."

"I heard that kid, Schwerin, today talking about being initiated by writing things about Ms. Coates on bathroom walls."

Fowler studied Marty. "Think there's anything to it?"

A little smile. "Maybe you should check it out, sir."

"I'll tell you what, Marty, instead of tailing me the next few days, why don't *you* make a report on all the bathroom humor we have at this fine institution, okay? By the end of tomorrow, complete documentation."

Marty Orloff's forehead seemed flushed as he took a long drag off his cigarette. "Sure."

"And stay conscious, okay?"

Fowler looked up and saw Ballard's big sluggish frame coming out the front door of Madison Hall.

"He must've got out early," Marty said, staring back into the classroom window.

Fowler ran around the grassy hill to intersect him. "Hang loose, Sergeant," he yelled back.

Ballard felt dizzy. He stood for a moment under the eave, at the entrance of the building, getting his bearings. Fowler came walking up the cement walk. "Cary?"

Ballard looked up in surprise. Fowler smiled, reached his hand out. "You got out of class early?"

Ballard pulled up his tie self-consciously. "Yeah. I have to go to Administration."

Fowler watched as the boy kept dropping his eyes. He knew he was either terribly shy or guilty as hell. "Look—have you got a minute?" Fowler said. "I have to talk to you. It's important."

"Sure."

Fowler started walking out from under the eave. Ballard ambled along beside him down the walk, under the stone arch, around the back of Ardsley Hall. There Fowler stopped in his tracks, pausing for emphasis. "Exactly why do *you* think the knees of your pants had dirt stains on them?"

Ballard felt little fists of air toiling in his throat. "I—didn't do anything, I—"

Fowler could see the boy turning colors, unable to get his breath. He took both his shoulders, shook him firmly. "Don't panic!"

Ballard looked back at him, his eyes welling up. "I didn't do it!"

Fowler still had the boy by the shoulders. "I'm not saying you did." He shook him again, less hard. "But you've got to help me out, I mean—it doesn't look good. Why were you trying to wash the stains out of your pants?

Ballard was shaking his head, moaning, "I thought I would be blamed again for something—"

"*Look*"—Fowler shook him again, this time violently—"*look at me, Cary.*" Fowler noticed the boy had snapped out of it; his green eyes were now looking clearly at him. "We found a knee impression in the dirt at the death scene—now, why do *you* think there were stains on your knees?"

"I woke up on the roof that night with my knees—"

"What night?"

"The night Finkelstein disappeared."

"How did you know which night that was?"

Ballard was trapped. He vamped again, trying to get air. Fowler tightened his grip on the boy's shoulders.

"I—I fell asleep before it happened—but it wasn't me." He started crying.

"Before what happened?"

"Before I saw that person in the window."

"What person?"

Ballard looked into the man's clear blue eyes. Fowler saw a whole world there. He saw his life when he was a child. He saw himself working with his father in the greenhouse. He saw his mother taking him to interview at schools after he had been expelled. It was as if the blue eyes were telescopes into his own life. Ballard disappeared into them. He kept disappearing into the eyes.

"The stranger," he said in a whisper.

Fowler had felt the boy looking at him the way he imagined a son might. He saw trust and fear battling against each other in the boy's face. "Tell me about the stranger," he said quietly.

"I see a figure of a person when I'm angry at people."

"Who were you angry at?"

"Crawford . . . Finkelstein."

"And you saw a figure."

"Yes."

"Could you describe this figure?"

"Tall, wears a black cape, a hat—a scarf pulled over the face."

"You don't remember what the face looks like?"

"Only the eyes."

"Is it a man or a woman?"

"I think it's a man, but something about him is . . ."

"What?"

"Seductive."

"So, it could be a woman?"

"Yeah."

"Where did you see this stranger?"

"Outside Finkelstein's window."

"When was that?"

"I always see him just . . . before people die."

Fowler released his grip on the boy's shoulders. "What happens after you see this . . . stranger?"

"I get sleepy."

"Then you wake up in a different place?"

"Yeah."

Fowler took Cary's hand and shook it slowly. "I'm glad you told me."

Ballard wiped his nose. "What's going to happen to me?"

Fowler got another whiff of the fear inside the boy. He put his hand on his shoulder. "We have to clear up the business with the dirt on your knees. Try and think about how you might have gotten those stains. Try to remember."

Ballard glanced down. "I'll try."

The boy started to walk away. Nick held on to his shoulder. "Cary, when I was a few years older than you, my father was badly wounded and it changed him so completely that *I* was deeply affected, in fact, I've never been able to get over it, my whole life."

Ballard was looking at him.

"When I read your file, Cary, I found out your father had died when you were very young. Do you remember what happened to your dad? That might be a place to look. A place where you started to block things."

"I'll try to remember."

Fowler watched Ballard walk back under the arch on his way to the administration offices. He walked to the phone in the parking lot of Ardsley. He fished in his pocket for change and dialed the van. Rodney picked up the phone.

"Yeah?"

"Did you find out about Ballard's old lady?"

"She lives in Lumberton, Eighteen West Orleans Drive, 555-5302."

"Great. Bill, where is the killer getting the drugs? Could we run that down?"

"If I had the cavalry at my disposal, sure."

"I'm going to take off. I'll call in later this afternoon."

"Weathers called, Nick. He wants to talk at you."

"I'll call him later."

Fowler hung up and swung his car down the hill, past the police station, toward the interstate.

When Ballard reached the administrative offices, his fear was gone. He stood for a moment beside the outer chamber of the office.

Through the window in the breezeway Ballard was struck again by the sight of the black wrought-iron fence surrounding Ardsley. The shafts hefted themselves out of the clipped grass beside the building. Ballard thought he could feel the points of the uprights shearing into his thoughts. He had become convinced that the fence, or one like it, was actually inside him, and that he would always be a prisoner to the kinds of thoughts that no one would believe.

Until now. Finally someone had heard him.

He walked from the window to the door of the assistant head-master's office. He turned the brass knob on the door but it was yanked inward. Goodson was awkwardly filling the entire width of the door opening. Ballard stepped back, startled. Goodson dropped his eyes, bustled through the doorway, and lumbered down the hall. He looked back over his shoulder once. Ballard stared after him, no-ticing how Goodson's thighs were so large they rubbed against each other and made the sound of a whisk broom, a sound that could still be heard faintly even after Goodson turned the corner.

From inside, Ms. Hall called, "Are you coming inside, Mr. Bal-lard, or not?" The boy closed the door behind him as he stepped onto the carpet inside the room. "Mr. Allington is expecting you," she said stiffly.

Once Ballard was ushered into the inner office, he heard the door close behind him. The motion of the door also made a sound that seemed to seal the room off, as if it were vacuum-packed. On the other side of the room, staring down, hardly breathing, was Allington. Without looking up, he spoke.

"You may sit down, Cary."

"Thank you, sir." Ballard slipped onto a dark green leather chair edged with brass studs.

Allington finished scratching across a sheet of paper that Bal-lard could tell, by the sound, was the school white bond. He placed an old-fashioned fountain pen in its holder, then screwed the top on the inkwell with his thumb and index finger. His eyes looked up, and as he peered from under his bushy eyebrows, Ballard thought he saw a frown. "Do you know who I'm writing to?"

"No, sir."

Allington picked up the sheet so it reflected the light from the windows. "I'm writing to the officer in charge of the state police station, a Captain Weathers." Ballard did not respond. "Would you like to read this letter, Cary?"

"Why should I, sir?"

At that point, Allington stood up. He smiled at Ballard, a little sadly. "Because it concerns you, young man."

"In what way, sir?"

"In a way that surprises me, Cary. You see, the headmaster has asked me to act as liaison to the police in this investigation."

"Oh." The boy looked around the room. He tugged at his collar.

Allington laid the sheet of paper neatly on the blotter. He walked around and leaned against the front of his desk. "First, suppose you tell me how you came to be rushing down the back stairway of Ardsley last week, the morning Crawford was murdered?"

"Because of a lack of air, sir."

"A lack of air?"

"When I saw Crawford's body, I—I felt I couldn't breathe, sir. I had to take a walk."

"You had to take a walk. I see. Where was your tie?"

"I don't know, sir," Ballard began to stammer. "That is, I don't . . . uh, remember having my tie with me."

"I heard it was found wrapped around Crawford's neck."

"Excuse me?"

"I had to talk to Captain Weathers today, as I mentioned. Surely you know your tie was the one found around the deceased's neck."

"No, sir!"

Allington stared at Ballard in disbelief. "Weren't you questioned?"

"Yes."

"By whom?"

"Lieutenant Fowler."

"Didn't he inform you that you were a suspect?"

"No. I mean, I always feel like a suspect, but he hasn't said I was one."

Allington was staring. "Why do you always feel like a suspect?"

Ballard looked down. "I always feel like I'm guilty, even when I'm not."

"Have your sessions with Dr. Clarence been helping you?"

"I'm not sure."

"Do you remember what happened to the white gloves you were issued at the chapel opening day?"

"No, I don't."

"I wish you did, for your sake."

Ballard felt the skin in his face tingle as a wave of needle points worked its way instantly across his forehead, and down the back of his neck. "Oh my God—"

"What is it?" Allington said, suddenly concerned, taking a step forward. "Are you all right?"

"Yes, sir, just—a little shocked. I thought they were in the coat in my closet."

"I wish they were." He dislodged his oxfords from the fringe of the Oriental rug and walked back, his heals squeaking. He reached down and pulled the white gloves out of his desk drawer. "Are these the gloves?" he said.

"How should I know?"

Allington was touching the edges of the white gloves. "What is this green residue?"

"I don't know."

Allington scraped the dried mildew with his fingernail. "Where is the other pair, Cary?"

"I—I don't know, sir."

"Are they in your room?"

"They must be, sir."

"All right," Allington said, taking a step toward him. "I want you to take a good look at these gloves, go home and get the other pair, and bring them to me."

"I can't see them, sir."

"Well, come over here then."

Ballard tried to stand, but his legs simply would not move. He tried to raise them, but they felt as though they were asleep. Not wanting to aggravate the master, Ballard attempted to raise himself out of the chair with his arms. His legs gave way.

He pitched forward onto the rug. It seemed to him as if he was falling, but in a very still way. Skydiving in the fetal position. Suddenly there was more air than he imagined existed. He didn't remember landing, but he thought he saw the white gloves floating by with a force of their own, guided by a strong hand. The same hand that had broken his fall, letting him slowly, gently down to the floor.

29

GREEN'S BAR AND Grill was hardly the kind of place Fowler had expected Muriel Ballard would want to meet. The bar was in a single, white frame house, just off the exit to the interstate. It had frowning green shutters on either side of two long clerestory windows. Next to it, a grocery store, run by the same man, had a sleigh bell nailed to the front door, and it jingled repeatedly as children ran in and out with candy bars.

Fowler walked inside. The venetian blinds cut the afternoon light into long sections that moved across the faces of the patrons like a ticker tape. Fowler opened the door and stood near the entrance. There was a large kidney-shaped bar around which mostly hunters sat, their colored hats pushed back on their heads.

One man, astride a barstool to his left, had a lock of loose hair hanging down in front of him. He was listening—as cigarette smoke curled up around him—to a man talking excitedly on the other side of him. The talker looked up. His face, blotched slightly along the cheekbones.

Fowler heard a hoarse voice from the other side of the bar.

"Lieutenant?"

He looked up and saw a tall blond woman, in her late forties, standing at the back of the bar near the cigarette machine. Fowler could see she was wearing a beige sweater dress and heavy makeup, trying, he thought, to hide her wrinkles—of which there were many. When he walked over and shook her warm hand, he noticed an imitation gold bracelet. Her eyes were blue-gray. She had razor-thin lips, a neck that reminded him of a swan, a voice like Bacall.

"I had to get out. Hope you don't mind."

Fowler saw a cigarette burning in her left hand. "No, this is fine," he said.

"I'm glad it suits you," she said, sitting down, "and if it doesn't, well . . ." She rolled her eyes up and shrugged.

Fowler started dragging the barstool over. "As I mentioned on the phone, Mrs.—"

"Is he in trouble again?"

Fowler paused, sitting down. An enormous bald bartender ambled over. Muriel jerked her head toward the man behind the bar. "What'll you have?" she asked.

"I'll have a draft." He glanced at the bartender. "Genny."

"Oh, a local boy, huh?" she said. "Where you from?"

"Buffalo. Grew up drinking Genesee." He put a bill on the bar as the large man positioned a mug on a cardboard coaster, took the bill, and leaned toward the register. Fowler cleared his throat as his change was slapped down on the wood. "Mrs. Ballard, you mentioned trouble. Has your son had a problem with discipline?"

"Oh please," she said, blowing smoke out. "He tripped his teachers, got in fights, stole things." Her bass voice dropped. "He's just—" She waved her hand. "Forget it."

Fowler was confused. "Mrs. Ballard?" he said.

"Call me Muriel."

"Mrs. Ballard, your son doesn't really seem to me like a troublemaker."

"Hahaha," she said.

"In fact, he seems painfully shy, withdrawn, and…"—he searched the striped faces near the window for the word—"defeated."

A sentiment pleated her top lip. Fowler couldn't tell if it was anger or sorrow. "Well, it's sad, really it is."

"What happened to him?"

"What do you mean?"

"He seems, I don't know, barely able to function."

"They contacted *me*, pal. I didn't want to send that kid to another boarding school, I'll tell you that much."

Fowler stared at her. "They contacted you—what do you mean?"

"No sooner was he suspended from Fieldcrest, that admissions director up there sent me a letter requesting I bring Cary for an interview."

"Who was that?"

"I can't remember his name. He said something about it being an experiment for 'youths at risk.' Hah."

"You don't think Cary's at risk?"

"Why are you asking—like I don't know? I mean—what the hell is this all about?" She drank bitterly from the tumbler on the bar.

Fowler took a sip of his beer. "You've read about the killings."

"Who hasn't?"

"There's been some unfortunate—let's call them . . . coincidences."

"You don't think Cary's involved, do you?"

"No, but some people do."

Muriel Ballard turned openmouthed to face him. "If you think that kid would hurt a flea, you're . . ." She stopped herself, twisting the corners of her mouth down like a circus mime.

"Does he have a temper?"

"*Oh, the worst*," she said, waving the air. "Just like his father, the bum. God save his lousy hide."

Fowler realized she had waved at the bartender.

"Jimmy, repair this for me, will ya?" she yelled, handing him the tumbler. It looked like a scotch on the rocks.

"What's Cary's temper like?"

"Look, mister, if you expect me to talk against my son, just forget it."

Nick Fowler adjusted his barstool. "Mrs. Ballard, there is a wealth of detail mounting up against him. He keeps showing up at the wrong time. I'm trying to—"

"Of course. Story of my life. The poor kid takes after me, always did."

"What I'm trying to determine is—"

"Oh, you want to pin it on me, don't you?"

"No, I—"

"I gave that kid anything he could ever want. I slaved for him, washed for him. You don't know what the hell I did for him, now do you?"

"No."

The bartender brought the tumbler back. She took it out of his hand and took a gulp. "You crumb, drive all the way up here and accuse me of such a thing."

"I didn't accuse you."

"You're all the same."

Fowler wanted to get out of there. Her whiskey voice was grating on his patience. "Yeah, all men are bums, right?"

Muriel looked up with surprise. "That's right," she said.

"Why? What did your husband do that was so—"

"Oh, you don't want to know. You might drop your halo, mister."

"Did he run around?"

She lit a cigarette, blew the smoke up into the air, and answered. "So you want to turn me into a cliché?"

"You don't need any help from me."

Muriel wheeled at him. He could see that one had stung. "All right," she said. "Yes. He did run around, okay? Are you happy? He also drank himself half to death and gambled. Anything else, nosy?"

Fowler laughed in spite of himself. "I'm sorry," he said. "This must be hard for you."

Muriel giggled. She sat up erect on her stool, opened her compact, and checked her makeup. "Oh Christ, I look like hell."

"Look okay to me."

"Don't lie." She stared over at him.

Fowler looked at her face in the small mirror. "You look good enough to tell me why your son's so troubled."

Muriel turned to him, her eyebrow twitching. "You got a nerve," she said, snapping the compact closed.

Fowler frowned. He stood up. "Did Cary hallucinate?"

"What?"

"Did he ever see things?"

"I don't know what you're talking about." She was looking unsure now.

"Did he ever say he saw something, a figure of a man, perhaps."

"A what?"

"A big, dark man, in a hat, a scarf pulled over his face."

"That was Roy."

"What?"

Muriel scratched her nose, suddenly very lucid. "My husband. That's the way he dressed. You know, it was kind of cool in the greenhouse, so he had a tendency to catch colds unless he bundled up. No, my husband dressed the way some houses look when people leave their Christmas lights up into February. Roy would still be wearing his coat, hat, and scarf right into spring. I'd say, 'Roy, it's April, you idiot.' He never listened to me."

"Roy's coat was black?"

"No, forest green, for God's sake."

"When Roy died, did the boy ever . . . see a man dressed like that, but in black?"

The lines in Muriel's face seemed about to crack. She started touching her skin, Fowler thought, to push the pieces back in place. Her eyes brimming, she looked perplexed. "Well, now that you mention it, he did say that he thought, wait a minute, yes, he saw something one time."

"When?"

She leaned forward. "I don't know, was it right after he died, or . . ."

"Right before?"

"I don't know. Sure. Whatever."

She picked her purse off the bar, slung it over her shoulder, and faced him.

Fowler was looking at her. "I didn't mean to bring back all these memories."

"Forget it." She put on her sunglasses and stood up. "Look, do what you can. I got him into that school. He has to keep himself there." She looked at him. A smile crept into her features. "See you around, kid." She swung her hip around the barstool. "Put it on my bill, Jimmy." She walked swiftly around the bar and pulled the door open. The afternoon light hit her like a flash camera.

Fowler looked through the blinds. He saw her get into a car and pull out. The bartender sauntered over again. "Anything else?" he said. He had a gruff voice; his thin mustache was lost on a sea of flesh. Fowler was surprised he could talk. Up to now, he had only grunted.

"No thanks." Fowler was fumbling in his trousers for a tip.

"Ah, I heard what Muriel was yammering about."

Well, he listened too, Fowler thought. "You did?"

"It's none of my business, but she's been coming in here for years."

Fowler nodded. "Yeah?"

"A lot of people thought it wasn't exactly kosher the way Roy went out."

"Oh, really?"

"I don't think she did it. She's a good lady, but some people, you know, think otherwise."

"What do you think?"

"If she didn't do it, I don't know who."

"Did her husband have any enemies?"

"Who doesn't, know what I'm sayin'? . . . but no. He was all right."

"But you think it wasn't of natural causes."

"No way."

30

BALLARD AWOKE, FACEUP, on a gurney in the nurse's office of the infirmary. He just kept seeing brushstrokes of white on an empty canvas. The strokes of white soon became a nurse's hat, the canvas, the lapels of her uniform. Ms. Ross bent over him, her soft face carrying a strong pair of hazel eyes. When Ballard blinked toward consciousness, she smiled and smoothed his hair back.

"We had a bit of a scare, but you're all right now."

"What happened?"

"I always said they put too much pressure on you boys at this school. It isn't right. They were going to call that Dr. Clarence in here to have a look at you, but I said, he's out cold!"

"I passed out?"

"It's stress, that's what it is, dearie. Too many tests, too many term papers. Why, when I came along, if I didn't want to go to school, I just took off, never thought twice about it." She punctuated this thought by adjusting her hat.

Ballard sat up on the gurney. He felt a little drowsy, but he thought he was all right. "Well, I'd better be going."

"Now, just hold your horses. It's not every day a boy passes out in a master's office and has to be carried out. What's the rush?"

"I have to get back to my dorm."

"Why?"

"To—clean it up. My room, you know."

"And what dorm do you live in?"

"Brookside."

Ms. Ross raised her head up and blinked. "Brookside? That's a good half mile from here. You think I'm going to let you go gallivanting out through those fields, and pass out again? No sir."

Ballard leaned forward. "There's something I have to find, Ms. Ross, really."

"It will have to wait."

"But how long? I mean, I've got to—"

"Long enough for me to pour you some hot tea, give you some medication if I have to, and call Mr. Willers, who drives me over the mountain. He can stop by Brookside on the way out. He'll be over when the canteen closes."

Ballard's eyes landed on the clock face. "That's three hours from now."

"Well, if you want to take those darn books and have me walk you next door to the library to study, that's one thing. But I can't let you walk home alone."

Ballard already knew she had made up her mind. He shrugged and mumbled something about the library. He heard Ms. Ross put the tea kettle on.

Fowler was on the phone with Orin, the handwriting examiner. "What?" he said, adjusting himself into the cushion of the chair in his motel room.

Again there was a long silence on the other end. Papers shuffling, labored breaths as if Orin was craning his neck to pick something off the floor that would verify what he was saying. Then the gruff voice. "I got nothin' with the standards you give me."

"So then the killer wasn't tracing the kid's writing?"

"No. Intentional disguise, yes—but these two letters in no way resemble the standards of . . . what's his face?"

Fowler sighed impatiently. "Cary Ballard."

"Right, or the other one you gave me—from the kid's folder. I go back to my original theory."

"Which was?"

"Nondominant hand."

Fowler pulled a sheet of stationery out of the desk, picked up a pen in his left hand. "Why do you say that, Orin?"

"Because in the killer's first letter, some of the words, okay, I'm lookin' at . . . the first sentence here: 'How did you know I was dancing?' The *o*'s are formed by draggin' the pen counterclockwise, the way a right-handed person would. By the end of the letter, in the postscript, the *o* in 'another enemy,' the pen has now been dragged clockwise the way a lefty would."

"How do you explain that?" Fowler was writing words with his left hand, studying the motion of the pen.

"Because whoever wrote this letter started to adjust and began naturally forming letters in a new way. And all through the second letter—there's an exception here and there—but, hey, for the most part, the pen was dragged clockwise."

Nick was still writing. "Isn't there a therapy that utilizes writing with the nondominant hand?"

"Yeah, some shit about . . . it puts you back into a child's state of mind or whatever, I don't know."

Fowler was watching his letters forming. "That's it. You start having primitive feelings and—" He suddenly dropped the pen from his left hand. He sat up in his chair. "Just like in the dance," he muttered.

"What?"

"The hands were reversed when he danced with his victims—they were leading."

"That fits."

Fowler was silent now. "Thanks, Orin," he said slowly. "You

may have just given me a key." He hung up the phone and leaned back in his chair. This was no coincidence. The killer had done two vitally important tasks with his hands reversed. Why?

The phone rang. He grabbed at the receiver, knocking it off the cradle. He took a breath to calm himself and picked up the receiver again. "Hello?"

It was Bill Rodney's voice. "Excited, Lieutenant?"

Fowler laughed nervously. "Yeah, a little anxious. What have you got, Bill?"

"I called the antique clothing store."

"Right."

"They sold another full tux, cummerbund, garters, bow tie, and all, just yesterday."

"Any description?"

"No one can remember. One clerk thought it was a tall woman."

"Did you get the size?"

Rodney was heard paging through his notes. "Size forty-four long. That's the thing, though, Nick. How many students in the school are that big?"

"Check the football players," Fowler said, then felt a cool tingling sensation running up and down his back. He had just remembered who else's size it was: his own.

31

NICK FOWLER STOOD in the early twilight outside Madison Hall. He was waiting for Dr. Clarence to come out of his last class.

After the students filed by, the main glass door opened. The

doctor's close-shaved head appeared in the opening, the pink-framed glasses—his signature—Fowler thought, reflected the streetlamps, glaring at him like two computer screens. The doctor stopped short on the sidewalk. "What is it, Lieutenant?"

"I have to speak to you."

"You'll have to make an appointment."

"I just need a minute."

Dr. Clarence seemed to stiffen. "Well, what is it?"

"It's about Cary Ballard."

"Yes, yes—what do you want?"

Fowler put his hands in his pockets. "You said once he hallucinates. I asked you before what he sees, and you refused to tell me. I'm asking again."

"Well, again, I have to tell you—that is confidential. I cannot reveal the content of a patient's sessions."

"All right, don't reveal content, just answer yes or no."

"I can't do that."

Fowler leaned against a stone wall. "Has he ever seen a masked figure?"

"A what?"

"A man or woman dressed in a dark cape and hat, a scarf over the face."

Dr. Clarence stared at Fowler. "No."

"I see."

"Will that be all, Lieutenant?"

Fowler looked distressed. He loosened his tie, his brow wrinkled. "Doctor, I'm at a loss here."

There was a flicker of a smile across Dr. Clarence's face. "Come come, Mr. Fowler," he said. "You don't expect me to buy that, do you?"

"What do you think of the killer?"

Fowler noticed a tiny light of interest glinting in the doctor's eyes. "He's violent."

Fowler stepped forward. "Why?"

Dr. Clarence seemed impatient. "Look, if you don't have any real questions, I'm going to have to ask you to make an appointment."

"Do you think Cary Ballard had anything to do with these crimes?"

The doctor shifted his weight. "Do you?"

"Yes."

Dr. Clarence stared at the lieutenant with surprise. "How so?"

"Well, the evidence against him is overwhelming," Fowler said sadly. "The first victim was hanged just outside his room, his own tie wrapped around the boy's neck. Now, with the second killing, we found a knee impression in the dirt at the scene; later we found Ballard's trousers with the same soil encrusted on the knees."

"I wouldn't say that's conclusive, would you?"

"No, that's why I'm looking for some indicator that Ballard might be violent. Who would know better than you?"

Clarence seemed taken aback. He cleared his throat. "It's a very complex topic, Lieutenant. Researchers have been looking for biological factors in the etiology of delinquent behavior for years."

"Biological factors, how do you mean?"

"Perinatal difficulties, physical trauma. When Ballard was born, for instance, he was dropped on his head in the hospital."

"I didn't know that."

"Of course you didn't."

Fowler leaned forward again. "You dealt with this fairly regularly before, didn't you?"

"Before?"

"Before you were let go from the psychiatric wing, Creedmore Children's Hospital, wasn't it?"

Dr. Clarence's complexion slowly began to turn shades in lapse photography, the hues of his skin flushing. He swallowed. "Yes, why?"

"Routine background checks are part of law enforcement, Doctor."

"That's invasion of privacy."

"Why were you let go, Doctor?"

"That is none of your business." The color had drained from his face now. He seemed pale and tired in the evening light.

"A source on the hospital staff said you were inappropriately associated with a patient."

"That's a lie."

"An underage patient."

"That is an outrageous accusation."

"It makes you a prime suspect in this case."

"How dare you take hearsay as fact?"

"I'm just telling you what we were told."

"I didn't let you stop me on campus a second time so I could be accused and insulted."

Fowler stared quietly at the doctor. "Why *did* you let me stop you?"

"To answer your infernal questions about the Ballard boy, but *now* I won't discuss it at all."

"Except in court?"

"What?"

"We discovered a number of court records carrying your testimony. Should there be a case, would you testify that the boy has a temper, for instance, is violent enough to—"

"He has an explosive disorder, for your information."

"What is that?"

"A violent temper one minute and—look—"

"Can you prove that?"

"With an sleep electroencephalogram—for your information." He waved his palms in a flat line. "But I'm not discussing this with you of all people."

"You're going to predict dangerousness?"

Dr. Clarence made an audible gasp. "I think we've reached our final impasse here." He walked around Fowler.

Fowler followed him. "So, without giving the boy any more than the standard intelligence tests, after seeing him for about a month, you're going to predict he is a criminal. What's your agenda here?"

Clarence stopped on the walk and turned, glaring at him. "That's it. This conversation is over!"

His raised voice turned a number of faculty heads on the porch of Booth Hall. Some students walking by stopped, staring.

"I hope that information about you doesn't get out, Doctor; might be embarrassing."

The doctor lurched down the walk. "Good night, Mr. Fowler!" He broke into a run.

THE DARK EYES watched carefully from behind the adjoining building's shrubbery. The figure caught the open edge of a dark cloak on a shrub, cursed, and rushed soundlessly along the walk to crouch between two automobiles. It watched the man pulling away in a black squad car, his headlights fanning across the façades of the dorms.

The figure slipped behind the wheel of a green compact, started the engine, and rolled silently down the street. The gloves seemed to peel away from the rubberized steering wheel cover with each turn of the road. A slight sticking sound in the empty car. Nothing else, no breathing, as if the figure had suspended the intake of air—all motor activity directed now through the eyes—vigilant, alert. The same eyes now saw the silhouette of a hand in the squad car ahead reach up to adjust the rearview mirror.

Fowler saw the car behind him turn off when he drove out the main gate. He wondered about it.

32

AT THE FRONT desk of the library, Ms. Leach flipped her gray hair up. Her battered face—tortured at first by a fierce intelligence, then by too many library cards demanding her attention—had seen the Ballard boy enter the library and slouch to a table. Instinctively she scratched one of the giant stains under her armpits and went back to her book.

Ballard opened his loose-leaf notebook and began reading from the section labeled "English." He wondered if studying would help clear his head. Actually he felt numb. He watched his hands turn pages as if from a great distance. The print on the pages seemed microscopic—all he could see were indentations for the paragraphs.

A grating noise from a leather chair came from the other side of the room. Ballard looked up. He saw a wide neck vault out of the chair. The back was muscular, the triceps quivered as the hands pulled some heavy trousers up and tucked in a white dress shirt. The skin on his arms and neck were tanned. Roy Gluckner turned around.

His bull neck protruded from his collar. He squinted at Ballard with a wide smile spreading across his face. There was a space between his two front teeth that seemed to grow larger as he smiled.

"I heard you fainted in somebody's office." He laughed.

"Yeah," Ballard said coldly. Ms. Leach glanced up from the front desk. Ballard just looked down at his notebook. He heard Gluckner's shoes squeal on the polished wood floor—they seemed like little animals stalking his study table.

Ballard kept looking down, remembering in an instant the first time he had met Gluckner, a postgrad student from Hawaii, a 235-pound fullback who had scored three touchdowns in the fourth game of the season—whose neck was too big to button the top button of his shirt, so even the headmaster never asked him to pull his tie up.

Ballard saw a pair of brown loafers step around the table and plant themselves next to his chair. He looked up. Gluckner leaned on the table, barely able to repress his glee.

"I thought only girls fainted, Ballard." The boy did not respond. "And all this time, I've been hearing you're such a ladies' man."

Ballard felt his breath quicken as he smiled back at Gluckner whose face, he noted, though handsome, bore some resemblance to a bulldog's. "Well, are you or aren't you, Ballard?" he said. "You're not the mover they say you are, are you?" he whispered viciously, bringing his jowls down toward Ballard's face. "You're scared, aren't you? Just like a girl."

Ballard felt sweat break out on his forehead. His stomach felt hollow. "Leave me alone, Gluckner."

Gluckner stood bolt upright in a mock imitation of an insulted female. "Oh my my!"

"Shhh," whispered the librarian.

Ballard looked back down at his book. "I've got no quarrel with you, Gluckner. Just go away."

"What if I won't?" Gluckner said, taunting, smiling casually down.

The boy kept staring down at his notebook, but the words blurred before him. "I'm trying to study."

"Poor little Ballard, now he's all upset," said Gluckner as he abruptly ran his hand from the back of Ballard's head forward so his hair fell down in his face.

Ballard stared up at him, pushing his hair back. "Where's your leash?" he said quietly.

Gluckner stared down at him. "What did you say?"

Ballard noticed himself standing to face Gluckner for some reason he couldn't explain. "I didn't know they let you out of your cage at night," he said, surprising himself, as he watched the words grab and take hold of Gluckner's jowls.

"Better watch your mouth, boy," Gluckner said, his neck growing in size.

"Oh, now I'm a boy. Maybe you don't know the difference."

"Step outside and I'll show you the difference, punk."

"Sorry, I'm busy."

"No, you're not," he said as he reached over with one fist, grabbed Ballard by the collar, and hoisted him up over the top of the table, which dragged against the wood floor.

Ms. Leach now moved around the front desk, "Here, here, now! What's going on?" Gluckner released Ballard's shirt and pretended nothing was happening as Ms. Leach rushed across the buffed wood toward the study table. "If you boys wish to rough-house," she said, "go outside."

"We were just leaving," Gluckner said calmly.

"He's leaving," Ballard said.

Ms. Leach uncrossed her arms and her underarms were now unveiled as her weathered face panned from one boy to the other.

Gluckner snorted and stared down at Ballard with contempt. "Can't always hide behind a woman's skirt, Ballard."

"I'm not," Ballard said, surprised by his own bravado.

"Especially Janine's."

Ballard suddenly saw Gluckner's face fall away, moving into the distance, past the front desk of the library, the infirmary, past the stone arch and the canteen, down the hill toward the lake, through a peeling wrought-iron fence, and into the graveyard. He remembered the day he first saw her. He felt the color disappear from his face. He looked up at Gluckner, who was still smiling down at him, pulling his sports jacket over his bulky chest.

"She told me about you, Ballard."

"She did not."

Gluckner laughed. "She told me all about you, everything."

"Liar," said Ballard. Suddenly he struck blindly at Gluckner, who ducked, then laughed again, pleased that he had hit a nerve.

"Ohhh, look out," he said derisively.

Ms. Leach stood between the two boys, her outstretched hands repelling them not by sheer strength alone. "Please, please, this is not a gymnasium—go outside!"

Gluckner dropped his voice to a whisper. "I'll tell you what she said some time, okay?" With that he clamped his fingers over his nose, glanced at Ms. Leach, broke into a high-pitched laugh, and tip-toed in mock fear, all atremble, through the door.

33

BY THE TIME Ballard had put on his jacket, gathered his books under his arms, and stepped out of the library, Gluckner was already striding under the arch. Ballard followed him at a safe distance. He didn't know what was giving him the courage.

Marty Orloff, the little cop who still had Ballard under surveillance, glanced up from his magazine when Ballard went by
him down the steps in front of the library. The boy was just disappearing around the corner of Booth Hall, heading under the stone
arch. He stood up and started walking.

Ballard watched Gluckner disappear over the crest of the hill
in front of the school. He stood at the wrought-iron fence by Ardsley, his eyes following the blacktop drive that dropped at a steep
grade. Halfway down, it split into a fork. Going to the right meant
passing through the main fence, out of the entrance of the school.
Going to the left led to South End, a small student house, then the
graveyard, the lake, and a steep incline down on to the main street
of Ravenstown.

Ballard observed Gluckner's cumbersome frame as it stopped
in the middle of the road, looking back at the school. He headed to
the left. Ballard stood in the shelter of the row of oaks that lined the
drive as it descended down the hill. He kept his eyes on Gluckner's
back, seeing the lines of his navy blazer grow indistinct. He mused
what would happen if he followed him all the way into town.

Then it occurred to him that Gluckner might stop at the waterfall, or cut back toward the graveyard. The thought that he might
be meeting someone there troubled him deeply. He had to know.

It was dusk by now and Ballard moved from one oak to another. His eyes remained fastened on the football player, whose
lumbering body was almost gone except for a white collar floating
like a specter in the dark.

Ballard moved behind the oaks, nearly breathless. He had
never done this before—never walked willingly into fear. He had
always run away. Again he glanced carefully around the trunk of
one tree, saw Gluckner again turn, glancing back toward the main

buildings of the school. Gluckner turned quickly and walked around the back of South End.

South End was a white clapboard house on the edge of a bluff that overlooked the town. As it grew darker, Ballard waited another ten minutes, twice having to creep slowly around the back of an oak to avoid the headlights of cars driving up into the school.

Finally, under the cover of darkness, Ballard cut along a rhododendron grove on the right of the fork. For an instant, he thought he heard someone behind him and turned around. He didn't see anyone though. He doubled back through a clump of cedars into the backyard of South End.

He stood near a hedge, looking up, trying to catch his breath. He saw a student on the second floor, through one window, in his robe, boiling spaghetti on a hot plate near the sill. Ballard smiled, as he knew hot plates were illegal. A blue reflection from a television set danced on the windowpanes. He knew TVs were illegal too.

Ballard moved along the hedge, then glanced down the back of the house. There was only a stoop and a back door hidden by the hedge. He thought the door must lead into the master's house but couldn't remember who the housemaster of South End was.

The windows on the back of the house were black. Ballard slipped up onto the stoop, lifting the top of the mailbox to see who the mail was addressed to—it was empty.

He tried the door, turned the knob, and stepped into a dark entranceway where his eyes were drawn to a shaft of light coming from under a door at the top of the stairs. Ballard noticed there was a door on each side of this entrance hall, probably leading to more students' rooms.

He put his weight on the bottom stair. A groan from the floorboard echoed like a human voice up into the stairwell. He immediately stepped back down and leaned out of sight against one of the doors in a corner of the hallway; in the dark, his hand fell on a doorknob as he tried to quiet the pounding in his chest.

No sooner did he step out of the entranceway than the door at the top of the stairs was flung open and a yellow light splashed against the inside of the back door, all along the stairs. At the same time, someone came bounding down the stairway. As the stairs sent up a chorus of grating wood, Ballard fumbled in a panic with the brass doorknob. It was locked.

Someone stopped two stairs from the bottom and appeared to be listening. Ballard could hear several labored breaths, each out-distancing the one before it, each pulled back like an undertow. Ballard was sure the drum in his chest could be heard for miles. He stood completely still.

Then the jowls and flared nostrils of Gluckner's profile moved around the corner of the stairwell. His eyes were fixed on the back door. He reached over, turned the knob, and pushed the back door out, staring through the screen door at the stoop.

Gluckner took two steps out onto the landing, and as the screen door began to close, the spring whining, Ballard stepped to the door on the other side of the hallway, and when the screen door slapped against the jamb, Ballard twisted the knob. It opened. He stepped backward into darkness. He eased the door closed just as he caught a glimpse of Gluckner's beefy face coming back inside. Ballard's hand was still holding the doorknob, afraid to release it, when more footsteps came rushing down the stairs.

During the sound he released the knob and leaned against the door. He heard a woman's voice, speaking very low. He couldn't tell who it was, but the voice purred in a quiet way, slowly in supplica-tion, like a cello. Gluckner's gruff vowels drowned out the music.

"It was nothing," he said on the other side of the door. "You ready?"

Ballard heard someone step hard on the floorboard, trying the doorknob. Ballard peered quickly around the dark room he was standing in and saw the outline of floor weights and a bench press. He groped sightless toward what he thought was an open door. He found himself inside a closet. He leaned his back against a row of hangers and tried to close the door—but a shoe on the floor kept the door wedged open.

The door to the room opened. The light on the stairs shone on Gluckner's forearm as he slowly opened the door. A woman walked into the darkened room. She was holding a purse along with his shirt and blazer. As she twisted fitfully, looking around the room, her face turned away and Ballard couldn't tell who it was. A wafer of light moved across her forehead, disappearing as the door slammed. For a moment, there was only the sound of two people breathing in unison.

A desk lamp went on as Gluckner strutted around the room in gym shorts and a T-shirt, closing the blinds in all the windows. He reached out suddenly and grabbed the things out of the woman's hands. He threw them on a chair. The woman crouched, moving in a circle away from him. A skintight red bodysuit twisted in the lamplight. She turned around, smiling—it was Ms. Coates, his math teacher.

Gluckner reached over, seized both her hands, and flung them up and down to loosen her muscles. She giggled and wrenched her arms away from him, straddling the bench press, lying back slowly. Gluckner stared down at her with an almost uncontrollable desire. He walked around behind her, fumbled, sliding weights onto the barbell that rested on the floor, all the time looking up at Ms. Coates lying there gazing at the ceiling.

"Having trouble?" she said breathlessly.

"No, I got it," he said, hoisting the bar over Ms. Coates's head and placing it in the steel supports. "One seventy-five. Ready?"

Ms. Coates smiled, inhaled and drove three short breaths out of her rib cage. "Move in closer."

Gluckner grinned and edged his thighs near her, on either side of the cushion.

"Closer."

He inched forward again so his thighs were above her. He stared down at her mouth, tightly creased, expelling breaths.

"Okay," she announced.

Gluckner lifted the bar out into air above her outstretched arms and placed it in her palms. Ms. Coates wrapped her fists around the bar and let the weight slowly down to her chest, thrust her hips up and in a coiling motion, pressed the barbell into the air.

"Good," Gluckner said. "Do five reps."

"No," she said, letting the weight down and pressing it up again. "Too much."

"Come on," he said, guiding the bar down, squatting toward her.

"No!" she yelled, straining the bar up into the air again.

"Yes." He squatted closer to her face, the hair on his thighs brushing her cheek.

"You son of a—" She strained the barbell up, her left arm sinking. "I can't."

"One more!" Gluckner yelled.

Ms. Coates let the bar down again, craned her neck back, her face turning crimson, pressed against his leg. She thrust her hips and hoisted the bar halfway up, straining, her arms wobbling. The bar stuck in midair.

Gluckner whispered. "Come on."

She wrenched her face over and bit Gluckner in the thigh.

"Ow!" The bar fell back to her chest and Gluckner squatted down, taking the weight. He stepped back, lifted the bar, and lowered it onto the support. He massaged his thigh. Ms. Coates's chest was heaving, her face covered with sweat. She stared up at Gluckner.

"Now," she said. "It's . . . your . . . turn."

"Oh," he muttered. "We're going to play games?"

"No," Ms. Coates said indignantly. "I just think you should get in shape."

Ballard watched Gluckner saunter around the bench. Ms. Coates took a step back, glanced at her watch, surveying Gluckner's muscle-bound body. "Take off that T-shirt." Her deep voice was detached.

"When is he coming?" Gluckner whispered slowly as he slipped the white fabric over his head.

"He's always late."

"Why are you doing this?"

"Get down," she ordered sullenly.

Gluckner was surprised at her tone, then began to smile. He lay down on the bench, his eyes darting across the ceiling.

She slid fifty-pound weights on the bar and locked them into place. She positioned her legs on either side of the cushion, then lifted the bar off the supports and squatted, lowering the bar to him. Gluckner took the weight in his hands, expelled air, and pumped the bar back into the air quickly four times.

"Ten more," she ordered.

His eyes burst open. "Forget it."

"Ten. Do you hear me?" She rubbed her hand across his face.

"Lay off!" he blurted, his chest swelling as he drove the bar up.

"Don't talk back." She squeezed the sides of his face with her thighs.

Gluckner's tongue had worked its way out onto his lower lip. He nibbled at her leg, taking the red elastic in his teeth.

"Come on," Ms. Coates murmured. "Be a good boy."

As the barbell was beginning to strain into the air, she lowered herself and begun slowly undulating her hips above his face. "And if you perform well, like a good boy, you can come back for a workout again sometime." Her gyrations began to slow down now, moving into prolonged circles, long slow arcs which drew every ounce of strength from Gluckner's arms as if her body was a magnet. His mouth was open, sluggishly following her pulsations.

Ballard raised himself up to see Gluckner's Adam's apple descend and reappear as he kissed up and down her thighs. The barbell sunk to his chest. Ms. Coates began to rub her thighs against the boy's face. Gluckner was grunting now, unable to lift the bar. Ms. Coates squatted down and yanked the bar into the air, her biceps bulging out. She shoved it onto the supports and swaggered around the bench.

"Couldn't do it, huh?"

Gluckner sat up and grabbed her hips like a vise with both hands and pulled her down. Ms. Coates hit the cushion facedown. He pinned her hands at her sides and tried to push her face into his lap. She pulled away, reddening, twisting her torso up into the air as she yanked her arms free, her chest heaving.

"You nasty boy," she hissed. "You dirty little boy." She began to writhe. "You naughty, dirty little—"

"*Shut up!*" Gluckner barked.

Ms. Coates pursed her lips. "You dirty little—"

Raising an open hand up, Gluckner said, "One more word and I'll—"

"Filthy," Ms. Coates whispered petulantly.

Gluckner brought his hand down hard across her face. The slap left a red blotch on her cheek. Her head had been thrown to the side and her open mouth emitted a scream. Gluckner pulled her into a sitting position and stood behind her, stroking her breasts from behind. He then leaned forward and closed his lips down over her mouth.

Her arched neck twisted back, yearningly. She sucked against his lips, moaning in a way that startled Ballard. Gluckner's mouth rubbed her lipstick across her face. She dug her nails into his back. Ballard thought he was becoming powerless to remain still in one position. The sounds that came out of her terrified him. His eyes seemed to fog over. He realized sweat was pouring down his forehead.

As Ms. Coates's strident moans began to get louder, Ballard lost perspective and imagined her cries echoing on the hills at the far side of town. He needed to calm himself but decided to settle for wiping his brow. He ran his palm across his forehead and knocked a hanger down inside the closet.

Suddenly the moaning stopped as Ballard panicked, pressing his body farther back into the closet. Then a winter coat came dislodged from a dowel—it slumped to the floor—the zipper from the lining rattling down the door molding. Ballard saw a flash of red through the cracked door stumble out of sight.

There was a long dead silence before he heard Ms. Coates's hoarse whisper. "What was that?"

"I don't know."

Another pause. Ballard realized again that his heart was hammering. Suddenly the closet was ripped open, and Ballard felt the light fall on his sweaty forehead as his hands instinctively covered his head. A massive hand wrenched him over the fallen coat on his knees out into the room. The boy saw the back of Ms. Coates's hand fly toward her face, swabbing the red blotch on her cheek.

"Cary?" she said in disbelief, pulling her bodysuit down.

Ballard felt the buttons on his shirt pop, then bounce against the wall as Gluckner ripped his shirt up into the air. His hands clamped around Ballard's throat. "You punk," Gluckner said, his voice in a free-fall. "Now you're gonna get it."

At this instant, the buzzer for the back door sent a shock through all three of them. Ms. Coates froze. Gluckner's arm was raised, his fist circling the air over Ballard's head.

"That's him," she whispered. "Don't make a sound."

She pulled out her compact and—standing there sweating, transfixed—with inhuman reserve, she covered the red blotches with makeup, applied lipstick, and matted her mouth against a piece of tissue in a matter of seconds.

Outside, the visitor had come inside and climbed the stairs. When Ms. Coates heard the feet stop at the top of the stairs, she smoothed the elastic down once more, opened the door into the entranceway, kicked the outside screen door open with her sneaker, turning her body, with a smile, up toward the stairs as she soundlessly shut the door to the room. She said, "Hello."

Ballard heard the muffled tones of an older man. The cadences sounded vaguely familiar. He heard the man's footsteps on the stairs, the screen door banging, then voices moving down the sidewalk, away from the house. The boy's attention was diverted as he realized Gluckner's hand was tightening around his neck. He heard Ms. Coates's deep laugh trailing off.

Then silence.

Gluckner's face, now impossibly red, turned toward Ballard. The wide forehead was covered with rivulets of sweat. The imposing jowls lifted into a hideous smile, a grin that grew wider, with more teeth appearing, as if a proscenium arch had been revealed, a curtain raised. Ballard felt for the first time he was center stage in a life that did not belong to him, a life he never understood and never wanted.

Gluckner's fist seemed to brood over the boy's features. It hung in the dim light, then slammed against his jaw and repeated this enough times that Ballard could no longer feel the blows as they struck him.

There was a moment when Ballard thought his face had caved in. He thought his insides were lying on the floorboards. There was something wet on his face, and, in his state of delirium, he was sure that Gluckner was washing his face for him. He tried to thank him but his lips couldn't pronounce the words.

He remembered his legs dragging and knew at the time his feet were plowing new ground. He knew with a certainty that people who are not really conscious know anything; fragments filter down into a submerged mass of dreams, that web of closed rooms beyond which no one can go, and there—where new thoughts are hurled against the wall of memory—strange connections are made.

BALLARD WAS RUNNING. In the distance a long gray corridor was laid out before him. He heard his feet hit the cement floor with uneven thumps. On one wall, a long, endless sheet of glass stretched as far as he could see. He looked over and noticed Gluckner behind the glass, in another hallway, sailing along as if he were a moving train; he smiled, holding up a pocket watch.

Ballard's legs felt rubbery. They struck the floor while his arms lurched to the side—straining—beating the air as if he had wings. Gluckner was practically floating over the surface.

Without warning, Ballard saw the hallway behind the glass change direction, twisting away from him. Gluckner waved good-bye to him and turned with the hallway, at the end of which two figures were beckoning him on. Ballard tried to break into the other hallway. He called out, but Gluckner's body was plunged against the light, getting smaller and smaller.

34

MAUREEN MCCAULEY NERVOUSLY kicked the gravel with her foot as the man behind her knelt down and looked into the keyhole. Sergeant Robby Cole turned and glanced at her legs, his eyes flitting up and down. He focused again on the lock.

He unscrewed a wide ball-point pen cartridge, pulling a black metal device out. He studied the irregular angles of the pick. He then twisted the squiggly end into the keyhole. "Usually these motel doors are cake."

Maureen didn't want to make small talk. Her eyes were frozen, looking away from him, out toward the highway. She had gotten an anonymous phone call suggesting vital evidence was being withheld in the case. She had agonized over what to do. Judy, the dispatcher at the station house, couldn't help; she was being closely watched. Then Maureen got a second tip from that teacher up at the school—same story—data was being withheld. She knew this was invasion but had to act. Her thoughts raced back to the scraping sound behind her.

The cop was working the pick, but his eyes kept darting back at her. "You'll have to conceal how you got it," he said.

"I know," Maureen said.

"If you could prove he was obstructing justice, then I could—"

"I don't have time for a warrant."

The lock clicked open. He stood up, slipped the metal piece back into his pocket. "You never saw me tonight."

"That's right," she sang quietly, brushing past him. "Thanks."

An arm reached out and grabbed her. "Wait."

She looked down at the arm, up into his eyes. Cole was leaning toward her. "I'll see you later, though."

"What?"

A low laugh. "You don't think I did this for my health, do you?"

She drew away from him. "No, your civic duty. Now—"

He was whispering. "Ever since you leaned over that fence down by the marsh and showed me your stockings, I've been thinking—"

She tried to jerk away—but he held on. "Look, Robby, I apologize for arousing you. It was unintentional."

"But I helped you. Now help me a little."

"Take your hand off my arm." She said this sharply, with authority, her voice echoing across the pavement.

He looked around, startled, releasing her arm. "You'll give me what I want—you watch."

"Get lost," she said over her shoulder.

She stepped inside, still hearing Cole's footsteps on the gravel getting farther away. When she closed the door, she sighed, her heart throbbing. Though she was rattled, she had to focus on why she was here. This had to be fast. Her mind was racing.

First she went through the drawers in the desk. Nothing. Then through his suitcase. She unzipped his bath kit. After-shave, razors, deodorant, toothbrush, hand cream. She lifted the shirts, ties, and underwear piled neatly in the suitcase. Again nothing. She looked around the room.

She saw a black briefcase sticking a few inches out from behind the bed frame. She smiled and pulled it out. It was unlocked. He hadn't been expecting this.

A sound in the bathroom? She looked around the dark room for a second, her breath quickening—must be her anxiety. When she opened the briefcase, she saw a number of official documents in a manila folder. Checklists for the latent investigation. Copies of initial offense reports. Copies of the reconstructions of both murders.

Underneath these documents, she found a leather flap that was snapped down into the bottom of the case. She unsnapped it and lifted it up.

"Hello," she whispered.

She paged through Fowler's supplemental reports; these hadn't been included with the others Judy Bayard had copied from the safe inside the station. She had already studied those.

She skimmed through them.

These follow-up reports hadn't had supervisory approval yet; there were no signatures. As she read them, it occurred to her they had never been seen by the department.

She knelt down in the edge of light seeping through the curtain, reading breathlessly. All the reports were about the same boy—the student outside whose room the first victim had been found.

She replaced the reports, sliding the briefcase back behind the bed. When she looked around the room, she didn't see the eyes in the dark corner—she didn't hear the squeak of shoes—the scrape of material. Her attention was elsewhere when she let herself out.

35

WOULD HAVE BEEN *fun, dancing the Cha-cha, cutting her.*

Start with the items in the medicine cabinet: pill bottles, prescription—some kind of ointment, aspirin, Pepto-Bismol, powder, witch hazel . . . pick up each, touch them, hold them, leave my energy, my germs, breathe on each of them, yes. Leave the voices in my head behind his mirror . . . he opens it, swarms, cries jump out at him.

Could have tied her down, gagged her, given her a little anesthetic for some major surgery—or no needle—just the knife. See if a woman's blood tastes sweeter than a boy's. Don't believe it.

Voices intensifying now, soaring through my head. Pick up his bath kit: shave cream, deodorant, disposable razors, after-shave. Fondle them, touch everything—Band-Aids—might need a few of those, mouthwash, toothpaste, cologne, antacid, touch all, keep the scissors. Into the main room.

Just the same, could have sliced off her tits and arranged them on the end table by the phone, called the desk, light blinking in the dark—he comes in, switches on the lamp, surprise!

Now touch the ties, the shirts, smell them, clothes folded neatly in the suitcase. There, a laundry tag: "Nk-Flr," carefully cut out, so he knows, remembers me, so he can worry. Use that antacid.

Could have just strangled her, made it look like a quarrel—he catches her in his room, subdues her, oops, pinches her larynx. No, then he'd be out of my hands. She's more valuable alive. She will lead you to me, Lieutenant.

Funny, don't get the same vibe as I do with boys, have to work on it, getting there though. Touching his pants, inside the cuffs, the pockets, feeling closer. Just for a minute, pull down the covers, lie on the sheets, voices blaring, conversations, a cacophony, then a terrifying stillness. Smell the fresh linen. Have to stop this—I'm losing my essence. You're taking it away from me, Fowler. Stealing my verve. Voices in my head say not yet.

I want to kill you.

They say wait.

36

FOWLER WAS PATROLLING the campus. The black Buick's head-lights swept up the steep hill in front of the school, under the stone arch that joined Ardsley and Booth halls. The sidewalks were empty as he rolled slowly past the library, the auditorium, the infirmary, up a slight grade to the gymnasium, and out into the parking lot.

He got out of the car and gazed at the tennis courts, the track, and football field beyond. The goalposts were visible from the floodlights outside the gym just behind him. His shadow loomed across the field.

He remembered how—before his Dad was shot—he had played football with Nick and his brother, Jim, now a career military officer stationed overseas. Jim was two years older. Like most fathers, Nick's dad was partial to his older son. It was unspoken. The ball just flew in Jim's direction more times. Jim got more attention, more love, and when it came time for Nick to choose professions, he chose his father's to compensate. Jim didn't have to.

It didn't really rankle Nick that much. It was something he accepted, but there was a distance between him and his brother. Nick knew that's what kept them separate as they got older. Now they were out of touch.

Nick saw his brother hike the ball back to his father. Nick was running downfield. He cut, made a crossing pattern. He saw the ball in the air. Sped up to meet it. Arms out, reaching for the ball. As it came toward him, he saw it wasn't a ball. It was Finkelstein's head, blood dripping from the neck, the mouth open, screaming right into his hands. Against his chest. He dropped it. Again.

Nick heard himself yell, the echo going across the field. His head was down between his knees, breathing hard. He stood up and looked around. There was some movement in the bushes at the edge of the track—between the woods and the gym, a dark shape. He was losing it now, seeing things, afraid he was being followed. Paranoid. He faced the bushes defiantly. He was about to break into a run.

He heard a crackle on the car radio. He jogged over, opened the door, listened to the transmission, got in, and turned the key.

IT WAS TOO bad that Ballard couldn't remember what had been running through his mind. For a long time, he didn't know where he was. He thought his eyes gazed up into a dark sky. He thought he was lying at the bottom of a primeval cliff where a red sun flashed over the horizon, sunk out of sight, only to reappear then sink again. He heard a crackling sound. Rattlesnakes, he was sure. Dinosaurs.

It was a while later he realized he was looking up at the hedge in the backyard of South End; the red sun was a police light revolving, throwing its beams along the wall of tiny leaves. A stick of smelling salts had been broken under his nose. A police radio came up into a hand above him.

"This is Fowler. We have a student down in the back of South End, one of the dorms up at the school. An EMS vehicle already on the scene. We'll take care of it, over." The radio answered in a garbled language Ballard couldn't understand.

Marty Orloff leaned against Fowler's car. He had found Ballard near the hedge and had called the emergency medical service. A young woman washed the blood off and examined Ballard's face. Nothing was broken. He would have two black eyes, terrible bruises. She lifted his head up, giving him a paper cup full of water to take a painkiller with. She held an ice pack on his face and asked him to keep it there. He was to come to the hospital emergency room the next day. Now he should get some sleep.

Fowler walked over to where Marty was leaning against the car.

"He was following a student named who?"

"Gluckner."

"Did anyone else come or go?"

Marty flipped the pad in his hand. "Ms. Coates, his math teacher, with another teacher—what's his name."

Fowler cranked the back door of the car open and pulled a bound book off the backseat. He handed the book to Marty. "The yearbook for last spring. See if he's in there."

Marty paged through the faculty pages of the book. "Okay, that's him. Mr. Toby. English teacher. Huh. Drama club. Webster Society."

"Marty, when did they go out?"

"About forty-five minutes ago."

"Then?"

"This guy Gluckner drags the Ballard kid out and dumps him by the hedge. Beat him up pretty bad."

"Okay, good work. Look, I'm going to drive the kid home. I want to talk to him. I want you to watch this house all night if necessary. I want to speak to Ms. Coates tonight."

"Shall I call this in?" Marty looked up at Fowler.

"No, I'll make out the offense report."

Marty glanced at Nick. "You're the boss."

Fowler let that slide. He gave Marty a look that let him know he was in no mood. He carefully led Ballard to the passenger side of the car, helped him inside, and drove slowly down the hill into Ravenstown.

They rode in silence for several minutes.

Finally Fowler loosened his tie, turned to the boy. "You all right?"

"Yeah."

"You said Gluckner made fun of you in the library?"

"He never used to bother me."

"But he suddenly starts picking on you . . ." Fowler turned the corner and drove up a hill past the waterfall. The road circled past High Street, around the lake. "What did he make fun of you about?"

"Nothing." The boy buried his face in the ice pack.

"Cary. What did he make fun of you about?" The tone in his voice was sharper now.

The boy's head was bobbing from weakness. "Janine."

"The girl in the graveyard."

The boy looked at him with surprise then shook his head. "What is it with them?"

"Them?"

Ballard turned groggily to face him. "First Finkelstein, then Gluckner does the same thing."

"You mean he also made fun of her?"

Ballard snorted. "Yeah, really."

Fowler was silent as he pulled the car into Brookside Cottage. He shut off the engine. "Cary, I need to ask you something." He turned slightly in the seat. "Are you as angry at Gluckner as you were at Finkelstein and Crawford?"

Ballard looked at him strangely. "What?"

"As soon as you get angry at someone, they . . . end up dead."

Cary stared out the windshield. "I didn't do anything."

"There must be a link, that's all I'm saying." Nick was deep in thought. "It can't be a coincidence."

Ballard's face was beginning to hurt. "What are you going to do?" he said, his eyes watering.

"Nothing, yet." Fowler reached over, ran his hand through the boy's hair. "But you got to help me out here, Cary. I'm running out of time."

Cary Ballard's young face was somber as he got out of the car and ambled over to the front door of the cottage.

WHEN HE OPENED the door to his room, Ballard saw Mr. Bendleby, his housemaster, seated awkwardly in his desk chair. Across the room, squatting on the sagging bedsprings, was Mr. Allington.

Ballard looked from one man to the other. Neither man moved much, but both opened their eyes in shock.

"What on earth happened to you?" Allington said, standing up.

"Nothing—got into a fight, sir."

"With whom?"

"Gluckner."

Allington stood up, pacing the room. He stopped near Ballard long enough to touch his chin and inspect the damage. "God," he exclaimed under his breath. "First you faint, then this."

Ballard lowered his head.

Bendleby moved awkwardly in the little desk chair. "Say, uh, Ballard, why didn't you tell me you were involved in this, uh, you know—"

"Just a moment," Allington broke in. "We're not sure of that yet, Mr. Bendleby. So, if you don't mind, I'd like to ask the boy a few questions."

"Uh, sure, I just, uh, like the boys down here to let me know what's going on, so I don't, you know, have to be the last to, uh—"

"I understand," Mr. Allington said. "You have every right to know. So does the entire student body and faculty of Ravenhill. As do the parents of these unfortunate boys. And the police."

"Ah," Bendleby said, setting his jaw against these facts.

"Mr. Ballard," Allington started. "This afternoon I asked you to bring me the other pair of white gloves. When you did not return, I decided to come look myself. In the meantime, I've had a long talk with Captain Weathers."

"Yes, sir," he said quietly.

Allington stood up and opened Ballard's closet door. "Let's stop playing games, shall we?" He slipped several hangers across the metal bar that was holding up his clothes. When Allington came to his dark winter coat, he thrust his hands in the pockets. Nothing was there.

"The second pair of gloves, Ballard?"

The boy looked down at the floor. "I must have lost them, sir."

Allington was about to close the closet door, when a sock hanging on the door hook fell down. He picked it up. Something caught his eye. It was a name tag on the neck of the sock. He walked slowly over to Ballard and held the sock down in front of the boy's face. He could plainly see the name on the tag: It said Harold J. Finkelstein.

Ballard looked numbly down at the sock. It was navy blue.

"I'm going to have to show this to Captain Weathers, Cary. I'm sorry."

Ballard nodded again. Bendleby sat very still in the chair.

37

WHEN BALLARD awoke, his eyes were full of stars. He was lying on the roof in a kind of half sleep. He had been having a dream about Crawford and Finkelstein, where they moved toward him in slow motion, their arms waving. They asked him why he had killed them. When they spoke, bubbles came out of their mouths as though they were fish.

He felt the soft tar under his back. He realized each image from the dream fixed itself on a star in the black sky. He rolled over and slowly got up to his knees. That was when he heard a sound on the pavement below. He walked silently to the edge of the roof but saw no one was there. He looked across the road at the woods. He thought they were dark and terrible. He walked to the roof door, then down the stairs to the rooms.

He shuffled into his room, not wanting to put on his light for fear that he would wake up Bendleby. He felt the gloom pressing in again and just stood there, thinking he should run away. Take off in the middle of the night, he thought, pack a suitcase and grab a bus home. Then he realized how that would go over. His mother would freak out.

He heard a footstep on the roof. His neck began to tingle as shivers chased up and down his spine. He stood stock-still, his eyes glued to his ceiling. Another foot scraped across the tar. Then the sound came from a place on his ceiling that was closer to the window. Ballard tried to remember what that side of the roof looked like. He had just been there. There was the small retaining wall, from which drooped the old mansard eaves, covered with slate. His window was cut into the side of the front eave.

His breath was racing in and out of his lungs. He now distinctly heard a spring as the weight of someone left the roof and started sliding down the slate next to his window. Again, he couldn't seem to move. He felt helpless to run.

A foot appeared on the wide sill. Then another foot. The knees of a figure started to bend down and the face came into view, as it always had, draped in the black scarf. The hat was pulled a little lower than usual. The eyes glowered down at the bed under the window, then seemed, like a cat, immediately to accustom themselves to the dark and raised up searching, finding the boy standing there frozen in the middle of the room. Hands crawled up the windowpane and slipping fingernails over the top window ripped the window down so there was nothing between the figure and the boy.

"Come here," it said in a hoarse whisper.

Ballard wet himself.

"Did you hear what I said?" the whisper came again.

"Yes."

Ballard took a step forward. The wet material on his thighs seized the loose flesh inside his pants, then broke loose as he strode toward the figure looming in the window. The hat wrenched down, the scarf whipped tightly across the face, the hunched shoulders, all seemed to lunge toward him—but it was he who was lunging toward the figure—his fragile hands reaching toward the face.

The figure drew back but didn't stop him. Then both hands, still shaking, were on the face, the black material snatched in his sweaty hands, pulling it down. There was a face that seemed to come at the boy from miles away, a face he knew, smiling.

It was Fowler.

"What are you doing?" he heard himself ask.

Fowler pulled off the hat and leaned forward, catching Ballard by the arms. "See? You did it."

"What?"

"You went through the fear," he said, shaking him slightly. "I'm proud of you."

"It's you."

"Yes."

"You're not—"

"No."

Ballard blinked. "I . . . went through it."

"That took courage."

"I thought, anything—death is better than this."

He pulled the boy closer. "This stranger who haunts you—this phantom—*who is it*?"

Ballard's thoughts raced by him. He felt as if he were on a roller coaster where snatches of memory whipped by like the cross sections of a track, lasting only a instant before they were out of sight.

His mind came to a stop. "The first time I walked in my sleep, my father found me in my room in the middle of the night. I think he heard a scratching sound on the wall and when he opened the door to my room he saw me running my fingernails up and down this wallpaper that had large ships printed on it. I was trying to get into one of the ships to get away."

"Okay."

"But now . . . when I remember that, I think maybe it wasn't my father, after all."

"You think it was this . . . stranger?"

"Yes."

"There's going to come a time, Cary, when you'll have to choose." He released the boy's shoulders.

Cary looked puzzled. "I don't understand."

"It's going to come down to this stranger's will, or your life."

Cary took this in.

Just down the county road that ran past the front of Brookside, Marty Orloff was kneeling in the shrubs, his head peering through the high grass. He stared up at the man dressed in black, kneeling on a window frame cut into the mansard roof of Brookside Cottage. He heard the man talking, then saw him say goodbye to the Ballard kid and climb back up on the roof. He watched Fowler walk down the stairs, get into his car, and drive away. He wondered what it was all about.

Ms. COATES GOT out of the car, tapped on the window, and waved goodbye as she scurried along the flagstone walk to South End. She stepped up onto the porch, looking for her keys in a waist wallet.

Fowler stepped out of the hedge. "Ms. Coates."

She jumped. "Ohh! You scared me."

"I'd like to talk to you."

She stared at him. "What about?"

"Oh nothing . . . murder."

"I'm sorry, I have nothing to say."

"We can either go upstairs or you can get handcuffed and take a ride across the highway—it's up to you."

She was frowning at him with distaste. "Do you get these lines from reruns, or what?"

He smiled. "No . . . just when evidence piles up."

"Here we go . . . more intimidation." She turned and walked up the stairs, her skintight red bodysuit swaying in a tantalizing way. At the top of the stairs, she gave him a glance, unlocked the door.

Inside, she sat down on the couch without a word. Fowler stood in the middle of the floor. "Where did you and Mr. Toby go tonight?"

"To the gym."

His eyes played over her bodysuit. "Was Harold Finkelstein in your math class also?"

"As I told you, all the freshmen take algebra one."

He glanced toward the bedroom. "Mind if I have a look around?"

"If you'll do it quickly, I'm tired."

Fowler walked into her bedroom. He went through the drawers of her dresser. He searched under the mattress, in back of all the furniture, through the whole closet. He went through the bathroom medicine cabinet. He rattled all the drawers in the kitchen. All the while Ms. Coates sat calmly, statuesquely, her legs crossed, staring straight ahead.

He walked back in, held up a string of pearls. "These yours?"

"Yes."

He walked over, laid a package of birth control pills on the table, a deboning knife, a pair of boy's underwear—size twenty-four waist—a lipstick, and a bottle of Shalimar. "Remember Harold Finkelstein?"

Ms. Coates looked sad but impatient. "Yes."

"His body had the imprint of a pearl necklace on the thigh. A cast was made because we thought it was a bite mark . . . I'd like to check these against that."

"Fine."

"The first boy had a tiny fragment of lipstick recovered from his mouth." He held up the lipstick, twirled it, looking at the bottom: L'Oréal *Sunset*. "The same brand and the same shade the letters were signed with."

"What letters?"

"Letters addressed to me from the killer. Letters that were also saturated with this perfume." He picked up the Shalimar. "The same scent you were wearing the day I interviewed you."

"I have lots of perfume."

"A druggist in town remembered a woman purchasing this brand recently."

"Is buying perfume a crime?"

"On the last victim, Finkelstein, a hair was recovered; after analysis it was discovered to be type A and it contained traces of progesterone—a hormone found in birth control pills. I'll also need you to take a blood test and let us analyze one of your hairs as a comparison."

"This is unbelievable."

"Both boys had cervical secretions present on their penises. Ms. Coates . . . whose underwear is this?"

"I was washing it for a student downstairs."

Fowler was getting impatient. "What's his name?"

"One of the boys, I don't know."

"Are you always in the habit of washing your students' underwear—and not remembering what their names are?"

"I resent the implication you're making."

"Let me be frank, Ms. Coates . . . I think you killed these boys."

There was a long pause. She gazed sadly around the room. She got up, walked less seductively into the kitchen, lit a cigarette, walked back into the living room, sat down on the couch all without uttering a word.

His eyes resting on her. "Can you prove me wrong?"

"Sure."

Fowler sat down on an ottoman. "I'm waiting."

"For what?"

"Ms. Coates, where do you keep the stationery, the costume you wear? . . ."

"Costume?"

"A black cloak, a hat, a scarf hiding your face."

"Someone wasn't very thorough."

He was still looking at her. "I beg your pardon?"

"Well, doesn't it strike you as pretty obvious that if I used all these items on my victims, I wouldn't leave them lying around."

"Sure, I thought of that."

"Someone went to a lot of effort to make it look like I did it."

"Did you?"

"No. I did not kill those two boys."

He stood up. "I'll need to take these items, if you don't mind, and tomorrow you'll have to submit to questioning at the station house. I'd like you to meet with a Dr. Koenig here in Ravenstown; he will be able to make the comparison tests."

"Look, Lieutenant, I'll be glad to donate my hairs, my lipstick—anything—but I'm not the killer."

He stood up. "If that's true, we'll find it out."

She stood up to face him. "Do you believe me?"

"No."

38

YES. HERE YOU are . . . beautiful things, prizes, keepsakes . . . let me run my hands over, touch my lips to you, perfect little treasures. Voices blaring, say kiss them, touch them—well I am, for fuck's sake!

Let me take off my clothes, here, lovely yearbook picture over an inscription . . . letter jacket, the varsity letter on the sleeve—let me put you on . . . let me lick your name—those letters ripped from your underclothes, perfect boring Fruit of the Loom, white and smelly . . . they fit! My tongue like a slug now, an urchin, a wet snail working its way across precious things.

Can't stop it, it's overtaking me . . . touch this other picture . . . I like this one, the way the boy is sitting: on granddad's knee—boy *looking up, admiring the old codger—not like mine . . . I cursed mine, wished him fouled by a thousand winds—by devils in all the heavens . . . I feel it inside, rising to the surface . . . what have we here—is it true? . . . our entire league, purple and gold, blue and white, gold letters on black felt, red and white, green and black, navy on gray . . . a pennant collection to envy—easily one of the worst sins—envy. Voices say I have it, no matter, can't wear the pennants . . . but I lick the name tag, the microscopic print in a sock, letters formed in English, sewn innocently into a sock that will never be worn. So much more space to fill.*

Here is the mirror, framed by dark wooden planks. Here we are. The face makeup . . . smooth it on . . . clown white, lips puckered, eyebrows accentuated, the cap, the books, the collar, the tie, the shorts, the socks—no name—and of course, the shoes, shined, buffed, reflecting back the light bulb, still swinging above my screaming head.

Move back and forth, here I am, changing, cutting the losses, years dropping away, turning slowly, dancing over my riches.

39

CAPTAIN ALLEN WEATHERS was drinking a soda when his dispatcher, Judy Bayard, dropped the morning edition of the *Tribune* on his desk, smiling as if she had swallowed a canary, and swung her hips back and forth until she negotiated the door. He always dreaded when she left memos with him because she tended to wear very tight jeans, and it depressed him that he enjoyed watching her move provocatively between his desk and door. It was a silent tradition between them. Today, however, it made him feel vaguely sick to his stomach. He thought about his wife at home and began to calculate his despair.

Weathers had just been reading Sergeant Orloff's informal report about his star plainclothesman dressing up in costume on a suspect's roof in the middle of the night.

The paper did not contribute to his digestion. There was a cover story, with the headline INVESTIGATOR WITHHOLDS EVIDENCE. It was an exposé that claimed Fowler had not filed any of his supplemental reports on one boy, Cary Ballard, reports that were so incriminating that the entire investigation was literally hobbled without them. The article asked why Lieutenant Fowler had done this.

Then citing "unidentified" sources, the article mentioned a pair of gloves and other clothes of Finkelstein, the second victim, found in Ballard's room. The reporter, Maureen McCauley, even went further. She quoted a source at the Buffalo PD as saying, "Former Sergeant Fowler was soft on crime, a real bleeding heart." Another policeman, obviously a rival, was quoted: "Sergeant Fowler had a tendency to pussyfoot around with criminals—he was too easy."

Weathers didn't waste any time. He called one of his ace sergeants, a man who had worked hard, had a decent forensic background, and was a good cop.

Sergeant Robby Cole got the radio call out on patrol. Actually he was idling behind the Tastee-Freez, biscuits and eggs jiggling on his window tray. He picked up the car radio, listened for a moment. The dispatcher was asking him to meet Weathers immediately at the crime van. He threw the car in gear, forgot about the tray, and left his breakfast all over the parking lot.

The captain found Bill Rodney and Nick Fowler sitting around the desk in the van, drinking coffee. Fowler had some lab reports in his hand and was on the phone arranging for Ms. Coates's interrogation and tests. Weathers's hairline seemed to bristle more than usual as he rapped on the door, then characteristically ripped it open, stepping up into the van. He threw the newspaper at Fowler who dropped the lab results, hung up the phone, and reddened slightly, opening the paper. He looked down, guessing what was coming. But this caught him off guard.

"You're fired," Weathers said quietly.

Fowler looked up. "I withheld those reports because the kid is being set up."

"That's against procedure in every department in the country."

"She got these out of my motel—that's breaking and entering."

"I don't care."

Fowler stared. "The murderer, whoever it is, is going to a hell of a lot of trouble setting that kid up and I intend—"

"No, mister." Weathers stared at him. "You're outta here."

"I'll give you the reports, Allen."

"Before you leave, yes, I'd appreciate it."

Fowler could barely contain himself. "You're closed off to what's happening here, Allen, believe me, I know what I'm doing. I have a suspect."

"It's been real, Fowler. I'm sorry."

"That woman at the paper is playing us both for fools."

"I've had about enough of it," Weathers said, turning his back. "You're not going to pussyfoot around my investigation."

Fowler squinting. "What?"

"Read your clippings, Nick. Now we're going to play it my way."

A long pause. "No, we're not."

Weathers was half out of the van. He turned in the doorway. "What?"

"All the work I've done, everything that's happened here will be lost. I'm not going to let you do this."

"It's out of your hands, Fowler. I've already replaced you."

Fowler blinked. "Sergeant Cole?"

"That's correct."

"You're going to put him in charge of this complicated investigation? He's not smart enough to rip out a summons."

"Look, it's over! You're history, Fowler. Better get packed."

Nick crossed toward Weathers. "Are you going to arrest me?"

"No, of course not!"

"I have your word on that?"

A puzzled look crept across Weathers's face. "What's this about, Fowl—"

Nick's fist came around and slammed him. Weathers fell through the doorway of the van, down the steps and stumbled to his knees. Fowler came out of the van swinging. Weathers ducked and caught him with an uppercut in the stomach. They traded fists until Nick's nose was bloody and Weathers had a nasty cut over his eye, blood down the side of his face onto a blue shirt. They kept swinging until a gunshot went off. Rodney's arm was up in the air. He was standing glaring at them from the van steps. "For God sakes, don't you two have any sense?"

At that moment Robby Cole stepped out his cruiser, strode over beside the two men. "What's the trouble?"

Weathers was getting to his feet. "Nothing," he said. He glared at Fowler. "I hope I never see you anywhere in this county."

"Don't worry." Nick took a step toward Weathers, ripped his shoulder holster and gun off, and smacked them on Weathers's chest. "I have extensive notes on this case. Rodney knows the file. Now all you have to do is teach him how to read."

He walked away.

Weathers wheeled. "I'll see you never work in this state again, Fowler!"

NICK PACKED SLOWLY, staring out the window of the motel room at the highway. The knuckles of his right hand were black and blue and his nose was swollen. He folded his clothes into two suitcases, put his desk items into the briefcase, without the supplemental reports, which he laid on the front seat of his Dodge. He took one final look at the cheap pink stucco walls of the motel, even looked back once as he pulled his car out onto the highway.

After he dropped the reports and the keys to the squad car off at the station, Fowler walked outside, got into his car and hurtled it up the exit ramp onto the interstate. He drove north, staring out at the dull landscape, his mind churning over the fragments of his weeks in Ravenstown. A familiar gloom set in. He stared out the window knowing he was depressed. What bothered him was why it felt so comfortable.

40

SEVERAL HOURS LATER the midafternoon sun was blazing off the windshields in the hospital parking lot. Nick got out of his car and masked his eyes as he approached the glass door.

Inside he found the front desk, where a middle-aged nurse was twisting an auburn strand of hair at her temple while reading a patient's chart. She looked up. Her wide eyes met his gaze. She smiled. "May I help you?"

Nick looked down at the counter, staring at his bruised knuckles. He couldn't seem to speak.

"Are you all right, sir?"

Nick looked up slowly. He saw a look of concern on her face. "I was wondering . . . I don't know if you can help me, but . . ."

"What is it?"

"Someone I knew was here many years ago and I was wondering if I could . . . see the room."

The nurse frowned. "See the room? I don't understand."

Nick was looking at his hands again. "I remember the floor. Five North. But I don't remember the room number."

"I'm afraid there's no way I could do that, sir."

"I remember the view out the window—like it was yesterday. Two very tall pines outside, close to the window, and rocks . . . some kind of a rock garden below." His voice shuddered slightly.

"A rock ledge?"

"Yes, probably."

"That would be five-oh-one, on the corner."

"That's right. It was at the end of the hall."

"Sir, I'm afraid there's someone occupying that room at this time. It would be against regulations to—"

"Ma'am, excuse me . . . the person I'm talking about disappeared when I was seventeen, became a missing person, in fact. He checked in here, alone, without telling his family—without identification—so no one could call. He died a month later."

"Sir, I—"

"It was my father." Nick was blinking back a wave of emotion. "I just need a few minutes. Please."

The nurse hesitated. "I think that patient might be smoking in the dayroom. Let's see if I can let you in."

When she opened the door, Nick walked into the unoccupied room and recognized it right away. He stared at the two single beds. In the empty closet hung one pair of pants, a shirt; a suitcase was on the floor, the flap open. White hospital gowns were hanging in a corner. A nightstand with cigarettes and a paperback, a little lamp, paper cups, Kleenex boxes. The light was poor.

Nick walked to the far bed and drew the curtain that wrapped around the metal bed frame. There was an empty bed, the sheets and blankets tucked in tight. Nick hovered over the bed. The nurse could see his shoulders tensing up, his hands out to the sides.

She blurted out. "Is this the room?"

There was a long silence. He was still looking down. "When he disappeared like that, I always believed he was hiding from me. I always thought I had done something wrong."

The nurse gestured slightly. "You didn't do anything wrong."

Nick was shaking his head. "I always felt like I failed him."

The nurse stepped forward and touched Nick's sleeve. "He might have felt he was failing you. Old age is a devastating thing."

"But why would he do that?"

"Could be any number of reasons. Depression, disease, sometimes they don't want the people they love to see them that way."

"It's something else." He turned to her, his eyes full. "Just a feeling . . . in here." He touched his chest. "I could have done something."

HE PULLED INTO the tiny driveway of his mother's white house on a back street that faced a river. Beyond the water was the mill, still running, though the smoke it generated was considerably less than it had been when he was a boy.

He stepped out of the car and looked around. It was chilly. He had taken a turn off the highway, thinking he would look around his hometown.

His mother came out of the porch, wiping her hands on her apron, looking apprehensively at him. The sun was in her eyes, and a wrinkled hand pulled a few wisps of white hair out of her blue-gray eyes, tucking them behind an ear. The other hand blocked out the sun.

"That you, Nick?"

"Hey, Mom."

She opened the screen door, came down the three steps, one stair at a time, her eyes searching his face as only a mother's can.

"Something the matter?"

"I'll tell you about it."

She slowly began to smile, wrapped her arms around him, then she tucked an arm under his and they edged together slowly up onto the porch and into the house.

An hour later, Nick pushed the crust of Sarah Lee apple pie away and took the last sip of his coffee. His mother was looking down, her hands folded, shaking her head. He noticed how her face still seemed to be continually on the verge of some tropical storm. When he was a child, he had thought her face was really the sky, sunny one minute then turning gray in an instant. As he looked at her across the table, he saw the clouds moving in.

"I wouldn't let the job bother you, Nick. People never know what they're doing when it's happening to them."

"Yeah."

"They just do what they think they should—that's what you did."

Fowler nodded but didn't say anything.

She rubbed her mouth, which was still puckish, still vaguely mischievous, though at this moment it was more serious than usual. "You did the best you could."

Nick Fowler stood up, took a few steps toward the window, glanced out for a moment at the wool mill, then sat down on the ledge with his arms crossed. He was looking down. "Now that I think about it," he said, "I don't know why I didn't hand in those reports. It was stupid."

His mother's eyes didn't move from the spot on the tablecloth. "You were afraid."

Nick looked up at her, then back down again. "For the kid."

"And yourself," she said almost inaudibly.

"Myself?"

His mother crossed her arms, then matted her lips together thoughtfully, raising her anxious eyes to meet his. "You didn't want to incriminate yourself, Nicky, have you forgotten?"

"What?"

"Well, this boy Cary sounds exactly like you."

"Come on."

"You were suspended from school like he was."

"Well sure, but—"

"For fighting, wasn't it?"

Fowler's eyes moving as he thought back. "Yeah."

"You were accused of things you didn't do, remember? Just because you wouldn't hang around with that crowd down at the square—I mean, the way those boys would spill out of that bar on Saturday night—you didn't feel safe in your own town. One of them started pushing you around, remember?"

"Vaguely."

"They made fun of you because you had a crush on that girl, what was her name, the girl with . . . the hair?"

"Margie."

"She was so prim they accused her of everything under the sun."

"Let's not go over all this."

She paused, rolling the edge of her napkin. "I never told you what they said to me at the school, did I?"

"What did they tell you?"

His mother rubbed her brow, where clouds were amassing, her face moving now into an electrical storm that she tried to hold back. "They—they called me into that dingy office . . . this was just after your father had disappeared . . ."

"It was *then*?"

"They had the audacity to tell me you should be put in"—she swallowed to push down the emotion—"a reform school!"

"You never told me that."

"They said you were dangerous."

Fowler stood up and turned, looking out the window. He smiled bitterly. "Only to myself."

"Yes."

He looked out over the roof of his car, beyond the side street to where the river water was gleaming in the afternoon light. He could see the shape of a mill raising its mottled walls in the water's reflection. "Mom, tell me about the night Dad was shot."

"Now, don't start on that again." She waved her hand. "I don't remember, dear."

He turned around to look at her. "Yes, you do."

Mrs. Fowler's face hardly changed, but she flung her hair back as if it was a memory. " . . . He was on radio patrol. Stopped into the grocery store to buy coffee . . . you know the rest." She turned away.

"No, I've blocked the whole incident—I'm telling you. And you would never discuss it."

"Because it hurts."

"They shot him by his cruiser?"

"No!" She turned back to face him. "He was away from the car, Nick. He just didn't know he had stumbled on to a holdup. They shot him through the glass as he was walking toward the door—then stepped over him with sixty-seven dollars and change. They were never found."

Nick was shaking his head. "Goddamnit."

"It was raining when they found him."

"Where was I that night?"

"I don't know."

He reached over and grabbed her shoulders. "Stop protecting me. I want to know."

Her lip began to tremble. She looked in his eyes, sighed. "You and your brother had a big fight that night. Your father took Jim's side as usual. You got very upset, yelled at your father, and stormed out of the house."

"What did I say?"

"I can't remember."

"What did I say?"

"You said—you hated him for loving Jim more than you! Why do you make me do this?"

"And then he went off to work that night?"

"It's not your fault, for God's sake. You didn't put those hoodlums there."

"Why didn't he shoot them? The report said he never drew his gun."

"I don't know, dear." She was backing away from him now.

"You know."

"It's not your fault, now come on!" Her eyes were scared now. She lurched around the table. Nick followed her, grabbed her forcefully by the wrist.

"So the report was fudged, wasn't it?"

"No."

"He was preoccupied, is that it?"

"Yes, yes, that's all it was. Now stop this!"

"Or . . . he didn't *have* a gun . . ." There was dead silence in the room. "Maybe he got so upset that night he . . . forgot it?"

Her eyes looked up at him and said it all. He let go of her wrist and looked away. A strange feeling swept through him, as if his father's spirit had just brushed by him in the room. He felt a chill, looked down at her.

"Do you still have that gun?"

She studied him for a long moment. She finally nodded, walked over to the walnut hutch, and opened a drawer. She moved some dinner napkins and pulled out an old cobalt-blue long-nose .38 Colt revolver in a scarred rawhide shoulder holster. She handed it to him.

"I should have thrown it away."

He slowly, carefully, as if trying on a silk garment, strapped the holster on his back, pulled the gun under his arm.

His mother was staring at him. "It's not your fault, Nick."

"Maybe not. But I owe him one."

She immediately pulled both of his hands sharply toward her. "You owe it to yourself." Her eyes were filled with tears.

His eyes were elsewhere. "I wonder."

"You're a rebel just like he was, and by God, you're twice as stubborn."

Fowler began to smile at her. "Think so?"

Suddenly her face broke through the clouds. She smiled and cried at the same time. "You know you are." She smacked him on his hard stomach, then hugged him around the waist. Nick touched her white hair and looked out the window, not knowing what had happened, only that he felt different.

Nick was running, out of breath, staggering, the street in front of him distorted, rain coming down, rivulets of water, mud puddles, the cement pitched downward, his feet slapping through water, stopping, gasping, staring into the downpour. Ripples of neon on the puddles reflected a sign above—lights over the grocery store, neon tubes, in script, Nick's Place—the tubes melting, oozing over the gutter, down onto the windows. Pulling the hair out of his eyes, he sees a man moving toward the glass doors. Inside two youths lurch away from the counter, black shapes in their hands, three shots, glass splintering, the man falls. Through the door, stepping over him, running away, laughing, footsteps receding in the dark. He walks up to the man, in slow motion, kneels down beside him. The man is trembling—a black cloak, hat, a scarf over his face. Nick's fingers reach down, lift up the scarf . . . his father's face.

Nick sat up. He shook loose the dream. Slices of light were bleeding through the sides of the window shade. He thought it must be the floodlight outside the mill across the street. Here he was, the middle of the night, waking up in his old room, head throbbing. He stood up, reached for his clothes.

Out on the porch, he let the screen door close quietly. He saw the mill across the river and raised his collar. He found the bridge over the water in the dark. Staring up at the old structure, he walked through the grass leaving a trail of footprints in the dew. The mill was leaning slightly toward the woods; he observed it— his mood now crowded with memories—seeing himself playing football on the grass in front of that mill on a hundred afternoons, his father calling to him. A voice in the distance.

He entered the woods in back of the building. The floodlight dappled the branches. When he had walked far enough in, he stood quietly, took from his pocket the last purple letter from the killer. He had never turned it into the police. He reread it, his face grim in the darkness. The lines about "his affinity for the dead" starting to disintegrate as the match struck and set the paper on fire, a harsh glow lighting up the trees, the blaze warming his face for a moment, igniting his conviction, the ash at the end of his fingers at low flame, released, falling down, his foot grinding it into the wet leaves.

41

CAPTAIN WEATHERS AND Sergeant Cole were determined to take Cary Ballard into custody that afternoon. They couldn't arrest him because he was a minor, but they could hold him in lieu of bail. They had intended to bring him downtown, make him admit that he had killed Finkelstein in a fight and hidden his clothes. They expected to grill him for hours, firing questions, intimidating him. Then they would start threatening him. He would confess. At least that was the scenario Weathers had in mind. When they walked out of Ballard's room at Brookside, Mr. Bendleby stood in the center of the boy's room scratching his gray head.

Ballard had disappeared.

Downstairs Marty Orloff stood by the squad car. He just kept shaking his head. His official story was that Ballard had never come downstairs. At least he had never seen him.

Weathers was walking toward him, glaring. "I should fire you too."

"Wouldn't blame you, sir."

"Go on home, Orloff. Take a few days off."

"Sir, I—"

"One more word and you'll be on safety patrol at the grade school."

BALLARD HAD AWAKENED that day with a start, a nervous unease flooding him. When he had opened his eyes, he was sure his vision was impaired. Everything was out of focus. He looked out the window and was able to vaguely discover that it was afternoon by the angle of the shadows.

He saw the kinky hair of the little cop sitting in the car just below the hedge that separated Brookside from the county road. Cary's eyes seemed to focus now.

He walked into the bathroom and threw cold water on his face. He dressed and climbed the stairs to the roof. He stood up on the mansard eave at the back of the house and, grabbing a hold of the drainpipe, inched his sneakers down each lip in the siding. About ten feet from the ground, he saw a torn piece of glove wedged into the corner of the gutter. He pulled it out, jumped free, and rolled. He knew with a sudden chilling awareness—as he sat in the leaves—that this belonged to the killer.

He plodded around the back of the marsh, climbed the fence, and threaded his way behind a clump of cedar trees until he came out on the road a half mile from Brookside. In the distance he could see the afternoon light on the grille of the little cop's car. He smiled.

He walked about a mile, then trudged up the hill to where High Street crossed. He drifted aimlessly around a bend of poplars. There he saw the brilliant green lawn of Raven House—originally a girl's dorm back when the school was coed—now preserved just behind a low stone wall. Looking at the fresh grass seemed to ease the pain behind his eyes. He slumped down on the smooth surface of the stone wall, his hand cradling his stomach, his chin propped up on the cornerstone. He squinted at the intersection of Academy Road and High Street in front of him, focusing his eyes on the stop sign.

He thought he saw Ms. Coates pull her yellow Mazda up to the stop sign, look both ways, glancing right past him, then turn left and putter off down High Street. This brought him up to a standing position. He swung himself onto the branch of an oak above the wall, peering at the yellow car in the distance. When he was satisfied where it stopped, he climbed down again.

He walked around the lawn, looking up at Raven House. It was a massive white structure, yawning through its black shutters, with a nineteenth-century widow's walk crowning its slate roof. It stood on a bluff overlooking the lake. Ballard remembered there was a bench around the back where he could sit down and look at the lake and the waterfall.

When he found the bench, the afternoon sun was still beating down on it. It was October but it felt like late August—the kind of Indian summer day he remembered from when he was a child. He looked down at the sheet of cool water in the distance. He saw the reflection of the trees on the far bank. He watched the water like this for a half hour, his sanity returning slowly as the sound of the water just out of sight roared over the spillway on the far side of the bluff.

Something caught his eye and immediately brought him up on his feet. He rubbed his eyes, sure that he was hallucinating. On the far bank of the lake, a girl in an ice-blue bathing suit was running. A tousled shock of blond hair was close enough to the shore that its reflection seemed like a fire moving over the surface of the water.

Ballard watched Janine as if she were a character in a dream. A layer of gauze seemed to prevent him from really seeing her. He reached out, as if toward a painting, thinking he could touch the small figure on the other side of the lake. He stared impassively, wondering where she was going, but decided to sit back down. Then his eyes were drawn away. A few hundred feet behind her, but gaining steadily, he caught sight of a hulking shape running after her.

Suddenly his eyes began to clear up again. It was as if a sheet of gauze had been ripped away. He saw the heavy arms pumping up and down in the distance, the ponderous legs striking the bank. He heard labored breaths echoing across the water and he knew.

Ballard didn't know what was forcing his legs down the hill through the high grass, or how his own breaths had replaced the ones that had driven him to his feet. His shoes were at an angle to the steep mound, throwing dirt into the air until he was down on a path near the water, where he broke into a sprint.

In the distance the pumping arms were getting closer to the girl. As Ballard panned the bank, he saw that Janine's face was flushed. Her unruly hair had fallen down in her eyes. Her limbs now flailed to the sides from exhaustion in her headlong pitch toward the bridge that extended over the spillway. Then she saw him, and something more than recognition came into her eyes.

Ballard felt his toes hit the wooden planks as he lurched forward across the bridge. He could see that Gluckner was only a few yards behind her. They were both winded, their lungs heaving as they bolted through the grass. He heard her yell his name.

"Cary! Help!"

Ballard grabbed the wrought-iron railing as he propelled himself in a run off the other end of the bridge onto the soft grass. He thought he saw desperation, fear, and love all exploding in her features as she ran by him, touching his outstretched hand, then she fell in exhaustion, rolled behind him onto the grass, her rib cage throbbing.

He turned back to see Gluckner bearing down on him, his shoulders seeming to swell with each stride. Ballard felt as though he were standing in the path of a locomotive. He knew he would be helpless to stop this mammoth hunk of flesh. He stood quite still, his eyes blinded now like an animal on a highway at night. At the last instant, something made him duck his head and throw himself under the churning legs.

A blast of pain against his skull. His shoulders struck Gluckner's shins, flipping him over, the momentum carrying the husky student completely over Ballard's back, where he hit the ground forcefully, skidding down the bank on his chest, over the embankment and into the water.

Ballard looked up and saw Gluckner come to the surface of the lake, furiously splashing, cursing him.

"Son of a bitch!" he yelled.

He was pulled slightly toward the cement wall that dropped precipitously where the rivulets of water disappeared over the spillway. He managed to grasp some reeds from the bank to keep himself from going over. The reeds broke and he drifted with the current, paddling furiously, until he caught a hold of the underside of the bridging.

Ballard stood up, grabbed Janine's hand, and hoisted her up. They ran up the hill as they heard Gluckner's voice cursing them in the distance. Janine was still winded and Ballard had to pull part of her weight as they ran through the old wrought-iron gate of the graveyard.

Gluckner was still clinging to the bridge but had brought a leg up over the side, trying to heave himself out of danger, when they disappeared over the crest of a knoll. They rushed around a circle of worn headstones, behind a small mausoleum. Janine flopped down on the marble, catching her breath for a moment, while Ballard looked down at her. The skin inside the elastic of her bathing suit was expanding and contracting so rapidly, it made him dizzy. He tried to look into her eyes.

"What happened?"

Janine was still gasping for air. She looked up at him. "I'll—tell you—about it—let's just—get away from him."

They started running again, this time around the practice fields, along a dirt road that split away and swerved into the woods. They found a path that wound up through a stand of pine. The path was covered with brittle orange needles. Janine didn't even look down.

"Don't you have any shoes?"

"I had flip-flops and a towel—but I dropped them," she said, holding a branch back so it wouldn't hit him.

"Where are we going?"

"Just wait."

The path curved out from under the shelter of the pines into a small meadow. They jogged on the dirt path through waist-high yellow thistles. On the other side of the meadow, Janine climbed up over some boulders, down onto a small mossy patch of ground. She threw herself down on the moss and it gave with her weight as her lungs rapidly caught air. Her breathing began to slow. Ballard just kept panting, looking at her, then back over the rocks and out at the meadow.

"I used to come here when I was little," she said, taking a deep breath.

"Good hiding place."

"Yeah," she said, hoisting her upper body onto her elbows. "If you listen, you can hear any cars on the road down below us. You can see the meadow."

Ballard sat down on the moss next to her. He didn't know what to say. He just looked around, panting.

"I haven't brought anyone here in a long time. It's . . ."—she pulled her knees up to her chest—" . . . special. What happened to your face?"

"Gluckner did a number on me."

"And you still helped me?"

"I—I don't know what came over me. Why do you hang around with him anyway?"

"I don't. I came down to sunbathe by myself. Had my suit under my jeans. He just came up behind me, started pushing me, pinching me. He stuck his hand down the back of my bathing suit."

"Bastard."

"Where did you come from?"

"I was on the bluff on the other side. I saw him chasing you."

She looked in his eyes and took hold of his arm. "Thank you."

She pulled her arms back, suddenly embarrassed, and lowered her eyes as they both fell silent. Ballard just kept looking down, pulling little tufts of moss away, letting his racing mind still.

"I haven't seen you in a while," he said finally.

"Well, is that my fault?"

"No," Ballard stammered. "I've just been caught up in something."

Janine pulled her bare feet in and sat cross-legged. "What?"

"The murders."

"What does that have to do with you?"

"It keeps looking like I did it."

Janine's eyes got larger as he talked. He told her about all the evidence building up against him. He told her about the lieutenant, the tie around Crawford's neck, the gloves on Finkelstein's body. She stared in wonder, her mouth falling open, her eyes getting softer, her limbs shivering. As he talked, he realized he had broken free of some of the fear. He knew he was on a journey out of a nightmare.

Ballard caught something in her eyes that tugged at him. He kept looking at her eyes. She was smiling shyly from under her tousled hair. He didn't know why he reached forward. It was just one of those moments when everything about her was conspiring to send him out of his mind—her tough yet soft features, her fear, her sadness. The way she looked in that blue bathing suit. He took her face in his hands and kissed her lightly on the lips.

She looked at him carefully and blinked. "That's not why I brought you here," she said quietly.

He leaned back. "I know."

She pulled her knees up again and wrapped her arms around them, looking off at the meadow. "It's not true, you know."

"What?"

"What they say about me up at the school."

"I haven't heard anything."

"Don't lie." She shook her hair out defensively.

"All right, I've heard things, but I didn't believe them."

Janine shuddered, her mouth crimped bitterly at one end. "I got in some trouble one time, but . . . they've never let me forget it. They started lying, I mean, spreading lies you wouldn't believe."

"Don't worry about it."

Suddenly her eyes welled up. "I can't help it. I didn't even like guys that much. They were like aliens to me. Nonpersons, you know? But they kept coming after me. 'Come here, sugar, here, babe,' making kissing sounds, shit like that. I wanted to prove something, I don't know, I . . . wanted to . . ." She started to cry.

Ballard took her in his arms, rocked her back and forth and stroked her hair. After she stopped crying, she lay down. He dropped down next to her and after a while they both went to sleep.

Ballard dreamed he heard a car approaching. First he heard the car in the distance, then it got closer and louder. He dreamed he was floating inside the hub of a racetrack. Then he realized the roar of the gasoline engines were his breaths, hot and furious, as he was kissing Janine and she was holding his face in her hands, kissing him back. They were half asleep, moaning, rocking against each other, awkwardly kissing faces, shoulders, arms.

Ballard found himself kissing down her blue bathing suit, gently biting her breasts through the elastic, until her tiny nipples began to harden. His mouth began to press into her belly, wondering as he touched her hips if she was part swan. Then he remembered a swan could break your leg if she wanted to. He edged his mouth down below her belly button, looking for feathers, when he felt her warm fingers come down and grab a hold of his chin. She pulled him back up. He landed on her lips again. He kissed her face, closing his eyes and opening them to see her skin sink beneath his mouth. He kissed her lips again and again, as a burning sensation shot through his stomach and legs, a feeling that set his insides on fire.

Janine flung her head out toward the meadow. Through a swirl of branches and hair, Gluckner's face loomed up behind her. Ballard shrieked and lurched back. With a knuckleful of hair, Gluckner snapped Janine back against the rocks and knocked the wind out of her. She began to gasp, her lungs clutching for air. He brought his other hand down hard against her face to stop her breaths. She tried to scream and kicked her legs up and down.

Ballard picked up a stone and hit Gluckner in the side of the head with it. There was a loud yelp as he fell to the side, letting go of Janine, who jumped away from him, still grunting, trying to get her breath. Ballard swung wildly at him.

"Run, Janine!" he yelled as he punched Gluckner on the shoulders and head. All he remembered was hearing her cry, yelling savagely toward the road for help. He glimpsed the blue bathing suit disappearing through the trees as Gluckner's fist came around and smashed him in the jaw. He looked up at the sky and thought it was blue elastic. He saw Gluckner tower over him as he felt a sneaker kick into his stomach. He was starting to pass out.

One of the last things he saw was a strap holding books fly up in the air. It appeared over Gluckner's head and came down hard, the bindings striking his head. After Gluckner slumped forward onto the rocks, the quick crack of a baton. A tall schoolboy was standing there behind him, in buckle-down shoes, shorts, a white shirt and school tie, a beanie. Cary saw a large jaw, white face makeup, a pair of clown lips painted on—but he couldn't forget the same burning eyes, as a black cloak swooped around the body. He thought he saw a syringe flash into Gluckner's arm.

He dreamed he was carrying a great weight and yet he seemed to be falling. He thought he stumbled down the hill, through trees, holding Gluckner's arm. At one point, beside a car, he remembered reaching wildly out for the schoolboy's face, was pushed against the car, then felt a sting on his arm. He was thrown back with vinyl slapping up against his bare arms. A door slammed. Then darkness.

42

FOWLER WAS SITTING in his car down the hill from the crime van. He had driven back down to Ravenstown out of curiosity, or so he told himself. He had called ahead to Bill Rodney, who assured him Sergeant Cole was out in the field, but now that he was here, he wondered if he should have come at all. He was lucky Weathers hadn't put the cuffs on him—but it didn't matter—he knew something was driving him back here. He heard a young girl's bare feet slapping the pavement near the van.

He recognized the girl from the descriptions Marty had given him. Fowler flung open his car door and yelled at her.

"Janine?"

"Are you Fowler?"

"Yes. You all right?"

Janine stopped in the middle of the road, shivered from head to toe, and blurted out. "Come quick, Gluckner is gonna kill Cary, I know it!"

Fowler stared at her a second as if not understanding. "Where is Cary?"

"Up in the woods. I'll show you."

Fowler hesitated, then ran toward her. "Get in the car," he said.

Fowler's Dodge skidded through the dirt and fishtailed out onto the old tar road. They drove up the hill. On the way Janine kept looking up into the trees, glancing wildly over the dashboard. They passed one car, a new Ford. A boy in a cap with a white clown face was driving. Nick saw an Alamo tag on the back fender through the rearview. That was strange.

They drove another mile up the ascent. Janine suddenly pointed to a path that led up the embankment.

"How long ago did you leave here?" Fowler asked as he jumped out of the car.

"About fifteen minutes," she said, still shivering.

Fowler led Janine carefully through the undergrowth beside the path so as not to disturb the heel marks he kept seeing in the dirt. By the time they climbed the hill and got to the moss beside the meadow, there was no one there. Fowler asked Janine to sit down for a moment while he looked around. Near the rocks, he found a clear green plastic tip that looked like the cap to a ball-point pen. He picked it up with his handkerchief and put it in his pocket. He saw some blood on a rock, kept it, noticed the impressions on the moss, then started following the footprints back down the hill through the trees.

"There're three sets of prints here," he said over his shoulder to her.

"Three? That's impossible."

"Come on, let's go. I'll have a team come back to take casts." Then Nick remembered he was off the case. Funny he should have forgotten that.

They worked their way down beside the path. He found another clear green tip in the leaves beside the road. They got back in his car. While he was speeding back down the hill, he thought he always wanted to go private. He could do that and still work the case without a conflict of interest.

It was still light out when he drove by the van. He didn't stop. At the bottom of the hill in town, he pulled into the first gas station and asked the kid pumping gas if he had seen any cars come down the hill. The kid scratched his head. "We don't get much traffic."

"Well, I passed a Ford going up, I know that," Fowler said.

The kid squinted at him. "Oh yeah. That was a Mercury, though, wasn't it? The silver one. Came by about forty-five minutes ago."

"Probably."

The kid twisted the gas cap on the tank of a car in the full-service lane. He slapped the nozzle back onto the pump.

"Where did it go?" Fowler said. "You remember?"

The kid took several dollar bills through the driver's window, paused, pushed his John Deere hat back off his blond hair, and stared at Fowler. He glanced over at Janine sitting in the front seat of the Buick. "Who wants to know?"

Fowler flashed his ID. The kid stared at it—he didn't know it had expired. He looked back at Fowler, walked to the road, and stared off to the other side of the small town. "He drove that-a-way, I think."

"Which way did he turn on the highway?"

The kid furrowed his brow. "Neither. Took the service road across the highway."

Fowler looked off in the direction of the highway. "What's up there?"

"Nothin'."

"Woods?"

"Yeah . . . and the old railroad station. Closed it down years ago."

Fowler stared at the kid blankly, then suddenly threw the car in gear, tromped on the accelerator, and squealed rubber out of the gas station, running a tire up over the curb. Janine looked back and saw the blond kid shaking his head.

"What is it?" Janine asked, turning around with panic.

Fowler was shaking his head almost incoherently. He pulled a photocopy out of his glove compartment as he ran the red light, gunning the car across the highway onto the service road.

Janine held the copy of a letter from Arthur Murray in her lap. Fowler just kept repeating the postscript: " . . . another enemy kissed out in nature, where time no longer runs."

The road to the abandoned railroad station was steep and wound through several switchbacks as it climbed the grade of the mountain on the other side of town. Janine watched Fowler press the accelerator. The Dodge was clambering around a blind corner when a silver car appeared in the middle of the road straining toward them down the hill.

There was an instant where Fowler saw it all happening in slow motion. The Mercury went into a skid. The white face behind the wheel was expressionless as the car hunted them. At the last instant he wrenched the steering wheel away. Fowler plowed his car into the weeds on the side of the road to avoid being hit. There was an instantaneous squeal of tires, a grinding of gears as the cars swiped each other—just missing a head-on collision—the sound of peeling metal everywhere as fenders scraped against each other. Fowler's car spun away, tearing through the brush, lopping down small trees, as leafy branches grabbed at them through the open windows. He tried to regain control of the car as it skidded down an incline. Janine screamed when the car finally slammed against the trunk of a tree.

Fowler helped Janine out of the car, and she lay down on the ground, crying, shaking with fright. Her knee was bloody. He made sure she was all right, then stood up to shake his head at the car. He saw that the damage was not that serious: The grille was mashed, yes, he would need a new hood, a new headlight, and there was that healthy scrape on the side.

He had installed a used police radio in his car when he first arrived in town, and now he was praying that it still worked. He turned it on. When he heard the familiar crackle, he barked into the microphone, identifying himself, the Mercury, a description of the person driving, and the direction the car was traveling. He said he thought it was the killer. He requested a wrecker.

A HALF HOUR later, it was dusk. Fowler was sitting on the side of the road with Janine cross-legged in the dirt next to him. From his medicine kit he had applied iodine to her cut and bandaged it.

The wrecker came chugging up the hill, followed by a squad car, with Bill Rodney behind the wheel. Fowler pointed out the position of his Dodge to the driver of the wrecker, handed him a credit card, signed a claim, then asked Janine to get into the second car.

Rodney was staring at Fowler in bewilderment. "What the hell are you doing here?"

"I'll explain, Bill. Let's take a drive."

"Don't you have any sense? Weathers finds out you're back here, messed up in this case, out of your jurisdiction, he'll not only arrest you, he'll probably sue the living hell out of you."

"Let him sue."

"You're lucky I was on duty. Nobody else would touch you with a long-distance phone wire."

"Give me a few minutes, and they'll be even more delighted. Drive me up this hill."

Bill Rodney gave him a look. "What's up the hill?"

"An abandoned railroad station."

They sat down in the car. Rodney put the car in gear and pressed the accelerator. "You're unbelievable."

"Anything on the person in the Mercury?"

"Nothing."

"If you check every rental place in the area, I'm sure you'll find one with a nasty dent on the side."

Rodney nodded in silence.

Three miles up the road, they rounded a bend and saw the deserted station. The brown cement structure looked like it had been shelled by F-1 bombers. Several of the uprights had caved in. The platform was buckled and slabs of pavement pushed up into the air. Rodney pulled his squad car up into the gravel parking lot. His headlights reflected in the broken windows.

Fowler turned around to Janine in the backseat. "Janine, we'll lock the doors. I'd rather you stay here just in case." She nodded. He turned to look at Rodney and they both got out of the car.

They shone their flashlights into the windows first. Fowler immediately saw footprints in the layer of dust on the floor, steps on top of oblong spirals, droplets, smudges of dust and blood. The place of death. He pointed at them, and Rodney nodded slowly that he also saw them. As they raised their flashlights, they thought the walls were covered with paint. There were streaks, great swaths of color.

They walked around the side through an open door. The putrid smell of fresh blood and excrement. Drops of blood on the door glass. The colors on the wall, smeared later?

Close now with the flashlight. Not just color, texture. Chunks of flesh pressed into the dusty plaster. A long snake, dripping red, black, splattered up at an angle. Rodney, choking, his handkerchief out, stumbling outside. Nick, one hand covering his nose, his flashlight up close on a long intestine. Nick, choking too, stepped outside. They were both dry-heaving, waving hands in front of their faces, clearing their heads, both coughing. Both looking up to take big draughts of fresh air.

That's when they saw him. Gluckner's feet had been noosed together, then he had been hoisted up the flagpole. He was hanging like a marionette. His upper body was swaying forward in the air, his limbs flying at angles. Their flashlights revealed he was strung up by small-gauge wires to different sections of the rope. The wires were wrapped around his neck, wrists, under his shoulders, around his waist. His eyes were bugged out.

"Good God," Rodney muttered.

Fowler shone his light up at the body. He didn't say anything.

Gluckner was leaning forward in the air slightly, as if bowing flamboyantly, one arm out in front of him, the other up in the air. He was dressed in a tux jacket, bow tie, cummerbund, shoes, and nothing else. His throat had been cut and he had been disemboweled.

From a corner of the building, they heard a whimper. Fowler walked over and he shone his torch down in the shadows; it fell on a form. Ballard was lying on his back, his head rocking back and forth. He was murmuring nonsense as if having a seizure. He was covered with dark red streaks. In his right hand, sticky with dried blood, was a long stiletto.

43

By the time twelve police cars had come roaring up the hill into the old station, Fowler was disgusted. Their revolving flashers sent beams of light out across the entire county, he thought, and their sirens erupting over the next few hours only announced their impotence.

When the EMS team loaded Ballard into the back of the ambulance, Fowler had to remind one of the team to make sure the boy was tested immediately to see if he had been anesthetized. He showed the two green plastic caps he had found to the crew men, who nodded, correctly identifying them as covers for disposable needles.

Fowler had managed to get his investigative work done before the police arrived. Rodney had given him a little time. Fowler had taken several photographs of the body, bloodstains, the walls, had found gloved prints on the ladder and on the doors of the old station lobby. Then he got one break: In the dust, among the blood-stained dance steps, he found traces of tar. His mind leapt back to the day he had stood on the roof of Ardsley.

Of course, first murder. Start over.

Before he left, Fowler waited for Sergeant Robby Cole to arrive on the scene. When Cole stepped out of the cruiser, the two men sized each other up, quietly, acknowledging each other with cold stares.

Robby Cole was astounded to see Fowler back in town and didn't exactly disguise his contempt. He stared at Fowler silently as the blond man told him everything he knew—respectfully handing Cole the needle covers—suggesting that he take the girl home and get out of his hair. He turned to leave.

"That why you left Buffalo, Fowler?"

Nick turned. "Pardon me?"

"Soft on crime, huh?"

Fowler just gazed at him, nothing to say, walking away. "Yeah, that's me, old softie."

"You're out of your league here, pussyfoot."

Fowler turned. "Don't *ever* say that."

"You better disappear, mister."

Nick kept walking. "Watch me."

When he was getting into Rodney's squad car, Nick saw Maureen McCauley getting out of her old blue Rambler in the dark. He froze when he saw her red mane in the revolving beams. He knew she saw him too, and he noticed her hesitate ever so slightly before she decided to walk past him.

Fowler couldn't help himself. He was angry as hell at her and he didn't intend to hide it. She stopped in front of him and put her feet together. He stared at her and an electrical current seemed to jump along the side of his jaw.

"Excuse me," he said, and walked around her.

She reached out and touched his arm. "I'm sorry. I never meant to get you—"

"Like hell you didn't," he said, and gave her a wide berth, whipped open the car door, and got inside. Janine was sniffling. He started the car and patted her shoulder.

"Don't worry. Cary's going to be all right."

He pulled the car out. The beams of his headlights caught Maureen's back as she climbed up the platform steps in her heels. She turned abruptly and stared into his headlights. He kept backing away until the beams swept away from her out onto the road.

Maureen showed her press pass to the duty officer and after asking a few questions, was handed a gas mask and led to the place of death. She took out her pocket camera and started taking flash pictures—mainly of the bloodstains on the floor. She glanced at the walls and shuddered. She took a half roll of film of the bloodstains.

Several policemen stood glumly around in the stray lights, smoking or staring off, some talking, some looking at her—especially one—Robby Cole. He stared at her as his men worked the scene, watching every movement of her body. She didn't pay any attention. She never spoke to Cole, only nodded at him before she left, and drove straight down to the darkroom at the paper.

As soon as Nick Fowler had rented a car that evening, he drove to the Thirsty Moose, sat down at the bar, and ordered a gin and tonic. He bummed a cigarette off the bartender and pulled on his drink. Somehow he had to figure out how the killer had managed to get Ballard to help in the killing—without the kid knowing it. Or had Ballard been unconscious?

He ordered another gin and felt the frayed edges of his composure begin to rebuild themselves. He knew if he had another gin, this would reverse itself and his equanimity would plummet off the graph. He had to do something before that happened. He planned to have several tonight.

He walked to the pay phone, and dialed the number for Ballard's mother, Muriel. When she answered the phone, he could tell she was sloshed. She seemed casual about the news, even flirty until he mentioned her son would need a lawyer, and a good one. Then she became argumentative, as if it had been Fowler's fault that Cary was involved. He explained he had been fired, and why, that he was still working on the case privately—for his own reasons—but for no money. That seemed to shut her up. She said she would think of something and rang off.

He called Edwin R. Koenig, who he guessed would be handling the autopsy. The doctor told him he could view the body unofficially after the police left. He thanked him and said he would call in another hour.

Fowler walked back to the bar, ordered another, and stared at the blue-and-red neon sign in the window. He watched the way the light in the tubes changed colors. He thought about the boy with the clown face in the car. Was he an accomplice? Was he Arthur Murray? He began to realize, when his faculties had been dulled enough, that the killer, whoever he or she was, would stop at nothing to achieve his ends. The end had already been stated as his own death. That's when he ordered a double.

AT THE TRI-COUNTY Hospital emergency room, Cary Ballard was on a gurney being pushed urgently through a corridor. At the side of his gurney was an armed policeman. The boy had been admitted an hour before in a state of shock. The tentacle of an IV was dangling into the vein of his left arm. When another patient was released, they had a room for him.

Ballard was installed behind a curtain in a drab blue cubicle surrounded by equipment. The policeman assigned to bring him in asked the attending physician, a pleasant dark-haired woman in green scrubs, what she knew about his condition. She asked the cop to wait outside the curtain while she administered more tests.

By the time Sergeant Cole and Marty Orloff arrived, the doctor emerged, telling both men that Cary Ballard was suffering from shock, had regained consciousness, but was now asleep.

"Was he given a drug?" Sergeant Cole asked.

The doctor looked down at a report she was holding. "There's a toxicology screen, Officer, so we need to know what we're expecting, or we have to test for every drug. And most of these drugs don't have antagonists."

"Was he knocked out? That's what we want to know."

"Well, the patient remembers being out, but doesn't remember for how long. We tried to narrow it down." She looked wearily down at her clipboard. "We ruled out volatile fluids. We tested him for benzodiazepines and barbiturates. We're running tests for Thiopental—which knocks people out for twenty minutes— Ketamine—about fifteen minutes—but which persists as analgesia for two and half hours. There are many others."

"When will you know?"

"If we say it's an emergency, the lab could have it tonight."

"It is," Cole said.

"He received a severe blow to the chin, but other than increased ocular movement and pulse due to emotional distress, his vital signs were normal."

Cole listened to this information quietly. "Doctor," he said, "the fact I want you to keep in mind is: Cary Ballard was found holding the murder weapon at the scene, was a suspect prior to this incident, and is to be kept under armed police guard at all times."

The doctor nodded, looking down at their guns.

EDWIN R. KOENIG admitted Fowler through the back door of the funeral parlor. They nodded to each other solemnly and proceeded in silence down the dim hallway into the examining room. Inside the room, the overhead lamp was out. Fowler didn't look in the direction of the body.

"This is very irregular," Koenig said, pulling on a pair of yellowish elastic gloves in the near darkness.

"I know," Fowler said quietly. "But as far as I know, the man now in charge of this investigation is not aware of the intricacies of the case."

Edwin R. Koenig's eyes seemed to be coming out of an eclipse. They flickered for an instant on the man standing across from him. He snapped the fluorescent light on above the examining table. The room was shocked into brilliance.

When he peeled the sheet down, they both tried not to look at the eviscerated midsection. The doctor started talking immediately. "The police were concerned with urine, bile, and gastric contents. These were sent to the lab an hour ago. Emergency results should be available shortly."

"Good."

"First, he put up a fight. I scraped the undersurface of the nails when I saw that several were broken. It revealed a layer of skin shaved from the perpetrator. An abrasion caused by striking is visible here on the knuckle of the right hand."

"All right."

He laid the hand back down and moved up the body to the head. "The back of the head sustained blunt trauma. You can see the layers of skin piled up opposite the direction of force. Subdural hemorrhages were produced." The elastic fingers roamed down to the neck. "Again, the victim's throat was slashed with a sharp instrument. Again, an incised wound, not as deep as it is wide, as you can see. Notice the ligature mark just below the chin, the deep lividity of the face. He was stabbed, then hanged."

"Like the others."

"Again traces of alcohol on the lips, salivary activity along face, neck, and upper body.

"I see."

"And notice the deep furrows along the wrists, underarms, waist—presumably from a thin-gauge wire."

"I found the body. They were piano wires."

Koenig's eyes lifted and fastened on Fowler. "I beg your pardon." His hands now floated below Gluckner's waist as if nothing was unusual. "An eighteen-centimeter medial laceration, very deep, multiple transverse lacerations severing portions of liver and spleen. Large intestine is ripped, a long section of large intestine appears to be missing . . . he's just . . . opened up—"

He broke off and pulled the top of the sheet up over the area, took a breath. "Excuse me."

"Thank you," Fowler said, turning away also.

Slowly Dr. Koenig regained himself. He was visibly upset. "This is the worst I've experienced in thirty years. I can't believe it."

"That's why I came back, Doctor. I've got to stop it."

In a rare moment of feeling, Koenig studied Fowler with blood-shot eyes. "Be careful."

"I will."

The doctor turned back to the body. He lifted the lower part of the sheet up to the pubic bone, exposing the legs. "Again, there were vaginal secretions present on the victim's genitals."

"Any foreign hairs?"

"In the pubic area, yes."

Fowler sighed, an early hangover starting to throb. "Were the hairs forcibly removed?"

"Some had roots, yes."

"Can we get a workup on the donor?"

The phone in examining room rang. Koenig pulled off an elastic glove and snatched up the receiver. "Yes?" He listened, scribbling words on a pad by the phone. "Yes," he said, writing furiously. "Are the hair samples ready? . . . I see . . . Then I'll speak to you tomorrow. Thank you."

He hung up and turned to Fowler. "There were traces of Sco-polamine present in the victim's urine—a drug that acts on the nervous system. It was delivered by injection, which means it probably took about ten to fifteen minutes to act, then knocked him out for about a half hour. That's the favorite of prostitutes in the city, I'm told, when they want to roll their johns."

"Okay."

"They won't have the microscopic characteristics of the various hair samples until tomorrow, but they were able to determine the hairs came from the victim and two other donors."

"Two others?"

"Yes. As before, we can't be sure of the sex unless there are residues of drugs that point to gender."

"Right."

Koenig sighed heavily. "Where can I reach you tomorrow?"

"At the Grotto, the motel out on the strip. I moved back in. Leave a message, I'll call you back."

"Fine."

Fowler took a step away from the examining table.

44

WHEN FOWLER LEFT the funeral home, he wanted another drink and walked back over to the Thirsty Moose, his shoes scuffing the gravel in the parking lot. There was a single sulfurous streetlight burning down, sending long shadows as he walked. It occurred to him he had spent far too many hours in places like this.

Just outside the bar's front door, he heard voices and loud music wafting from under one of the windowsills. He stepped up to a pay phone cupped in a silver egg-shaped receptacle and shoved a quarter into the slot. It rang four times, then was picked up.

Bill Rodney's dry voice rasped into his ear. "Yeah, hello."

"Bill, it's Nick, sorry to bother you at home."

"Not to worry. Just got in. What's up?"

"Anything on the rented car?"

There was a hesitation on the line. "You're going to love this."

"What?"

"We found the car. It was parked behind the Taco Bell out on the strip. Stolen."

"Great."

"Nontraceable, of course. The men are dusting it for prints now. They're supposed to call me if anything unusual shows."

"Son of a bitch," Nick said under his breath.

"The kid at the counter said a man, kind of husky, wearing a black cloak, drove up, bought a diet soda, and walked back across the strip into town."

"Any further description?"

"They all said he wore heavy white makeup, was tall, had a deep voice."

"A clown face painted on?"

"You know him?"

"Sure, we go way back . . . Bill, this is the first time the killer has appeared without the scarf."

Rodney laughed on the other end. "Nick, go to bed, huh? It's too late to worry yourself—just think, you have all day tomorrow."

"You're a walking affirmation, know that?"

"I'm just jealous of all the money you're making."

"Shut up."

"Look, if you want to stay here, I think the wife could be talked into it."

"But she wouldn't love it. No thanks. I appreciate the offer though."

"Talk at ya later."

"Bill, do you know the results of Ms. Coates's tests?"

"Good news and bad news. The tests linked her to the perfume, the lipstick; the blood test linked her to hairs on the body—but under severe interrogation, she proved not to crack. The kicker, of course, she was still in custody when Gluckner was slaughtered today."

"I had a feeling. Bill, can I call you for further developments?"

"Of course you can." There was a silence on the line. "But you know, you're putting me in a spot."

"You mean, if Weathers found out you were passing me official information?"

"Of course."

"Tell you what, Bill, I'll follow all this up on my own."

"Cole is in first thing tomorrow. When he pulls out, if I'm alone, I'll buzz you."

"Thanks." He hung up.

Fowler stepped toward the door of the bar, but as he pulled on the handle, something caught his eye in the reflection of the glass. He turned around.

Standing at a distance, silhouetted by the streetlight at the end of the parking lot, a tall woman was staring at him. The figure stepped forward and a glimmer of light picked up red hair.

She stood perfectly still. Her voice was quiet and—from that far away—merely a whisper. "You didn't believe me," he thought he heard. "I never wanted you to get fired." The voice seemed disembodied, almost an echo.

"It didn't look that way," he said quietly across the parking lot.

"I went too far." Her voice was getting closer, a murmur on the still air. "And I'm incensed that Mr. Sleaze, Robby Cole, has taken over. Serves me right." She stepped forward and the face went into shadow again. The words seemed to be floating very faintly toward him.

"Forget it. You did me a favor."

She was moving slowly. "How so?"

"I always thought I could go private, now I'm forced to."

The high heels entered the light. It shot up the calves, across the green dress, onto her face. "Is that why you came back here?"

He looked at her. "No. Why did you kick me around like that in the paper, Maureen?"

The corners of her mouth squirmed. "I'm sorry. I felt stuck here. I was trying to hold on to the story, and I was mad that you wouldn't work with me. I'm really sorry."

A rush of anger shot up the center of his chest. "You should be," he said harshly. He shifted his weight. He was looking up at the streetlight when he realized she was five feet away now.

She took a breath. "Did the police talk to you?"

"Oh yeah."

"I heard you found the body."

"Let's not talk about it."

She looked down at her purse, opened it, and pulled out several photographs. "Look, I have something to show you."

He heard the gravel under his shoes as he stepped next to her, looking down. "What is it?"

"The bloodstains on the floor. Maybe you haven't developed your pictures yet, but look. See this?" She pointed down. "I learned this step in the gym at school, when I was thirteen. It's the She Go, He Go."

"The what?"

"See how the victim is taken from an open break position, then looped into a half turn?" She shuffled a diagram of the dance she had photocopied to compare the steps. "It's like a half a dance, but it's there."

She shuffled the pictures again. "And this is called the Sugar-foot Walk because from promenade position the killer is going triple to the left, then make a quarter turn, then triple to the right, then it's smudged but . . . you can . . ."

"Never heard of these dances."

"It's the Lindy." She pulled another picture. "This is a variation called the Mooch, another hop favorite. See how the killer kicks his left foot forward, see the smear, replacing it, then the right, the same, always replacing the weight, see the heel print? . . . Then it all gets confused. They seem to switch."

Fowler looked down. "That's because the victim is leading."

She stared at the pictures, shaking her head pathetically. They both seemed to go silent, their minds drifting away from the horror of it. "How can I make it all up to you, Nick?"

Fowler looked touched. "You'll have to do penance."

"What do you have in mind?"

"Well." He smiled. "I could make you teach me these dances."

She dropped the pictures on the pavement. She threw her purse behind her and bowed, arched into dance position, waiting. He stared at her for a prolonged moment, feeling an uncontrollable hunger for her. Simulating a regal air, he stepped closer, ready to dance . . .

He clamped his arms all the way around her and kissed her hard on the mouth. She threw her arms around his neck, her soft lips wide open, her tongue searching his mouth. Their mouths were rubbing hard across each other's faces, moaning, kissing, tasting each other. Maureen began moving her breasts up and down on his chest.

Nick ran his rough hands over her body.

Maureen was blushing, her cheekbones pierced with color even in the dark. "Stop that."

He pulled her closer, pressed his lips down along her neck and arms. She started moving her hips ever so slightly against his, pushing against him, smiling. He was grinding back into her now, his hands sliding down her green dress, onto her buttocks. Both smiling now, kissing, laughing, clutched to each other right there in the parking lot.

They didn't see Sergeant Orloff in the adjoining parking area. He was leaning against his car in back of the Thirsty Moose, smoking a cigarette. They didn't see him turn down the volume on the police radio. How could they see his lips moving, silently, calling in information that might be of interest?

In front of his room at the Grotto, Nick nudged Maureen so her back was against the door. He struggled with the key. "Maybe I should let you open it," he said, winking at her.

"I'm off work."

"Besides, this is your atonement."

"And rough justice it is."

The key finally turned. Nick nudged the door open, picked Maureen up in his arms. She screeched, then slapped a hand over her own mouth, giggling. Nick planted kisses up and down her neck, heaved her across the threshold of the darkened room, and kicked the door closed.

He threw her down on the bed, a bead of light shot from the curtains across her aquiline body. He leaned down, bit her neck, kissing down her front, his mouth into green material between her breasts. Maureen emitted tiny moans. Nick kept kissing down her body, stroking her hips, her thighs. He felt her arms rubbing his shoulders, then pulling his hair. He lifted the green dress up. He noticed her eyes flaring in the darkness.

"Is it okay?" he said.

She shrugged. "I'm nervous." She crossed her arms and pulled the dress up. Nick watched it slide up her body, over hips, belly, breasts, neck, face, her hair finally up in the air floating down over her shoulders. The green material sailing to the floor.

He stared, suddenly unbuttoning his belt, struggling awkwardly out of his trousers, tripped once, laid the gun and holster on the floor. He tried a few buttons on his shirt, gave up, ripped it over his head and lunged on top of her long, soft body, kissing face, arms, breasts, hands. His mouth rushing down, searching hips, buttocks, and thighs, finally between her legs, his tongue inside her, a man dying of thirst, deep draughts from a well, her moans getting louder, hands cupping breasts, squeezing her hard, rubbing her all over.

She slapped him, trying to break free—the game too delicious—she had to prolong it. He grabbed a handful of hair, tugged her back onto the bed; she squealed, a flail of punches on his chest and shoulders. He spanked her. She howled, flattened her bottom onto the sheets, giggling, kicking him away. He fastened a tight-waist on her, held her still, kneading her thighs, his mouth again between her legs. Her back beginning to arch like she was having a spasm, thighs taut, crying out, she shuddered, again, her arms thrashing, grasping his hair, grating her torso up and down against his face, something carnal and violent overtaking them, riding it out until it subsided. He crawled on top. Then he was inside her, pushing into her. Pushing slowly in, slowly out. They didn't see the face waiting, watching, the strange inhuman gleam of the eyes between the crack of the door.

THE SMELL MUST *be flesh. Odors mounting through the room, can hardly stand it . . . almost pass out from the sound of skin sliding against skin, endless cries, kisses, grunts . . . NOW LOOK OUT THE BATHROOM DOOR, see the Day-Glo palette of color, bodies moving through the air, vibrating: my father beating my mother, making her jitterbug, pulling her into a turn—she twirls—he won't let go, now choking her, lifting her dress, raping her, smiling, humping her from behind, his tongue shining like a snake, clinging to her mouth, my mother whimpering—a dog crying from her own mouth—inhuman sounds, voices, small screams smothered by his tongue, then sighs, terrible defeats, thrashing of arms, her face flogged, then tears.*

I want to kill him. He smiles at me through the darkness, laughs at my cries, still mounting her, driving hard, violating my room, fucking her on my desk, her fingers against my bulletin board, her back arching, relaxing, her voice crying out, shedding tears, begging, the cry of an animal. Hear them like machines, pumping, disgusting, fleshy, smelly forms spoiling the walls.

Voices spring from inside my head. Drowning her out. Ascending higher, whispers, soaring into the walls of my skull, telling me—I should be there on that desk—not her. I should protect her. I should be raped and killed, not her. I should do something, why can't I do something, stop him, kill him. Can't. I'm afraid.

I look out into the room—darkness—then Day-Glo—darkness—then Day-Glo. I used to follow you, Fowler, used to tell you things. Now you're hurting her, just like my father. Her legs in the air, ecstatic cries . . . Day-Glo pigments applied at angles, sharp upward strokes. You thrusting, her crying, me dying inside, walls getting brighter, decorative coating, swatches of rouge, cosmetics, skin. Traces of flesh, paint, blood, all hitting the wall, splashing, roaring out of me. Yesssssssss.

I have to protect her.

NICK WAS DRIVING harder, slowly arching into her, inching her against the headboard. Her thighs trembling, wrapped around him. He started pushing faster, pulling her hair, high-geared now, with each thrust her eyes seemed to spark, her face flushed, her parted lips mouthing silent words.

He rolled over so she was on top. She laughed, threw her head forward, a red curtain drawn back across his face, then flinging her hair back, began to rock. Her face flinching between loose strands of hair. Nick gripping her, a tension there, she pulling, he pushing, slowly, like that for a long time.

She fell forward on his chest and grasped his shoulders. She rolled the other way as if they had done this for years, he still inside her, still thrusting, she nudging against him, locked in for the ride. He pushed her toward the headboard. Now they were on the far side of the bed.

There was a slight crackle under her back.

"What is that?" she whined softly.

He smiled, reached his hand under her shoulder, and pulled out what looked like an envelope. The bead of light picked up the purple color. They both smelled it at the same time.

Maureen screamed, pulled the bedspread over her.

Nick was scrambling across the floor. He found the gun. She saw his shape faintly rush through the room, heard him kick open the bathroom door. Through the back window she saw his silhouette, saw the gun lunge in first. She heard a loud thud, a shattering of glass. She screamed. A cloaked figure leapt out of the bathroom, grabbed the steel frame around the window, pulled himself up, and jumped out of sight.

Nick was lying on the bathroom floor, bleeding. He had been sapped, the bathroom mirror thrown open in the dark—over his gun hand—into his forehead. Maureen switched on the light.

"Jesus, Nick, oh my God." She started dabbing the blood with tissues. Nick looked dazed, then was abruptly on his feet, switching the light back off. He ordered Maureen onto the floor. He peered out the window, blood dripping into his eyes. In the parking lot behind the motel, he could see a cloaked figure running away. He leaned out the window and fired at the shape, which immediately dropped. He kept firing, the gun sending a spray of sparks out the window, the sound deafening in the small room. He dropped below the window, crawled to the holster, reloaded, crawed back, then slowly raised his head up to see.

The glass exploded.

A round of bullets cut chunks out of doorjambs, snapped curtain rods. A clay lamp shattered as they dove down.

Nick dragged Maureen between the two double beds, whispered, "stay here." She was crying. He managed to pull on his trousers, had wrestled the shoulder holster on his bare back, and was out the door, running around the side of the motel, ducking between cars, his gun trained on the place where the figure had fallen. He saw nothing but the woods beyond.

A police car hurtled into the parking lot, its floods whirling. The car pulled a one-eighty, spun around so the grille was facing Fowler, both doors opened and two policeman ducked down, firearms leveled through the windows. One was a shotgun. Fowler was wiping the blood from his forehead in confusion. He saw blue forms running out of the woods, coming from the direction where the killer had fled. They had their guns drawn. One of them was Orloff.

Maureen was wrapped in the bedspread, running along the side of the motel in her bare feet. She had seen the police car. She stopped at the corner of the pink stucco building where she saw Nick—spread-eagle up against the wall—being frisked. Marty Orloff was running his hand down Nick's leg, checking his pant leg. She saw Robby Cole pull Orloff out of the way, take the shotgun out of another man's hands, and drive it up into Fowler's gut. She started running. Nick was on his knees, coughing up blood and phlegm.

Maureen ran up behind Cole and dug her fingernails into his face, trying to scratch his eyes. He yelled, jerked away from her, his hat falling, then easily shoved her down on the pavement. His eyes lit up when he saw her state of undress. He was still holding the shotgun. He stared at her, a sly smile, then pitched the butt of the shotgun against Fowler's head. There was a dull thud—Nick flipped over on his back—unconscious.

Maureen screamed, "You son of a bitch!"

"Shut up!" he yelled back at her. "He's under arrest for firing on a police officer." He strode slowly toward her, still smiling. Cole reached down, pulled her brusquely up to her feet, pushed her against the wall, leaned in, a whisper. "It's pay-back time."

"Take your lousy hands off me."

Another whisper. "Wouldn't want to see his face messed up now, would you?"

She stared over at Nick, out cold. Orloff was kneeling by him, watching Cole.

Cole's face was in closer. "I think you'd do almost anything not to see that happen, wouldn't you, honey? Wouldn't you?" He was resting the shotgun against her neck, the steel cold. A whisper in her ear. "Say a word and I'll hurt him, trust me, I will." He started feeling her breasts through the material, pressing her harder along the wall, acrid whiffs on her shoulder.

He yelled over his shoulder, "I'll have to search the suspect's room— you men, hang loose." He pushed her farther down the wall. She felt his hand probing the material between her legs, his fingers through the folds, up between her thighs now, sweaty palm rubbing her vulva. She couldn't seem to make any sounds. Her lips were moving.

Out of the corner of her eye, she saw the barrel of a pistol make an indentation in Cole's cheek. She heard Sergeant Orloff's voice.

"You won't enjoy this with a hole in your face, Cole. Now drop the shotgun and stand away from her or I'll have to pull this trigger."

Cole turned his face and stared into the muzzle. "Orloff, you piece of shit."

"Drop it."

Maureen heard the shotgun fall against the foundation of the motel; she looked down and saw it lying in the dirt. Cole stood away from her, his arms out to the side with a swagger, glaring at Orloff. She took a long step forward and kicked him squarely in the balls. Cole bawled like a hyena, falling to the ground, both arms between his legs, rocking, crying out, his face red with agony, saliva pouring out of his open mouth into the dirt.

Orloff was shaking his head. He looked over at Maureen. "I'm sorry about this."

Maureen was shaken. "I want an ambulance for that man," pointing at Fowler.

"Call emergency medical!" Marty yelled to one of the other men, who reached down to a dashboard, pulled a microphone up.

"And the killer got away." Maureen pointed toward the woods.

Marty turned and looked beyond the parking lot. "The rest of you men, arm yourselves and search those woods."

Maureen crouched over Nick, stroking his hair, blotting his forehead with the bedspread.

Cole was still rocking in the dirt, groaning. His head was straining, kept falling back. He rolled over, tried to sit up, his eyes full of fury. "Orloff, I'll fix your ass!"

Maureen suddenly stood up and walked over. "No you won't," she said quietly, leaning down toward Cole's ear. "This man came to my aid. If you so much as harm a hair on his head, I'll not only slap you with a lawsuit for police brutality and assault, I'll write a firsthand account of what you did to me tonight, and there were witnesses." She faced the other men who were still checking their guns, staring at her. They dropped their eyes. "I'll see you ousted, Robby Cole. I'll see you convicted."

There was a stillness at the corner of the building. Maureen stood up, looked at Marty. "You've all been gunning for Nick. Help me get him inside." Marty looked at the beautiful woman with the red hair. He smiled and nodded at her.

THE LIGHT BLAZED on in the motel room. Nick walked to the shattered windows, applying the ice the medics had given him to his jaw. They had also given him a shot to dull the pain, a dressing for his forehead, cold packs for the crack on the head. He was staring at the blue shirts moving back and forth in the woods behind the motel. He turned and looked down at the purple envelope on the edge of the bed. He looked up at Maureen. They didn't say anything, just stared at each other.

He walked across the room, a little shaky, found a handkerchief in his pants pocket, picked the letter up with a handkerchief, turned it over, sniffing it carefully. He switched on the desk lamp. It was addressed to him in the same scrawl. He slit the top of the envelope, spreading the purple stationery out under the light. Maureen stood by him.

Dear Mr. Fowler,

I see you've returned. Something is happening to me. I'm changing, becoming, but I find it hard to explain. Surely you can guess. You know me so well.

Save the last dance for me.

My best to Maureen,

Arthur Murray

P.S. This next one is the cause of it all.

Maureen pulled a chair away from the desk and sat down, her upper body giving slight, involuntary shivers. She looked at Fowler who was still naked from the waist up, staring at the letter, his shoulders tense, face sad, eyes shot through with red lines. He suddenly threw the ice pack against the wall. "I can't believe he was in here."

"Or is it she?"

"It's definitely a man." His eyes were roaming the top of the bed. "How did he know you were here?"

"He watched us in the parking lot."

Fowler gave her a quick glance. "Had to be."

"What are you going to do?"

"I'm thinking."

He noticed that she was sitting on the edge of the chair, leaning toward him. His eyes climbed up from the rug, her bare legs pulling his attention across the bedspread she was clinging to. He noticed her expectant eyes.

She arched her eyebrows and leaned her head forward. "I have an idea."

"I bet you do."

"A few short hours ago we were angry at each other, right? . . ."

"Yes."

"People reveal themselves when they dance."

"Did we dance? I didn't notice."

"Let's throw him the prom he's always wanted."

Fowler blinked. "What do you mean?"

"Have a dance. Invite ballroom teachers, experts, enthusiasts. How could Arthur Murray resist?"

"Why should he come?"

"*You'll* be there. I could run a promotional piece on it."

Fowler lifted his shirt off the floor and slipped it on. He parted the thick curtains, catching sight of a Ravenstown police car whizzing by. He looked back at Maureen. "What kind of promotional piece?"

"Well, announcing an authentic ballroom dance . . . at a nice hall somewhere in town. After this murder today, and this close call tonight, he might want something more civilized. Invited are: selected faculty, prominent citizens, *and* any suspects you want. Then on the gossip page, I'll arrange for a small chatty paragraph—my friend Chris will do it—about the rumor that you will be in attendance."

Nick raised his eyes and let them bathe on this woman. "Let me sleep on it."

She stood up, took a step toward him, touching the smooth surface of his shoulders. "Let me sleep on it with you."

Fowler reached a hand up and ran it gently along her cheek. "I'm worried about you being involved in this."

She moved closer. "You can't do it alone, Nick. I'm with you now."

He picked up his gun, walked to the door, and pulled the chain on. "I have to think."

45

IN THE EMERGENCY room the next morning, Robby Cole was limping, walking around bowlegged, staring at the drab blue curtain surrounding Ballard's cubicle. A small man with curly hair and gold wire-rimmed glasses stood scratching his bald spot, watching the sergeant.

He was the same young man who, years ago, had handled Muriel Ballard's divorce when he was fresh out of law school. Michael Lichtman now placed his briefcase down where the legs of the boy's steel bed were visible from under the curtain. The blue material rippled slightly in the draft. He had yet to speak to the boy. Ballard was still asleep.

Lichtman kept crossing his arms and staring at Sergeant Cole, who returned the stare. Finally he spoke. "The doctors have said repeatedly my client isn't well enough to go home, yet you people are determined that he should, as sick as he is, now go to the state police station for further questioning. That is not only illegal, it's inhumane."

"Mr. Lichtman, Cary Ballard is a suspect. Do you know what that is? I'll spell it for you."

"Even a suspect has rights."

Sergeant Cole was standing with both hands on his thick belt. Marty Orloff was standing next to him, his back arched away from the wall, doing neck extensions. Cole signaled Lichtman away from the curtain that separated Ballard from the wide hallway of the emergency room. He hobbled a few paces. "Mr. Lichtman," he began quietly. "Maybe in New York City, lawyers like to stick their noses where they don't belong and distract everybody. The fact is, I have to question this kid. I don't care where I do it."

"Why don't we question him here?"

"I intend to, but *we* are not going to question him. *I* am going to question him."

Michael Lichtman's face fell in exasperation. "Sergeant Cole, I think it not only fair that I be present, it's a virtual necessity."

Cole bent forward slowly from the waist, in pain. "For who?"

"My client."

"Lichtman, do you know anything about this case?"

The bushy head of curls was nodding emphatically. "I've been studying the reports, of course."

"Have you finished?"

"Well, not every single document, after all—"

"Then why don't you get up to speed and let me do my job."

Lichtman shuffled the papers under his arm. "I insist on being present during the questioning."

Cole turned to another hefty policeman standing next to Orloff. "Would you escort Mr. Lichtman to the waiting area?"

The policeman and Orloff each took Michael Lichtman under one arm, nearly lifting him off the ground. The tiny man's face turned beet red and he began to flail his legs and talk excitedly in the hefty policeman's ear. "I'll nail you with a case of assault if you so much as touch me." By now his shoes were skating above the waxed floor.

"Ask him if he wouldn't mind waiting just a few moments," Cole said dryly.

"Police brutality!" Lichtman yelled.

Cole watched the wire-rims being yanked around the corner. He walked over to the curtain of Ballard's cubicle and pulled it aside. Ballard's eyelids were drooping but they were open.

"You well enough to talk?"

Ballard looked around the room, slightly dazed, wondering who Cole was. He looked up into the man's dark, somber eyes and shook his head.

"Come on," Cole barked. "What happened?"

"I don't know."

"If you tell me the truth, I'll let you go home."

Ballard did. He stumbled through what he remembered from the moment he saw Gluckner chasing Janine. He left out the part about kissing her and dreaming he had burned his way onto the table of elements.

He couldn't remember much after being thrown into the backseat, the drug taking effect. When Cole began to describe the train station, flashes of memory came knifing back, shocks of light through a haze. He remembered holding Gluckner around the waist for an instant at the station. He remembered blacking out, being revived. He thought he recalled lying nearly unconscious, looking across a small room at Gluckner's back. A tall schoolboy had his arms around him. That's all he knew.

Ballard's account sounded true enough for Cole to arrange that the boy be released on his own recognizance, pending further interrogation. He could leave as soon as the doctor felt he was well enough.

When the boy left the hospital late that afternoon, he found himself in the agitated presence of Michael Lichtman. He was forced to repeat everything he had just told Sergeant Cole.

By the time Ballard was up in his own room relaying the events for the third time, Lichtman was still not satisfied. Not until the persistent and annoying lawyer's sweaty hands were squeaking down the stairway railing did Cary Ballard feel a sense of relief.

IT WAS DUSK. Cary stood in the doorway of his closet, staring up at something on the edge of the shelf above his hangers. It was a hat. It was black with a gold brim, and had the word "Cat" printed on the front. Ballard stared at it and a new wave of fear overtook him. It was Gluckner's hat. He had seen him wearing it at the pep rallies when he wanted to seem truck-driver tough. Everyone in the school knew it was his hat.

Ballard pulled the hat down from the shelf, ran a fingernail over the scratchy felt. He shuddered, feeling a swell of rage surge through his body. He knew his emotions had shifted. A kind of resolve crept into his face. He found himself staring out the window, wondering when it would be dark enough.

MR. BENDLEBY'S GARAGE door sent up a mournful rasp when Cary lifted the door. He stood for a moment, listening to his breath as his eyes got used to the dark. He could just make out the handle of the shovel leaning against the wall in the corner by the workbench. He reached out and touched the smooth cold handle.

IN THE FIELD behind Brookside, Ballard could feel the rye grass rub the side pockets of his tan jacket. In his left pocket he had folded Gluckner's hat. On the far side of the field he brushed by the bough of a pine, wet with dew. About twenty yards into the grove, he struck the ground with the point of the shovel and found that it was soft enough to dig.

All this time a car had been parked across the county road. It was hidden just inside the entrance to the school beside a white dilapidated garage where the wombats stored the lawn mowers for the west campus. When the woman behind the wheel saw Cary slip out the front door, she stepped on the gas pedal and coasted silently onto the dirt road behind the marsh that circled the edge of the field.

She watched the boy lope awkwardly through the tall yellow grass carrying a shovel. She eased the car door shut as a light fog settled over the edge of the field. She felt the mist against her legs as she folded something into her hand, and had to duck under a pine branch, she was so tall. She stepped down on a floor of soft needles, listening. She heard the shovel strike a rock in the distance. She crept closer and positioned her body behind the trunk of a tree. She watched Cary put the shovel down. The boy was staring down at a hat. Her eyes fell also on the hat. She saw the boy pick it up, drop it into the hole, immediately shoveling dirt on top of it. Ms. Coates placed the small flashlight back in her pocket, picked out the yellow branch of a poplar near where the boy was digging, memorized it and walked quietly back through the pines.

46

THE NEXT MORNING Ballard was sitting in his English class when another notice came. Mr. Toby looked down at the white slip of paper that had been shoved through the crack in the doorway by an underclassman. His eyes swept across the room and fell on Ballard. "It seems you're wanted in the headmaster's office," he said.

Ballard stood up, seeing the slightest glee appear in Mr. Toby's features, just a feather of emotion. He edged past the master, excused himself, and staggered out into the hallway, in the grip of a nausea that caused the walls to blur as he edged down the stairs.

In the headmaster's suite, the secretary nodded amiably, gesturing Cary toward a heavy brown door. Cary took a breath and pushed. The door opened soundlessly. The headmaster rose up from his desk.

"Come in, Ballard, come in."

As Cary sat down in the leather chair in front of the long desk, he thought he saw himself staring back from the burnished wood panels that surrounded the room. Dr. Hickey looked solemn. He sat back down at the desk, clearing the stack of papers away from the center of his blotter.

"This is not a happy occasion, Ballard."

"I know, sir."

"I mean for you."

Ballard could see the reflection of the headmaster's skull like a rare artifact perched on top of a spindle in the glare of the polished wood. "I don't understand."

Dr. Hickey dropped his wiry eyebrows down and peered at the boy for a long moment. "Do you understand this?" He opened the drawer to his desk and pulled Gluckner's hat out and tossed it with disgust into the middle of the blotter.

Cary Ballard stared down at the gold brim smudged with dirt. He didn't think he could speak, yet he heard words coming out of his mouth. "Where did you get that?"

"A faculty member brought it in. It seems you were seen burying this in the woods. The hat of the last boy murdered. It doesn't look good, Mr. Ballard."

"It was in my closet, sir. I didn't know how it got there."

Dr. Hickey frowned at him, half smiling, as if the boy had made a ridiculous statement. "Of course you don't. You didn't know how your school tie ended up around the neck of one body and your white gloves on the hands of the other." He suddenly stood up, adjusting his gray cuffed trousers up over his skinny hips. He pulled the door to his office open. He called out into the hallway.

There was a flurry of sounds, the secretary whispering outside, then Ballard heard footsteps slowly nearing the door. Mr. Allington appeared in the doorway. There was an ironic expression on his thin lips. "Hello, Cary."

Dr. Hickey closed the door and turned to face the boy as both men stood stiffly against the wood panels. Dr. Hickey crossed his thin arms. "We're going to have to notify the police."

Ballard nodded slowly, more out of weariness than anything else.

Allington was shaking his head. "I think we should try to work this out among ourselves, Brandon."

"No!" Dr. Hickey said.

"You asked me to take charge of this."

"I want the *police* to take charge of it now. This is over your head, Elliot." He reached down onto his desk, picked up the receiver of his phone, then glanced at Allington. "Go ahead, just say it."

"It's nothing, Brandon. Seven more students have withdrawn from the school this morning. The last thing we need is more publicity. And having one of our own boys arrested will—"

"I don't care anymore." Dr. Hickey's facial muscles were trembling. "I want an end to it. If we have to close the school, that's what we'll do." He dialed the phone.

Allington's eyes drifted over to the boy. "I tried to shield you from this, Cary."

"Yes, sir," he stammered.

"Don't worry."

The headmaster spoke into the phone. "Captain Weathers, please."

The two men both stared down at the floor as they waited for the voice on the other end of the line.

CARY BALLARD SAW the booking sergeant's distracted eyes keep looking away. The boy stood before an elevated, dirty, yellow Formica counter topped by a tall row of silver bars that framed the sergeant's wide, sallow face. The face glanced at Sergeant Cole. "This is a detention?"

"Yes. Since the suspect is underage, the captain has requested an investigative detention, to be signed by the magistrate. If probable cause is found at the hearing tomorrow, he'll be moved to the state juvenile detention center until trial."

"So this is one day at most, right? The kid's a minor."

"Correct."

"What about bail?"

"Let him call his mother."

The man asked Cary his name, address, age, occupation, social security number, and made him empty his pockets.

Sergeant Cole stood near the desk, his hat pinned under his arm, still sore, his weight shifting from one leg to the other. A woman with bleached blond hair was typing every word the booking sergeant said. Finally the man behind the counter pushed the report away from his belly, stared off at what Cary realized now was a television. The man was briefly amused, then looked back at Cary, shrugged, and told him he could make a phone call.

Cary Ballard dialed his mother and let it ring. She picked it up on the seventh ring.

"Hello?" Her voice was flat.

"Mom, it's Cary."

There was a pause. "What's the matter?"

When he told her he was being thrown in jail, she screamed. Cary started crying. He had held up well until now.

"Do you have any idea how much that lousy lawyer has cost me already? Do you?"

"Will you stop yelling at me? Come and get me."

"Your father didn't leave me a cent, kid. How do you expect me to pay for all this? Huh?"

Cary didn't know. She was still ranting when he was tapped on the shoulder. A guard threw a hand in the direction of a long yellow corridor. Ballard could hear his mother's voice begin to sob through the earpiece.

"Come get me," he yelled. He hung up.

The man led him down the hallway, where with each step the lighting grew dimmer. Cary started to panic, a terror building inside. They turned farther into a maze of more bilious yellow hallways. Strange faces. Eyes staring at him—making him cringe. He hugged one wall when a scrawny hand came out to grab him. He rushed to catch up with the guard's dull footsteps. They stopped in front of an empty cell. The man gestured him in. The door echoed when it shut. Footsteps retreating. Then silence.

For several minutes, Cary sat breathless, still as a statue, listening to bar doors slamming, men's voices in the distance. He was cold. His mind was a blank. It occurred to him that he wanted to die. He would stop breathing, crush his skull against the wall, anything to be released. He had to die. His life was an endless torture. There was nothing that mattered anymore. He stood up, slowly grabbed two yellow bars in both hands, his breath quickening.

He threw his head forward and bashed it against the steel. A shock of light, then specks twirling in the distance, a maelstrom of soaring falling dots of fire, like a flock of birds against the twilight, swooping down, flattening out to fly overhead. Then blackness. Then a face. Eyes. Over a black scarf. There it was. It would never go away. It would always be there to taunt him.

Cary hit the cell floor.

He felt the bump on his forehead. He closed his eyes. There was the face again. He suddenly found himself driving his fists at the image, tearing his fingernails across the face, gouging the eyes. He started screaming. "Leave me alone! Leave me alone!" He was kicking, scraping at the face, in a free-fall of rage, trying to tear the face from his mind.

The guard appeared through the bars. He saw the boy now lying on his stomach, pounding his small fists against the floor.

"Shut up!" he yelled. "One more sound out of you and we'll put you in the basement."

Cary didn't even hear the man's words. He saw the face in his mind moving quickly now. He could feel his heart beating against the cement floor as the face receded into the distance. He blinked, opened his eyes, noticing the dirty floor under his chin as if it was sacred ground. He reached his hands out. When they touched the cold floor, he knew. Something had changed.

47

NICK FOWLER RAPPED on the screen door. It rattled against his knuckles. He dabbed the bruises on his jaw, winced, opening his mouth slowly, the pain still with him. A small face appeared behind the screen. "Yes?"

"Mr. Pullen? It's me. Nick Fowler."

The door was unlatched and swung open. "Come in, Lieutenant."

He stepped in. "This is unofficial now, Mr. Pullen. I'm no longer with the police force, but still working on this case."

The little man was peering up at Fowler with a fierce look on his face. "I don't want my name in the paper anymore, is that understood?"

"Yes."

"All right then." The elderly man led Fowler through a small kitchen, in need of paint, dishes stacked in the sink. They moved silently through a hallway into a dark living room. He pointed at a battered recliner next to a couch. Nick sat down, looking around at the old heavy furniture, covered in wine upholstery and faded macramé doilies. The windows were encased in sheer white curtains, all covered with dust. There was a dank smell in the room. Fowler watched the old dance instructor seat himself nimbly on the couch.

"When you were mentioned in the article, Mr. Pullen, it said you have been teaching dance for . . . ?"

"Nearly half a century, young man."

"Have you ever taught dance to any of the faculty of Ravenhill School?"

"Of course. You think this town could sustain a dancing school? I get a few locals, but for the most part, it's faculty wives."

"Mostly women, then."

"Occasionally I get a master. I had to teach them all the basics for the Golden Jubilee two years ago."

"What was that?"

"A ball commemorating something or other. I had to take every master in hand and teach him to waltz. It was a nightmare only Diaghilev could have produced. You've never seen so many left feet."

"Do you still have any records on their progress?"

"What do you mean?"

"Did you take notes?"

"Are you kidding? Why?"

"No reason."

"It was all in my head, Lieutenant."

"Well, can you remember anything about the dancing skills of any of the teachers, any of them?"

"That was a long time ago, Mr. Fowler."

"Any names at all pop into your head?"

"Not really." Mr. Pullen was beginning to fidget.

Fowler looked down at the dusty patterns in the Oriental rug. "Would any of it come back to you, if you actually saw them dance *now*?"

"Well, of course. Dance is nothing more than expressing emotion through movement."

"So you would remember?"

"Primitive men danced with joy for a good harvest," he said, lifting his arms to the ceiling.

"Mr. Pullen?"

"They danced with pain at their initiations into manhood, they—"

"Sir, excuse me, but we have our own initiation going on here. It's more like a sacrifice. Three boys have been murdered by someone who is dancing with their bodies. I need your expertise, your help, but most of all, I need your full attention."

Mr. Pullen's eyes widened as he sat up, visibly chastened, his posture becoming more erect by the second. "For your information, I can talk on many different topics and still know exactly what's going on in this room."

Fowler nodded. "I'd expect nothing less."

Mr. Pullen's eyes seemed to soften. "I don't really care for the attitude you're taking with me."

"I'm sorry, but I'm up against the wall here."

"That's not *my* problem."

"No, it isn't. But if you would agree to help, then . . ." He made a imploring gesture.

"I told you I would."

Fowler shifted forward in the chair. "Then listen carefully. If there was a dance at a hall here in town—I'm just saying *if* there was one—would you be willing to come and observe?"

"As long as there is no mention in the paper and no publicity. I value my life. You may not care, but I do."

"I value every life, Mr. Pullen." Fowler held the man's eyes for an extra second. "Just observe, that's all. No fanfare. Not a word about you in the paper. Just sit in the back and study the guests, think back to when you were teaching the faculty, and talk to me afterward. That's all."

Mr. Pullen sighed heavily. "So is there such a dance?"

"If you say yes, there will be."

The little man made a quick movement, stood up, and stared through the dusty curtains. "How I got involved in this, I will never know."

THE STATE POLICE range boss didn't ask to see a badge. Nick still had his ID; he flashed it, working his jaw in pain as he glanced at the gun racks. He saw the Colt .38, Smith & Wesson 9 mm, and Beretta—all good, solid, duty pistols. He noticed a shelf of 45-caliber Colts reserved for tactical units.

The man reached his hands up. "Try something different today, Lieutenant?" His fingers slid down onto a fat barrel. "I acquired this Bulldog .44 Special myself, equipped with speed loader. One hell of a mean pistol."

"Got this old .38 I had fixed up." Nick pulled out his father's gun.

The range boss cocked his head. "I lost my faith in .38s a long time ago."

Nick was looking at him. The man pulled a .45 Colt off the shelf. "This will take a man down, no questions asked."

Fowler nodded, looking up at the arsenal of startling firepower. "No thanks, I'll stick with this antique."

He walked out on the range, swinging a pair of earmuffs. It was late afternoon and he had the place to himself. He strode along the firing line, stopping at the last stall. He liked the feel of his father's gun. He touched the blue-black metal casing, the long sighted nose, the thin grips. He had taken it to a shop to be reconditioned. The gunsmith had offered to vent the barrel to keep the muzzle down on recoil. A good deal on ammunition.

The silhouette target was nine yards in front of him. Nick thought of the first time his father had taken him out for target practice with a .22, can on the fence, sunny afternoon just like this one. He loaded the chambers with shiny brass .38 bullets.

He leaned into a bent stance, left leg slightly forward, arms straight out in front of him, a two-handed grip on the revolver. He squeezed off six rounds. Five in the X ring. Not bad.

He reloaded, tried drawing fast from the old holster, missed the target once altogether. He kept reloading, faster, squatting, moving, drawing, and shooting. After a while his pumping motion and his aim became more fluid.

The range boss watched out of his Plexiglas booth at the man working so hard. He was puzzled. After a while he yawned when the rounds kept popping the inner circle.

48

Up into the chamber. Switch on the light bulb, swinging, light splashed on yearbooks, light then dark, pennants, bulb swaying back and forth, pictures of boys flickering, swatches of hair, shine then dull, curled photographs, light then dark, name tags pinned on dank wooden walls, still squirming like live butterflies—the wind from below—close the trapdoor. Stop the fucking bulb—reach up. There.

Have to apply dressing to the wound, not healing, pull away gauze, mute the scream, my mouth open, a silent howl, now chills, cold in here. But, quiet. Just the wind. My breathing. No adults.

In the skin, a graze, furrow in the flesh where the bullet went by, bleeding for a night and a day, starting again—this is too good for you, Lieutenant. You get the end of a razor. You shouldn't have raped her. Cut off your genitals and hang them on the clothesline. Let you bleed into a pit of rats, let them crawl inside you, munch your innards, while you're still alive—how would that be?

Dab the blood. Now pressure. Apply the salve. No voices. No rhythms. Just look at my work. There they are. Souvenirs from life. Keepsakes from a time before screams, changes. My change. Inviolate, perfect, out of fire, bones and blood, out of pain, and lovely terror.

One more now. Just one sacrifice—then deal with them. By then my change complete, my new form shaped from psychic flaws, lead into gold, a perfect childhood, flawless revenge.

All sweetness and light.

49

THE NEXT MORNING Ballard was standing before a magistrate in Reliance, the county seat, with Michael Lichtman standing next to him. The short lawyer was twitching. He moved his briefcase dramatically from one hand to another, sighing, scrutinizing the man behind the gavel with a petulant expression on his face.

All Ballard could think about was the cold cell he had spent those five hours in: the nauseating yellow walls and bars, a bed with broken springs, the one square window, barred. His mother had arrived to bail him out at two in the morning. They had stayed in a motel under police surveillance. Cary was in a daze, his neck still aching from his fitful sleep. He stared over the massive bench at the frizzy gray eyebrows of the magistrate. He watched as if mesmerized by the vaporous blotches of hair that seemed to float over the small eyes of the balding middle-aged man in the black gown.

The magistrate was poring over the request from police authorities for Ballard's detention to the state juvenile center until his trial. On Cary's other side, the prosecutor for the county, a tall gaunt man of fifty in a dark brown suit, was standing in silence, looking intently at the magistrate. He had just handed the man behind the bench an "information" naming the boy as the prime suspect in all three killings, stating the times and places of the crimes, aspects of evidence, as well as the nature of the charge: first-degree murder. After what seemed like an eternity, the magistrate raised his eyes and nodded to the attorneys that the hearing could begin.

Fowler sat beyond the rail that surrounded the bench, leaning forward, listening to the hushed tones of the lawyers in front of the magistrate. Next to him was Mrs. Muriel Ballard. On the other side of the aisle, sitting grim-faced, Sergeant Robby Cole.

Muriel whispered to Fowler that she had borrowed her aunt's life savings to post bail for her son. Fowler nodded sympathetically. He was straining to hear the voice of the prosecuting attorney making his opening statement. After a pause, the magistrate's bushy eyebrows seemed to hover over the other attorney's head.

Michael Lichtman spoke in a slightly tremulous tenor. "The defense would like to request a waiver of the preliminary hearing, due to a lack of direct evidence."

"Denied," the magistrate said quickly. "We have exhibits found in the defendant's possession, affidavits from faculty and students alike swearing that the defendant was enemies with all three victims."

"The police took sworn statements from everybody but their mothers, Your Honor. That doesn't make them true."

"Watch your tone, Mr. Lichtman."

Lichtman stared upward, impervious as the magistrate's voice continued. "More important, Counselor, we will have depositions by an expert witness, a psychiatrist."

"You mean Nathan Clarence, the Doctor Death of Ravenstown?"

The magistrate was slightly taken aback. "We have every reason to believe the defendant's doctor could provide testimony as to the boy's mental capacity to perform or abstain from certain acts."

"Has the doctor testified in closed session yet?"

"This afternoon."

"Your Honor, first of all, the defendant is a *child*. The prosecution should not prefer a charge of murder in the first degree against a minor."

"I'm aware of that, Counsel, but the heinous nature of these crimes forced me to—"

"Has to be manslaughter, Your Honor, or it's a mistrial."

"I'll take your request under advisement, Mr. Lichtman."

"With all respect, Your Honor—"

"We have a statement by a witness who saw the accused trying to conceal an article of clothing belonging to the latest victim. The file of evidence against your client is exhaustive."

"Your Honor, the defense also asserts there are extenuating

circumstances that may point to my client being unfairly questioned. We suggest that this preceding amounts to a mistrial."

"In a multiple-murder case?" the magistrate said, opening his eyes in amazement as he stared at Lichtman. "Where did you take your law degree, young man?"

"In the great state of New York, Your Honor, which allows that a defendant may secure his release from custody, especially if the allegations are false."

"You have to prove that, Mr. Lichtman."

"I can also prove that Cary Ballard was not read his rights before he was interrogated by the police."

The magistrate shook his head as if assailed by a bothersome fly. He gazed out over the small courtroom in Sergeant Cole's direction and raised his voice. "Did you tell the boy he had the right to remain silent, Sergeant?"

"Yes."

Lichtman turned and stared at Sergeant Cole then back at the magistrate. "My client has no recollection of this, Your Honor, and furthermore he did not sign a rights waiver before being interrogated."

The magistrate sighed wearily and looked over his glasses at the dark-haired policeman. "Robby, did the boy sign a waiver?"

"He was not in custody, Your Honor. I spoke to him in the hospital. He was not interrogated."

Lichtman was up on his heels. "He was for all intents and purposes under police control, Your Honor. *And* he was denied counsel. I know, because I was forcibly taken from his side in the emergency room."

The magistrate sighed, looking over at Sergeant Cole. "Robby, you're familiar with the laws. I suggest in the future that you allow counsel to be present." He looked slowly at Lichtman. "No matter how difficult he is."

Lichtman stared at the magistrate. "*Miranda v. Arizona.* Do I have to quote cases? I've never seen such a dog and pony show."

"I'll hold you in contempt if you don't watch your mouth, Mr. Lichtman. The boy was not in custody when he was questioned. The arresting officer has said so."

Michael Lichtman was ready for takeoff. He pulled his blue suit down. It was riding up his heat-tempered limbs. "Your Honor, may I remind you, if there is any intent to use what the boy said against him in a court of law, he must be advised of his rights *before* questioning—I don't care if he's in the Dairy Queen."

The magistrate's eyebrows were getting singed. "Don't lecture me on the laws. If counsel can retrace a few simple steps, he will recall: The reason the boy was detained in the first place was because he was seen burying incriminating evidence—that was *after* he was interviewed by the police."

"Now we're calling it an interview?"

"I have no choice but to see the defendant bound over for detention in the juvenile center until his trial, Mr. Lichtman. And the charge of murder is too serious to allow release at this time."

A silence fell across the room as Muriel Ballard inhaled, almost gasping, from the front row. A different silence entered Cary's insides, as if he was no longer standing in the musty courtroom. His eyes glazed over. In his mind, he was already behind bars.

AFTER THE HEARING, Fowler stood outside the county courthouse, squinting into the sun next to Muriel Ballard, who put on her sunglasses and stood in silence.

He turned to her after a long pause. "You know, something isn't right here. I remember when I studied Cary's school file, there was an abnormal interest—an obsession really—in the details of his past, his father's death, his psychological problems, his behavior."

"Really? How strange. They never said anything to me."

"Almost as if that information was poised, waiting to be used against him—which now it has been."

"Can you check on that?"

"Yes I can, but, Mrs. Ballard, I'd like to ask you for some information of a . . . personal nature."

"All right."

Fowler worked his jaw uneasily, as he took his hands out of both pockets and rubbed his face. "I'd like you to go home and think back over your life. Then make a list of every man you ever dated during Cary's childhood."

Muriel turned suddenly around and she looked at him aghast. "Are you crazy?"

"No."

"That's none of your or anyone's business." She stood away from him on the steps, bristling, caught in a moment of indecision, not knowing whether to stay or go.

Fowler put his hands back in his pockets and walked past her down the steps, stopped, then turned back to look up at her. There was an uncharacteristic emotion in his voice. "Someone is trying to frame your son, in case you're interested, and I have to know everyone he's come in contact with—even when he was a child."

"I have never in my life dealt with people like you. What do you want from me?"

"Mrs. Ballard, I'm asking nothing more from you than—what someone is trying to take from your son. His soul."

Muriel stared at him, her mouth closing resentfully as she turned and strode across the grass toward her car.

Fowler watched her, then rubbed his neck, feeling cramped from sitting in court so long. He decided to stretch his legs. He walked down the sidewalk in front of the courthouse, letting his mind roll.

Fowler saw a blue newspaper machine and wondered if the "dance story" was out yet. He slipped in two coins and lifted the glass cover, pulling out the paper. In the social pages there was a two-column article about a dance being held in town at the Rotary Club auditorium, to which the community was invited. At the bottom of the page, a tentative guest list was announced; it included noted dance teachers and ballroom experts from New York City. Near the bottom of the list it said "former Lieutenant Nick Fowler."

Fowler nervously wiped the back of his neck as he read the small type. On the page facing the announcement, he saw that Maureen had managed to interview prominent figures from the town on their reaction to the idea. Most of them, it seemed, had not followed the dance evidence on the case and therefore were not in the least shocked or even mildly disturbed by the idea. The mayor said it was just the kind of thing to "lift the town's spirits."

Fowler was uneasy but understood this as a possible spiderweb in the making. If only the killer would come. Certainly Arthur Murray had proved himself to be an avid reader of Maureen's columns.

Nick stepped up to a pay phone and called the Rotary Club. He was told that tickets were selling out. He hung up and was about to put the paper away when he noticed a small headline and an article in the corner of the facing page. It said HEADMASTER OF RAVENHILL RUSHED TO EMERGENCY ROOM FOR NERVOUS EXHAUSTION.

Nick thought about his father's lost month in the hospital. At this instant, a flash hit him: He was sitting on his dad's lap in a police station squad room, no more than ten years old, looking up at the man's face. He remembered the muscle along his jawbone working in and out. Out of a clear blue he said, "Why did you become a policeman, Dad?" A couple of officers standing around overheard, laughed, said something about taking bribes, not having to wait at traffic lights, like that. Nick recalled a serious expression coming over his father's face. He took the boy's hand, looked down at him, and said, "Avenge evil, son. That's the real reason." This of course brought an uproarious reaction from the men. His father was slapped on the shoulder, jabbed a few times; finally he looked embarrassed and smiled. Nick shook off the memory. He knew his father was by no means perfect, but he also knew the man was utterly sincere, had meant every word, and had put himself in the line of fire to prove it. Nick dialed the van, feeling his father's gun against his ribs.

Bill Rodney's voice was thick with smoke on the other end.

"Yeah. Rodney."

"Bill, it's me."

"Well, if it isn't the Lone Ranger."

"Anything on the Scopolamine?"

"Oh yeah. Same drug used on Orloff, the Ballard boy, and the victim. Extensive checks, Nick. No druggist anywhere in the county has dispensed it in recent memory. The hospitals, of course, use it, but infrequently."

"Then it was either stolen, or someone had a stash."

"No shit."

"Where are the needles coming from?"

"A medical supply warehouse. We're checking mail orders. It takes time."

"I want to jog your memory, Bill."

A sigh of impatience. "I'm waiting."

"Remember back a few weeks, I requested two R&I clerks be

detached from county police to run record checks? Did that ever happen?"

"Like molasses, but yes."

"Good, okay, remember I gave you a list of townspeople and faculty members? I'm curious about auto registrations, DMV requests, anything—utilities, Ma Bell—we've got to run histories on those people."

"You're a dreamer, Nick, that's what I like about you."

"Bill, it has to be coming from the inside. Someone who works on campus or who in some way is connected with what is going on. How else?"

"Why histories, anyway?"

"I have a gut feeling the killer is acting out some drama from his or her past."

"How could you know that?"

"I just sense a great passion behind these killings—I'm talking years of rage, lethal stuff—and it's escalating now. The killer's transforming himself. He came after me the other night."

"I heard."

"Early childhood experiences determine a lot."

"Why don't you give it up, Nick. You're obsessed. Go back to Buffalo. Find yourself a nice reporter."

Nick paused on the line. "Anything but that."

Bill laughed. "Look, I'll try to feed you whatever they have."

"Anything on where a disguise might be stashed? Maybe a rental?"

"What am I, your personal secretary? You don't work here anymore, did that slip your mind?"

"What about a dorm room?"

"Sergeant Orloff checked the entire housing list for empty rooms. Jesus."

"Where is Orloff now?"

"Fourth floor of Ardsley."

Fowler was feeling impatient. "Do what you can to get those backgrounds, Bill. Wouldn't hurt the police to look good for once." He clicked the phone down, his thoughts racing.

ON THE FOURTH floor of Ardsley, Marty Orloff was sitting in the office, alone, his feet up on the desk. He jumped out of his chair when Fowler opened the door.

"Mr. Fowler," he said, relaxing. "Didn't expect to see you here."

Nick stood looking at Marty. He walked up to him. "Listen, Marty, there's no way I can thank you for what you did the other night—how you helped Maureen—kept her from possibly being raped, me from getting beaten more than I already was. Thank you."

Marty was smiling. "You're all right, Mr. Fowler. I'd expect you to do the same for me."

"If they come after you, let me know."

"I will."

"Call me Nick, will you?"

"Sure." They shook hands.

Nick was sheepish. "Anything I can do?"

"No . . . unless you want to read some of the reports I've generated since you were fired. Don't worry about Sergeant Cole—he bailed out to watch the football game."

"What reports?"

"Remember that silly assignment you gave me to get me off your butt? The bathroom detail. Well, look what KP did for me . . ." He handed Nick a detailed list of the scribblings from bathroom walls.

"Refresh my memory."

Marty sat down again, leaning back. "Some kids in the tunnels were initiating that kid, Schwerin, by making him write stuff about Ms. Coates on a bathroom wall or something, remember?"

"That's right."

"There's lots of interesting stuff in there—check it out."

Nick looked down. "Okay."

"It makes sense, too. You want to know who someone is balling, ask the students. Better yet, go where they can write forbidden stuff. You know, these fuckin' kids: cooped up in here day in and day out, having to wear a tie and jacket six days a week, required chapel, required sports, required activities. It's got to seep out somewhere."

Nick was leafing through. "Lot of washroom philosophy in here?"

"Oh yeah. All the greats are quoted . . . Plato, Nixon, the girl next door."

"This must have taken you days."

"I searched every boy's room, men's room, and ladies' room on campus. Three floors on Madison. Every floor in Ardsley, in Booth. I checked the infirmary, the gymnasium, even the chapel. The language arts facilities. Even walked into a senior dormitory on east campus and had to wade through a mob of guys who had caught a freshman inside. 'Freshman in the dorm! Freshman in the dorm!' they yelled. Two of the seniors were so giddy they ran into the showers themselves, clothes on and all. I walked in, checked the stalls. They thought I was weird, called me a 'Fed.' "

"I'll study these tonight."

"Behind the attacks on the school, dick jokes, pornographic artwork, and phone numbers—you might find something."

Nick turned a page, started reading a poem. He scratched his head, tucking the report under his arm. "Thanks, Marty."

50

Ms. COATES PULLED a purple dress over her head. Her brown hair, worn in a pageboy, sprung out of the crew neck like a freshly cut bouquet. She tousled the hair, put a dab of perfume on her neck out of habit, rubbing the residue behind her knees, looked once more in the mirror and, as she was walking out of her bedroom, flicked off the light.

When she brushed by her office door, before turning off the light, she stopped short. A puzzled expression came over her face. Her typewriter was missing. She started searching for it under the desk.

"That's strange," she muttered to herself. She hesitated as if not knowing what to do. She looked around the room, then down at her watch. "I wonder where I put it," she said out loud, clicking the switch by the door, the bulb dying.

Outside she started her yellow Mazda. The engine turned over the third time, and as she waited for the car to warm, she pulled the rearview over and scrutinized how she had applied her makeup. She looked bored and sat for a moment in the fading light with a sour expression on her face.

Her mind raced back to the night Cary had seen her lifting weights with Ray Gluckner. She had been frantic enough when two students from her math class had been murdered. Now Gluckner.

She resented that as soon as she had began to touch the boys, something terrible happened. No sooner did she taste their young lips than they were murdered. She felt cursed. She woke in the middle of the night from unsettling dreams where raging fires tore the boys' faces away from her hungry mouth. In the early hours, she wondered if she hadn't killed the boys herself. Her skin would begin to burn as she heard steel cylinders sliding onto barbells in her mind—the hard breaths coming out of the boys' chests as they lifted her weights—then turned their breaths to her.

No coincidence could cause three of her math students to die as soon as she had taken them. She was terrified to think that she might have caused their deaths. The guilt was staggering. She had even gone into therapy.

She kept racking her brain, wondering if it was fate. At the school in Canada, when she first began teaching, she was only a few years older than the students she took home. Now, even though she looked young, she was usually fifteen years older than the boys she seduced. Yet that made it all the more exciting. She had been especially close to Gluckner. He was one of the few boys strong enough to handle her. She had discovered an almost uncontrollable desire for the rough talk, the hard muscles that pinched the breath out of her. His death had quietly shattered her.

She put her car in gear. This would be her third session, she thought. She had already decided she would tell the doctor tonight, at the end, that she wasn't coming back. She pulled the Mazda out of the driveway at South End.

She gunned her car so it climbed the grade to Academy, turned left on High Street. She parked, pulled the key out of the ignition, grabbed her purse before slamming the car door. She trotted along the sidewalk, up a walkway to a front door. A man with clear pink glasses, his hair cut close to his skull, opened the door and admitted her.

The tall figure in the cloak came out of the woods behind Dr. Clarence's house. He walked around the house, crept up the flagstone steps, his shoes nearly silent. He snuck along the deck to a window from which a ribbon of light was emanating. He put his eye to the glass and through a break in the curtain saw a strange sight inside. Ms. Coates was sitting in an easy chair with a blank expression, staring into space. The man with the pink glasses was bent over behind her, talking softly into her ear, so softly the figure couldn't hear him. He placed his ear against the glass to hear better.

For a time, he wondered what it would be like to be just a boy, seeing the doctor bending over the woman through the windowpane. As the light fell across the pupils of the figure's eyes, that thought seemed to take possession of him. He wouldn't have to imagine for long. He would soon *be* that young schoolboy standing there, feeling vulnerable, without a care, yet yearning to be part of what was inside, not knowing what was inside, looking for a way to be. Changing.

He walked swiftly along the deck, around the side of the house, opened the back door, closing it again silently. He walked into the room where the doctor was still talking softly to Ms. Coates. The doctor didn't move when the figure came into the room. He glanced over once, but kept talking in subdued, velvety tones. The figure walked up to the window and looked out for a moment. Then he drew the curtains back together.

"Is she ready?" he murmured.

"Shhh!"

The figure turned to stare at the doctor. The eyes above the scarf betrayed a deep annoyance at this outburst. He let his pupils rest contemptuously on the doctor, who was still speaking softly to Ms. Coates.

"When I clap my hands," Dr. Clarence said softly in Ms. Coates's ear, "you will do exactly as I say. Ready?"

He clapped his hands. Immediately Ms. Coates sat up alertly, her spine as straight as a board. The figure sighed impatiently and walked across the room, his back against the mantel of the fireplace, staring at them. He watched the doctor pull on a pair of surgical gloves, tediously pressing the latex down around each finger.

Dr. Clarence carefully placed a small writing table in front of her. He then pulled a portable typewriter out from behind the couch, opened it on the table in front of her, and plugged it in.

"Now," he said to Ms. Coates. "As you can see, this is your own typewriter. Turn the machine on." She did. "You will type exactly what I tell you to." The woman placed her finger on the keys.

"I, Ms. Coates . . ." She began to type.

" . . . did willfully help Cary Ballard murder three students . . ." Ms. Coates stopped typing.

Dr. Clarence bent over her. "I realize you didn't really murder them, Ms. Coates. Remember this is an exercise to help you get rid of the guilt, the tortured feeling of having been involved with these boys, that's all; if you understand, nod your head." She did.

"All right," Dr. Clarence continued, "begin typing again." She placed her fingers on the keys.

" . . . murder three students . . . enrolled at Ravenhill School. The three boys . . . named Crawford, Finkelstein, and Gluckner . . . had become very annoying—what's the matter?" Ms. Coates had stopped typing again.

"I loved him . . ." There was a mournful expression on her face.

Dr. Clarence's voice was sharp. "I'm waiting, Ms. Coates."

"What was it again?"

" . . . had become very annoying to us both."

Ms. Coates typed quickly across the parchment paper, her fingers unaware of any strain. She made a mistake. Dr. Clarence let her backspace and correct it, then continued.

"However, now I am filled with revulsion at my horrid acts . . . and have decided to take my own life."

Again Ms. Coates stopped typing. Dr. Clarence leaned over her, as if pouring poison into her ear. "I know you're not really going to kill yourself, Ms. Coates. This is a metaphor; you're killing off the part of you that feels guilty, don't you see? If you do, please nod your head."

She did.

"Now begin again . . . I leave young Mr. Ballard to his fate . . . but I can't live with myself any longer."

The doctor paused, gazing toward the tall figure standing at the fireplace, a strange smile wrinkling his small precise mouth.

"Signed, Ms. Coates . . . alias Arthur Murray." He paused and silently read the letter over her shoulder. "Now, shut off the machine." She did. "Now close your eyes and relax. You will not remember any of this. You are going to be taken home to sleep. To rest. Now . . . sleep . . . sleep." Ms. Coates's body seemed to go limp very slowly in the chair.

Dr. Clarence smiled. He took out a prescription bottle of pills, rolled it against her fingertips. Ms. Coates's hand numbly clasped it, then let go as she drifted deeper into hypnosis. He now set the prescription bottle on the table. There was a strange silence in the room. The doctor looked across at the cloaked figure as if waiting for him to approve, to say something. He didn't. He just stared contemptuously at him. Dr. Clarence began to fidget. He walked across the room to stand next to the figure, his thin body wrenched slightly to one side as if embarrassed.

"All you need to do now is sign it."

The figure reached into his cloak and pulled out some lipstick. He twisted the bottom and a dark pink stick twirled into sight. He placed the lipstick in his left hand and walked over toward the letter Ms. Coates had typed. He stood poised over her for a long time, breathing heavily, his back to Dr. Clarence. The doctor started to become edgy. The huge form just stood there over her, swaying, beginning to speak.

"I loved you. And you betrayed me. You rejected me when I needed you most. At a time when no other woman, ever, had been good to me—you gave me trust, then you took it away. I'll never be the same."

Dr. Clarence began twisting his hand unconsciously. "Not now."

The figure kept his frenzied eyes fixed on Ms. Coates. "You shouldn't have done that."

"You'll get worked up."

The man looked down at the woman, bent down closer to her, whispering, beginning sadly to touch her face. "There was a brief moment when the light was changing around me." The words seemed to pour out of his mouth. "The days were getting brighter. I actually thought I could have a life, that all these things in my head would go away. But then you violated me, you slept with . . . children . . . with my students . . . with other men, no doubt."

The doctor moved silently toward him. "This is not the time for this."

The figure was still fixed on Ms. Coates. "How many other men?"

The doctor touched his sleeve. "Don't think about that. Say goodbye to her."

The figure reached down and shook Ms. Coates. "How many?"

Dr. Clarence wrenched the man's hands away, whispering in his ear, "Her reward is in that bottle of pills. Release her. Then you'll be *free*. This is no time for anger."

The cloaked man turned around to face Dr. Clarence. "I've changed my mind. I want her to see me as I am."

The doctor's restless pupils darted from one of the man's freakish eyes to the other, then froze, arrested by a foreboding. "No. No. Everything has been prepared."

"You have to be more flexible, Doctor."

"You're going to ruin it!"

"Wake her up."

Dr. Clarence began to blink repeatedly. "Now you listen to me. I've been against any violence from the beginning. I will not—"

"What violence? This is a gift."

Clarence backed up almost imperceptively. "You said—"

"I'm going through a transformation. My psyche longs to let go, you said that yourself."

"Of course you twist what I say, but don't you dare attribute these unspeakable acts to me!"

The figure leaned toward him, cloak spreading. "I thought you were supportive of my change."

"Yes, I am, but the horror later, the—"

"You didn't like it?"

"I did, but . . . I can't. I won't."

The figure capped the lipstick, dropped it in his pocket. "Wake her up."

"No, please," the doctor said, his face now puffing up, filling with dread. "We worked this all out. You said—"

"What did you say to me?"

"Wh—?"

"*You said 'shhh' to me before!*" The voice thundered out of the tall man.

"I'm sorry," the doctor began to stammer nervously, backing away from him. "I had no right to do that—you must have felt attacked, terribly dismissed. I was wrong. I'm sorry."

This seemed to satisfy the figure, who looked down at Ms. Coates, her carriage still untroubled, her eyes still closed. "Now."

The doctor hesitated. "Of course, you decide, after all, you're the great, the only Arthur Murray. The brilliant tactician behind this, but . . . if I might just mention . . ."

"What?"

"We decided that you should no longer dance. That it was too risky."

The figure suddenly towered over the doctor. "What did I tell you?"

As if by will, the doctor curbed his trembling. "That you were changing form, and your new embodiment would . . . decide everything . . . even our fates."

"That's very good, Nathan." The man turned, tore the scarf off a hideous white clown face, monstrous red lips painted on. The cloak whipped open and flew across the room. Standing there was a giant schoolboy, buckle-down shoes, knee-high socks, round-collar shirt, bow-string tie, and satchel of books. His eyes fell on Ms. Coates. "Now, wake her up."

Dr. Clarence rubbed his face feverishly, managing to still himself. He stumbled over to Ms. Coates, bent down, and whispered in her ear. "When I clap my hands, you will wake up and remember nothing of what has happened here."

He clapped his hands.

Her eyes fluttered open. She smiled at the doctor, who blanched, backing away from her, his anxious eyes flying toward the strange figure in front of her.

The schoolboy loomed over Ms. Coates. She looked up, startled, not understanding, as this strange tall boy above her smiled, his clown lips spreading across his white face. He seemed shy, embarrassed.

Her mouth parted gently, in slow recognition. "Is that you?"

"Yes," he said.

"What are you doing here?"

"Can you hear the voices?"

Her troubled eyes fell on the doctor, still backing away. "What's going on?"

Dr. Clarence shrugged. "I couldn't stop him."

She sat up in the chair. "You couldn't—"

"He insisted on speaking to you. I'm sorry," the doctor murmured, then walked out of the room.

A panicked look, an escalating dread was strewn across her features. She looked up to face the boy. "Well, it's nice to see you."

He just stood there, eyes distorted, swaying. "Is it?"

Nervous. "You're looking—fine."

"Can you hear what the voices want me to do?"

"Why are you dressed like that?"

Tears started running down the boy's face, leaving tracks across the white makeup. "I dressed for you."

"What?"

"You like boys, don't you?"

Her skin turned visibly pallid, lines of sweat appearing across her forehead. "Look, dear, we were married a long time ago. You and I were never meant for each other, you know that."

"I loved you."

Waving him off, a jittery glance. "Oh, you did not." She attempted a laugh, looking around the room.

"I worshipped you, wanted to protect you."

She went silent, staring up at the dangerous man—a man she once loved—standing there dressed like Buster Brown. "Look, I have to be going." She leaned forward.

"I have something to tell you."

Standing up. "I'm sorry, I have to go."

"Sit down!" The voice was deep, stern.

She swallowed. "All right." A placating tone, as she sat. It only made it worse.

"I took care of your boys."

"*My* boys?" A slow terror coming into her eyes.

He looked at her and shook his head. "I've come full circle now. You are the cause."

Very agitated, rubbing the back of her neck repeatedly. "The cause of—what?"

"The voices say you failed me—they're rising, falling—they're in the room now, they're—"

"What did you mean—took care of what?"

"You know."

"No . . ."

A silence . . . then his eerie voice. "I absorbed them."

She started crying silently, her shoulders bending forward. "*You* did it?"

"I wanted to be the only boy in your life."

She jumped out of the chair, the horror finally hitting her. "You monster, you—"

"I did it for you."

"Don't say that! I had nothing to do with this!"

"You betrayed me."

"Well, of course! You're less of a man than those boys were."

Now the room was full of silence. She saw the rage in his face, the clown features distorted—then the strange smile. She picked up her purse, moved tensely toward the door.

He blocked her. "Kiss me."

She put her face in her hands. "Those boys were beautiful!"

He slowly raised the knife into the air. "No, *this* is beautiful! *You're* the reason I started, *do you understand*? My reason for becoming."

She was backing up now in terror, her mouth opening, nothing coming out. "N—n—no." A shriek. "NO!"

"The *reason* I came into being."

Her eyes flew up to the hand that was holding the knife. It all became clear. She leapt across the room, screaming.

In one hand he grabbed a tuft of hair as the screams continued. Then the knife flashed through the room. It fell, as if from a great height, the cold steel streaking the air. The flawless mouth and long lashes and stylish hair were left untouched. The freckles under the makeup on her cheekbones were still shining, evanescent, as the terrible gagging began and her arms thrashed the air. For a few brief seconds, her lashes rose and she glanced up at him, through a hypnotic haze, the blood seeping through fingers tearing at her throat. Her eyes searched his face savagely, until the blue pupils began to plead, then gradually went empty, a vacuous clarity filling them, until, almost drained of color, the irises fixed on the void.

51

LET ME KISS you . . . your lips so soft, still warm . . . never mind the blood . . . let me smell your skin, your soft ripe sweet perfectly moist—even though you're dead—skin . . . are you listening? . . . finally listening to me? CAN YOU HEAR ME?

I didn't think so.

Now scissors . . . what to take . . . of course, the brassiere . . . let's see. On her side . . . now unbutton the dress, easy, there, pull the halter down around her shoulders, don't wrinkle, goddamnit! . . . Oh, red lace . . . that's nice, so nice . . . God, how can I, what can I, where . . . now, be calm . . . reach behind, unsnap, unsnnnn-naaaaaaap it, yes. Lift the cups off . . . Oh. Oh. Let me just, please just once, let me. Yes.

NO, NO, NO, NO PLEASE, quiet the voices, just this once leave me alone, please leave me—JUST—

Fine. Pick her up, where? Here, out the back door, fast, doesn't matter, he's gone, out the back, now—leave it unlocked. Where do I take her? . . . here, outside, just run, doesn't matter, no place to take her, run, carry her, run, watch out for the branch, crash through leaves, branches cut, doesn't matter, just carry her through the woods, find a place for her . . . prickers, thistles, thorns, keep going, her hair swaying, feel the mist, it's wet, moist like her, wet leaves, twigs, sounds, voices, owls, doves, crickets. Keep going, find a place, must be a place, some way to show the world, branches cutting my back, now see—these branches don't hurt, do they? . . . they're soft, feel the branches, feel the night, leave your smell in these dark woods, these soft . . . quiet . . . terrible . . . cold . . . where to take you. . .

CAN YOU KISS ME NOW?

I didn't think so.

NATHAN CLARENCE WAS on his knees, mopping up the swirls of blood on the hardwood floor. He had watched hopelessly as the boy had grasped the woman's lifeless body, flailing it around the room. There was no attempt to dance actual steps; the turns, the dips, the sways, had all come out of a kind of rage he had never seen before, the hands clutching the inanimate limbs, the boy's lips kissing the dead woman's face with fury.

He washed and rewashed the blond wooden planks until all the dried red splatters were gone. He scrubbed the wall with cold water until he was sure the stains were out. He looked over at Ms. Coates's body lying peacefully on a piece of plastic he had dragged in from the garage. She was lying with her arms at her side, while the boy lay drenched in the corner, his face hidden.

When Nathan Clarence had finally washed everything he could think of, he burned the letter. He wiped all the doorknobs, the wooden handles of the chair she had sat in. He drove Ms. Coates's car out in the middle of a fairway on the school golf course, the typewriter in the backseat, the purse on the passenger seat; he then walked back through the playing fields—in the dark—all without being seen.

When he got back, he found the boy had done a bad thing—he'd taken her body and hidden her in the woods, behind the doctor's house. They had to go with flashlights to find her, and there she was, lying in the leaves. They had to bring her back inside and discuss where she should go.

The tall boy finally cleaned up, washed the blood from his body, and wrapped the figure's clothing over his schoolboy's uniform. He put the scarf back on and was lying on the couch now, his eyes raking the ceiling plaster. The doctor stood over him, not knowing what state of mind he was in. "We have to put that body somewhere," he insisted.

He saw breaths deflating the scarf on the figure's face as he sucked them back through a cavity that appeared through the black material.

"We'll find a place."

Dr. Clarence took his pad and pen and pulled a chair up next to the couch, crossed his legs and looked over at the feverish eyes. "Tell me."

The stranger pulled the scarf away from his lips. "It was . . . more poetic this time. When the knife went in"—he adjusted his body on the couch—"her skin was like paper, the kind I used to cut up as a kid, workshop paper, that made that crisp sound when the scissors—"

"What happened with Gluckner?"

"What?"

"Why did you disembowel him?"

There was a long tense silence in the room. "Why are you asking that *now*?"

"I'm interested."

The stranger glued his crazed eyes to the ceiling. "Would that turn you on?"

"Should it?"

The stranger turned toward the doctor. "You don't want to hear about a woman's flesh?"

The man in the chair stiffened. "We missed our session on the last boy."

"Of course you'd prefer a boy." There was a caustic tone in his voice.

"No, I'd rather hear about someone *else*, actually."

"Look, I always tell you what I did, and THEN YOU TELL ME—"

"Like *all* your promises."

"What?"

The doctor put down his pad. "I sense you have completed the guilt and punishment you have directed at yourself all these years. I believe you have resolved the issue."

"Resolved?"

"With the boys. Now I see, intuitively, you've moved on to other concerns: your mother . . . more work to do there, of course, but I think you should tackle the biggy."

"WHAT?"

"You know who I mean."

A tense pause in the room. The figure's forehead reddened beneath the makeup. "Not *him*?"

"Yes, him. You said he had a studio?"

The stranger rolled his head back and forth. "Not now."

"I gave you Ms. Coates, now it's your turn to give *me* something."

The doctor watched the hands of his watch click around. The man on the couch kept distressing an area of flesh between his eyebrows. He lay there silently, jiggling his feet uncontrollably.

After several minutes, he took a deep breath. "It all started because of the gloves."

"What about them?"

"I didn't want to wear them."

"He made you?"

"I didn't care that my mother wouldn't—that she couldn't—"

"Couldn't what?"

"Do it with him."

The doctor trembled. "She couldn't do *what* with your father?"

"You know."

"No I don't."

"She said it depressed her."

"Why did it depress her?"

"It reminded her of when she . . . was young."

"So *you* had to take her place?"

"Yes."

The doctor paused, carefully, said, "What was it you had to do?"

"Wear white gloves."

"And?"

"You know."

The doctor's breathing began to quicken. "What did 'doing it' remind you of?"

"How much I hated his studio, hated the people there—the way they smiled at me in the mirrors."

"What way did they smile?"

"Smug, self-satisfied smiles, as if I was such a good little boy."

"Were you?"

"Yes. OH YES."

"Why did they smile at you?"

The figure rolled his head. "Because I had to demonstrate every . . . single godforsaken . . ."

"Say it."

"As if I . . ."

Dr. Clarence licked his lips. "Go ahead, say it."

"As if I was *her*."

"In front of his classes, yes?"

"Yes."

"How did that make you feel?"

"I didn't feel anything. I couldn't feel my feet. My hands. No breath coming out."

"You just put on the white gloves and you . . . ?"

The figure paused. "Yes. I danced with him."

The doctor dropped his pad and pen on the floor. "With your father."

"The Waltz, the Swing, the Fox-trot . . . all the ballroom dances."

"The Rumba?"

"Do you know it?"

"*No.*" The doctor rocked back. "*No, I don't dance.* I—I—"

"I had to do the Bolero Break, the Varsoviana, Tuck and Spin, the Dishrag."

Dr. Clarence's neck began to twist over the back of the chair. "So you made your victims . . . do it?"

"I even made them lead."

Dr. Clarence was leaning back in his chair, beginning to swoon. "No more," he said almost inaudibly. "Don't. Please."

"I made them dance the way I had to."

"The whole time."

"What?"

Dr. Clarence was mewling, rocking his head back and forth. A small rivulet of spittle draining from his mouth had attached itself to a button on his shirt. His eyes had disappeared up under his lids. "The whole time . . . you were killing yourself!"

The stranger frowned. "No, I was showing those boys how—I was demonstrating how I—I—" He gave a quiver.

"You killed them because . . . because . . ."

"The way their strung limbs beat the air. It was beautiful. Kind of like a moth at night—when it lands on a light bulb, you can almost see through its body—that's the way those boys were. I could almost see the blood inside them stop moving, start to congeal, the organs going into failure one by one . . ."

"Like you!"

"What?"

"You made them feel what you felt!"

"NO!"

"And your mother." Dr. Clarence's legs were each coiled around a leg of the chair, his neck swelled out, his pelvis arched into the air. "You've killed her now."

"She had nothing to do with this."

"She betrayed you." His legs were vibrating as his body arched into the air. "Just like Ms. Coates."

"What do you mean?"

"What other women betrayed you? Ohhhh!"

"I don't know—I . . ."

"It's so . . . Freudian! Oh! Oh!" The doctor's back seemed to vault toward the ceiling as he began to achieve orgasm. His hips and thighs shuddered, his head fell back over the chair, rolling wildly, as he screamed. "Ahhhh!" Then he pitched back and forth quietly in the chair for a long time, singing softly.

It was a lullaby.

AN HOUR LATER, the figure was staring through the same thin break in the curtain, lost in thought. The lights were low. Nathan Clarence was behind him, nuzzling him like a newborn calf, prodding his back with his shoulders. He pulled at the edge of the black scarf, blowing on the black hairs along the tall man's neck. "Come on, Masked Man."

"Leave it alone."

Nathan whispered in his ear. "You promised."

The figure pulled away solemnly and once more walked to the other side of the room. Dr. Clarence followed him around the room, gesturing, beseeching him to pay attention, reaching out to touch his arm. The figure continued to pull away with indignation. "I can't," he finally said flatly.

"Then why did I help you? These murders were useless to me."

He looked at the doctor. "How about a useful one?"

"Why can't we make love?"

"I thought I could, but . . . I'm changing now . . ."

"I'm changing too. For you."

The man shook his head. "Not now."

The doctor touched a brass lamp that was by the couch. He was talking again to the man's back. "Well when?"

"I don't know. Soon."

"You keep saying that, but you never—"

"Just try to be patient."

Dr. Clarence's stricken face turned and seemed to float out of the light as he walked to the other side of the room. "I'm nothing if not patient." He left the room.

The figure put on his hat and slipped out the side door onto the deck. He stood in the dark for a long time, gazing out over the town, thinking about the dance.

52

WHEN MS. COATES did not show up for class the next morning, all the students left when the clock ticked to the tenth minute after the hour. They piled out of the room and scattered down the halls, disrupting the other first-period classes. The voices of a few of them could be heard as they chased each other under the stone arch, the soles of their shoes slapping the cement. They threw books at each other, yelled at the top of their lungs.

In his office, the headmaster heard the students' voices and looked down at his watch. He had been startled out of a daze that followed the phone call. The call had come at nine A.M. sharp, just as he was sitting down.

Dr. Hickey limply stood up and opened the door to his office. He walked across the hall into the assistant's office. Mr. Allington's secretary was not in yet. The headmaster walked through the outer office, rapped on the door, and entered. Allington was seated at his desk, on the phone. When he saw Dr. Hickey enter, he rang off quickly and rose.

"That was the chairman. He told me."

Dr. Hickey moved gravely toward the window, not making eye contact with him. He seemed to be staring into the chrysanthemums outside the window. "The last straw was me being hospitalized. They lost confidence in me."

"I'm sorry, Brandon."

"Did Hungerford sound relieved when he called you?"

"No indeed, he was very sad."

Hickey turned to face Allington. "Are you sad?"

"For you, yes, of course."

"And for yourself?"

Allington paused. "Have you chosen a replacement?"

Dr. Hickey pulled his wrinkled hands out of his perennially

gray trousers, carefully adjusted the Windsor knot on his tie, and looked into Allington's eyes. His smile was ironic. "Well," he said, "I guess you've gotten your way after all."

He walked out of the room.

BY EIGHT O'CLOCK that evening, as people were turning off Main Street to park behind the Rotary Club, a rumor had spread through the dorms up on campus that Ms. Coates's car had been found on the golf course. Faculty members and friends of the math teacher tried to convince themselves she had been called away for some emergency.

Nick Fowler was standing across the street from the auditorium. He saw some students skulking around in the parking lot, smoking. He tried to manage a smile when he saw Maureen drive up. He was hardly surprised at how great she looked in her dress. Aquamarine with matching shoes; around her neck, a simple string of pearls. When she approached him, he took her hand, but he was nervous, on edge.

Nick had managed to get a fresh suit out of the cleaners. He had cut himself shaving and was on his second white shirt. They both noticed two police cars in the parking lot. He took Maureen aside. "Ms. Coates is missing."

"Oh no."

He unfolded a sheet of white paper from his breast pocket. "This poem was on a bathroom wall in one of the dorms. What do you make of it?"

Maureen was looking into his eyes as she took the sheet of paper in her hands. For a long moment, she couldn't look down.

ALGEBRA I

She presses weights and barbells—and such.
Because he hits her whenever she fucks.
The tar on her thumb,
The soot on her bum,
She can't appreciate living that much.

So then—she takes off all of her "Coates"
For boys on whose affection she dotes.
She opens her knees,
The greatest of ease,
Don't let him catch her sowing your oats.

Maureen looked up at him. "I don't know . . . 'tar on her thumb'?"

Nick was studying her face. "That's what struck me, 'tar,' 'soot.' Wonder what it means." He folded the poem into his pocket. They walked inside.

They stood in the corner of a large room decorated here and there with black and white art deco cutouts. They watched a few faculty members come in. They saw Mr. Pullen enter, bowing to several ladies who knew him. The little man made polite conversation, then awkwardly excused himself.

The ceiling was veiled in a canopy of red material, thematically correct; on a closer look, Fowler realized it was a parachute. The masking tape holding the black and white streamers to the walls disappeared when the lights went down. Mr. Pullen was making his way to the top of the bleachers in the dark when the band started to play.

Mr. Toby arrived in a flurry, preened his way across the dance floor, his courtly gestures becoming a parody of old-fashioned manners. His black hair was elegantly matted in a forties style. Mr. Carlson, the German teacher, who had seen the first victim in Ardsley, kept looking down at his cordovan wing tips—as if they had a life of their own. Mr. Curamus, the Latin teacher, managed to spill some punch on his suit; that seemed to baptize the evening as people became more relaxed and actually started to dance.

Nearly all the faculty came. There was an electricity in the air. People were standing around in groups, laughing or being dazzled by the professional dancers from New York City, elegantly attired, doing impeccable turns around the floor.

On the stage was an eight-piece band that played tunes from the forties. They started out the first set with "Tangerine" and ended it with "Midnight Serenade." People flooded the dance floor and began to pull out the old steps. The musicians themselves were old-timers and understood the music—getting quickly to its heart. The elegance of the ballroom dances were punctuated by swing tunes like Count Basie's "One O'clock Jump" and Duke Ellington's "Take the A Train." The floor was completely full when they picked up the tempo even more with Glen Miller's "In the Mood."

Finally Dr. Brandon Hickey and his wife arrived. The headmaster was dressed, to everyone's surprise, in a dark blue suit. He seemed serene. Right behind him was Elliot Allington, dressed casually in gray slacks and a blue blazer, as if he had appropriated the headmaster's uniform.

Fowler didn't see Nathan Clarence come in. At one point, he just noticed the man was on the dance floor, dressed in a white suit, jitterbugging with the librarian. Ms. Leach was already sweating, her armpits dispatching the aromatic warning that gave her whatever dancing room she needed. The doctor looked quite flashy.

Nick Fowler was dancing slowly with Maureen in the middle of the floor. His eyes were panning the room, reporting in her ear what he was seeing. He tried not to look at Mr. Pullen, hunched in the distance, not moving, a statue in a black polyester suit.

Nick held Maureen's hand loosely, his other hand on the small of her back. They were cheek to cheek.

"I'm exhausted," he said.

"You look tired."

"I don't see anything, do you?"

"No."

Fowler was staring at Mr. Toby, who had been dancing from the beginning, negotiating the steps discovered at every crime scene. He was whirling one of the masters' wives around, doing slip-aways, arch turns, pivots. He did the Charleston, the Polka.

"That guy's a regular encyclopedia of moves."

"Who?"

Fowler twirled her around so she could see. "The guy in the gray suit, what's his name, Astaire."

"Oh yeah. I saw him before. He's good."

In the other corner of the room, Fowler could see Dr. Brandon Hickey, after several more drinks, putting down some steps too.

"The old headmaster. Look." Again he turned her around.

"Not bad for an ancient."

Elliot Allington sat in the grandstand sipping punch. Finally Dr. Hickey's wife pulled him up with great ceremony. She maneuvered him behind several groups of people so that Fowler could see only his head and shoulders. Some time later, he was twirling Mrs. Hickey around the room. They were reckless and livened up the floor. At one point Fowler thought he saw Allington holding her hand as she bent down to pull up the strap on her shoe. She shook her hair out with an uncharacteristic abandon.

Maureen had already sat down. An hour had passed. Fowler was threading his way back to her from the bar. He was not wondering any longer who was a good dancer, but why nothing had transpired. He had the realization that this was too obvious a trap. Nothing would happen tonight.

When he reached Maureen and handed her a plastic cup with punch in it, he told her he had overheard a group of people at the buffet table asking how Ms. Coates—easily the most attractive woman on the faculty—could have missed this dance. One of the wives had even gone to the pay phone to call her, she told them, but there was no answer.

The band announced the last dance, a slow one called "Everything Happens to Me," and the lights were dimmed. Fowler looked around the room. He saw all the faculty members and town officials either dancing or sitting and suddenly felt that it was none of them. He looked from one person to the other, discouraged, and although he couldn't locate the doctor in his white suit—all his suspects looked remarkably tame.

In the middle of the last song, the lights abruptly came on as something tore through the parachute in the ceiling. It fell in slow motion, sending the red material ballooning back up into the ceiling, until the rope pulled instantly taut. At the end of the rope was the body of a woman, hung by her ankles still jerking up and down. She was wearing a fitted purple dress now bunched down around her thighs. Her arms were frozen rigidly above her head with 45 rpm records glued between her fingers. Her throat had been cut.

The entire room went silent. People stood where they were, mute, in shock, until the grotesque features of the hanging woman sent a roll of panic across the room. Here and there people began to scream. Then a chorus of screams. Women and men alike got sick and fainted. In the course of a minute or two, the entire room was in pandemonium. People were rushing to get out of the door, others were crying, some were in hysterics; people who had been close to Ms. Coates were calling out to the heavens, shrieking above the chaos.

Fowler fought his way to the body, saw that it was the math teacher, grabbed one faculty member and demanded that he run outside and get the police. He stood at eye level with the corpse, now dangling at the end of the rope; he reached a hand up to stop it from swinging. He looked into her face, overwhelmed with remorse that he could have prevented this. He made himself look at her. Now the victim was a woman, he thought. He glanced around the room. Mr. Toby's petrified face was staring at him.

Fowler looked back at the body. His eyes welled up. Ms. Coates's features were hideously distorted in death. He closed his eyes, shaking his head repeatedly.

Elliot Allington's voice came over the loudspeaker. He was up on the bandstand, speaking into the microphone in front of the stunned band, trying to quiet people down.

"Ladies and gentlemen, please . . . faculty members, please be calm, I beg you. I'm told the police will be here presently. Just, if you can . . . get a hold of—" There were more screams from the floor. "Please everyone? . . . Just . . . everyone? . . . Please leave quietly. We're sorry. This is a terrible tragedy. Please just drive safely. Please . . . be careful."

Fowler had his hand on Ms. Coates's shoulder as if comforting her when Captain Allen Weathers walked through the gym doors and strode over to him. The burly man couldn't believe what he was seeing.

"Fowler, what the fuck are you doing here?"

"Never mind what I'm doing here."

"I thought I told you to stay away."

"I tried."

"You make trouble wherever you go."

"The trouble was already here, Allen."

"I'm beginning to think *you're* the trouble."

Fowler was in no mood. "Tell that to her."

He stepped out of the way and Ms. Coates's body swayed toward the captain.

53

AN HOUR AND a half later, red lights were still flashing against the storefronts beside the Rotary Club. Fowler was pacing, watching the façades on the street blinking on and off, when he saw Bill Rodney coming out of the same side door of the auditorium that the crime unit was using. He ran up to him.

"Bill, what's up?"

Rodney's old leathery face looked startled, worse for wear. He glanced over his shoulder nervously. "Let's talk over here." They walked around a line of police vehicles sitting out in the parking lot.

"He's on the rampage," Rodney said.

"Weathers?"

"Yeah. Tech services is almost finished. The woman has been dead over twenty-four hours, we think. She was dragged through the freakin' woods. They found crushed leaves in her hair, bits of moss. Seems the crew had the parachute up for a day or so. Somebody strung her up there and tied off a rope that fed down into the squash court next door. Whoever killed her just walked into the next court, untied the rope, retied the end and let her fall thirty-five feet. Then he flicked on the lights."

"The lights went on just before."

"Couldn't have."

"I was there, Bill."

"But the switches are on the other side of the gym, pal."

Fowler was thinking. "Then we have two people. The lights may have been the signal to let the body go."

Rodney looked away. "Hmph," he grunted, and pulled out a cigarette.

Fowler watched him strike a match. "Do you mind?" he said, reaching for his pack.

Rodney looked at him in surprise. "You smoke?"

Fowler lit the cigarette and blew the smoke out. "No."

"Neither do I."

"Anything on the background checks?"

"We're trying," said Rodney, "but it's a logistical nightmare."

"Let me help you. Get me to the computers in the station house."

The old detective looked at him out of the corner of his eye, almost laughing. "You got to be kidding. Tonight that place'll be a madhouse."

"Tomorrow?"

"Look, I'll try. Can't promise anything."

Fowler's head felt dizzy when he took another drag. "I want to do a search according to theme. A serial killer who goes after young boys . . . now a woman. I want to check field reports, autopsies. These aren't the first murders. This person is seasoned."

"I'm sure they've already done that, Fowler."

"I also want to check DMVs for past addresses. I'm going to match those against personal files from school administration."

"We've already subpoenaed the school records. They're tied up in litigation."

Nick paused, staring intently at Rodney. He looked at the pavement. "I'll have to get around that."

Rodney pulled on the cigarette uneasily, and as he blew the smoke up, it turned red in the flashing lights. "Why do you think he murdered this one, Nick?"

Fowler looked up at the building, shaking his head. "Not sure. Some kind of hate . . . some passion . . ."

"Though the way he displayed her was too calculated."

"Maybe to conceal the real place of death?"

Rodney looked at him. "That's what I think."

ONE THING FOWLER realized, driving up into the campus, was that Cary Ballard was still at the juvenile detention center awaiting trial. Nick had made sure Maureen kept any news of his detention out of her paper. At least the boy couldn't be blamed for this one.

Nick parked his car in back of the school kitchen. He tried all the windows on the ground floor of Ardsley Hall. He had to get into the administrative offices, which dominated the floor, and tonight with everyone too frightened to come out, there would be little foot traffic. He checked the grates to all the basement windows and found one loose. He rattled it until he was able to unscrew the bolts with his pocketknife. With the butt of his .38, he tapped a windowpane through, then listened to the glass sprinkle the cement floor inside. He reached in and unlatched the window. After he crawled in, he jumped to the floor below.

He caught sight of a figure moving against a far wall. Nick shifted between steel columns, breathing hard. He watched as a shadow crept on all fours toward a door that had a crack of light underneath it. Fowler rushed to the next column, aimed his gun, and shone the flashlight on the figure. It broke into a run.

Fowler yelled, "Freeze!" His voice echoed off the walls. He saw a flash of brown trousers, heard shoes sliding as he ran toward the figure.

The light revealed a small man wearing a khaki uniform. His two front teeth were missing. He was flattened against the wall, sweating, eyes senseless with fear.

"Who are you?" Nick pointed the beam onto the floor.

The cracked, nervous voice said, "Stanley. I work the graveyard shift here and over on the boilers at the power plant.

"Do you have any identification?"

"Yeah." The shaky hands pulled out an old tattered wallet. Fowler looked at it quickly under the flashbulb. He handed it back to him.

"Didn't mean to scare you."

"I thought you was that killer." A line of spit issued from his teeth.

"Do you know who I am?"

"You're that lieutenant fella."

"Right. Sort of. Look, could you help me out?"

"What?"

"I'm still investigating these murders, and I need to get into the administrative offices and have a look at the faculty files. Now, what I'm doing is important, but it's technically illegal because the lawyers for the school won't release these records."

"Anything against lawyers, I'll do it. They've ruined this damn country."

Nick smiled. "Can you get me upstairs?"

"Sure, have keys to all the offices. Them sons of bitches have a double-locked door to the basement anyway. You would have had a hell of a time. Probably would have ended up in the tunnels."

"Stanley, you're a lifesaver."

Upstairs, the little wombat ambled back down the hallway as Nick drew the blinds in the administrative offices. He had targeted seven files. The personnel records were locked up. After a long search through all the drawers, books, the secretary's desk, he finally found the file keys at the bottom of a brown monogrammed pencil cup that matched the desk blotter.

He studied the files with his flashlight for quite a while, spread the manila folders down on the carpet. He had it narrowed down to three people. He was leaving when he noticed the smudge on the carpet. He knelt down, holding a dab to his nostrils. No doubt about it: tar.

THE GREEN COMPACT pulled across the strip, rambled soundlessly around the Grotto, parking in back of the pink motel. The figure behind the wheel got out, carrying a large suitcase. He walked around the building, rapped on the door of the room at the end. The door opened.

Dr. Nathan Clarence was standing there, still in his white suit, a cheerless look on his face. A champagne bucket was sweating on a black-veneer table. He stared incredulously.

"Where have you been?"

"Shh," the deep voice reverberated around the room. "I brought something for you." He closed the door.

Dr. Clarence was nervously adjusting his tie, trying to pull the lapels of his suit jacket down as if it didn't fit. "I've been waiting and waiting..."

The figure gestured around. "Is this okay for our first time?"

The doctor gave a brief, jaundiced glance around the room. "It's enchanting."

"Have to start somewhere." The man thrashed at the cloak, which floated down onto the shag carpet. The scarf was lifted. A schoolboy smiled now at the doctor, the white face with the clown lips becoming more distorted each time he saw it.

The doctor seemed discouraged. "Did you have to—?"

"What?"

"Can't you be yourself?"

"This is me."

Dr. Clarence's face was solemn. "All right, fine."

"You don't like it?"

"Yes, yes—of course, but—I've been waiting so long, frankly, I won't believe it until it happens."

The schoolboy excitedly touched the doctor's wrist. "I've found a way to keep my relationship with *her*."

The doctor sighed impatiently. "She's dead, don't you understand? We've been over this."

"She's not dead, she's coming back."

"You killed her."

"*You're* going to bring her back for me."

"Look." The doctor inhaled, trying to calm himself. "Killing your ex-wife made you feel a primal loneliness, as if you'd killed your own mother—or wished you had—I don't know."

"She was good to me."

"You're being maudlin. Ms. Coates hurt you."

The schoolboy's lips were curled down, then just as quickly, his face seemed hopeful. He lifted the suitcase onto the bed. He snapped open the clasp, drew out a wig of curls, high heels, a makeup bag, and a woman's dress. He held the dress up in the light. There was an adolescent eagerness in his movements. "Would you be her?"

Dr. Clarence stared at the boy as if he'd asked a preposterous question. "No."

The boy looked sad. "Why not?"

Dr. Clarence was clearly at wit's end. "You work that out in *session*, don't you understand? This is something else. This is *fun*."

The boy stared at him, achingly, the white face twisted with regret. "Fun?"

The doctor was suddenly touched. "What about that woman you were involved with before, the boy's mother."

The clown face looked even sadder. "That was a long time ago."

The doctor knew he could influence the boy. "She could dress up for you, I'm sure she could. You liked her. Reach out to her."

The boy was no longer miming a pitiful face; instead, his eyes were contemplating something, envisioning possibilities. The same eyes ascended slowly through the congested air of the motel room to behold the doctor, who was smiling with his usual contempt.

The clown didn't have anything else to say.

OUTSIDE THE THIRSTY Moose, Fowler stood at the pay phone, dialing, looking up at the sky. In the back of his mind, he tried to make connections: the files, the tar, the poem about Ms. Coates. He wondered if Maureen, who had sped off to write the story for the morning edition, might be finished yet. The sky was dark and hazy. The air was close. Mr. Pullen's phone was ringing. A high-pitched voice came on the line.

"Yes?"

"Mr. Pullen, it's Nick Fowler."

"Oh." A chill in his tone.

"Look, under the circumstances, I'm sure you're not in the mood to comment."

"Oh for God's sake—yes—that's correct."

"I'm sorry you had to see that."

"I have never been so disgusted in my life."

Fowler didn't know what to say. "It's terribly sad."

"What a travesty. I can't believe I'm involved in this."

"Mr. Pullen, they think Ms. Coates had been killed long before the dance."

"Well, I don't have much to say. Aside from the pros they brought in, Mr. Toby certainly was the best dancer there."

"I could see that myself, Mr. Pullen."

"The headmaster wasn't bad himself; I remember at the Jubilee he was quite nimble. Now he's a little stiff. What a ghastly business."

"Anything unusual you noticed, Mr. Pullen, anything at all?"

"I'm afraid not."

"Well." Nick paused, looking again at the sky. "Thank you for your help." He started to hang up.

The high voice stuttered. "Th—th—the only thing that puzzled me was one man, I can't remember his name. He just seemed so unsure of himself."

"A lot of the men were."

"But this man was the most naturally talented, most adept, most graceful dancer I had ever coached. Now he has two left feet."

Fowler's breath quickened in his chest. "Could you describe him for me?"

NICK PULLED THE car up to the Grotto. He felt strangely nervous. He turned off the car and just sat there, letting the quiet soak into his racing thoughts. He could hear cars going by in the dark. He weighed what Mr. Pullen had just told him. It fit with what he had found in the files.

He could make the arrest tonight.

He got out of the car. He stepped over to his motel door, unlocked it, and when he pushed on the doorknob, again he smelled the strange aromatic perfume. He turned on the light, and there on the floor, in front of him, was a purple envelope.

He opened it.

Dear F,
    Well, how did you like my girl? Wasn't she stunning?
    Bet you think yours is nicer.
    Too bad we always hurt the ones we love.
    Fondly,
    Arthur Murray

    P.S. Meet me tonight. I'm in room two-oh-one, down at the end.

Nick shone his light in the window of room 201. The curtain was drawn. He listened for a long time. He pulled his gun, tried the doorknob. It turned. The door clicked open, a fetid smell drifting out. He swung the door open, the gun pointing into the room. The streetlight from the parking lot was dim at this end of the building. The room appeared to be empty. Nick shone his light in the room. Nothing. He stepped inside. Dead silence.

The door slammed behind him.

At the same moment a hand whacked the gun to the floor at his feet. A fist knocked the flashlight out of his hand, driving it against the wall, the light blinking out. He felt strong hands behind him clutch his neck, fingers crushing his windpipe. He couldn't get his hands under in time, was blacking out, legs buckling—he threw his head backward and banged it against another skull, saw stars—but the hands fell away. He threw himself to the carpet, waiting. He heard nothing, no breaths. He found the gun in the dark.

Then the door flew open, a shape coming at him from behind the door, a white thing, its arms raised. Fowler fired, emptying the gun. The body fell on top of him, knocking him to the floor of the room. He could smell blood and gunpowder, felt a slight residue on his hands. It had happened so fast. He saw another figure burst through the doorway, heard footsteps retreating.

He slid himself from under the body, located the flashlight, but the bulb was broken. He reached in his pocket, found Rodney's matches. He struck one.

He rolled the body over—saw pink glasses, a nearly shaved head. The match closer. Dr. Clarence with six bullet wounds in his face and chest.

54

CAPTAIN WEATHERS WAS bustling down a thin hallway, a small entourage of uniformed policemen at his heels, one gaunt plainclothes tech in stride with him, sidestepping, talking rapidly in his ear.

"We turned the room upside down, Cap, not a single goddamned print, except from the corpse. But we did recover some threads from clothing, a few hairs down at the lab already—back in a day—

yielding blood type, other factors, who knows? . . . Fragments of tar on the rug: We're checking the composition, what else . . . uh . . ."

Weathers stopped outside a door, staring at the tech. "I want that room locked up tighter than a ram's ass."

"Oh yeah, some different carpet fibers we're checking out . . . and makeup."

"Makeup?"

"Yeah, that white face stuff circus clowns use . . . the real article too—it's kind of cream-based—"

"All right, all right. Put the report on my desk." He opened the door and stepped out of the hallway into an interrogation room, slammed the door.

Fowler was seated in a straight-back chair in the middle of the small room. There was a strong wooden table, concrete walls, reinforced doors, a square hole cut into the wall with black Plexiglas set into it.

Robby Cole was leaning over him. "I didn't hear you."

Silence. Nick didn't respond.

"I said, did you kill him?"

"I fired my gun, yes."

"So, you *did* kill him."

"Not necessarily."

Cole hit him hard across the head with the heel of his hand. Fowler slumped forward, his face coming up with furious eyes.

"You lay another hand on me, I'll take that arm off."

"You gonna kill me? You're good at that."

Weathers restrained a smile. "All right, come on, Sergeant, relax." There was a pause in the room. "So let me get this straight," he said, facing Fowler. "You broke into this motel room . . . how'd you break in?"

"The door was open, Allen. Come on, the killer is out there right now while you're—"

"Shut up," said Weathers.

"Sure, I'll shut up."

"Yes you will," said Cole. "Believe me, you will."

"Whatever you say."

Cole's blood was up. "Think you're smart, don't you?"

Fowler looked up. "He's planning his next murder while you two are dicking around."

"We're dicking around? Is that what we're doing?" Cole was righteously indignant, strutting around the table now, the hands on his hips shaking with emotion. He reached over and struck Fowler hard on the side of the head.

Fowler sprang to his feet, grabbed Cole by the shirt collar, swung him around, slamming him down on the table. "Don't *ever* do that, do you hear me!"

"At ease!" Weathers separated the two men with his burly arms. "Another outburst from either of you shitheads and I'll book you both!"

Fowler sat back down, his face altered by the fury coursing through him. Cole leaned against the wall—still the tough act—but shaken.

Weathers sat on the side of the table reading Fowler's statement. "Okay . . . there was a struggle in the room . . . someone choked you . . . and you claim pushed this doctor at you . . . you fired . . . and whoever it was got away—are you kidding me?"

"Yeah, I'm kidding you, Allen. I killed this doctor, then drove his body over here so you could charge me with murder."

Cole leaned into his face. "Don't get smart, fuckface!"

Weathers stared at Fowler. "I heard there was some unpleasantness between you and the doctor."

"Nothing major."

"The county prosecutor has stated the doctor wouldn't testify because you threatened him."

"That's common practice, Allen. It's happening right now."

"A motel room is sure a nice place to stash a body."

Fowler was looking up at the two men. "I didn't stash any body. Use your heads. The killer checked into *my* motel. He either kills the doctor, or knocks him unconscious, leaves me a note, waits for me to show up, then throws the body at me when I walk in. He set me up."

"This killer is pretty smart. He sets you up—he sets up the kid . . ."

Fowler became very still. "He's not pretty smart. He's *very* smart."

"Too bad you weren't smart enough to stay away."

"Allen, you underestimate him—that's how *you're* being set up."

"What else aren't you telling us, Fowler?"

"Nothing."

"I told you to get off this case, didn't I? Well, now you're going to learn."

"I don't have to do what you tell me. I don't work for you, re-member?"

Weathers swallowed. "First you withhold evidence on a sus-pect, now you kill the one person who could have proved in court that the kid is violent."

Fowler stood up. "I change my opinion of you, Allen. You're going soft between the ears."

Cole was in his face again. "Sit down!"

Fowler glanced at Cole then back to Weathers. "He's a thug, but, you've sold out to the D.A. If you had any guts, you'd admit you have no idea who this killer is, you just want a conviction. Allen . . . you've become a bureaucrat."

Weathers was scrutinizing him, clearly stung, the jaw lowered, breaths drawn in, eyes watery. "Outside, Cole."

Cole eyed Fowler resentfully, then walked to the door. "My fucking pleasure." Weathers followed him into the hallway.

Outside the closed door, Weathers turned to him quietly. "Get some help, I don't care how you do it, if you have to beat it out of him—I want a confession."

Cole had a grin now forming on his lips.

55

THERE SHE IS. Out of the car. Have to follow her. How many years? Don't let her see me. Mustn't see me. Won't recognize me—down the sidewalk, oh, she's turning . . . looking . . . but people don't know me, never know who I am, the way I look. But she knew me when.

Out across the highway, trotting in high heels, now where? Funny how people can't hear the voices . . . whispers descending down through my brain, almost to my chest, heart in a free-fall, the whole sensation to my toes, then back up.

Into the state police station . . . perfect . . . follow her right into the station, right up to the booking desk, wouldn't that be fun? Walk right up and file a complaint, hurry, run, after her, now she's jogging up the steps, oh, have the years changed us, you there, me just a step behind you, yet light-years away. Maybe I could change you. Cut the laundry tag off that cotton dress.

She's in the revolving door . . . step in, two doors behind, yes, I'm in, now here we go, round and round the mulberry, she's almost halfway around, now STOP!

She bumps into the glass door, looks down, thinks something's jammed, oh, beautiful, looking up and . . . now, here we are . . . she turns, eyes through the glass, a thousand shattered memories, she is gaping, her mouth falling open . . . she sees I'm the man who stopped the door—doesn't know what to make of it yet . . . now getting irate . . . still doesn't recognize me . . . just now, a flicker, a glint in the eye, a faint recalling . . . now dawning on her, or just scared . . . yes, that's it . . . transfixed.

You don't remember me.

56

SHADOWS OF BARS divided the grit on the wall. Loud voices could be heard in the distance. A rusted cot. A grimy floor where a pair of shoes were being pulled onto a man's feet, the shoelaces tied, the hands withdrawn. The feet took Fowler's weight as he stood up, turned around, put on his jacket.

A black, stocky guard was standing outside the cell, swinging keys. He peered in. "They haven't asked you to address Congress—it's just a visitor."

The sound of locks clicked through chambers. The door swung open. The guard stepped in next to Fowler, a dangerous edginess in his arms. Nick buttoned his suit jacket, looking at the guard, and for a moment paused, glancing solemnly around the tiny room.

The guard stared at him. "Miss the place already, huh?"

"Oh yeah."

"Don't worry, you'll be back."

Fowler walked through the door. Up the stairs.

Muriel Ballard was seated in the waiting room at a cafeteria table. The guard let Nick in, surveyed the other tables—two with visitors. He backed out, locked the door.

As Fowler walked toward her, he saw her stand up. "What happened?" she asked. "They told me you'd been arrested."

He sat down at the table. "Yes."

"For what?"

"Murder."

"God's sake."

"I just hope they don't make it stick."

She looked shaken. "This is crazy."

"They claim I killed your son's shrink."

She sat down, was silent for a long time. "I'm sorry . . . One thing after another."

Nick was looking at her. "What?"

She looked to her side, as if trying to prevent some thought from recurring. "A man just now . . ."

"What?"

"Just some man . . . he stopped the revolving doors at the police station, looked at me kind of . . . like he knew something about me . . . he looked so familiar . . . I know I've seen him somewhere before."

Nick was studying her. "Who was he?"

"Just a stranger." She shrugged.

They both fell silent.

"Have you thought about what I asked you?" Nick said finally.

She turned and looked at him sharply. "Of course I thought about it, what do you think?"

"Have you made a list?"

"No, I haven't made a 'list.' You think I counted my lovers on both hands? It was very rare that I saw anybody in those years. God's sake."

"I don't mean to suggest—"

"If I did see a man when Cary's father was away, it was on a friendly basis. I didn't sleep around."

"I understand."

"Once or twice, maybe."

Fowler was feeling uncomfortable under her frowning gaze. He didn't know what to say exactly, how to phrase it. He paused for a moment. "Were you ever in love?"

This question staggered Muriel Ballard completely. She turned to him again, clearly horrified. "Of course. With his father, the louse. He didn't deserve it."

"But was there ever anyone else? Someone special?"

An irritable tone. "Everyone has one of those."

"Who was it? Do you mind if I ask?"

"Yes, I mind very much, Mr. Fowler." She paused as she tugged the russet skirt down over her knees. She adjusted herself on the edge of the bench. "Of all the nerve," she muttered to herself. Fowler sat patiently watching her bristle, glare at him, then turn away.

"If it's going to cause you that much anxiety, Mrs. Ballard . . ."

She snapped at him. "What anxiety? I don't have anxiety."

"I just thought if it could help your son."

"It's because of him that . . ." She stopped.

"What?"

She was still edgy, readjusting her clothes obsessively. "I *was* in love once. Don't look so surprised. I was a pretty slick chick in those days."

"I wasn't saying you weren't."

"When I was a hostess at the Algonquin, they ran a piece on me in the society column. 'Who's the gal with the electrifying legs?' they asked. That was me."

"I'm sure it was," he said flatly.

She reached over and slapped him. "Don't you patronize me, you bastard."

Fowler was taken completely off guard. He felt the burn on his cheek as Muriel Ballard stood up, burst into tears, and hurried across the visitors room. A few prisoners stared at her blankly, then resumed speaking in low tones. Fowler saw her list to one side as she scuttled on her high heels to a table by the window.

She hunched at the table, sniffling. He walked up behind her.

"I'm sorry, Mrs. Ballard."

"He was very tall," she said, turning around suddenly. "You know, dark and handsome, the whole bit." She dried her eyes on a handkerchief.

"What was his name?"

She thought back for an instant. "I can't remember now."

"Where did you meet him?"

"I don't know. At some mixer." She paused. "Wait, it was ladies' night. That's right. A dance or something."

"A dance?"

"At the country club. Well, anyway, the man was to die for. I was head over heels, of course. So when we made love, I persuaded him not to use anything. Can you imagine?" She paused again. "I wanted to get pregnant, I don't know why."

"What did he look like?"

"He had beautiful, fiery, intense eyes. He looked like F. Scott Fitzgerald with jet-black hair."

"This was fifteen years ago?"

"Yes. And he was so suave, so gallant. But a temper, let me tell you."

"What kind of temper?"

"He'd just get very upset over little things, over nothing."

"Like what?"

"Well, for instance . . . we made love for months but I never got pregnant. So silly me, I asked him to go to a doctor. Well, it turned out he was infertile." A tear started to work its way down her cheek, leaving a trail of mascara.

"I see."

"We were both crushed. Something happened. I really wanted a baby, God knows why. Look what good it's done for me." She started to tear up again, the memory pulling at her composure.

"Can you remember his name?"

"Elton Avery. Yes, that's it."

"Where did this man go?"

"I don't know. We lost touch." She cried some more.

"This man . . . was he a good dancer?"

"Oh. Just . . . sublime."

"And you went dancing often?"

"On ladies' nights, mostly."

"Why?"

"Oh, it was just a tick of his. He said something about how, on those nights, I could lead."

"I thought so." Nick Fowler had been piecing together the information, his thoughts hunting one another. Now he made the connection. "Mrs. Ballard, the man in the revolving door today, could it have been him?"

She looked at him, horror-struck. She froze as if years were peeling away from her. She looked despondent. "Yes . . . it could have been him."

He stood up. "All right, I'd like you to go downstairs immediately and see a sketch artist."

"Why?"

"Why did the man spend years haunting your son? I think he's the killer."

She was now giving him a numbing stare. "I have to think about this."

"Don't think about it. Do it."

The metal door at the end of the room scraped open. The guard stood quietly in the doorway. "Fowler? You're wanted in interrogation."

Nick looked over uneasily. "Do you still have that lawyer?"

"Yes."

The guard's voice boomed. "Fowler? *Now*."

Signaling to the guard. "Just a minute." He leaned down to Mrs. Ballard. "Does he remember where Cary lives?"

"I think so."

"If he does what I tell you now, it may nullify the evidence a prosecutor will use against your son."

She leaned toward him.

57

WITH HIS HANDKERCHIEF, Michael Lichtman lifted a pair of blood-soaked high heels off the floor of Cary Ballard's closet. He studied them for a moment and wondered if Fowler was right about whose shoes they were. When he turned them over, he noticed there was blood smeared on the bottom of the soles. He didn't understand.

Lichtman called Mr. Bendleby, the Brookside housemaster, with an anonymous tip that Ms. Coates's shoes were in young Ballard's closet, then hung up. Inside of a half hour, the police arrived.

Fowler had advised Muriel to tell Lichtman that Mr. Bendleby, the Brookside housemaster, should be the person to get his teeth into this. He knew Bendleby would whip the clue into a frenzy around the police's ears.

Fowler had suggested that the killer, not knowing that Ballard was in custody, might again plant his latest victim's clothing in the kid's room. He was right.

BILL RODNEY'S WEARY face was staring through the doorway of the interrogation room. He kept looking at his feet as blue shirts bustled by in the hallway behind him. "They're obsessed with you, Fowler."

"They think they have a case against me?"

"They do."

"Give me a break."

"They're gunning for you. You always have to ruffle their feathers, don't you?"

"Call Dr. Koenig, see if he's doing the autopsy."

"All right."

"And do me a favor? Tell Maureen I'm here, would you?"

"Sure. There're a few assholes still down in computers," he said.

"Can you get into the NCIC?" Fowler asked quietly.

Rodney held up an operating manual entitled *National Crime Information Center*. "What are friends for, huh?" He paged through the manual. "It says . . . 'the files in the data base are divided into known active and inactive and usually containing, if available, the suspect's description, MO, and a summary of the criminal record.'"

"Let me give you the name."

"Okay, I'll put in a few keystrokes, see what I come up with. What is it?"

Fowler looked down at the book. "Elton Avery."

Rodney wrote it down as Sergeant Cole's voice echoed down the hall.

CARY BALLARD WAS on the campus of the juvenile detention center, sitting in the Great Hall—a gigantic room with murals from the thirties painted on the walls: faded scenes of men with bulging muscles hoisting girders, erecting buildings; planes flying overhead; trains smoking through a landscape bleached white from the sun.

Today the sun was bright and lit a large square on the table where the boys were eating. The light cut across Cary's table setting. The noise was deafening. There were over six hundred boys in the gigantic room. It was lunch. Cary was feeling the old nausea. Several of the boys at the table, particularly Albert, a Spanish kid from the city, didn't like that Cary kept to himself and always looked troubled. As Albert was serving the food, he anointed Cary with a new nickname. He avoided the pink strips of corn beef, just plopped a boiled potato in a pool of water on his plate.

"Pass this down to Shitface," he said casually.

The plate was passed, each minuscule face wary, a few taken off guard, laughing out loud, all staring down at the plate as it traded hands. The broken boiled potato on Cary's plate was steaming up at him when he got it.

"Hey, Shitty, is this a beautiful meal, or what? Talk to me."

A bunch of boys at the table tittered, others just ate the corn beef and cabbage with disgusted faces.

Cary couldn't even imagine eating the watery potato. He looked out the window, calculating how many more days there would have to be to his life.

"Oh, Mr. Shitface, yoo-hoo? What—you're too good for us, too white for us, maybe? You don't want to associate with us?"

Cary looked blankly up the long aisle of faces at Albert. "Beg your pardon?"

Albert put down his fork, his mouth still full of food. "I'll beg your fucking pardon, Shitbrain. You got a problem?"

"Yeah I do," Cary said.

Albert wasn't expecting an answer. He looked up, finishing his mouthful. "Say what?"

"Yeah, I got a problem." The expression on Cary's face had gotten increasingly embittered. "You didn't put any meat or cabbage on my plate, numb nuts."

A roar went up from the chairs. "Ohhhhhhhhh!" Most of the faces at the table were now suddenly alive, staring from one corner to another. No one said that to Albert.

The Spaniard calmly put down his napkin. "What did you call me?"

"I called you 'sir.' "

The table exploded with laughter.

Albert's face was drawn now, his chin down, his honor maligned. He stood up slowly. "Didn't get any meat, huh, Shithook?" He took a pair of brass knuckles out of his back pocket, slipped them on his right hand. "Guess we'll have to serve up some of your face!" He strode down along the table. Cary put his hands up over his head. The brass went up in the air.

A beefy hand grabbed Albert's face, wrenched him around backward. The boy's right arm was twisted up behind his back. Albert cried out in pain. One of the administrative guards had put the boy in a half nelson after he stood watching the exchange. He'd been asked to come get Cary. "Drop the knucks, son, or I'll have to break your arm."

Albert was silent, staring with fury at Cary, but dropped the brass knuckles. They clanked on the floor. The man pushed Albert into another guard who already had his stick out and, with a mean smile on his face, jabbed the boy along the aisle, out of the lunchroom and down a corridor.

The administrative guard leaned down beside Cary. "Come with me," he said, and led the boy away, the faces at the table following them. They left the room, walking fast down a hallway.

"Where are we going?"

The big man was stony, walking briskly. Cary had a good view of his nostrils. "Your lucky day, son. Some magistrate upstate rescinded your detention. Paperwork will take about an hour."

58

DR. KOENIG SLIPPED off his lab coat. He methodically brushed the jacket of his best gray suit. He walked out into the lobby of the funeral home to greet the two policemen.

"Captain Weathers?"

The thickset man shook hands, introducing Sergeant Robby Cole. They followed the doctor back down the hall into his office. They both stood sullenly as the doctor pulled on his lab coat and surgical gloves. Weathers's complexion was flushed, his face stern.

Koenig slowly uncovered the body, drawing the sheet down to the chest. Dr. Clarence looked different without his glasses.

Weathers shuffled his feet. "Uh, Doctor Koenig, we have an authorization signed by a magistrate . . . the county prosecutor ready to move on this case . . ." There was a lapse in his speech as he gazed at the doctor. "We need you to corroborate the confession given by the suspect in custody."

"May I read the statement?"

Weathers's tone was conciliatory. "We don't have it here at present. The suspect has admitted to the killing and did sign the confession—that's all you need know."

"You're speaking of Lieutenant Fowler?"

"He's no longer a lieutenant, Doctor. He was stripped of his rank when I fired him for withholding evidence."

"Yes."

"There was considerable malice between him and Dr. Clarence, apparently. They had arguments in public. There are witnesses to this."

"What time did Mr. Fowler supposedly kill Dr. Clarence?"

"He was taken into custody at four-thirty A.M.; we estimate the murder took place between three and four."

Dr. Koenig shrugged. "Well, the body speaks for itself."

"What?" Weathers was glaring.

"Let me give you my findings . . . then we can talk."

The two policeman gave wary nods.

The doctor cleared his throat, bending over the body. "There are methods for calculating rigor mortis, first of all." He pulled on the arms to demonstrate. "Weighing also the quantity of potassium in the ocular fluid and the state of the digestion, I would place the time of death somewhere between eleven P.M. and two A.M."

Robby Cole was twitching. "That's impossible."

Koenig glanced at him. He lifted the eyelids on the body. "Petechial hemorrhages are present beneath the conjunctivae." He poked the mouth open. "A trace of blood and mucus present, due to extravasation from membranes of the nasopharynx. Vomitus is present. He was strangled."

There was a hush in the room.

Weathers pointed his finger down at the face and chest. "There're six gunshot wounds, for Christ's sake."

"Captain, there was little or no blood loss. Wounds of this nature would have resulted in enormous bloodletting, but there wasn't much loss because the fluids had already begun to congeal over several hours. No, there's no way I can justify this. I'm sorry."

Cole stepped forward, lifted up the corner of the sheet, tossed it back over the face. "Well, Doctor, it's like this . . ." He strode over very close to him. "Either you find a *way* to justify it . . . or we'll do it for you."

Koenig's fastidious voice hardly changed inflection. "You'd better make sure that when you finish with me, Sergeant, that I'm no more alive than the doctor on this table, otherwise I'll bring this whole conversation down around your ears."

Cole took the doctor by the arm. "Not if you're being fed by a tube."

Dr. Koenig went pale. He lifted his chin. "I've already released my findings to a third party, who is ready to publish them. You're too late."

Cole shot a look at Weathers, who had already dropped his eyes and was shaking his head.

THE BOOKING SERGEANT slid an envelope down off the shelf. He unclasped it and handed Nick Fowler his possessions, which included a computer search from Bill Rodney. He glanced up at Nick's face, gave a low whistle. One eye was black-and-blue, the left side of the face was swollen, there were cuts and bruises. He watched Fowler grimace in pain as he strapped on his gun and shoved a wallet into his pocket. Nick looked at the man. "Mrs. Ballard still down with the sketch artist?"

The man shook his head slowly. "I heard something about she burst into tears and had to go home. They're going to try again tomorrow."

Nick was reading the computer report. "That'll be too late."

It was still light out when Fowler stepped outside the police station. He thought about the poem for Ms. Coates.

When he had climbed the last flight of stairs to the roof of Ardsley, he found himself running to the west wall. He saw the impression his foot had made weeks ago in the tar.

He walked the roof, exploring every chasm, every corner. He didn't know what he was looking for, and but for the fact he was having that feeling again, he would have stopped. The same dark, heavy vibe, the cold wash through his bones.

With the strap off his gun holster, he climbed up the slate dormers, thinking there might be a way into a hidden room in the abandoned attic. The enormous attic was used as a storage area. He had already explored it.

He stared up at the giant water tower and remembered he had read how the installation of a new sprinkling system had rendered the tower obsolete. It was just a massive round wooden bowl with a rounded shingled roof pirouetted into the sky.

He walked around it. It sat on a steel platform. Wire cables that were strung at sharp angles to stone partitions held the structure in place. No ladder, but a set of rungs up the outside. He climbed up slowly. They ended. Strange. The roof must have been new. He noticed the shingles were recent. Very strange. He climbed down.

Fowler crawled underneath, with his flashlight, and found what he had suspected. A trapdoor had been cut into the floor of the tower. It was locked with a heavy-gauge padlock and bolt.

Fifteen minutes later, after a trip to maintenance, he climbed up the stairs with a giant pair of snips. He had to hold one arm against his chest and with all his might pull the other end toward him. He finally cut the lock.

He slid the bolt and climbed up inside. The flashlight revealed the killer's lair. The walls were covered with exotica from all the victims. Fowler saw the name tags ripped out of Crawford's underwear; they were taped over his picture that had been cut out of the yearbook. His letter jacket, family pictures, clothing, all were displayed.

Nick saw Finkelstein's name tags, his picture, blotches of hair ripped from his scalp, a pennant collection, photographs of the boy with his grandparents, articles of clothing—all arranged on another clammy wall.

Then he saw Gluckner's yearbook picture, his letter sweater. An autographed five-by-seven in a football uniform, no helmet, a straight-arm to an imaginary tackler, flashing a grin. A stick of deodorant was taped down below a lump of flesh on a hook that Fowler realized was the dead boy's belly button.

He moved his flashlight along the wall. There he found the rest of the hunted. On an empty section of wall, he found a small bottle of Shalimar, a yearbook picture of Ms. Coates, a dried rose hanging upside down. Her lipstick. Her brassiere.

He saw Dr. Clarence's faculty picture from the yearbook. The light revealed a dog-eared paperback of Freud's *Theory of Psychoanalysis*, pictures of the doctor smiling while on staff at Creedmore Hospital, one of his laundry tags, and something Fowler didn't understand—a dress, a wig of curls, and a pair of high heels.

He flashed his light on the opposite wall on his way down. His heart started pounding. On the dank wall was a photograph of himself that had been taken years before. He anxiously grabbed for his back pocket, shone the flashlight in his wallet, and saw that the photograph was missing. He looked up and saw all the news articles written about him, his name in newsprint cut out, taped up, a laundry tag he had never missed cut from one of his own shirts. That sent a shiver through him. A headline cut from magazines spelling out "preoccupied with DEATH."

Nick backed down out of the tower, closed the trap, slid the bolt into place. He had to decide quick: a full police force stakeout, evidence teams in to fingerprint everything, get hairs to the lab— NOT AFTER WHAT THEY DID. He would wait for the son of a bitch tonight himself. He had a few things to take care of first.

He didn't see the eyes watching him from behind a cornice on the south wall. He didn't notice the figure slip across the roof, down the stairs, the feet racing, fists pounding the walls. He didn't hear the cries of anguish in the stairwell. How could he know the eyes were frightened, panicked, giving off an alien glow.

MAUREEN WAS JUST getting back when it happened. She had put in a phone call to Dr. Koenig and he had, in turn, sent her details about the autopsy. She had rushed to the bank to withdraw bail money for Nick, had lost most of the morning in meetings with her editors regarding the scathing, inflammatory article written about her experience with State Police Sergeant Robby Cole. Nick's arrest had been the last straw for Maureen. What was needed now was a bold stroke to reverse the events she herself had set in motion. She wanted to put the story in the evening edition.

Her editor in chief, however, had asked that she put the potentially explosive material on hold, for a matter of days, try to bail Fowler out, and give the justice system a chance to work.

Maureen was glad to hear that Cary Ballard had been released from detention. She had been driving herself hard since the terrifying night at the dance. She kept waking up in the middle of the night in cold sweats, dreaming about Ms. Coates falling out of the sky. She was comforted when she heard that the woman had been murdered a full day before the dance, but somewhere deep down, she felt responsible.

She knew she would be kept waiting hours at the hall of justice, so she came back to have her assistant proof the transcript of Dr. Clarence's autopsy. She was standing over the desk, her coat on, her keys in her hand, when the phone rang. She thought it might be Nick.

"Hello?"

"Maureen McCauley, please." A boy's voice, high and eerie— hadn't had his tonsils out.

"Speaking."

"I have some information about you know what."

"Who is this?"

"Never mind that. Do you have a car?"

"Can you at least tell me who I'm speaking to?"

"No names, ma'am. I'm a student. Drive a half mile past the back entrance to the school golf course, okay?"

Maureen was scratching the directions down. "Yes."

"There's a rest stop on the left, overlooking the creek. Pull your car in there and leave the motor running. I'll get in and we can drive somewhere safe."

"Look, I have a deadline that—"

"This won't take long. Meet me in fifteen minutes. No police."

"Young man, I have to know who—"

But there was only a dial tone. Maureen put the receiver back on the phone, chewed the inside of her lip, then walked down the hall.

The sun was down when she pulled onto the highway just outside of town. The fading light made the old gray pavement seem as though it was moving under her tires in slow motion. She drove past the back entrance to the golf course, and when she saw the rest stop, she pulled in.

Maureen didn't see anyone. She glanced impatiently at her watch, tapping the steering wheel. Her mind drifted. Suddenly the passenger door was ripped open. She jumped. An oversized boy, a hard mannish face, clown white. An antiseptic smell.

Maureen jammed the car in reverse—a round-collar shirt, a cap, the mouth painted a ghoulish red—all moving toward her. A hand came out of the air. She pressed the gas. The car shot backward but was too late, the boy was inside the car, the handkerchief had hit her hard in the face, clinching her mouth and nose—the other hand came around and grabbed the back of her head like a vise. She fought against the hand, gunning the car, spinning the wheel. The car screeched around and slammed into a bank of flower beds.

For one instant Maureen wrenched her face away, but the pressure of the handkerchief was clamped back over her nose. She tried not to breathe while she got her wits, then flailed when she felt her vision clouding. All she could remember was the strange dark eyes burning down, the clownish red mouth contorted until, as she began to fade, it spread into a smile.

How could he? Break into my world, my abode, MY PLACE and violate me—touch my things, my treasures . . . fondle my trophies, mementos, articles from which my change is constructed. How could he!

He has to die. You'll bring him to me. Voices beseeching, rising,

a chorus of sounds. Now, a WOMAN in the flowers. Move over . . .
I have a use for you. Let me kiss you . . . your lips so soft . . . let me
smell your skin, will it be this soft, this ripe after you change? . . . are
you listening? . . . CAN YOU HEAR ME?

 Now scissors . . . what to take . . . of course, the label of your
dress . . . what else? . . . now, slip dress up, let me get my hands up
your thighs . . . come on, yes, peel panty hose down, stretch, over hips,
easy, out of the crease, yes, down your legs, off your feet. That's nice,
so nice . . . voices whisper now . . . be calm . . . don't stretch them!
Easy. Now cut the nylon, along the thigh, over the hip, up around and
under the tummy, now—yes—got it. Oh. Oh. Smells nice. Let me just,
please just once, let me change you—with this knife. No. Wait. Linger.
 Savor the delay.
 Anticipate.

WHEN CARY WAS walking up the main road into Ravenhill
School, he felt exhilarated. A state vehicle had escorted him to
the entrance of the school. He took a deep breath, looked up and
saw the array of chimneys along the roofs of Ardsley, Booth, and
Madison halls—the gray stone, the brick chimneys, the ivy, the
tall wrought-iron fence—all of it gave him a somber rush.

On the walk in front of Ardsley, he saw a strange sight. A tall
boy had appeared from behind a parked car, on his knees, crawling along the grass. He was moaning as Cary approached him.
The student was apparently hurt. As Cary got closer, he just saw a
black collar high over the face, a cap on the head.

"I've sprained my ankle," the student pleaded in a high-strained
voice, his face down in pain. "Could you help me to the car?"

"Yes, but . . ." Cary was flustered, wondering how he could lift
him up. He bent down, placing his shoulder under the upraised

arm. Before he could lift, the arm yanked his neck down, pulling his face into the grass. Another hand slapped a handkerchief hard against his face, the impact almost knocking him out. A stench like bug spray entered his nose, forcing him to heave. Cary flailed his arms, watching the boy's face now appear, coated in white, straining, the sweat appearing on the forehead, the makeup running.

Cary knew this face. His free hand lashed the grass. He twisted away, gasping, but the giant boy grabbed him again and clamped the handkerchief to his face.

Cary stared helplessly into the mammoth boy's eyes, the pressure over his nose beginning to lighten. He thought someone was smoking. Everything, the eyes, the makeup, even the hard red lips, were floating away, getting blurry, until the face was far in the distance.

59

FOWLER WAS BEGINNING to feel a knot in his stomach. Maureen hadn't answered the phone the last hour. At the *Tribune* they said she had been called away on an urgent matter. He stood in front of the chapel. A terrible thought occurred to him.

Inside the hall, the entire faculty, the officers of the alumni association, the board, and the trustees were all in attendance. The student council members of the four classes were there, each wearing school blazers.

On the stage, Dr. Brandon Hickey was making his final speech as headmaster of Ravenhill. In a few moments, he would hand over the crest of the school to Elliot Allington, who would take the helm of the school as the new headmaster. The school crest was a round fourteen-karat-gold plate of the school insignia that hung over the headmaster's desk. It was always presented to the incoming man in a formal public ceremony.

Fowler mounted the stairs, two at a time.

On the stage, flanked by his administrative staff, Brandon Hickey was extolling the merits of his past administration with anecdotes designed to distract attention from the murders that had driven him from his post.

He didn't notice Nick Fowler standing in the back of the auditorium. Dr. Hickey finished his speech and, hoisting the gold school crest, presented it to Mr. Allington as the room burst into spontaneous applause. The new headmaster, flushed and proud, began to give his acceptance speech.

None of the men on the dais noticed the man following them over to the reception room in Ardsley after the ceremony. None of them realized that he observed which of them had left early.

THE HINGE ON the roof door directed a sharp rasp against the bricks. Nick ran toward the water tower. He pulled down the trap, flashed his light inside to see if it was safe. He vaulted up. He shone his flashlight up along the walls. He saw all the victims' possessions just as he had left them. Then, what he most feared was waiting for him. There was new memorabilia. When he shone the light on the other side of the dank wooden slats, he saw it all. Maureen's picture, a label from a dress Fowler had bought her, her column photo smiling at him from faded newsprint—and a round section of her panty hose—could it be? ... yes ... the crotch.

Fowler slammed his fists against the wall.

Wait.

A purple envelope on the floor. He opened it.

Dear F,

Come and get it. You'll recognize them by the sound of two
voices . . . screaming.

Ever yours,

Arthur Murray

A pair of black shoes stepped over an unconscious man. A pair of gloved hands quietly flipped the man over. The gap in his front teeth glowed in the light from the furnace. Stanley had been hit hard on the head.

The shoes kicked the ribs, pausing to see if the wombat was still unconscious, then began walking slowly toward a grimy door.

The man in the cloak pulled open the door and stared out upon a cavernous room that dropped three stories underground. Through the gigantic wooden crossbeams, on the floor far below, he saw they were still tied to the old greasy turbine engines, both bound with ropes. They were gagged, looking up.

On the cement floor underneath the power plant, Maureen and Cary were startled when they heard the door in the rafters abruptly open. They looked up and saw a man in a dark cloak and hat, climbing down the steel ladder on the wall. When he reached the floor, he turned to them.

Cary froze. Maureen drew in a breath, thinking at first she had seen a specter. The scarf over the face, the hat corkscrewed on the head—he was almost laughable—like a figure in a cheap melodrama. Yet when he approached her, the laughs that were due his appearance turned to cries in her throat.

He was moving stealthily toward them, something glimmering in his hand. It was a long stiletto.

NICK FOWLER'S FACE was pressed again at the panes of the lead windows to the Ardsley reception room. His overwrought eyes combed the room. All the men were gone now. He was uneasy and moved through the flower bed, back under the arch in silence.

He was staring up at the buildings. Booth Hall was a mass of black stone and chimneys against the night sky. Ardsley Hall loomed over the tall fence.

Something caught Fowler's attention.

He noticed a white shape in the half-light bobbing in the distance, a high voice whimpering. It looked strangely like an apparition floating away through the fog. He broke into a run.

He realized it was a head of white hair as he came, winded, pounding across the wet grass. The sound startled Mabel, the wombat who worked the graveyard shift, cleaning the classrooms. She was crying, running across the lawn toward the infirmary. She turned when the footsteps approached her. "Who is that?" she said, her voice hoarse.

Nick stopped running. "It's Fowler, Mabel. What's the matter?"

"Stanley's been hurt!" A withered hand drew a strand of hair out of her face. "I was making my rounds and I found him out cold."

"Where?" Fowler whispered.

"The power plant."

60

THE FIGURE HOVERED over them, the knife hanging loosely at his side. He paced, anxiously, a coiled spring with burning eyes. Then he stopped. He swayed in front of them, dangerous, unpredictable. Insane.

He pushed his scarfed face next to Cary's. "Hope we don't have to wait too long," he mumbled. The gag warped under the boy's straining chin. The figure moved along the wall until his face was opposite Maureen's. He smiled. "I might not be able to stop myself if he doesn't come soon."

Maureen couldn't move. She was frozen with terror. She saw the knife rise in his hand. It was levitating in the air above her. She resigned herself to death and held her breath, waiting for the blade to fall, but inexplicably, the man paused.

He moved away from her. He ran his fingers along Cary's throat, almost caressing the white skin.

The blade moved slowly back to Maureen. She watched the eyes with a sinking feeling now. The wavering had stopped. The last shred of accessibility had disappeared from the eyes, leaving black holes in the face. He had made his decision and the knife went high in the air. It came down. She felt cold steel by her neck. She looked up. The eyes in the face were glinting. The blade suddenly dug into something. The rope across her shoulder snapped. She shut her eyes.

That's when she heard the gunshot. A bullet glanced off the floor inches from the man's feet. The man in the scarf dove to the floor and cut her ankles free. He grabbed her hand, backpedaled, dragging her across the floor, behind the old turbine. There was another flash from the ceiling door, high in the rafters. The bullet ricocheted off the wall above the turbine.

"Drop the knife," said a voice from the rafters. Fowler was descending the metal stairs one at a time, his gun aimed down at the cold boilers. "Throw it out in the middle of the floor!" he yelled. There was no sound in the room, only his shoes on the rungs. He paused halfway down the wall, listening.

Silence.

He shoved the gun back into his holster and took the rungs two at a time all the way down the wall. Once down, his hand went back into his coat as he rushed across the cement floor, in a crouch, both hands now on the gun. He moved around the side of one boiler, thrusting his gun in. Nothing. He moved now to the second boiler, his gun in tight, and threw himself around the side of it.

There, in the stone wall, was a jagged opening into an underground passageway.

An old wooden door was ajar.

He pulled the small wooden door aside, looking into blackness. He shone his flashlight into a passageway. He understood immediately he was staring into the tunnels.

He opened the small wooden door and crept into blackness.

Fowler's light illumined a short passageway with stone walls, not high enough to stand, so he crawled. About fifty feet in he came up against another wooden door. This one was locked. He could see fresh prints when he shone his light down on the dirt near the door.

Then he heard Maureen's voice. She was calling into the passage, her voice far in the distance, whimpering, pleading for help. He banged maniacally on the door, drawing blood on his fist. Nothing. He maneuvered around and crawled back.

Nick found Cary unharmed. He cut the ropes binding him, and without a word, they ran across the floor. With his arms around the boy, they climbed.

Fowler coached him up one step at a time.

"Where's Maureen?" Cary asked slowly.

Fowler kept inching him up. "In the tunnels. Don't look down."

"With him?"

"Yes."

"Do you know where they lead?"

"Ardsley." Nick glanced down. The floor below began to look like a cavern in the distance. When they got to the top, they ran outside.

Nick got on the police radio in his Dodge to call for backup. He asked Cary to get in the car and wait. Cary refused. The boy was determined to go up on the roof with him.

Fowler stood in the dark weighing what to do. In the silence of that moment, the boy looked at the great black fence surrounding Ardsley. He studied the waists of scrollwork, the steel shafts thrust into the dark sky. He knew in an instant those bars would forever imprison him if he didn't go along. Fowler glanced down at the boy. He must have sensed this.

MAUREEN WAS ON her hands and knees crawling in the dirt down a long tunnel. She had quieted down, trying to get a hold of herself. She could hear just breaths behind her, nothing else. The ghastly breaths of a killer so vile he would cut people open and paint walls with their organs.

She tried not to think about it. She focused on the breaths. Behind her was a light source. It illuminated the arched railroad-tie bridging that held up the tunnels.

"Where are you taking me?"

No answer. Just the breaths, short plodding sounds. Hands against moist dirt.

"Are you going to hurt me?"

No answer.

She kept crawling, bits of sand and gravel falling in her hair from above. Had to get through to this man.

"Do you know when these tunnels were built?"

No answer.

Crawling. She flinched as her kneecap pressed down on a stone. Only then did she realize her panty hose was off her body. This sent cold needles across her forehead, a shudder down the back of her neck. She had to quiet her fear.

"I did a story on these tunnels," she said nervously. "They were gouged during the war, when the school was used for military training. Did you know that?"

No answer. Has to be something to make him talk.

"They dug a series of underground tunnels in case they were bombed," she said. "At one time, they ran up under all the major buildings."

She cringed when she heard the unearthly voice. "You can get to other dorms from here?" The words seemed to fall out of the ether.

"Only Ardsley. The others caved in."

She realized then *why* he had asked this question. The thought made her sick to her stomach. She started to feel dizzy. Her wrist collapsed and she fell forward into the dirt. A hand grabbed her hair and pulled backward. She felt a sliver of cold steel against her neck.

"Don't make me cut you down here. The rats will finish you off."

She sprang helplessly forward. The blade fell back out of sight. Just the breaths again.

"Are you going to kill me?"

No answer.

She had to reach him. There was a human in there somewhere. "You don't have to hurt me. I could help you."

No answer.

"I'm very interested in why you do this."

Nothing.

"I could interview you. Would you like that?"

No answer.

She began to feel faint again. She stopped to shake her head clear. The piece of steel pressed against her buttocks. She shivered, started crawling in a panic. She heard the voice.

"Don't pretend you like me. I know who you like." The voice was angry. Breaths.

"How do you know that?"

"Because he and I had a vibration."

"Don't you still?"

"No. He went too far. He violated me, desecrated my home."

She had an uneasy feeling now. "How did he do that?" Sounded patronizing. Think!

"He's a rapist!"

Maureen was feeling hot beads of sweat breaking through the back of her dress now. It was stifling down here. No air. Her knees were bruised. She had to say something.

"You still have a connection with him though."

An eerie pause. "No."

"He wants to be close to you."

"Too late."

"Why is it too late?"

"You came into the picture."

It all hit her suddenly. He was going to kill her out of jealousy, out of some primal force she couldn't control. Her imagination began to run. There were her own breaths, the breaths behind her, the hands and knees trudging through the dark loam. She started to cry.

"Don't hurt me, please."

Maureen heard squeaks, wails, little cries in the distance. Her voice was hoarse. "What's that?"

"Be sure they don't run up your dress."

Little scramblings in the dirt.

"What is it?"

"Rats."

As the screeching increased, the light behind her shone down the tunnel. She heard him begin to laugh. She saw red eyes, a sea of them moving toward her.

She screamed.

61

MAUREEN OPENED HER eyes. It took her a moment, then she realized: She had been chloroformed again. A rope was tied under her chin, forcing her head up, another was around her chest, and her arms were strung up above her head, ropes taut across her breasts. The rope holding her weight was strung to heavy wire cables above her. She was bound to the top of the water tower. She was gagged.

The figure appeared in front of her standing on the slant of the roof. He leaned in so the black scarf almost blotted out the sky.

"He should be here shortly."

Maureen couldn't scream. She was too busy thinking. The figure took a stiletto out of his cloak. He flicked the razor-sharp tip just below Maureen's Adam's apple. A sprinkle of blood emerged.

He ratcheted the blade this time just over the Adam's apple. Another trickle of blood sprang to the surface. He pressed the knife under her neck and let the cuts ooze droplets of blood along the blade.

Maureen wanted to wrench her body from side to side, but she reasoned that if she stood her ground, she might live longer. She held perfectly still.

The knife's point again grazed the flesh of her neck. The line of blood was so thin, it was almost invisible for a moment, then it began to seep down along her skin. Maureen was beginning to tremble.

Drops of blood began to hit the tar shingles.

He again held the stiletto under the fresh wounds; red dripped on the blade. Then, as if a primeval bird had flapped its wings, the cloak was off, the scarf down, a strange distorted clown face moving toward her, the eyes iridescent, the lips frozen in a smile.

A rasp of the roof door stopped him cold. He turned.

NICK HEARD THE grating sound echo over the tar. He and Cary stood staring across at the chimneys, the skylights, the immense cornices that dominated the corners of the building, and the sky beyond. The water tower was dark against the sky. A single star was hanging in the heavens.

Fowler stopped to catch his breath, moved the bundle to his other arm. He pulled his gun out, reloaded it, and closed the chamber. He whispered in Ballard's ear.

"Stay behind me."

They crept along the west wall, occasionally bringing their heads over the top of the wall to stare into the gloom. They saw nothing. Suddenly Fowler heard a moaning sound, a woman's voice. He crawled faster. He paused at a corner, staring at a section of the roof where hundreds of chasms were hidden in the brick facing. Fowler pointed silently in that direction and crawled around the corner.

The boy had fallen behind. He was tired, scared, physically

dragging as he strove to catch up with Fowler. He heard a sound above his head. He wheeled, raising his hands. A black winged figure descended upon him and, like a vulture, grasped him around the neck. The figure took his fist and punched the boy viciously across the face. Cary fell down, appearing to be unconscious. The hands readied a syringe, lifted up the boy's sleeve.

Cary abruptly reached up and pulled down the scarf.

He was staring into the stunned white face of Mr. Elliot Allington, the new headmaster.

They looked at each other.

Ballard felt a flood of memories pouring into his mind as he looked quietly up into the man's eyes, now watery and ashamed.

"I saw you when I was a child. You killed my father. Didn't you?"

The eyes seemed to reignite. A quiet sneer spread across the thin lips. "And what if I did?"

Cary stared into the man's eyes. "Why?"

"Your mother deserved to know what it was like to *lose* someone . . ." Allington murmured. "She left me to have a child with your father. That child was you."

"So you've tortured me all these years."

Allington nodded silently. The shock at being discovered had passed quickly out of his dark features. An evil resolve broke across his face.

Cary raised his voice. "I'm not afraid of you anymore."

"Oh no?" There was threat in his tone.

"You'll never haunt me again."

"Because you're dead inside, little boy."

"Like you?"

A sadness on the clown face. "Yes."

"You can't control me anymore," Cary said calmly.

The hands were suddenly on the boy's throat, pushing him down. "The spell is over!" Cary choked out. "I've broken free of you." The syringe went into the boy's arm. Within a few seconds, his eyes had rotated up under his lids. The man placed a bloody stiletto in the boy's hand and crawled away.

MAUREEN WAS SHIVERING, her neck marked by streaks of red. She heard steps, felt tension on the ropes binding her. The figure stood up behind her. She stiffened, fear twisting through her body. She saw a cloak catch on one of the ropes. A knife appeared in front of her face—but her eyes widened when she saw it was a pocketknife. It sliced the rope around her chest, then the one holding her arms. Behind her the masked figure whispered, "It's me."

It was Fowler's voice.

He ripped the tape away from her face, dabbed her neck with his hand. "I'm going to get you down. Hold on."

Maureen turned around to smile at him. She saw something loom in the sky. It rose up even higher than the figure standing behind her. It was another figure. She screamed. Suddenly hands were around one figure's neck. The man behind Maureen was wrenched backward, the other man rooting under his cloak. A gun fell to the tar. The two men began striking each other, a rain of fists against the scarves. They clasped each other's faces, the masks pulled down, and rolled off the side of the water tower, as one white face kept coming up like a new moon rising. They both plunged ten feet into a crosswork of cables, which broke their falls. More fists, figures scrambling across the shingles. Nick could now see the face he had known belonged to the killer.

Allington kicked the revolver and it slid along the tar into a corner. Fowler sprang forward and threw his weight against the man's knife arm. They rolled across the shingles, grunting, kicking, clawing at the weapon. He lost his grip on the stiletto arm. The blade plummeted. He rolled away just as it dug into the tar. He pitched himself under the water tower. Above him Maureen was trying to wriggle free.

Nick crawled out from the other side of the tower just as Allington flew at him, his cloak billowing behind his white face. They thrust their knives, parrying around the side of the water tower, lunging at each other along the west wall. A single star plunged down between their straining faces.

Suddenly Allington feinted high, but charged low, piercing Fowler's leg. Nick grunted, falling on his hands and knees, gasping at Allington's feet. The tall man lifted the knife in both hands, about to bring it down on Fowler's neck.

Maureen threw the brick at the back of the head. It struck Allington with such force the knife was jolted from his grasp and flew off the side of the building, the tall man collapsing for a moment on Fowler's body. Allington wheeled and stumbled to his feet, dazed. He instinctively leapt toward Maureen.

Maureen ran toward the north wing of the roof. She ran hard, her adrenaline pumping. She could feel the heavy gasps of air fueling the deadly machine behind her. She heard the huge legs striking the tar right where her feet had been a split second before. Behind them, Fowler somehow struggled to his feet, fell, then started to crawl along the tar.

Maureen was only inches ahead of Allington. She saw the fire escape ladder and darted, throwing the man off. She then vaulted her body toward the metal ladder, turning around to climb down when Allington grabbed her by the hair and yanked her back up onto the north wall.

The first bullet caught him in the shoulder. From the west wall,

Fowler had found the gun and was pulling the trigger. Maureen saw the blood squirt out of the body above her. Allington staggered backward. There was a crushed look of disbelief on his face.

He started to clamber along the wall of the roof. The next bullet grazed his neck. The blood sprinkled the ledge of the building. The pattern of the drops was not a dance but an emblem of evil, a mythic bloodletting that showered the stone.

Allington jumped the Ardsley wall and landed on top of the stone arch. He was limping away, bleeding badly now. Fowler jumped the wall too, landed and rolled. He took several steps along the top of the arch, approached the man, his gun raised. "Why did you kill the boys?"

Allington stood very still, breathing hard. Fowler advanced slowly, the gun aimed. Allington stared down the muzzle. "I had to . . . finish the drama."

Fowler looked down at his father's pistol. He understood at that instant what the man meant.

Allington let out a wail and lunged toward him. Nick fired two rounds into his chest. The body was still coming, hands around Nick's neck, choking, squeezing. Two more shots. The hands still garroted around his throat. Nick was starting to asphyxiate, his legs collapsing, his vision blurred. He arched his neck forward, fell underneath the man and, with all his might, heaved.

Allington pitched over his head, off the arch.

His legs caught the stone gargoyle above the vault and his body flipped over twice. Fowler watched him somersault, his white face coming back to see the sky halfway down, twisting in the air down seven stories until he landed, skewered on the great fence. The gigantic steel uprights rang out as they plunged through his body, throwing up a spray of blood. He hung limply, his intestines tangled with wrought-iron shafts, his spine crushed, his face still staring up with a strange look of shock.

62

MAUREEN HAD BEEN so traumatized by the incident she quit her job and flew back to San Bernardino. She wrote Nick a letter, saying it was good to be back. She was spending a lot of time in the sun, letting the desert air bake down on her. She might even look for work out there. She was sorry, she said.

Nick was sad she had left. He thought he loved her, but he wasn't sure after all what that was.

He drove back upstate, spent a few weeks in Buffalo, but most of his time fishing high up on the Niagara River. He saw some friends, even took his ex out for a drink. He told her what had happened. She didn't get it. She criticized him, still in the grip of some old anger.

Nick drove back to Ravenstown. It was the last race of the cross-country season, and Cary had called to tell him the coach had let him come on the team late. The boy had been training hard. He felt good and was applying for a full scholarship for his sophomore year.

Nick parked his car and sat in the stands. It was one of those blustery fall days when the wind was high and the trees were swaying and the leaves were blowing across the fields with a kind of reckless, wild incontinence. Gray cirrus clouds were knifing across the horizon.

Nick kept his field glasses trained on the far side of the golf course, where the runners passed in the middle of the race, only visible for about a mile before they disappeared into the woods until the finish. Through the glasses he saw a few runners out in front, coming down the hill, then came the pack, and finally the rest. He saw Cary struggling far back, but not in last place. He could tell even from this far, the boy was having a rough time. Still, he looked strong and Nick was proud, given his short time on the team. He was going the distance.

When the runners threaded behind the oaks, out of sight, he put his field glasses down and realized Allen Weathers was standing beside a cruiser down on the side of the stands. Robby Cole was getting out of the passenger door. They looked up at him. Cole was wearing shades. It seemed incongruous to Fowler that someone would wear sunglasses on a cloudy day. He watched them stroll up through the bleachers, making a number of spectators uneasy. They turned around to see where the cops were headed.

Weathers stopped a couple of rows down. He nodded. "Lieutenant," he said.

Nick nodded, didn't really have anything to say.

"Look . . . uh . . ." Weathers sighed, uncomfortable at best. "I owe you an apology, Fowler. I was running scared. The brass were coming down on me . . . it's no excuse, I know."

"No," Nick muttered.

"Guess I lost my principles. You taught me a big lesson, though. You saved lives. Saved my ass too. I've asked the governor for a special commendation."

"Thanks, Allen."

Cole wandered up, looking ashamed, reached a hand out in silence to Fowler. "I'm sorry."

Nick couldn't bring himself to smile, but he took Cole's hand.

Weathers cleared his throat nervously. "And I'm sure you wouldn't be interested, but in case you are, I'd like to offer you your job back, with a raise." A long silence. "Think about it."

Nick nodded with appreciation. "I will, Allen. Thanks."

He watched them leave. Both men seemed embarrassed to have to do this, yet relieved, perhaps. He knew he would never work with them again, but it was nice to be asked.

Nick picked up the field glasses and swept the fairways looking to see if the runners were coming in. Out in the middle of a grassy field, something caught his eye. A flash of red. He focused the glasses on a woman turning in his direction. He saw a smile, but it was the wrong face. An older woman. He instantly felt an ache of longing reach down inside. He looked up at the clouds for a moment. He put the glasses back up to his eyes.

Maybe he would buy that plane ticket.

He saw the pack coming down the homestretch. Cary had come from behind and was moving up. The people in the bleachers were up on their feet, cheering. Cary rode out his kick and placed third.

In the distance the trees were bent over in the wind, the leaves still swirling across the grass. Higher up, the sky was threatening to clear.